CROSS TO BEAR

THE TERRY DAVIS SERIES
BOOK 2

CLAY E. NOVAK

SILVERLIGHT PRESS

PRAISE FOR CROSS TO BEAR

"*Cross to Bear* isn't just a thriller; it's a reckoning. It digs deep into what it means to protect your people when the system's broken and the rules don't apply. Novak's voice is authentic, unflinching, and full of heart. If you've ever asked yourself what kind of person steps up when everything's on the line, that person is Terry Davis."

MICK BETANCOURT, EXECUTIVE PRODUCER, AMAZON SERIES, *REACHER*

"*Cross to Bear* is the kind of story only a soldier who's been there can write. It's raw, unvarnished, and rings true on every page. Clay Novak captures the cost of duty, the weight of loyalty, and the quiet violence of men who've seen too much and done what's necessary."

BRIGADIER GENERAL GUY JONES, U.S. ARMY (RET.)

The conspiracy continues with Terry Davis in *Cross To Bear*! This story takes off like a rocket ship, and it is nonstop until the very last page. It was impossible to put down; every time I tried to stop, I thought... just one more page. When it was over, I felt like I had sprinted a marathon. Every chapter and every page leaves you wanting more. Full of excitement and danger, this is a fitting second chapter to the Terry Davis series!! I can't wait for the next installment from Clay Novak!

ALLEN J. LYNCH - MEDAL OF HONOR RECIPIENT AND AUTHOR OF *ZERO TO HERO*

Cross to Bear

The Terry Davis Series

Book Two

by Clay E. Novak

ISBN 979-8-9993621-4-8 Hardback

ISBN 979-8-9993621-6-2 Paperback

Published by Silverlight Press

Malibu, California & Austin, Texas

www.ThroughPenandLens.com

Silverlight Press has a Speakers' Bureau for its Authors. Please direct all inquiries for Author Clay E. Novak to Susan Sember, Publisher, at the above website for speaking engagements, appearances, book signings, and media interviews. Wholesale and bulk sale orders may also be directed to the Publisher.

Cover Design: Daryn Rowley

Cover Photography of Chicago skyline: Connal Novak

Interior Design: Susan Sember

CROSS TO BEAR

Dedicated to the Police Officers, Nurses, Firefighters, Ambulance Crews, and First Responders who risk their lives daily to save ours.

And to the members of Task Force 2 Panther, Baghdad 2008-2009

TABLE OF CONTENTS

Chapter 1	1
Chapter 2	9
Chapter 3	17
Chapter 4	26
Chapter 5	34
Chapter 6	41
Chapter 7	49
Chapter 8	58
Chapter 9	65
Chapter 10	72
Chapter 11	79
Chapter 12	88
Chapter 13	96
Chapter 14	103
Chapter 15	110
Chapter 16	118
Chapter 17	125
Chapter 18	132
Chapter 19	139
Chapter 20	145
Chapter 21	150
Chapter 22	157
Chapter 23	164
Chapter 24	171
Chapter 25	178
Chapter 26	186
Chapter 27	191
Chapter 28	199
Chapter 29	205
Chapter 30	212
Chapter 31	217
Chapter 32	222
Chapter 33	228
Chapter 34	236
Chapter 35	241
Chapter 36	248

Chapter 37   253
Chapter 38   260

Acknowledgments   265
About the Author   267
Afterword   269
Sneak Preview of Book Three   271
Also by Clay E. Novak   273

CHAPTER 1

T he grey Toyota 4Runner stopped on the Chicago suburban street with a hint of a slide. It was early in the season, even for Chicago, to have this kind of wintery weather. Terry Davis put the SUV in reverse and parallel parked the vehicle like he had been doing it his entire life. It was the day after Thanksgiving, and the precipitation was coming down in that rainy-snowy mix that most people referred to as sleet. Terry just thought of it as shitty weather. He was almost hit by a passing car as he climbed out of the driver's seat, closing the door and hitting the lock button on the key as he dropped the ring into his pocket. Wearing his ever-present baseball cap and a Filson waxed-cotton coat, he braced himself against the wet as he walked two houses down the sidewalk.

The inside of the house was lit, and he could see people milling around through the large picture window of the brick structure. It looked like every other house on the street, both sides of the street in fact, but he knew this one like the back of his hand. He bound up the seven steps to the covered porch and reached for the aluminum-framed storm door. He was almost run over by two women coming out, both about the same size and moving quickly. He recognized one of the women, but not the one dressed in hospital scrubs.

"Wow," he said as the women brushed by him without a word. "Not even a 'hello' for the love of your life. I see how it is." The women turned. The woman Terry recognized jumped into his arms and kissed him. The woman in scrubs stood there, confused.

"Holy shit!" she said. It was Mary, or Mary Anne, as her father called her. "What the hell are you doing here? Does Jimmy know you're coming?" She hugged him again. "Oh, I'm sorry, this is Dana," she introduced the woman in the scrubs. Terry held out his hand, and she took it. "Pops is out of Old Style; we were running to the store."

"I'll be here," he said. She hugged him again.

"It's so good to see you," Mary said with a huge smile. "We will be right back." The two women went down the icy steps quickly and turned left down the sidewalk, opposite the direction of Terry's 4Runner. Dana looked over her shoulder as they walked, and the two women giggled. Terry turned and took a deep breath, opening the door.

The house was raucous. There were only a dozen or so people inside, but it sounded like fifty. This was the house Mary grew up in with her brother Jimmy and their adopted parents. Jimmy was the closest thing Terry had in the world to a brother. Closer than any of his Army buddies, including Brian. The two of them met as kids and were inseparable from that day until Terry left for the Army. The family held this event on the Friday after Thanksgiving for as far back as Terry could remember. Jimmy and Mary's dad, known affectionately as 'Pops,' was a retired Chicago Police Detective who usually worked on Thanksgiving. Hence, the family started celebrating the day after, and it just stuck. They invited all kinds of different people over every year. The crowd changed, but the house was always full, there was always plenty of food and drink, and it was never dull. Terry was smiling as he walked through the door.

The only face he recognized as he walked through the living room was Pops. He was sitting in his chair at the head of the dining room table, laughing and smiling. There were two other men, about his age, sitting on either side. Terry was betting old cop stories were being shared among the three of them. Pops was in his eighties and still in relatively good shape. He was a big German, probably six feet three inches, and weighed over 230 pounds in his prime. A small woman came from the kitchen in the back. She was tiny and frail, but she was laughing and smiling as well, carrying a glass tray covered in ten varieties of holiday cookies for the men to eat. It was Jimmy and Mary's mom, and that is what Terry had called her from the beginning. Mom and Pops were second parents to Terry as a kid. Terry had probably taken as many beatings from Pops as he had from his own father. Terry and Jimmy were 'mischievous' in Mom's words. Pops called them troublemakers.

Terry shook the moisture off his coat, causing Mom to look up at whoever it was coming through the door. She quickly put the plate of cookies on the table and threw up her hands with a bigger smile. Pops clearly didn't recognize Terry, especially with the beard that had grown back in the last few months.

"Who the hell are you?" Pops yelled from the table. The two men turned and looked at Terry. Mom slapped Pops on the shoulder and maneuvered quickly to Terry to hug him. Terry could feel, even though his coat, her Italian frame had shrunk over the years.

"It's Terry," she yelled back at her husband, "you blind S.O.B." Mom rarely cursed. Saying S.O.B. instead of son of a bitch was about as close as she came. The big man rose from his chair and came to greet his 'other' son.

"You need a shave," the old man said as he stuck out his hand. It wasn't really a hand as much as it was a paw; it engulfed Terry's hand as the two men shook.

"Thanks, Pops," Terry said with a smile. "Good to see you, too."

"Holy Shit!" Terry heard from behind the big man. It was Jimmy. "What the fuck is this?" He maneuvered through the small cluster of people to his brother, and the two men hugged. Mom struck her son on the back.

"Seamus," she said, using Jim's given name, "I'm not telling you again. No bad language."

"C'mon back in the kitchen," Jimmy said. Terry followed him, shedding his coat and laying it over a plastic-covered armchair. Terry looked around the kitchen and was instantly transported back to his teenage years. The avocado-colored appliances were still there, including the refrigerator, stove, oven, and even the sink—same kitchen table. Nothing had changed. "What's going on, brother?" Jimmy asked, handing Terry a beer. "Did you see Mary? She just left."

"Yeah," Terry said, taking a sip from a can of Miller Lite. "I ran into her on the porch with some other chick."

"Dana," Jim interrupted. "That girl is fucking fine. You'll love her. She's a nurse at Cook County. She won't go near me because I'm Mary's brother. You'd probably have a pretty good shot if Mary would let her near you." It was like the two men had seen each other yesterday instead of the three years it had been. Terry was feeling the nostalgia he knew would accompany this visit, but also nervous. He had been in town for almost four months without telling anyone. The aftermath of Nebraska and Tampa was still on his mind, making him reluctant to see any of his family or friends. The last thing he wanted to do was put them in jeopardy, but after four months, he decided the risk was low and to make his first appearance. He could think of nowhere safer than a house full of cops.

Mary and Dana came into the kitchen, shaking off the snow and carrying a case of Old Style and a bottle of Early Times whiskey. Comparatively, the whiskey was terrible, but it was a household favorite, and there was always a bottle of it around. It made Terry flash back to the glass of Old Charter he shared with the Vietnam veteran named Larry, who saved his ass just a few months before. Terry just now noticed Mary had her badge on her belt and her Chicago Police issued Glock 17 in a holster on her hip. *I must be slipping.*

"Beer and whiskey while on duty, officer?" Terry said with a smile. "Pretty sure that is against department policy, even here in Chicago."

"Well, smartass," Mary said, "I'm not on duty, but this neighborhood is going to shit, so walking at night without a gun is ill-advised. And I haven't even had a drink yet, so go fuck yourself."

"Mary!" Mom yelled from the living room. "I heard that. No bad language!" The foursome in the kitchen all laughed. Terry caught Dana's eye. She smiled. Mary saw the exchange.

"No," she said as she stepped between the two of them. "No, no, no. You stay away from her,' she said as she poked Terry in the chest. Then she turned to Dana. "And I already told you he is dangerous.

And he's mine." It was a running joke that someday Mary and Terry would end up together. They even kissed once, long ago, but it never took; there were too many brother-sister feelings going on, and they decided it was too weird. It didn't mean Mary was going to let her friend run off with the man she had a crush on all through her childhood.

"And what about you, officer?" Terry turned and looked at Jim. "You off duty, too?"

"Fuck yeah, I'm off duty," Jimmy said with a smirk. "Especially now that you are here." Jim and Mary both followed in their adopted father's footsteps and became cops. Jim was a grinder; he always had been. He worked hard, and he was a good cop who worked his way up and got selected to be a member of the SWAT team. Mary was smart and had used her brains and her attitude to make detective. Pops was as proud as he could be of his two kids.

The four were laughing and joking in the kitchen. The bottles of Miller Lite ran out, so they were sipping on the cans of Old Style meant for the old men at the dining room table. Mary grabbed the bottle of Early Times and four glasses.

"Nah," Terry held a hand up. "I'm good. I have to drive home."

"Yeah," Jim said with a hint of a slur in his speech, "where the hell are you staying anyway? And how long have you been back?" Terry had been dreading this conversation since before he walked in the front door. He knew everyone would be pissed when he told them.

"I'm back out by mom and dad's old place," he said. "In a little apartment." He left it at that.

"Dana lives out that way," Mary said. Terry looked at Dana. She smiled again and sipped the whiskey and water over ice that Mary had handed her. There was a gold chain hanging around her neck, the matching gold cross dangling down near her breasts. She caught him looking and furrowed her brow in disapproval. He quickly diverted his eyes.

"You could give her a ride home," Jimmy said with a devilish smile. "Or she could give you a ride. Or you could give each other a ride." Terry rolled his eyes. Dana turned red. Mary punched her brother in the chest.

"You're a fucking asshole," the detective said.

"Mary Anne!" This time, it was Pops. "Last time. Watch your mouth!" It was a warning that echoed through the house since the trio were teenagers. They laughed at the empty threat. Dana was suddenly close to Terry, standing next to him. She was short, maybe five feet two. Her hair was a very light brown with just a few strands of grey in it. Terry assumed she was about Mary's age, just over forty. Her scrubs were baggy, but Terry could tell there wasn't any fat on her. She was cute. Mary stepped between the two of them.

"Oh, no, you don't," she grabbed Terry's shirt. "I know those eyes. Hundreds of women have fallen prey to those eyes." She was holding the whiskey and water in her free hand and pointing at Terry around the tumbler. She spilled a little. "I need to talk to you anyway," she said. "We will be right back." She never let go of Terry's shirt, leading him out the back door onto the cold enclosed porch. It was dark except for the streetlight in the alley shining through the windows.

"I don't think sexual assault is the way to get promoted, officer," Terry said as she closed the door behind them.

"You fucking wish," she said. She was suddenly earnest and more sober than he thought. "I saw your name about four months ago. You were on a BOLO that ran through the division. Two days later, it was lifted." Terry stood emotionless. Inside, he was surprised, but he couldn't react in front of her. "What was that about?"

"Got me," he said, playing dumb.

"Bullshit, Terry," she said with emphasis but keeping her voice low. "Stuff like that isn't an accident. They don't tell every detective in Chicago to be on the lookout for someone and then say, 'never mind.' Something happened."

"Mary," he lied through his teeth, "I really have no idea what you're talking about."

"Terry," she said, changing the subject. "I have to tell you something. I can't tell Jimmy, and I can't tell Pops."

"You're pregnant," he said, half joking. "Who is it? That Italian kid from down the block? I'll kick his ass."

"Such an asshole," she said. She turned away from him. This was something serious. He touched her shoulder.

"Hey, Mary," he said softly. "I was just joking. You know you can trust me, and you know I will help, whatever it is. If there is anyone in the world who is here for you, it's me. Now, what is it?"

"It's a little complicated," she started. Terry stood quietly. "There are two guys who have been recruiting people to work undercover. They aren't cops, though. They are looking for people to work gangs and they came to me." Terry interrupted.

"Mary," he said. "No offense, but you're the whitest white girl around. If you looked any more Irish, you'd be a fucking leprechaun. Why in the world would they want you to work gangs undercover?"

"I started asking the same questions," she said, looking him in the eyes. "They brought up the family. Asked if Pops was my old man and if Jimmy was my brother. Of course, I said yes. It's not a secret; everyone in the CPD knows who we are. This family is like a Friday night TV cop show."

"Mary," Terry said. "You're rambling." She was definitely shaken by whatever was going on. Mary wasn't wound tight, but she always had her shit together. This was very out of character. Terry was trying to get her to focus.

"I know. I'm sorry," she said. "Terry, they aren't cops, and they aren't recruiting people to do cop work. It is definitely gang related, but it isn't law enforcement. This is warfare. They are going to war with the gangs. No warrants and no arrests."

"Mary, they can't be going to war with *all* the gangs," he said with disbelief. "That's like a hundred thousand people in Chicago."

"Not all the gangs, just one," said. "It's an offshoot of MS-13. They are just gaining strength and size in the city. They are taking over whole territories. Whole neighborhoods. It's insane. And these guys are going to war with them. That's what they said."

"Are these feds?" Terry asked. "FBI, DEA, some other federal agency?"

"No," she said. "They didn't carry badges, and they didn't carry guns, and they didn't identify themselves as agents or any other title. They just called each other 'mister.'"

"OK, so why can't you just say no?" Terry asked her. "And why can't you tell Jimmy or Pops? I am sure they would have some input or advice."

"Because they didn't really give me the option to say no," she said. "Terry, I don't know how I got into this or why they came to me, but I am supposed to report to them on Monday. I've already been cut away from my division. I am supposed to report to them with all my tac gear in a bag. No weapon. They are going to issue me new ones. And drive my own car."

"What do you think happens if you don't show?" he asked quietly. His brain was spinning.

"They showed me what happens," she said. He couldn't see the tears in the dark, but he could hear them in her voice. "They put two files on the table. It was my file and Jimmy's, but they were changed. Altered. All kinds of disciplinary shit in there, all made up. They are going to fire me, and then they will fire Jimmy. Do you know what that would do to Pops? And Jimmy?" Terry had a sinking feeling. He could hear that voice on the phone in Tampa. He had seen this kind of power before.

"Did they *actually* recruit anyone else that you know of?" he asked her.

"No," she said. "My supervisor said it was just me. Maybe people from other departments or divisions or units, but just me from my division."

"Mary," he was trying to calm her down, "I think you are making a bigger deal out of this than it is." He didn't believe that himself, and he doubted she did, but it was worth a shot. "Listen, if it will make you feel better, I will be wherever it is you are supposed to meet these guys before you get there and sit there the whole time until you come out." She nodded, sniffling back some tears. She hugged him.

The two of them went back inside. The kitchen was empty, so they followed the sound of laughter into the dining room. Jimmy was at the table with the old cops, drunk and laughing with them. Dana was nowhere in sight. *Damn.*

CHAPTER 2

Terry walked out of the house, turning right down the sidewalk to the 4Runner. He was thinking hard about whether or not he had an ice scraper in the back of the SUV. He knew his truck would be covered in this shit mix of snow and rain, and he would have to clean it off before he drove back to his apartment. He didn't hear the steps behind him before he heard the voice.

"Hey," Mary said. Terry's hand fell reflexively to his hip, reaching for a pistol that wasn't there. She jumped back. "Shit, are you carrying?"

"No," he said as he shook his head. "Old habits." She handed him a piece of paper.

"That's the address where I have to be on Monday," she said. She was standing there with no coat. She wrapped her arms around herself, the oversized wool sweater her only protection from the cold. "I have to be there at six in the morning." He nodded his head. "And Dana needs a ride home. She fell asleep in my room. She worked a shift and a half, eighteen hours, before she came over. She isn't drunk, just tired. Can you get her home?"

"Sure," he said, looking at the piece of paper. "I'll start my truck."

"And, seriously," she said. He looked up. "Keep your fucking hands to yourself. Or I'll cut them off." She was smiling. He knew that look; she wasn't joking. Terry just shrugged. Mary turned and jogged back to the house. Terry climbed in and started the 4Runner. He was digging through the back for an ice scraper when Dana walked up.

"Go ahead and get in," he motioned to the passenger door. "I'll get it cleaned off, and we can go." He looked at his watch, 0103 hours. It was already Saturday. Dana stopped as she looked into the cargo compartment of the SUV. While he was digging for the scraper, Terry moved his poncho liner and exposed the case for his AR-15. The two locked eyes, and Dana furrowed her brow again, then walked up and got into the passenger seat without a word. Terry found the scraper and cleaned off the truck, climbed in the driver's seat, and buckled in.

"Where to, young lady?" he asked.

"Young lady?" she said mockingly. "Mary wasn't kidding. You *are* full of shit. Just head west, I'll give you directions as we go." The ride was quiet, other than Dana giving turn-by-turn directions leading him to Interstate 55.

"You could have just told me to get on I-55," he said. "I've been gone a long time, but not that long."

"Things change," she said. "And Mary said you've been hit in the head a lot, so I didn't want to assume." He turned and looked at her. He suddenly had a flash of Peggy sitting in the passenger seat of his Jeep, driving the backroads of Nebraska. The fog cleared, and Dana was still talking. "She said you were in the Army for a long time. Total badass is what she said."

"Mary is the one full of shit," he said flatly. "I just did my time and retired."

"Yeah?" she said. "All retired guys just carry a rifle around in the back of their car? I know what I saw back there." He sat quietly. No sense getting into an argument with someone he didn't know over something she probably didn't understand. "I worked as an ER nurse for a long time. You know the damage those things can do?" He looked at her again.

"I do," he said, looking back at the expressway. "Up close and personal, I do." It was her turn to look at him. "If it makes you uncomfortable, you could have gotten another ride home." Terry was writing off any possibility of getting laid by the fiery little nurse.

"Ha!" she snapped. "It takes a lot more than that to make me uncomfortable. Even when men I don't know stare at my tits," she said. Terry looked at her. "Yeah, I caught you looking in the kitchen. Get off up here." Terry signaled and exited the highway into the heart of the suburbs. Dana resumed her turn-by-turn instructions. He thought about explaining that it was the cross he was looking at and not her chest, but realized she wasn't likely to believe him. *Don't waste your breath.*

They drove quietly through residential neighborhoods until she told him to stop in front of a small house. It wasn't much, probably fifteen hundred square feet or so, but in this neighborhood, it was worth a small fortune. He was curious how she afforded to live here on a nurse's income.

"Nice place," he said, looking past her as she climbed out.

"Thanks for the ride," she said. She was about to close the door when Terry stopped her.

"Hey," he said. "I only stay about ten minutes from here. If you need anything, I'm nearby." Terry had made offers like that to people his entire adult life. He was honestly trying to be friendly, but Nurse Dana didn't think so.

"Like what?" she said. "A little booty call? I don't think so." She slammed the door and walked up the drive to the dark house.

"Well, fuck you very much," Terry said aloud as he put the 4Runner in gear and drove to his apartment. He was off in his estimate; it took almost twenty minutes to get there from Dana's place. Terry pulled the SUV into the apartment complex parking lot and climbed out. The moisture falling from the sky had stopped, and the night was quiet. He looked at his watch: 0215.

Inside his apartment, he dumped his coat over a kitchen chair and went through the same ritual as any time he came in the door; watch, wallet, Benchmade knife, keys, and cash all went into the tray on the kitchen counter. Terry took off his hiking boots and put them by the door, and his hat went on the counter next to the tray. He was headed for the bedroom when he remembered the piece of paper Mary gave him. He reached back into the pocket of his Filson and fished out the scrap. The address for Monday was on the front. He flipped the paper over and found phone numbers for Mary, Jimmy, and Dana.

After Tampa, Terry tried to stay off the grid as much as possible. He only had a pay-by-use phone, which he bought from Walmart, in case of emergency. It was out of the plastic but never used and sitting in the nightstand next to his Glock 19. He couldn't stop thinking about what Mary told him. Who were these guys? CIA wouldn't be starting a war with a criminal gang inside the borders. If they were FBI or any other federal agency, they would have said so. And they damn sure wouldn't have threatened to have her fired if she didn't cooperate. She said they weren't cops, and he trusted her judgment on that. Cops know cops, pure and simple. In his bones, Terry felt these guys were somehow associated with the organization that tried to put General Dawson into the Director's seat at CIA, but he had nothing more than his gut feeling.

In his bedroom, he lay on the bed, staring at the piece of paper. He would do a recon of the location on Sunday so he could find a place to park or sit and keep an eye on the address. He flipped the paper over and looked at the three phone numbers. Terry reached into the nightstand, grabbed the basic cell phone, and typed a very generic text.

THIS IS MY NUMBER - FOR EMERGENCY ONLY – TD

Before he hit send, he typed in the phone numbers for Mary and Jimmy. On a whim, he included Dana. Within two minutes, he got a response. The phone vibrated on the nightstand.

THX – M

Terry put the phone on the nightstand and turned off the lamp. He pulled the Army issue poncho liner up over his head and was quickly dozing when he heard the phone buzz again.

GFY – D

"Go fuck yourself," he said. "Boy, she's a real peach." He put the phone down and turned out the light. He fell asleep quickly. It felt like a matter of minutes before he heard the phone buzz again. When he pulled the nylon blanket off his face, it was light outside. He looked at the phone and realized it was almost nine. He never slept like that, never that late. After all the years he spent getting up early for physical training or operations, he was always up before the sun. *I must be getting old.* Terry picked up the phone and looked at the text message.

SRY. COFFEE? – D

"You've got to be kidding me," he said as he got out of bed. He didn't even answer the text; he just got dressed. Terry realized something in the days before he went to see his second family, the Friday after Thanksgiving; he was lonely.

Terry Davis left Nebraska over four months ago and did his best to wipe his life clean and put only himself at risk. After he shot Peggy in the bedroom of the farmhouse, he drove into Iowa, where he stopped and took all the money from his bank account, leaving only what was required to keep it open without penalty. In the same town, he sold his Jeep and bought the 4Runner, only having to add a little bit of cash to walk away without requiring a loan. The next time he stopped for anything other than gas or food was at this apartment complex, less than a mile from the house he grew up in. His parents had sold the place about a half dozen years ago, but this was his neighborhood. He knew these streets better than any town on the map.

Terry knew another fight was coming, and he felt that terrain would be important. He knew this terrain. The agreement was 'live and let live', but killing Peggy violated that, and he knew it wouldn't go without notice or repercussion. The nameless, faceless organization would eventually get around to coming after him, so he kept to himself. His sister lived within fifteen minutes of his apartment. His dad had passed away shortly after they sold the house, but his mom was less than an hour away. He hadn't seen a single friend or relative in the last four months. He did nothing but heal, rest, and keep his eyes open, waiting for what he thought was inevitable. When the unavoidable didn't come, he decided to reach out. He needed to. The isolation was driving him crazy. He was lonely.

Terry didn't have a permit of any kind to carry a gun in Illinois. He knew the state had some of the most restrictive firearm laws in the country. It took a specific, state-issued identification card even to buy ammunition. His body almost ached when he left the little one-bedroom apartment without a gun on him because he knew the threat was out there. He kept the FNX-45 Tactical pistol and his rifle stashed in the 4Runner, and he had the rest inside the apartment. Even though that was against the law in the great state of Illinois, he assumed the risk. It was as good as it was going to get, and he learned to live with it.

He walked out of the apartment and out to the parking lot. It was already warming up, and the wet snow from yesterday was melting. Everything was a muddy, wet mess. Terry drove the 4Runner through a Dunkin' Donuts that he passed on his way home the night before and got two large, black coffees and a bag full of various sweeteners and creamers. He pulled up in front of Dana's house and got out with the two coffees, almost spilling them as he slipped on the ice. She called to him from the front door.

"Don't bust your ass," she was in oversized sweats and a robe. "I'd hate for you to spill my coffee." The tone was much lighter than it was a few hours ago. Terry got to the front door.

"Good morning, dear," he said loud enough for the neighbors to hear. "You were fantastic last night." She rolled her eyes and let him in. He followed her into her kitchen, where she grabbed two mugs from the cabinet.

"I didn't mean for you to *bring* me coffee," she said. "I was wondering if you wanted to *get* coffee." She transferred the black liquid from the paper cups into ceramic mugs. He drank his as soon as she handed it to him. "Straight black, huh?" He nodded.

"No sense drinking coffee," he said, "if you're going to ruin it by putting all that crap in it."

"Well," she said with a smirk, "I'm going to put all that crap in mine." She proceeded to put more sweeteners and cream in her coffee than anyone he had ever seen. It looked like milk when she was done stirring. The cross was still hanging around her neck. He assumed she slept with it on and possibly never took it off. She caught him looking again.

"You're not very subtle," she said. "Eyes are up here, soldier-boy." He let out a heavy sigh.

"As nice as they are," he said, stopping to sip coffee, "I wasn't looking at your chest. It's the cross." Dana looked down, almost surprised to see it there. She never took it off.

"You got something against Catholics?" she said with tension. He exhaled again. He wasn't in the mood for an argument.

"No," he responded. "I grew up Catholic. Went to Catholic school and everything. My experience is that most people who wear those nowadays wear them for fashion and not faith. I was just curious about which one you were."

"Well, it's a long story," Dana said. She changed the subject. "So, you're going with Mary on Monday?" He almost spat out his coffee. "We texted this morning. She was mad at me for telling you to go fuck yourself."

"So much for this being a big secret," he said. "What did she tell you?"

"Everything," Dana said. "That she is scared and doesn't know what to do, and you're the big protector guy, and you're going to go with and keep her safe. Blah, blah, blah." She smiled at him. "I want to go, too." He stopped the cup before it got to his lips.

"No," Terry said and then resumed drinking.

"No?" she said with irritation in her voice. "Listen, buddy, while you were running all over the world for the last however many years, I was the one protecting her. You don't just get to walk in and take over."

"No," he said again. Whether he wanted it or not, there was an argument happening.

"Who the fuck do you think you are?" she said. "You can't keep me from going."

"I can't," he said. "You're right. So, go ahead. And when bad things start happening, and I mean really bad things, you can run in and save her."

"What do you mean by 'really bad things'?" she said, taken aback.

"I'm a 'worst case scenario' kind of guy," Terry said as he stood in front of her. "In your world, you fix things *after* really bad things happen. You patch holes in people, that's what you do. I'm the guy who puts holes in people. That's what I do, what I've always done," Dana leaned back against the counter. "These people, the people that she is dealing with? I have a bad feeling about these people. So, I am going to be there to keep things from going bad, not fix them after."

"You said, I patch people up after really bad things happen," she said defiantly. He knew what was coming next, and he almost winced. She was about to use his own words against him. "So, *if* things do go really bad, wouldn't it be better to have me there?" And there it was, she outflanked him. *Shit.*

"Why do I get the feeling," Terry said, "I'm not talking you out of this?" She stood there quietly and sipped her coffee. Smiling.

CHAPTER 3

Coffee with Dana was short and relatively uneventful. Terry tried several times to talk her out of going with him on Monday morning to watch over Mary. He was unsuccessful and realized that whether he took her with him or not, she was going to be there. He might as well keep her out of trouble, too. Before he left, they agreed to take a drive on Sunday to recon the address Mary gave him and then pick up her car from Mom and Pop's place. She didn't have to work again until Tuesday and didn't seem to be in a rush to get her wheels back.

Terry went back to his apartment and settled in. He knew the recon the following day would be important, but not being able to see inside the building while Mary was inside was killing him. He would have to check the building for entrances and exits, windows, doors, parking lots, and garages. This wasn't going to be a drive-by to check the address. He was worried that his 4Runner, as bland as it was, would draw attention being in the area two days in a row and driving around as if he were casing the place to rob it. *Maybe we can pick up Dana's car and use that?* He was running through options in his head and looking at an old paper street map when he realized it was already getting dark, and he hadn't eaten since the day before.

His head was in the tiny refrigerator looking for something to eat when he heard the cheap cell phone buzzing on the counter. He had taken it with him that morning, and it was sitting next to the tray full of his pocket items on the counter. If he offered to help Jimmy, Mary, and Dana in case of emergency, he knew he needed to carry it. He looked at the phone; it was Jimmy.

MEET AT THE TRAIN STATION WHERE WE SMOKED CIGS @ 2300 – S

Terry would have been smiling if he hadn't had a sick feeling in his stomach. "S" at the end of the message was about Jim's birth name, Seamus. The train station was the local commuter station, not far from Terry's apartment. When they were kids, Terry lived in the suburbs and Jim lived in the city, so the two would ride the train back and forth to see each other. One night, the two stole a pack of unfiltered Pall Mall cigarettes from Terry's dad and went to the train station so Jim could head home. The station building was small and butted up to a hill. The pair discovered you could easily climb the hill and step onto the roof of the building, looking over the downtown area of the small suburb. They smoked the stolen cigarettes until Jim's train came, and he headed back to the city.

Terry didn't know why Jimmy was being secretive, but he didn't like it. He looked at the time on the crappy cell phone: 1839. He had just over four hours before he needed to meet his best friend, so he went back to focusing on his recon tomorrow. Terry wasn't paying for internet and didn't have a computer, and his little cell phone wasn't a smartphone. He was doing old-school paper map work, and it was refreshing.

The building was on a four-lane city street with a turn lane in the middle. It was a large building, according to the grey outline on the map. That was what he had to work with, roughly building outlines on a paper street map. The veteran infantryman went over the map, again and again. He knew the size and scope of the buildings on all sides and the direction and distance to each major highway. He found the closest police station and even the closest emergency room. Terry was planning as many contingencies as he could without seeing the building itself, all while watching the clock ticking down to his meeting time with Jimmy.

The train station was less than a mile from his apartment. Terry was tempted to walk just to be outside, but didn't want to draw attention to himself. A guy walking the streets at night, in the winter, was exactly something a suburban cop would take an interest in, and Terry didn't need that. He decided to drive, knowing the parking lot would have at least a few cars in it; there were always suburbanites who took the train into the city on a Saturday night for dinner. He could park there without raising any suspicion. Terry decided to go early and get eyes on the area. That feeling in his stomach was getting worse. His watch read 2238 when he walked to his 4Runner.

The drive to the station was quick, less than five minutes along the quiet suburban streets. Terry parked in the lot and sat, watching the building and the minimal activity in the area. Not much was moving tonight. Finally, he climbed out of his truck and walked to the back of the building. There were no footprints in the snow or mud on the hillside that led up to the roof. He had beaten Jim to the spot. Terry climbed the slippery slope and stepped onto the shingled roof. He suddenly had the urge for a cigarette.

Terry was keeping one eye on his watch and one eye on the two roads that led to the parking lot. He had no idea what Jim was driving, so he was looking for headlights. A small Nissan pickup pulled into the lot at 2302, and Terry watched Jimmy get out and survey the area before he headed toward the station building. Jim was halfway across the parking lot when a squad car pulled in, the driver slowly heading toward him. Terry crouched down, keeping only his eyes above the roofline. After a brief exchange, Jim clearly showed his badge to the officer, and the squad car turned around and drove back out of the lot. Soon, Terry heard Jim coming up the slope.

"Hey, James Bond," Terry said as Jim stepped onto the roof, "what's with all the fucking secrecy?"

"Terry," Jim said with a serious look, "No bullshit, I need some help."

"If we are meeting on the roof of a train station," Terry said, "this can't be good. What the hell is going on?"

"It's Mary," Jim said.

"You talking about her meeting on Monday morning?" Terry interrupted. He was starting to feel the cold seep in and rubbed his hands together.

"You know about that?" Jim asked. Terry nodded. "Brother, there is something seriously wrong going on, and she is in the middle of it."

"I got that feeling too," Terry said. "Did she tell you? Or someone else?"

"One of the guys on my team said something," Jim replied. He was rubbing his hands together like Terry was, fighting the cold air. "I guess they tried to recruit him, too. He started asking them a lot of questions, and they dumped him." In a weird way, that actually made Terry feel better. If these guys, whoever they were, were actively recruiting other people, then Mary being pulled in wasn't tied to Terry.

"How did he know about Mary?" Terry asked.

"I guess they passed each other in the hallway. She was leaving as he was going in," Jimmy said. "He asked our SWAT commander if he knew the two guys, who they were, whatever, and he mentioned Mary. Pops was the SWAT commander's TO when he was a rookie, so he did some digging, and then he came to me." Terry was following along, realizing the Chicago PD was more inbred than the Army. "Terry, these guys aren't cops."

"That's what Mary said," Terry told him. "Who do you think they are?"

"Honestly?" Jim took a breath. "I think they are military. Special ops or something. I thought maybe you would know."

"Is that why we're freezing our asses off up here?" Terry asked. "Because you think these are some super-secret special forces guys? Like they are going to track you or something?" Terry knew it was a possibility. It may even be a probability at this point, but he didn't want to scare Jim. Coming here, discreetly, was the best idea Jimmy could have come up with, whether he knew it or not. "Listen, I am going to recon the place for her Monday meeting tomorrow. I'll let you know what I find out." Jimmy shifted his body in the cold, and it probably saved his life.

Terry never heard the report of a weapon or saw a flash from a muzzle, but he heard the supersonic crack of the round and the impact it made when it hit Jimmy in the right shoulder. He fell flat onto the roof and yelled in pain. Terry grabbed him by the collar and dragged him off the roof. He didn't know where the shot came from, but he knew staying on the roof wasn't an option. He needed to get to the 4Runner. Terry propped his best friend against the base of the hill and looked him in the eyes.

"You got your gun on you?" Terry asked. Jimmy nodded. "Good. Stay here. I'm going to get my vehicle. Open your fucking eyes." Jimmy stopped wincing and looked at him. "Put pressure on that. Shoot anyone who isn't me. Got it?"

"Yeah," Jimmy said. "Got it." He tried to control his breathing. Terry turned and moved around the building. His instinct told him the shot came from across the railroad tracks, which meant he had the building between him and the shooter, but that guy was probably moving already. Terry made a dash to the cluster of cars closest to the building, hesitating just for a second and then moving to the 4Runner. He climbed inside and fired up the SUV, whipping it around to the backside of the building. When Terry got to Jimmy, he was already on his feet with his pistol drawn.

"Get in the back," Terry opened the liftgate. "There is a first aid kit back there."

"What?" Jimmy said as he moved to the back of the vehicle. "Take me to a fucking hospital!"

"If we go to a hospital," Terry said with sincerity in his voice, "whoever shot you is going to find you there and finish you off."

"Where the hell are we going?" Jimmy asked as he lifted his body into the cargo compartment. Terry slammed the liftgate shut. A bullet hit the roof rack of the vehicle. *Thank God this fucker can't shoot.* He moved to the driver's seat in a low crouch and climbed in. They sped out of the parking lot, Jimmy wailing as he was thrown against the plastic interior of the grey Toyota. Terry reached down and hit the button to lower the rear window of the vehicle.

"Throw your fucking cell phone out the window," he yelled as he drove.

"What?" Jimmy yelled.

"Your cell phone," Terry responded. "They tracked your phone. Get rid of it." Jimmy fished his phone out of his pants pocket and tossed it out of the moving vehicle. Terry raised the window and then grabbed his phone from his pocket. He typed as he drove.

INBOUND W J. HE HAS GSW. NO HOSPITAL. PREP TO TREAT.

Terry was running through possibilities in his head. They could have a drone overhead; he learned that after Tampa. They could track his cell phone as it was pinging off the towers; he did that in Iraq over ten years ago to track down terrorists. They could be monitoring Dana's phone. He thought the first was unlikely, especially with the air traffic in and around Chicago. The second was primarily unlikely because he had only used his phone in the last day or so. The third was possible. Dana was Mary's best friend, and if they were tracking Jimmy's phone, they were likely tracking Mary's. Anyone with a background in signal intelligence would be linking as many of the devices as possible. Dana's phone may be on the board somewhere, judging by her call and text volume with Mary. *Shit.*

"Hey, brother," Terry yelled back to Jimmy. "You still with me back there?"

"Yeah," Jimmy said. "This hurts like hell."

"We are heading to Dana's," Terry said, looking in the rearview mirror. "Don't get out of the car. We will pick her up and head to my place."

"Copy," Jimmy said from the back. It was a pet peeve of Terry's, but he knew it was the difference between cops and soldiers. Cops used 'Copy' on the radio, and soldiers used 'Roger.' In the military, if you say 'copy' on the radio, it means you physically wrote something down, or you've seen too many bad movies. They pulled up to Dana's house, and she was standing in the door wearing scrubs.

"We're leaving," he told her. "Grab your med gear and leave your phone here."

"What?" she asked, very confused.

"We can't stay here," Terry told her. "I'll explain later. Just leave your phone here and grab your shit." The fiery little nurse hesitated for a second, but she could see in his eyes that this was no time to argue. She stepped back into the house and came back with a black backpack loaded with medical gear. Before Dana closed the door, Terry tossed his phone inside. She looked at him. "Let's go," he told her and headed for the 4Runner. She bounded behind him and could see Jim stuffed in the cargo compartment, so she climbed into the back seat.

"I'll treat from back here," she said. Terry was impressed. She was all business now. Terry maneuvered the SUV as quickly as he could through the little suburb while trying not to draw attention. *Maybe it was the cop Jimmy talked to.* Terry flashed back to Peggy's garage and the Sheriff's deputy handcuffed to the step on the side of the Audi. He was trying to drive and put pieces together at the same time.

"We're going to my apartment," Terry said to Dana. "You can patch him up there. We will be there in about fifteen minutes. Don't dig too much out of your bag."

"You drive," Dana snapped at him. "Let me do my fucking job."

"Yes, ma'am," Terry said. She was right, he needed to focus on the road. She knew what she was doing and certainly didn't need a grunt telling her how to be a trauma nurse. Terry was happy the wound was simple, mainly because it meant Jim was going to be fine, but also because he was going to come back and watch Dana's house once she got Jim stabilized. If they were tracking their phones, having both devices in one place would certainly draw the attention he was hoping would confirm his suspicions.

The trio pulled into the parking lot at Terry's apartment complex. Jim was still in pain, but Dana had his wound dressed in a bandage to at least contain the bleeding until she got him inside. Terry turned and looked behind him before he shut off the engine.

"Hey brother," Terry said, "we are going to act like you're drunk. Dana and I will help you get inside, but if anyone sees, that's the story. Got it?" He looked at Jim, who flashed a thumbs-up. Dana nodded. Terry got out and walked to the back, opening the cargo hatch. He draped his Filson over Jim to conceal both the wound and the bandage. Dana got out of the backseat and packed her bag back up. Terry refrained from giving her the 'I told you so' look; he knew this wasn't the time. Jimmy leaned on him, and he helped his best friend, his brother, down the sidewalk and to his apartment. Dana caught up to them by the time they hit the front door.

Inside, they put Jimmy in a chair, not because it made it easier for Dana to treat him, but because Terry didn't have a couch. To say the apartment was bare was an understatement. Dana looked around and shook her head as she put the bag of medical gear on the kitchen table. Terry didn't realize until now that Jim was still holding his CPD Glock in his hand. Taking the pistol from his friend, Terry put it on the counter. He stood back and watched Dana work. She was good. In a matter of minutes, she had the wound cleaned, packed, and bandaged.

"Let's go put him on my bed," Terry said as he tried to pull Jim out of the chair.

"Looking at this apartment," she said, "I'm surprised you have one." She reached in and helped Jim out of the chair. He wasn't completely dead weight, but he was fading. His adrenaline had run out, and his body was shutting down to rest and heal. The two got the SWAT officer into the bedroom and laid him on the bed. Jimmy wasn't as tall as Terry, but he had a chest like a beer keg and was solid muscle even in his late forties. Terry and Dana backed out of the room and closed the door.

"He is going to sleep for a while," she said. "It's gonna hurt like hell when he wakes up, though."

"It's a good thing you'll be here when he does," Terry said, moving to the linen closet. "Keep an eye on him. I'll be back before sunrise."

"What?" she grabbed his arm. "You're leaving? Where are you going? And when are you going to tell me what is going on?" He turned and looked at her. She was cute.

"I'm going to watch your house," he said. "I think whoever shot him was tracking cell phones. His, maybe yours, and mine, too. That's why I left them there. Now I'm going to go watch to see what happens. If someone comes to visit, we will know for sure." He handed her some towels and rags.

"What the hell am I supposed to do?" she asked as she followed him into the kitchen.

"You know how to use this?" he said as he handed her Jim's Glock.

She never unfolded her arms. "I asked if you knew how to use this," he said flatly.

"Yes," she said, taking the pistol. "Mary taught me after I got mugged."

"Good," he said, turning to the door. "Clean yourself up and keep an eye on him. Anyone besides me who comes through this door, shoot them." He walked out and closed the door behind him. Dana stood there with the pistol in her hand, wanting to put it back on the counter but hesitating. Something inside her knew he wasn't being dramatic. She found herself thinking about him for a few seconds longer than she realized.

"Dammit," she said to herself. "Mary was right; he *is* fucking dangerous."

CHAPTER 4

It didn't take Terry long to find what he was looking for. He spotted the house with the For Sale sign the morning he brought Dana hot coffee from Dunkin' Donuts, not because he had any desire to buy a home but because it reminded him of the one he grew up in. The sign in the yard was part of it, but the front walk and the driveway hadn't been shoveled after the snow on Friday.

The house was empty, and he needed a place to park the 4Runner inconspicuously. Terry pulled the SUV into the drive, casually walked into the yard, and took the sign down. Now it just looked like any other house with a car parked in the drive. If you weren't from the neighborhood, you wouldn't notice it, and Terry wasn't planning on being around when the neighbors started to roll out of bed.

He didn't need anything sophisticated for this minor operation. There were plenty of streetlights, house lights, and porch lights shining throughout the neighborhood, allowing him to move around without night vision. He grabbed the FNX out of the console between the seats and screwed on the suppressor. He hadn't fired the pistol since he shot Peggy at the farmhouse, but he knew it was clean and was confident it would function as it always had. He held the FNX close to his body as he moved, minimizing the silhouette of the big pistol.

Terry moved between the houses and through the backyards. Here and there, he set off a motion-activated backyard light or two. He thought about all the times he snuck out his window as a teenager to go drinking with his buddies or hook up with some high school girl. *Glad they didn't have shit like this back then.*

He made his way to the back of the house that was across the street and up one from Dana's place. It was a big grey house with a covered porch and bushes around the front. Terry quietly slipped between the bushes and the porch railing and sat quietly, watching Dana's house. His watch read 0234. The retired Army officer realized that if anyone had tracked them to Dana's, they could easily have come and gone in the time it took to get Jim to the apartment and patch him up.

Terry was a young Captain the first time he heard the phrase 'Hope is not a course of action,' and it stuck with him. He watched a fellow Captain, the battalion intelligence officer, get destroyed by the battalion commander during a briefing when he said he 'hoped' the enemy was going to do something. The young officer sat down and never finished his portion of the brief after getting his ass chewed. Terry never uttered the word 'hope' in a briefing in his career after that. This was a case where he hoped he hadn't arrived too late, but he would never say that out loud.

The minutes dragged by as Terry sat in the cold, wet mulch behind the bushes, waiting to see if the bad guys showed up. Shortly after 0300, Terry caught some movement off to the side of Dana's house. In the rush to leave, she left the porch light and the interior house lights on. He didn't see a person, but he was confident he saw a shadow, and it was too big to be an animal. Terry blinked quickly and opened his eyes wide, trying to clear his vision and expand his field of view. Another shadow on the other side of the house, too soon to be the same person. There were at least two of them, and these guys knew how to stay concealed just like Terry did.

Terry saw headlights out of the corner of his eye. It was a police car, just like the one he saw in the parking lot of the train station. It was a Ford Explorer police model, something many police departments had been forced to adopt as the big automakers moved away from making four-door cars with big engines and Rear Wheel Drive.

The police SUV stopped in front of Dana's house, and the cop stepped out. Terry watched his movements, trying to determine if he was part of whatever was going on or if he was just a cop responding to a call about prowlers in the neighborhood. He held his breath as the officer walked up to the front door, knocked, and peered into the windows. After a second knock, he walked off the porch and strolled casually to the right side of the house. He looked to be older and a little overweight, but he was wearing a heavy coat, so Terry really couldn't tell.

The cop clicked on his huge MagLight as he walked around the side of the house, making a cursory check to see if anyone was there. You could see by the way he moved and the way he checked with his flashlight that his heart wasn't in this. The uniformed man walked to the other side of the house and repeated the half-hearted check for peeping toms and then returned to his cruiser. Before he got in, he transmitted something into the radio mic on his shoulder, then drove off into the night. Terry watched and waited. *At least the local cops aren't involved.*

Terry knew someone had called the police, and they had reported something or someone outside Dana's house. Whether they were being tracked by cell phone or another method, he knew they were being tracked. The combat veteran didn't believe in coincidences, so in his mind, this validated his theory; whoever was behind this had considerable capability. His gut told him the unnamed, unknown organization he encountered in Tampa was behind this.

Terry waited another half hour, watching Dana's house and not seeing anything, before he extricated himself from the bushes and worked back to the 4Runner. His mind was spinning as he drove back to the apartment. He deliberately took a different route and went with his eyes in the rearview mirror, trying to identify a tail if there was one. On the empty roads just after 0400, it would have been pretty easy to spot, but he wanted to be sure.

Terry wheeled the SUV into the parking lot and tucked the FNX back into the console before he got out. He hadn't slept, and being out in the cold for the last hour had sapped his energy. He needed to get inside and get some rest. At some point, he needed to get hold of Mary, but they had ditched all their cell phones, so he would have to see her in person. Terry knew if she wasn't being watched before, she certainly was after Jim took a bullet in the shoulder. It was going to be challenging to talk to her, let alone convince her not to go to the meeting on Monday. Even knowing she is putting her life at risk, the cop in her was going to want to investigate and find out who shot her brother and why.

"It's me," Terry said as he came through the front door. He didn't know what state Dana was going to be in, but he wanted to announce his presence before she shot him. The apartment was quiet but still completely in order. There were bloody bandages in the trash can, and Dana's medical backpack was still on the kitchen table. Terry was confident no one had been there. He moved to the bedroom to check on Jim and found Dana asleep on the floor next to the bed. She was wearing a pair of Terry's athletic shorts and one of his old Army physical training shirts. He peered into the bathroom and saw damp scrubs draped over the rod for the shower curtain. She must have cleaned them up before she went to sleep.

Terry walked in and spotted the Glock on the floor next to her. She may have been reluctant, but at least she listened to him. He moved it away from her before he leaned in to make sure Jimmy was breathing and checked his pulse. Terry looked at his best friend, his brother. He shook his head with guilt. He didn't know if he was, but he felt responsible for this. Chances were he had nothing to do with it, but he was in the middle of it now. Terry's second wife always said he was the 'bad penny' while he was in uniform. Every unit he was assigned to ended up deploying to combat, and trouble seemed to find him no matter where he was. Trouble had indeed found him again.

Terry picked up the Glock, walked quietly out of the room, and closed the door, walking down the very short hall to the living room. He surveyed the mostly empty living space. *I really need a couch.* He didn't have much choice, so he grabbed Dana's medical bag off the table and put it on the floor to use as a pillow. Terry had spent twenty-five years in the military and had spent hundreds of nights sleeping outside in various countries and under the worst of conditions. Sleeping on a floor with a pack for a pillow was not foreign to him, but he wasn't a young man anymore, and he anticipated waking up with an aching back or sore muscles as a result. He put the pistol on the floor next to him and lay on his back, head resting on the backpack.

Terry's mind started to drift to the same place it had gone every single night for over four months: Tampa and everything that led up to it. He thought about Peggy and the trip to the National Guard armory to call General "Boo-Boo" Dawson. The Sheriff's deputies came to the house. He could see George and Juanita and their little gas station and grill. He could smell the blood from the man he killed with his Benchmade knife in the dark—the carwash. Brian and Emma, along with the four of them, were talking and laughing around their kitchen island. Terry thought about the brave old man, Larry, who helped him fight off some contractors and, eventually, a Platoon of SEALs. That same old man, Larry, dying alone on his couch. He thought about the shitty little motel—the explosion. Then, Dawson's basement, and killing the General with his government-issued General Officer pistol.

Terry thought about the two priests who helped him because they were good men and not just because they were priests. The skinny, tattooed waitress who helped him steal a car was murdered as a result. Then heard the voice of a faceless man and recalled his words.

"We are powerful people. We aren't Democrats or Republicans. We aren't politicians or soldiers. We are Americans, and we are doing what we think is best for America. We are the media. We are the government. We are the people who can move mountains. We are going to get our way whether we allow you to live or not."

Those words were burned into his memory, even after all the concussions and the head trauma throughout his life. He would never forget those words. Then he remembered Peggy. How she betrayed him and even tried to get him killed for whatever cause she and this nameless organization were involved in. He remembered her lying on her bedroom floor with two bullet holes in her chest, holes from his hand.

At some point, his conscious thoughts became dreams, and he transitioned into sleep. The next thing he knew, he could smell coffee. He grabbed the Glock and sat up, pointing it at Dana as she stood at the kitchen table. He startled her, and she spilled hot coffee on her hand. It was daylight, although Terry had no idea what time it was.

"Dammit," she said, shaking the hot coffee off her hand. Terry didn't apologize. He hauled himself off the floor and walked over to find the only two mugs he owned filled with black coffee.

"Sorry, I don't have all that crap you like in your coffee," he said flatly. Terry put down the Glock and picked up one of the mugs.

"How about 'I'm sorry for pointing a gun at you?' or 'I'm sorry for scaring the shit out of you?'" she said. "You sorry for that?" Terry didn't answer. Another argument not worth having. He sipped his coffee.

"How's Jimmy doing?" he asked her. She gave him an incredulous look.

"Boy," Dana said, "you're some piece of work. He's fine. He's been up once and has been to the bathroom. He is resting again, but he is mobile. Blood loss wasn't too bad, and I already changed his bandages. He is going to need to see a doctor." Terry nodded his head. "I'm fine, by the way," she continued. "Now, do you mind telling me what the hell is going on?"

"I'd prefer not to," Terry said. She opened her mouth to speak, and he put his hand up. "*But* I know you aren't going to let up, so I may as well tell you." He just realized she was still wearing his shirt and shorts. They were huge on her tiny frame. "Nice outfit, by the way." She opened her mouth to speak again, but Terry cut her off. "I'll make you a deal. I'll tell you what's going on if you tell me about that cross around your neck."

Mary was confused. He could see it on her face. She didn't understand his fascination with her necklace, but she would play along. "Deal," she said. "You first." Terry nodded.

"You already know about the guys trying to recruit Mary into whatever war they are planning with the gangs." She nodded. "I am pretty sure this is related to that. Well, maybe not the war with the gangs, but related to the guys Mary is supposed to meet tomorrow."

"How do you know that?" she asked. Terry got the feeling Dana was more than just a good nurse. He could see the wheels turning behind her eyes.

"You need to trust me on this," he said. "There is something much bigger going on, and the less you know, the safer you are."

"No way," she said flatly. "No way you're dragging me out of my house in the middle of the night, to patch up bullet holes in Jimmy, and then tell me 'you're safer not knowing.' So, you'd better start talking, or I'm leaving."

"You're a real pain in the ass," he said. "I'm trying to protect you, Dana."

"Yeah?" she said. "I don't need your protection," she paused. This was a game of chicken to see who blinked first. She knew he needed her to take care of Jim, so she held all the cards. "Last chance or I'm walking."

"Jesus," he said. "If you want to know, I'll tell you. You're not going to believe me, but I'll tell you anyway." She folded her arms, holding her cup of coffee. She won, and she was quietly gloating with a shit-eating grin on her face.

One of the things Terry always enjoyed about being with Peggy was the sparring between the two. Peggy was brilliant, and she gave as good as she got, but Terry almost always came out on top. Dana was different. She was unimpressed by who he was. Terry suspected that part of her even loathed who he was. With Peggy, it was an intellectual game of chess, trying to outmaneuver and outthink each other. Dana seemed unafraid to smash the chessboard and declare victory.

"These guys that Mary is going to meet?" he started. She sipped her coffee. "My gut says these guys are either former or current military. Probably high-end special operations guys or maybe from the tactical teams at CIA." He waited for a reaction from her, but got nothing. "Those guys are part of a bigger thing. A bigger organization that moves behind the government. They influence our country and our leadership. They use the media. They have money. They have power. They can do whatever they want." She giggled and sipped her coffee. She didn't believe a word of it. "Never mind," he said as he turned away from her out of frustration.

"Wait," she said. She was still smiling. He turned back around. "You're trying to tell me there is this big conspiracy. These people who can do whatever they want and get away with it? Like a...what do they call it...shadow government?" Terry stared at her. "And they are going to start a war with the gangs. And they shot Jimmy. And they are after us." She suddenly felt very nervous. "You're some kind of nut, you know that?"

"There were people at your house last night," he said. The smile left her face. "There were people outside your house when I was there. They went to your house because that's where our cell phones were. They tracked them." Dana put her coffee cup on the table. "The only reason they don't know where we are is because we left the phones there." She was staring at the mug on the table, trying to decide if she believed what he was saying.

"So, what about Mary?" she asked. "If what you are saying is true, and I'm not saying I believe you, then we can't let her go meet them. And if you're wrong, and she doesn't go meet them, then she and Jimmy get fired."

"I know," he said. "But I'm not wrong, and I need to go talk to her."

"This is crazy," she said. "People like this don't exist." Dana was starting to consider the real possibility that she was in danger just by being here, but not from the people Terry was talking about, but in danger because of Terry himself. *He may be insane.* She didn't know what to believe.

"I know this is hard to wrap your head around," he said. She gave him a look. "But think about it. Two guys who even Mary says aren't cops are recruiting cops to start a war with the gangs in Chicago. Someone shoots Jim for no real reason. But not just someone; someone with a suppressed weapon in the dark. And then people come to your house in the middle of the night because that is where our phones are."

"You know what I think?" she said. "I think you're nuts. You may have shot Jim yourself. And the only person who said someone was at my house last night was *you*." He resigned himself to the fact that she wasn't going to believe him. "I'm leaving." She went to the bathroom and put on her scrubs. Terry stood there, watching her. "You can keep the bag to take care of Jimmy." Dana walked out the door without another word.

CHAPTER 5

"**B**rother," Terry said to Jimmy, "I need you to get up. I am taking you to Mom and Pops." The SWAT officer stirred a little and then let out a soft moan as he felt the pain in his shoulder. He opened his eyes.

"This fucking hurts," he said with a wince.

"I know," Terry told him, "but we need to get moving. I need to get you to your parents, and then I need to find Mary."

"Nah," Jim said as he sat up. "I'll go with you. Where's Dana?"

"She left," Terry said as he helped Jim to his feet. "You don't need to come with; you need to rest. I know Mom will take care of you just like she did when we were fifteen and Pops got shot in the ass by the drunk Italian guy. Remember that?" Jimmy laughed and then winced in pain again. He was on his feet and moving.

"Yeah, I remember," he said. "Dana took off?"

"She did," Terry said. "Let's get going, and I'll fill you in while we drive." The two men struggled with getting Jim dressed and out to the 4Runner. It wasn't easy, but the stocky man powered through the pain and got into the passenger seat. He was breathing heavily when Terry climbed into the driver's side.

"So, what the hell happened?" Jimmy asked as they pulled out of the lot. "Who the fuck shot me?"

Terry began to recount the story of what happened after they got off the roof. Jimmy only remembered parts of it, so Terry was filling in the gaps. He hadn't decided until now if he was ever going to tell Jim, his closest friend, the whole story about what happened in Nebraska and then Tampa. He felt like he didn't have much choice, and Jim not only needed to know but deserved to know.

The drive took over an hour with traffic, and by the time the two men pulled up to Mom and Pops' house, Terry had revealed the entirety of what happened four months prior. Jimmy was neither surprised nor judgmental. Terry was closer to him than any man on the planet, including his closest Army buddies like Brian. Jim took every word on faith because he trusted Terry.

"So, what does all that mean?" Jim finally asked him. "Like right now. What does it all mean in what is going on now?"

"Other than I am confident the two are connected, I don't really know," Terry said. "But I need to get to Mary to make sure she is OK and that she doesn't meet with those guys tomorrow. Let's get you inside." Terry got out and shuffled around to the passenger side of the SUV. He pulled Jim out of the vehicle and threw his arm over his shoulder, bearing most of the SWAT Officer's weight. Getting up the front steps was a challenge, but the two men fought through it and opened the front door.

Pops was in his chair, in front of the TV with a can of Old Style in his hand as they came in. The big man never stood up.

"Mom," he yelled as he looked at his wounded son. "You'd better get in here. Terry and Jimmy have been out causing trouble." He sipped his beer. The Bears were playing the Packers, and there was no way Pops was getting up from watching the game. Mom came in from the kitchen.

As the wife of a cop and the mother of two more, her lack of reaction shouldn't have been a surprise, but it made Terry realize the strength the little woman possessed. There was no real shock or wailing of 'my baby' coming from Mom. She just threw her hands up and then motioned for Terry to move upstairs.

"You can tell me what happened after the game," Pops said, staring at the screen. Terry looked at him and chuckled. The trio turned left at the top of the stairs and moved Jimmy to his old room. Another wave of nostalgia came over Terry. The room seemed frozen in 1990, with the same posters on the walls and trophies on the dresser. Terry would have bet his retirement check that there was still a Playboy under the mattress, a bottle of vodka in the closet, and condoms in the top left drawer of the desk.

Mom scurried off to the upstairs bathroom and came back with a plastic tub full of first aid supplies. There was blood seeping through Jim's shirt, so Mom cut it away with a pair of orange-handled Fiskars scissors. She went to work and wasn't saying a word. The wound was cleaned and the bandages changed in a matter of a few minutes. Even Dana would have been impressed. Jim was immediately back to sleep before she could even pull the blue comforter over him. She looked at Terry.

"I would have thought," she said with disappointment in her voice, "this sort of garbage would have stopped when you two grew up. Maybe you still haven't grown up." The little woman got up and walked out with the plastic first aid tub. That was as close as she got to yelling at Terry. It hurt.

Terry looked at his brother for a second before he lifted his sore body off the bed and headed back downstairs. Pop wasn't in his chair, but he emerged from the kitchen as Terry hit the bottom step. The two men shared a look.

"It's halftime," the old man said. He was still huge, Terry realized. Pops sat back in his chair and popped the fresh can of Old Style.

"Pops," Terry said. "Jimmy got shot last night."

"Did you shoot him?" the old man asked tossing a cashew into his mouth. Terry couldn't help but smile.

"No, Pops, I didn't shoot him," Terry said. The old man shrugged. "Pops, Mary is mixed up in something at work. She might be in trouble. I need to go talk to her." For the first time since they walked in, Pops showed some emotion. Mary was his baby girl, and the idea that she was in trouble caught his attention.

"What do you mean she is in trouble?" he asked Terry, locking eyes with him.

"It's tough to explain, Pops," Terry was sidestepping. The old man had seen this from him and Jimmy since they were ten years old. His eyes narrowed. "I'm not bullshitting you, Pops. I can handle this, but I need you to do a couple of things."

"You're still a scroungy little shit, but I believe you," Pops said. "What do I need to do?" Terry smiled at him.

"You still keep a gun in the house?" Terry asked. The old man reached into the magazine rack next to his recliner and pulled out a .38 snubnose Smith and Wesson. "OK, that answers that. The people who shot Jim may come looking for him. Second, I need to get hold of Mary, but I don't have a phone."

"You don't have a phone?" the big German laughed at him. "Hell, even I have a phone." He reached into his pants pocket and pulled out a flip phone. Terry shook his head. "Hit star and four. That's her." He handed Terry the phone.

"Thanks, Pops," Terry took the phone and walked through the kitchen and onto the back porch. Mom only glanced at him as he passed through. He opened the phone and pressed the speed dial combination Pops had given him. It started ringing.

"Hey, Pops," Mary's voice came through the phone.

"It's me," Terry said. "How soon can you meet me at the swing set?" There was a noticeable pause.

"The swing set?" she said. It wasn't really a question. "Are you trying to get me to make out with you again? And why are you on Pops' phone?"

"Mary," Terry tried to express the urgency of the situation without revealing too much on the phone. "How quickly can you meet me there? We need to talk in person."

"I can be there in half an hour," she said.

"I'll see you there," he said. "Mary, leave your phone at home."

"Copy," she said. That damn cop habit. He was confident she heard his tone and would do as she was told. He hung up the phone and went back into the house. Mom was in the living room with Pops.

"I'll be back in a little while," Terry said. He tossed the phone to Pops. "Thanks." He turned to walk out the door.

"You know you don't live here, right?" Pops said. He had been telling Terry that since he was a kid. It was like traveling back in time. Terry walked out the door and was heading for the 4Runner when a car pulled up in front and double-parked, blocking him in. Terry made a quick estimate and didn't think he could get to the 4Runner in time to get his pistol. *Shit.*

Dana popped out of the backseat of the black Honda Accord. It was an Uber, and she was back to pick up her car. She was surprised to see Terry but gave him an evil eye and walked past him to the house. Terry was inside the 4Runner and waiting for the Uber to move when Dana reappeared and jumped into the passenger seat. Terry stared at her.

"Get out," he said.

"You're going to see Mary," she said. "I'm coming with, so you can go fuck yourself." Terry had never felt the urge to hit a woman in his life, but this one was trying his patience. The Uber finally pulled away, letting Terry out of his parking spot.

"I should have locked the doors," he said to no one in particular. He looked over at Dana before he pulled away from the curb. It was the first time he had seen her in regular clothes. She didn't wear any makeup and her hair was in a ponytail, but she looked good. Terry had never felt so conflicted about a woman in his life. "So, do you believe me now?"

"No," she said. "But I don't think you're crazy either." Terry looked at her. "I went back to my house and looked around. There were footprints in the snow around the house, so I called the police. They said they responded to a complaint from the neighbors last night about someone prowling around my house. So, you weren't lying about that." Terry felt a weird sense of vindication.

"Wait," he said as they stopped at a red light. "Where is your phone? Do you have it on you?"

"No," she said. "I knew you'd freak out on me if I did. I left it at Mary's mom and dad's." Terry pulled away as the light turned green. They were headed for a park inside the nearest forest preserve. Jim, Terry, and Mary hung out there as kids and then went there to drink at night as teenagers. The forest itself provided cover for more than one getaway when the local police arrived to break up a party of underage drinkers. They called it the swing set for short. It was also the place where Terry and Mary kissed before he left for the Army.

The two were silent as they drove a few miles to the preserve and sat quietly after Terry pulled into the lot by the park. He positioned the vehicle where he could see the road in his sideview mirror, and the park itself was in front of him. He was constantly watching, eyes moving from one to the other. He didn't notice she was staring at him until she cleared her throat. He looked at her.

"What?" he snapped at her.

"Jesus," she said. "Chill out. I was just wondering what that burn scar is on your neck." He stared at her. "Call it professional curiosity," she said, trying to ease the tension. He looked at his mirror again.

"It's from a hot casing," he said. "A training exercise a long time ago. It got caught and burned my skin." Terry looked at his watch, and it had been almost half an hour since he spoke to Mary. He opened the door and climbed out. Dana climbed out of the passenger side and followed two steps behind him. There were a few families in the park, braving the cold. Terry went over to the pavilion and leaned on a post, watching the road coming in. He reached into his back pocket and fished out his can of Copenhagen. It seemed like his first dip in days.

"Well," Dana said, "that's disgusting." He could hear the disdain in her voice and looked at her. He looked back at the drive without saying a word. There was a car coming up the road, and Terry could see Mary in the driver's seat as she pulled into a parking space. She jumped out and hugged Dana.

"What's with all the secrecy?" she said, looking at Terry.

"Jimmy was shot last night," Terry said. He could see the shock in her face.

"Way to ease into it," Dana said with a smartass tone. He snapped a look at her, and she cowered.

"He is at your parents. Dana patched him up last night, and Mom is taking care of him now. You cannot go to this meeting tomorrow. Period," he said.

"I'm trying to process all of this," Mary said. "Where did Jimmy get shot? Like, where was he? And where did he get hit? Were you with him?"

"Yes, I was with him," Terry started calmly, hoping to keep Mary calm. "We were at the train station by my parents' old place. He asked me to meet him there. He knows about your meeting tomorrow through his SWAT commander. He was worried." Mary's face went white. "Someone shot him with a suppressed weapon, a rifle. It went through his shoulder. I evacuated him to Dana's. We picked her up and went to my place. She patched him up. He is at your parents. He is going to be fine."

"He needs to see a doctor," Dana interrupted. Terry snapped a look at her. "But, yes, he is going to be fine." She put her hand on Mary's arm to calm her.

"I went back to Dana's and people were moving around her house," Terry continued. "Thankfully, a local cop scared them off. They tracked us there, most likely by our cell phones. Listen to me, Mary. I don't care if you get fired or not; you cannot go to that meeting tomorrow."

"But what about Jimmy?" Mary said with a desperate tone. "He'll get fired, too."

"Mary, Jimmy got shot," Terry said. "I don't think he gives a shit about getting fired right now."

"I think she should still go," Dana interjected. Terry and Mary both looked at her.

"No one asked you," Terry said. "She's not going."

"Yes," Mary said. "I am going. We need to find out what the hell is going on." Dana smirked at him.

"I knew this was going to happen," Terry said. "Mary, you can't go. You must trust me on this."

"This is my job, Terry," his pseudo sister replied. "I can't just look away from this. These guys are starting a war with the gangs, and now they have shot my brother. Give me a good reason not to go." Terry exhaled with exasperation.

"This is the part," Dana said in her smartass tone, "where you tell her all about the big boogeyman that is out there controlling the government."

CHAPTER 6

"**W**hat the hell is she talking about?" Mary asked. Dana stood there with her arms folded and a smirk on her face. She was pissing him off.

"Not here," Terry said. "I'll tell you the rest, but not here. Did you leave your phone at home?" Mary nodded. "Let's head back to Mom and Pops, we can talk there. Dana left her phone there, but I put Pops on guard duty, and it is still daylight. No one will try anything there. At least not right now."

"What do you mean by 'right now'?" Mary asked. "I swear to God, Terry, if you put my parents in danger, I'll kill you." Terry knew she had put her own parents in danger the minute she agreed to meet these guys, but placing blame wasn't the thing to do right now.

"Let's just talk there," Terry said. "And you're riding with me," he said, pointing at Dana. It wasn't a request. The three walked back to the vehicles and split up. Dana climbed in with Terry, reluctantly. As soon as she closed her door, Terry laid into her. "Goddammit, I don't give a shit whether you believe me or not, but keep your fucking mouth shut. You're about to hear the whole story. Shit that you don't want to hear and that you won't want to believe. I tried to keep you out of this, and I tried to get you to trust me, but you're invested now and you're going to hear all of it." She was leaning back against the door, trying to stay as far away from him as she could. "Until we get there, hell, even after we get there, just be quiet."

Terry put the 4Runner in drive and pulled out of the parking lot. Dana didn't say a single word during the short drive to the house, going up the walk, or even once they got inside. Pops was still in his chair when they came through the door. He held up the revolver to show Terry he was still on guard duty. Dana followed Mary into the kitchen to say hi to Mom.

"How'd the Bears do?" he asked Pops, trying to keep things as normal as he could.

"Lost," he said. "Again." Mary and Dana came out of the kitchen, and the three headed upstairs to Mary's room. "No boys in your room, young lady," Pops called behind them. They kept moving, ignoring him. Terry poked his head in to check on Jim. He was awake but still lying in bed.

"Hey, brother," Terry said. "I've got Mary and Dana here." Jim turned his head and looked at him. "I'm going to fill them in on everything I told you on the way over. Everything. I'll have Dana come check on you after we are done."

"Cool," Jim said and lay his head back on the pillow. Terry knew he was in a lot of pain, and they had nothing but Early Times to take the edge off. It was cool in war movies for guys to take a shot of booze to numb the pain, but Terry knew it wasn't the best option. He would let Dana decide if there was anything else that could be done for Jimmy's pain. Terry hated seeing him like this.

If there was one person in the world who didn't need Terry's protection, it was Jimmy. Terry could see an image in his head from when they were about twelve and Jimmy wrecked his skateboard going as fast as he could down a big hill. He was covered in road rash; his skin looked like he had been in a fire. He lay in pain in that same bed. It made Terry sick back then, and he felt the same way now. That was also the first ass beating Terry took from Pops.

Terry closed the door and headed for Mary's room, taking a deep breath before he went in. When he told Jim on the way over, he knew his best friend would take everything on faith and trust, but it was still difficult to recount the story. Mary, and especially Dana, wouldn't be an easy audience like Jimmy was. When Terry came into the room, Dana was sitting on the bed with her arms already folded. Mary was in the chair at her old desk. Terry forgot how small the room was, but it was still pink. Everything was pink.

"I'm going to tell you everything," he started. "Some of it is awful to hear. Some of it you won't believe, but I promise you it is all true." Just like he had done with Jimmy, Terry told them the whole story from Peggy chopping wood to shooting her in the chest and everything in between. Surprisingly, the two women didn't utter a word or even ask a question until Terry was done. Dana broke the silence.

"I would have shot that bitch, too," she said flatly. It caught Terry completely off guard. He didn't even know how to respond.

"That's what the BOLO was," Mary said. "Four months ago. The BOLO with your name on it that was sent out and then recalled. That's what it was about." Terry nodded. "We are the people who can move mountains," she repeated Terry's words. "If they can have a BOLO sent out and recalled that quickly, they aren't lying."

"A BOLO?" Dana said. "These people have drones and spies. They have people killed and then cover it up," she was getting animated. Mary moved to her to settle her down, but she wasn't getting hysterical; she was mad. Dana looked up at Terry. "You're not bullshitting, right? This is all true."

"Hand to God," he said. It was something he had heard his Italian great-uncles say around the dinner table as a kid. It had been replicated in mob movies for decades and seemed cliché on most occasions as a result. Today, it seemed very fitting. Dana put her head in her hands. "Mary, this is why you can't meet these guys tomorrow."

"This is *exactly* why I have to meet them tomorrow," she countered. "I'm calling Jimmy's SWAT Commander. I'm telling him what happened to Jimmy, and I am getting the SWAT Team over there in the morning."

"They will be gone before you get there," he said flatly. "As soon as that call goes out, they are gone. They will be out of there before he can assemble his team. They know everything. They hear everything. I am not trying to overstate this, but it's damn close to true." Terry's brain was moving quickly now, trying to decide their next move. The smart move was to break contact, get Jimmy, Mary, Dana, and even Mom and Pops, and take off. He knew that wouldn't happen. Jim needed some rest, and Mom and Pops hadn't been pushed out of this house by rising crime, gangs, or anything else, so he knew they wouldn't leave.

Mary was a different story. Terry wasn't convinced they wouldn't kill her walking in the door tomorrow; it was a definite possibility after they shot Jimmy. At a minimum, they would take her and move her somewhere, and Terry would lose contact with her. His gut still said she shouldn't go at all, but he knew for damn sure she couldn't walk in there alone.

Then there was Dana. For the first time, Terry felt sorry for her. She got caught in the middle of all this because she was friends with Mary and came to a holiday party. Now she was stuck. This poor nurse is in the middle of this big mess that she had no business being exposed to. He looked at her as she lifted her head out of her hands. Her face was beet red.

"Why don't you go check on Jimmy?" Terry recommended. She nodded and got up from the bed.

"I'm sorry for everything I said," Dana said to him, putting her hand on his chest as she passed by, walking into the hallway. Terry watched her over his shoulder.

"So, what do we do now?" Mary asked him. He turned and looked at her.

"That's what I am trying to figure out," Terry told her honestly. "I know Dana can't go home. They know her house. Mom and Pops aren't leaving, and Jimmy needs to rest. That kind of keeps us here, at least for now." Mary nodded. He could tell she was thinking through this, too. "If we are staying here, I need to make a trip to my apartment. I have some gear there that is better to keep close at hand." She looked at him.

"I need to go tomorrow to meet them," she said. Terry started to object, but she cut him off. "You need to come with me. I can't go by myself because you know what will happen. They will kill or kidnap me. If I don't go, they are going to come looking for me, for us. That means the only option is for you to come with me. We go in there together. If Jimmy were good, I'd have him too, but he can't. That leaves us."

She was right, it was the only viable option. At least if he walked through the door with her, she had a fighting chance. Mary was tenacious and could be downright mean if she needed to, but in a room full of professional operators, she didn't stand a chance by herself.

"Yep," he said with an exhale, "you're right. I have to think about how to do this. I'm going to run back to the apartment and get my kit. I'll be back in a couple of hours, and we can plan this out in detail." She stood up and hugged him.

"I'm glad you're home," she said. Mary hit a nerve. Terry had been wondering, since the minute he loaded Jim into the back of the 4Runner with a bullet hole in his shoulder, whether any of this would have happened if he hadn't come home. Did he bring this on? Did Tampa and Nebraska follow him here? Had he put the people he loved in jeopardy again? Mary let go of him and walked out of the room. Terry shook his head in an attempt to get rid of those thoughts of self-guilt. He turned to find Dana standing in the doorway.

"How is he?" Terry asked his best friend.

"He will be OK, but he needs lots of rest," she said. "I'll repack and rebandage the wound, but it didn't hit anything solid, and he is strong, so I don't anticipate any problems healing." That made Terry feel better. Mom did a great job taking care of her son, but having a no shit nurse on hand was a blessing.

"Thanks," he said as he tried to walk past her.

"You know," she said, "sooner or later we are going to figure out we don't actually hate each other."

"You kept my best friend from bleeding out," he said. "I couldn't hate you if I tried." He smiled at her as he walked past. She stood there for a minute before she followed him down the stairs. "And you still have to tell me about that cross."

Pops was watching the local news from his chair when Terry hit the bottom step. He was planning on heading to his apartment to get his gear when something on the TV caught his attention.

"Pops," he said as he came around to see the TV screen, "can you turn that up?" On the screen was a street reporter, wrapped up in a winter coat with the station logo on the chest. The graphic at the bottom of the screen read *"Gang War Escalating."* Pops turned up the volume.

"In an overnight shooting, seventeen gang members were killed at the house behind me," the reporter said. *"Chicago Police are telling us this is nothing like they have ever seen. This was not a drive-by shooting. Rival gang members entered the house in a military-style operation and killed everyone inside."* Terry's eyes went wide. *"Initial reports from the police say this took planning and training. The police fear militant gangs are beginning to take over major portions of the city, and this extreme level of violence will continue."* It was starting. Exactly what Mary said was happening. This was a war, but not between gangs.

"Bunch of shitbags," Pops said quietly. "Fuck 'em." Pops was still a cop, no matter how old he was. In his head, gangbangers killing gang-bangers was a victimless crime, especially if no bystanders were hurt. He had no idea what had happened the night before, only what he heard on the news.

"Mary," Terry called out to the house in general. He didn't know where she was, but the house was pretty small, so it was likely she heard him. She emerged from the kitchen. "You need to look at this." She looked at the TV and her face turned grey. The production crew was on the ball; they had already changed the graphic at the bottom of the screen: *"Military-Style Gang Operation Leads to 17 Deaths".* She looked at Terry.

The desk reporter in the studio replaced the on-scene guy. Her voice was crisp and clear, *"Police currently have no leads, but believe this is the work of the ultra-violent faction of MS-13 that has invaded Chicago."*

"MS-13, my ass," Mary said.

"Mary Anne," Pops said. "Not saying it again. Watch your mouth." He threw out her middle name, so he wasn't kidding. Mary was in her mid-forties but looked like a kid who got caught with her hand in the cookie jar.

"Keep an eye on that," Terry said, looking at Mary but pointing to the TV. He looked outside and could see the sky turning a darker blue as the sun was going down. He had two hours on the road, to and from his apartment, in front of him, and needed to get moving. "Stay here," he told Mary in a low tone so Pops couldn't hear. "I'll be back in a couple of hours. No one leaves." Mary nodded. Dana had been standing by quietly. Terry had almost forgotten she was in the room.

"I'm going with," she said. Terry wasn't in the mood for an argument, but the sigh escaped his lungs anyway. "Jimmy is stable. Mom is here if he needs anything. If anyone is going to need medical in the next couple of hours, it's you." She was needlessly making her case, although in his head, he applauded her assessment.

"Fine," he said with mild exasperation. "Get your coat." Dana bounded back up the stairs. Mary eyed him suspiciously. "I don't need any shit from you," he said. She just smiled and walked away. Dana came back down the stairs with her coat, and the two of them were heading out the door.

"You two keep your pants on," Pops said from his chair. Terry couldn't help but laugh. Dana turned red again. "You're too old to be having any babies," the old man added and then sipped his beer.

"Thanks for the advice, Pops," Terry said with a smile. The pair headed out the door and climbed into Terry's 4Runner. There was a light snow coming down again, melting as it hit the street. Terry reached into the console and pulled out the big, tan pistol. He screwed the suppressor back on and stuck it between his seat and the console. Dana watched him intently. He waited for the lecture he assumed was coming. Instead, she was quiet. "If anything happens, get into the backseat and get as low to the floor as you can." He put the SUV in drive and pulled out of the parking space. Ten minutes into the ride, Dana broke the silence.

"I really am sorry for not believing you," she said. Terry used to give Peggy a hard time about being what he called 'chatty.' She was a brilliant woman, but struggled to articulate her thoughts in a concise manner. Dana was a nurse. She was constantly talking to patients, families, doctors, and other nurses. Being chatty was part of her job and part of who she was. Terry sat quietly. "And I'm sorry you had to shoot your girlfriend. That's what she was, right? Your girlfriend?" Terry kept driving without saying a word; he wasn't interested in having this conversation. "You know, veterans like you come through the hospital once in a while. They don't talk very much either." He looked at her. "I know a lot is going on, and you've been through a lot, so if you need to talk to someone, I'll listen." Terry turned his eyes back to the road. He desperately wanted to change the subject.

"Tell me about the cross," he said.

"You're like a dog with a bone," she replied. "My parents bought it for me on a trip to Ireland. We were in a little shop in Galway. I saw it and I wanted it, and my dad said no. I was being a brat and throwing a fit. My mom went back later that day and got it. My dad had no idea she bought it until she had to claim it at customs."

"So, it's a gift from your parents," he said. "That's the significance."

"Let me finish," she said, with a hint of exasperation. "Mom held it until my confirmation and gave it to me then. Two years after she bought it. She kept it secret the whole time." Terry nodded. He could see her holding the cross in her fingers out of the corner of his eye.

"Are your parents still around?" he asked.

"No," she said quietly. "They died a long time ago." She didn't continue, and he didn't press.

They drove the rest of the way in silence. Terry's mind was spinning. He was thinking about tomorrow, about walking into that building with Mary. Do they go in with guns drawn? What were they going to find inside? Just the two recruiters? More? He was building the contingencies in his head. He almost missed the off-ramp because he was focused on tomorrow. When he jerked the wheel to make his exit, Dana slid in her seat. Terry saw headlights behind him jerk to follow him down the ramp. *Shit.*

"Jesus," Dana said. "Did you doze off or something?"

"Get in the backseat," he told her while he looked in the rearview mirror. She stared at him. "The backseat. Now. There is someone following us."

CHAPTER 7

Dana unbuckled her seatbelt and climbed between the seats. Terry realized how tiny she was as she moved through, barely touching him. The headlights were still in the mirror. If it were a cop, he would have turned on his sirens by now. Terry eliminated that possibility. If they were trying to be discreet and follow him to the apartment, they were doing a shitty job. That's not it either. It had to be an ambush. The vehicle accelerated, and Terry could see the headlights get closer. He reached down and pulled the pistol from between the seat and the console.

Terry had been trained to set in ambushes of all types throughout his years in the Army. He had been taught how to react if he ever got caught in one, too. All of those scenarios involved a squad or larger of infantrymen, on foot, carrying weapons and grenades. This was certainly not that, but he had another arrow in his quiver.

Before he became an aide, Terry was sent to a combat driving course put on by the Army's Criminal Investigative Division, or CID. CID manned and trained all the security detachments that provided security for generals around the Army. Part of the responsibility laid on those young men and women in the security detachments was to transport generals safely by air and ground, so they needed to know how to drive with the intent to keep their general alive. Aides didn't usually receive this kind of training, but Terry knew some people, made some phone calls, and got himself into the course.

"Keep an eye on them," he said to Dana, trying to keep calm. "If they move out from behind us, tell me which side they are on." He could see her head poking over the back seat to peer out the rear window. Terry was focusing forward. He didn't know if there was another vehicle waiting for them somewhere, but he wanted as much warning as possible. He assumed they were on his bumper, trying to get him to go faster and maybe even lose control of the vehicle. He knew if they got out from behind him, they would try a PIT maneuver to spin the 4Runner. In either case, it would be much easier to finish him off if the vehicle were in a ditch.

"Driver's side!" Dana yelled. Terry looked in his side mirror. They were coming up next to him. There was only a curb and sidewalk on his right, but the roadside was lined with telephone poles. Too risky to head that way.

"Braking!" he called back to Dana. She reflexively braced herself against the back of his seat. He slammed on the brakes. It was a black Chevy Suburban. Private security and even government security had gone almost solely to that vehicle for their services. It was predictable at this point. The driver of the Suburban didn't react quickly and flew by the 4Runner. The big Chevy took a long time to stop; Terry's brain registered it and assumed it had armor plate, adding the extra weight and causing the braking distance to increase. Terry cut left and accelerated into a U-turn. He knew it would take a few seconds to get the black SUV turned around, so he needed to make the most of it.

Terry accelerated and headed back to the highway, turning onto the ramp and continuing south. He got into traffic quickly, keeping an eye in the rearview mirror as he looked for the next exit.

"Do you see them?" he asked Dana. She was looking out the back window.

"No," she said. The next exit was less than a half mile ahead. Terry started to slow down. He was torn between heading back to Mom and

Pops and risking the trip to the apartment to get his gear. If they knew where his apartment was, they would have just ambushed him there instead of on the open road. It was worth the risk. He got off at the next exit.

"Keep an eye out," he told her. "See if anyone follows us onto the ramp." He turned right at the end of the ramp and headed toward the apartment, sticking to the residential streets. Dana climbed back into the passenger seat. Terry was convinced they had lost whoever it was following them. He tucked the pistol in next to his seat.

"Whether I believed you before or not," Dana said, clicking her seatbelt, "I certainly do now."

"You did well back there," Terry said. "Thanks."

"I'm good in backseats," she said, smiling at him. His eyes got wide. She started laughing. "Sorry, I make inappropriate comments at the worst times. It's my defense mechanism."

"Well, I don't get surprised that often," Terry said as he navigated the side streets, "but you certainly did. I just saw a different side of you."

"Yeah," she said, still smiling, "you saw my ass when I climbed between the seats." She laughed again. Terry didn't know if she was just stressed or if she was hitting on him.

"Um, yes," he said. "Yes, I did." He was treading lightly.

"You suck at this," she said. Now he knew she was hitting on him. It never failed to amaze him how incidents like this affected people. He knew soldiers, back when he was in uniform, who would spend a firefight with a hard-on because of the excitement and near-death experience. Maybe she had the same type of reaction. Terry saw the Suburban headlights in his mirror; they were coming fast.

"Shit," he said. "The Suburban is back. How the fuck..." he stopped mid-sentence. "Do you have your phone on you?" She looked like she wanted to throw up. "Goddammit. Throw that thing out the fucking window!" Dana hit the button in the door, and the window went down. She tossed the iPhone out the window and rolled it back up. "Now I need to lose them again." Thankfully, Terry was on his home turf. These were the roads he learned to drive on, and he knew every intersection, every corner. Dana unclicked her seatbelt and moved to the back seat. "As much as I'd like to see your ass in my mirror again, stay where you are." She sat back down.

Terry made a hard left turn. He knew exactly where he needed to go. The weight of the Suburban was going to work against them. He could accelerate faster and corner quicker, but he wanted to keep them close. He was slowing for a stop sign when he put the gear shift into neutral. As soon as he got under fifteen miles per hour, Terry pushed the transfer case into four-wheel high. The orange light on the dashboard appeared, showing '4H'. He put the truck back into drive and accelerated as the transmission reengaged. The Suburban was still behind them—two more streets.

"What the hell are you doing?" Dana asked him as he slowed down.

"This was supposed to be a through street that never got put in," Terry said, turning right. "Every winter, we would take my buddy's Jeep Cherokee through here." Terry could feel the wheels starting to slip. They were on mud and grass. The Suburban turned right and followed them. "Right up here used to be a pretty deep puddle. I hope it is still there. Hold on." The front end of the 4Runner dropped, and water came over the hood. Terry pushed hard on the accelerator, and the Toyota pulled out of the backside of the puddle and regained traction. "Keep coming, you guys," Terry said as he looked in the mirror.

The driver of the Suburban had to make a choice. He could try to stop, but if he slid, they would be buried in the puddle. If they stopped in time, he would have to back up all the way to the pavement and go around or back up far enough to gain enough speed to try to get through the puddle. His other choice was to gun it and hope they made it through. Terry was counting on two things: the driver hadn't put the big, black SUV into four-wheel drive, and that the armor plate was going to make it so heavy, it was going to get stuck regardless. The driver decided to gun it.

Terry watched in the mirror as the front end of the Suburban dropped, and he held his breath. The headlights started to rise out of the water and then stalled. They had gotten stuck. Terry got to the paved cross street at the other end and turned left. He finally exhaled.

"Damn good thing no one ever filled in that hole," he said. At the next intersection, Terry put the SUV back into two-wheel drive, and they made their way back to the apartment. Terry drove by it once to make sure nothing seemed out of place. He knew every car of every person that lived in the complex. He didn't see a single car he didn't recognize.

"Is it safe for us to do this?" Dana asked. "Do they know you live here?"

"I don't think so," he said. "But we aren't going to waste any time. We will get my stuff and get back on the road." He pulled into a parking space and decided to take a shot. "By the way, I don't suck at it," he smiled at her. "I'm just playing hard to get." He got out before she could answer, tucking the FNX under his coat as he moved.

Inside the apartment, he worked quickly. Terry knew he had paid for an entire year in rent, so the apartment was his for another eight months or so. He didn't need to clean the place out, and it was probably a good idea to leave at least a small portion of his arsenal at the apartment. He had his AR-15 with the Trijicon ACOG sight in the back of the 4Runner. He built that gun a few years ago, making it as close as he could to the service rifles he had carried throughout his five combat deployments. He knew he wanted the short-barreled AR-15 with the suppressor attached, and the two guns he had been given by George the moonshiner in Nebraska. The old man had given him an original Colt 1911 pistol and a fully automatic AK-47, his son had snuck back from 'Nam in his duffle bag, both with the serial numbers removed.

Terry knew those two weapons would come in handy because he could ditch them anywhere and they couldn't be traced back to him. Terry was shoving the weapons into an Air Force-issued green canvas aviator's kit bag when he noticed the look on Dana's face. He could only assume the extent of his weapon supply shocked her, but he didn't care. Terry looked twice, and then a third time, at the Winchester Model 12 shotgun in the corner. It was handed down from his grandfather, and Terry had been shooting it since he was a teenager. He was more comfortable with that weapon than anything else, but he didn't think it was going to be of much use in this fight. He left it where it stood.

Terry handed Dana a green backpack. It was the same assault pack he bought before his first deployment to Afghanistan almost twenty years ago. It was filled with spare magazines and ammunition. It was heavier than she assumed, and she nearly dropped it when he released his grip on the pack. Terry knew he needed to keep one hand free as they left the tiny apartment, in case the bad guys did know where he had been hiding out. Instead of carrying the body armor in his hand, he ditched the Filson and threw the plate carrier over his head and then covered it with the waxed-cotton jacket. Terry threw a second assault pack on his back, this one containing a helmet and an AN/VPS-14 night vision monocular, along with his 'war belt'.

The pair moved quickly without talking. Dana was turning into a valuable teammate. Terry led them out the door and headed to the 4Runner. He opened the cargo compartment, and the interior lights revealed Jimmy's blood still on the back of the seats. That was going to reduce the resale value. Terry was trying to get them out of there quickly. The apartment seemed to be a safe harbor that he didn't want to ruin if he could avoid it.

He tossed the assault pack and kit bag into the back of the vehicle and laid the FNX on the floor of the open compartment. Terry ditched his jacket, pulling the body armor over his head and straight into the back. Dana was still shaking the heavy backpack off her back when he grabbed it from her, pulling open the zippers. Terry grabbed two, thirty-round magazines from the pack, zipped it closed, and tossed it in the backseat, handing the magazines to Dana. He reached into the kit bag, grabbed the suppressed AR and the FNX, and closed the rear hatch. She stood there looking at him. It was the same look she had inside; he could see it even in the dark.

"This is serious, isn't it?" she said. He handed her the pistol and took one of the rifle magazines, looking around to see if anyone was watching. It was dark, but it was November, so it wasn't exactly the middle of the night. Terry slipped the plastic magazine into the magazine well and pulled the charging handle back, letting it go and loading a round into the chamber. He took the pistol back from her.

"Keep that one in the front seat with you," he said, referring to the magazine she had in her hand. Over her shoulder, he saw the headlights of the Suburban coming down the block. He handed her the pistol back and grabbed the second magazine, shoving it into his back pocket. "Get in the car, now!" he hissed at her. "Get in there and get down." Terry got behind the 4Runner and kneeled down, getting into a covered shooting position. He flipped open the plastic caps covering the red dot scope mounted on the little rifle, turning the dial to bring the dot to its lowest brightness setting. The Suburban stopped about twenty yards away, with the nose pointed in their direction.

Terry knew the vehicle was armored, and the vehicle armor and the engine block would protect anyone coming out of the driver's side. Anyone coming out the passenger side would have to clear the armored doors for him to have any chance of killing them. Terry raised the rifle to his shoulder. He knew to be patient. He had been in enough firefights in his career so that he was able to think clearly and not get jumpy. Many inexperienced soldiers would have started firing as soon as the doors opened. Terry needed to verify his targets and let them get clear of the vehicle before he fired. He just had to wait.

The mud from the puddle covered the hood and halfway up the doors of the big SUV. This was the exact vehicle. The passenger door opened, and a man stepped out casually. He was in jeans, and Terry could see they were covered in mud after the man stepped from behind the door. Terry smiled. The rear passenger door of the vehicle opened, and a man in a suit stepped out, careful not to get any mud on himself as he moved. The driver remained in the vehicle, and no one opened the rear driver's side door. Terry couldn't see any weapons.

The two men spotted his 4Runner and started walking in that direction. *What the fuck is going on?* Terry waited as the men closed the distance. When they got inside of ten yards, Terry spoke up from behind the SUV, still pointing the rifle at the two men.

"That's far enough," he said loud enough for the two men to hear. The man in the suit froze. The man in the dirty jeans dropped his hand to his hip as he stopped. "If I see a weapon, I *will* shoot you." Dirty jeans raised his hands.

"Mister Davis," the man in the suit spoke up. "Mister Davis, we spoke on the phone a few months ago." Terry recognized the voice. It was the voice in his head that had been haunting him for months. He felt a chill run down his spine. "Mr. Davis, we need to speak again." Terry stood up, the suppressed rifle still on his shoulder, trained on Dirty Jeans. Terry wasn't aiming. He kept both eyes open so he could look through the scope and still see his surroundings while he moved forward.

"He moves or anyone gets out of that vehicle," Terry said plainly, "I'm going to put a round through your brainpan."

"Mister Davis," the nameless man said, "I am going to send him back to stand by the vehicle. Is that OK? I need to speak to you."

"You, in the dirty jeans, drop the weapon before you move," Terry said. Dirty Jeans looked at his boss, who nodded. The man slowly removed a pistol from his belt and set it on the ground. He stood erect with his hands up. "Go ahead. Back up." The man stepped backward slowly until he reached the Suburban. The man in the suit moved closer. Terry snapped the barrel of the rifle a foot to the left, pointing directly at the finely dressed man's face. He stopped.

"Mister Davis," he said. "We had an understanding. Live and let live. You killed Ms. Baron. That wasn't part of the agreement."

"I could kill you, too," Terry said. "Right here, in this parking lot."

"Mister Davis," the suit said. "You have a habit of making a nuisance of yourself. I'm here to give you a final warning. Stay out of our way."

"I didn't go looking for this," Terry said. "This, whatever this is, this found me."

"We know that," the older man said. Terry could make out his face now. He had the face of a Hollywood character actor. Something told Terry that was part of his role in this organization. "That's why we haven't killed you. Or your friends, like the little nurse in the back of your car. Now, we need you to stop. If you don't, there will be no more warnings." Terry flipped the selector lever on the rifle from 'SAFE' to 'FIRE.' The audible, metallic click made the old man flinch.

Suddenly, Terry heard glass shatter behind him. He fired two rounds and hit Dirty Jeans in the face—the suit dove to the ground. Terry turned to see a man lying face down next to the 4Runner, and the driver's window shot out. The driver's door of the Suburban opened, and the driver got out. He fired a suppressed pistol from between the open door and the A-Pillar of the truck, missing Terry and shattering the rear window of the 4Runner. Terry returned fire with five rounds. Somewhere in the middle, the driver's head snapped back, and he disappeared.

Terry looked down, and the man in the suit was gone. *Shit.*

CHAPTER 8

"You OK?" Terry yelled to Dana as he moved forward, attempting to find the man in the suit. He was moving quickly, rifle up, toward the black Suburban. The rounds from his rifle and the driver's pistol were all supersonic rounds. Although both guns had suppressors on them, the rounds still made a *crack* as they broke the sound barrier. To anyone in the area, they probably sounded like firecrackers. Add that to the sound of the glass breaking out of the 4Runner, and he knew someone nearby was probably calling the cops. If he couldn't find the man in the suit quickly, he had to get back to the vehicle and take off before they got here. He was working against the clock.

The old combat veteran moved around the rear of the big SUV and cleared the backside like he was the lead man in a four-man stack, entering a room full of bad guys. No one there. He scanned the rest of the parking lot, using his peripheral vision to look for any movement. Nothing was moving in the darkness. Running in any direction would most likely be a wasted effort. He hadn't heard a response from Dana, so he backtracked to check on her.

"Dana," he said in a tone only loud enough for her to hear. "I'm coming to the back of the vehicle. Don't shoot me." He moved forward slowly, constantly looking over his shoulder to watch for any sign of movement. When he reached the Toyota, Dana was still on the floor of the backseat, holding the FNX-45 at the ready. Her eyes were wild. Terry was afraid she was going to shoot him when he opened the door, but he needed to get her back to reality. He pulled the handle and cracked the door open a hair. Only her eyes moved.

"Hey," he said softly, "it's me. Let me have that." Terry reached inside and pulled the pistol from her grip. She didn't offer much resistance, and he could see her body release the tension in every muscle. She was showing signs of shock, but she was at least hearing him. He guided her out of the backseat. They needed to move.

Once the nurse got her feet on the pavement, Terry opened the front passenger door and tried to get her to climb in. She wandered around the back of the vehicle, looking for the man she had shot just a minute before. He tried to stop her, but she looked him in the eye.

"I want to see him," she said.

"No, you don't," he told her. "Trust me." He tried to grab her, but with the rifle in one hand and the pistol in the other, she went by him easily. There he was, a man dressed in muddy jeans and a black jacket, face down on the pavement in a pool of blood. Terry tossed the rifle into the backseat and pulled her away from the corpse. He could hear sirens in the distance. He didn't have time to be gentle. "We need to go, now," he said urgently. He pushed her into the passenger seat and closed the door, quickly moving around to the driver's side and getting in. He backed out the parking space and drove out of the lot, away from the incoming police cars.

After about two blocks, he turned on the headlights and moved through the neighborhood streets, trying to move as quickly, but as inconspicuously, as possible. Dana was staring out the windshield like a zombie. Terry knew it wasn't the blood, or even the pieces of brain and skull, which bothered her. As an emergency room nurse, he was confident she had seen more of that than he even had.

"Pull over," she said before he got to the highway onramp. Terry quickly pulled the SUV to the side of the road and turned off the lights. Dana opened the door and vomited, more than once, out onto the pavement. It was like driving a drunk friend home who needed to puke but was courteous enough not to do it in your car. He knew she wasn't drunk, and it wasn't the blood and guts. Dana had never killed before. She was a nurse and had seen people die, but never by her hand. The man on the ground was dead, and she did it. It made her sick.

"I'm sorry," Terry said as he touched her back. "I'm sorry you were forced to do that. You never should have been involved with this." She took a deep breath, sat back in her seat, and closed the door.

"Let's go," she said, staring out the windshield.

"You sure?" Terry asked her.

"I'm fine," she snapped back at him. "Let's go before the cops show up." Terry knew she was upset about killing the man, and now she was embarrassed about throwing up as a result. He put the 4Runner in gear and headed for the highway without saying another word.

On the highway, Terry stayed in the center lane as much as he could. The rear window was missing, as well as the one Dana shot out in the door behind Terry, and he didn't need any curious State Troopers to spot them and pull him over. Terry had the heat blaring to make up for the missing windows as they cruised at highway speed. It was about fifteen minutes before she spoke.

"I…I've never done that before," she said over the wind and the blowing heater. Terry had been through this before with young soldiers after their first fight. It wasn't uncommon for the shock of taking a life to impact even the toughest people. "I'm sorry for throwing up like that," she said.

"There is nothing to be sorry for," he told her. "You saved my life. That guy was going to kill me. Probably, he would have killed us both. You kept us both alive. Don't apologize for that." Dana turned and looked at him. "And don't worry about puking," he said, trying to lessen her embarrassment. "It happens to a lot of people after the first time."

"Did it happen to you?" she asked.

"Yep," he said, lying through his teeth. Terry never felt remorse or shock the first time he killed a human being. He didn't know if it was because he grew up hunting, or some other reason, but he just didn't. She forced a smile when she heard it. Terry knew she would replay this night in her head for the rest of her life. She had saved his life; he didn't lie to her about that. The man was within three feet of him when Dana pulled the trigger. Whether he meant to kill him there next to the 4Runner, or just subdue Terry and kill him later, the result would have been the same.

Terry was wondering where the man in the suit had disappeared to as they drove. His mind was spinning. It was possible, he learned after the firefight with the SEAL Platoon at Peggy's farm, there was a drone overhead and they were being tracked right now. Was it even worth trying to lose the aerial tail? What would happen when the police found the SUV and the three dead bodies in the parking lot? Would it be on the news when they got to Mom and Pops? Would it be covered up like Tampa? Terry was coming away from the encounter with the suited man with more questions than answers.

One advantage of Mom and Pop's neighborhood outside Chicago was that it still had alleys behind the houses. Terry pulled his Toyota into the alley and stopped in front of their garage. He knew he couldn't leave it there, but it would be a lot more discreet to unload all the gear in this alley and walk through the fence than it would if he parked out front. He resisted the urge to turn the flashers on and looked at Dana. Her eyes were still glassy, but she seemed to be at least conscious of where they were.

"Stay here," he told her. "I'm going to drop this stuff in the back yard and then I'll park around front." She just nodded. He knew the postage-stamp-sized lot had an eight-foot privacy fence all the way around, mainly because Pops just wanted to sit in the yard and drink beer without being bothered. Terry pushed open the back gate and stood for a second. When he was a kid, he and Jimmy used to play wiffleball in the backyard. They had an epic game when they were teens that lasted for two hours, and they consumed an entire case of Pops' Old Style in the process. He smiled quietly to himself.

Unloading the gear was quick; Terry got it inside the fence and stacked it behind the garage, then closed the gate. The only spot he could find to park in front was about seven spaces down from the house. The street was crowded with cars and even some foot traffic, which surprised him but also made him happy that he didn't try to sneak a pile of guns and tactical gear in the front door. He was crossing his fingers that Dana would be able to get to the house and up the steps without significant help. When he opened the passenger door to help her out of the truck, she almost fell into his arms.

Terry got Dana to her feet, and he could almost see the clouds lifting behind her eyes. She was somewhat lucid and had her balance before he closed the door. By the time the pair reached the house, she was moving completely normally. It was a good sign. They got to the front porch, and she reached for the door, but he stopped her.

"Dana," he said, "look at me." The petite nurse turned her eyes to him. "I am going to tell them everything that happened. If you want me to leave out what happened to you, I will. It's a tough thing..." She cut him off and opened the door, pushing her way inside. Terry followed her and quickly shut the big, oak door behind them. Pops was still watching television, and Mary came out of the kitchen.

"I fucking shot someone," Dana blurted out. Terry's eyes went wide, and he slapped his forehead, pushing his ballcap up onto the top of his head in the process. Mary stopped mid-stride. Pops just chuckled.

"Welcome to the club," Pops said and raised his beer in a mock toast. Dana looked at him. Mom came out of the kitchen, wiping her hands on her apron.

"You shot someone?" Mary asked. "What the hell happened?" No one corrected Mary for cursing. Mom pushed past Mary and hugged Dana, guiding her to the dining room table. Terry stood in front of the door, flabbergasted by Dana's change from almost falling out of the 4Runner to announcing she shot someone in less than a minute.

"You're a hell of a date," Pops said to Terry, still smiling. The old man got up from his chair and walked over to the table to hear the story. Pops was always up for a good story about a shooting.

"Pops," Terry said, "a lot is going on that you two don't need to know about." Terry had no intent of insulting the older couple, but that was precisely what he did. Pops turned back to him and opened his mouth to speak, but Mom beat him to it.

"Terrence," Mom started. Terry knew he was in trouble. "I have a son in bed upstairs with a bullet wound. You have Pops sitting there, on guard, with his pistol for crying out loud. And now, this poor young lady just announced…in my living room…that she shot someone. We deserve to know everything that is going on." Terry waited. He knew there was more coming. "I am the wife and mother to police officers. Police officers have surrounded me for my whole life. I know the bad things that happen in this world. Now, you sit your butt in that chair and tell us everything. I'm going to start some coffee."

Terry took off his coat and sat at the kitchen table. Everyone was quiet, waiting for Mom to come back from the kitchen with coffee. Terry could smell the fresh brew from the kitchen and realized he needed to get his gear from the back yard. The chances of anything being stolen were almost zero, but it wasn't a risk he was willing to take. He stepped into the kitchen to see Mom, busying herself with a tray and coffee cups.

"I have to get some stuff from the backyard, Mom," he said. "Is it OK? I'll be right back." He was twelve years old in an instant. The small, Italian woman waved her hand at him as if to say 'go.' Terry went out through the porch and hauled the gear back up to the house. When he sat down at the table, Pops was laughing and sipping black coffee.

"What's so funny?" Terry asked.

"I'm laughing at Mary," Pops said. "She just found out she is the only one in the house that never killed anyone." He laughed again. It took Terry a second to process what Pops said, then he saw Mom with her head in her hands.

"What?" Terry said. "Mom? When did you…?"

"It was a long time ago," Mom said, with a sharp tone. "We will talk about that some other time." Terry caught himself speechless again. He knew Mom was a tough woman; she had to be to put up with Pops and with Jimmy and then with Terry, too. He had no idea, and never would have guessed, that the little lady was capable of killing someone. Everyone was looking at Terry.

He started into the story of Peggy, Nebraska, and Tampa. He felt like a broken record. It was the third time he repeated the story in the last day or so. Forty-eight hours ago, only his close friends Brian and

Emma knew anything about it. Now, it seemed the whole world was being told.

Jimmy came down the stairs in the middle of it, his arm in an old, battered sling that had probably been used and reused a dozen times over the years. Jimmy looked at Dana for half a second because she was in his traditional seat at the table. Once he realized what Terry was telling the family, he took the chair next to his younger sister. Jimmy looked better than he had just hours before, right up until Terry got to the part about the firefight in the apartment parking lot.

"Jesus, man," he finally spoke. There was a crackle in his throat. "Do you go anywhere and *not* get shot at?" Terry hung his head a little. Everyone sat quietly. Then Jimmy smiled. "Hey! That means Mary is the only virgin in the house!" He wasn't talking about sex.

"Seamus!" Mom snapped at him.

"You know what I mean, Mom," Jim said as he patted his sister on the back. Pop stood up. Standing over the table, with everyone else sitting, he looked as big as Terry ever remembered.

"Alright!" the big German said. "Here's the plan…"

CHAPTER 9

"Pops," Terry said as he started to stand. The old man cut him off.

"Sit down, you scroungy little shit," Pops said, pointing at Terry, "or I'll knock you down." Terry put his ass back in the chair. He knew this was bluster, but Pops was protecting his family, and Terry needed to let him do it. Pops turned and pointed his finger at Dana. "You, nurse girl. Take this dumbass back upstairs and check his wound." Pops tossed his thumb at Jimmy. Dana and Jimmy got up and started moving; they knew, like Terry did, that this was not the time to protest. "Mary, call Rocco and tell him that I need a case of beer." Rocco Moriarty was the SWAT Commander and Jimmy's boss, and Pops had trained him as a rookie a long time ago. Terry assumed the message about the case of beer was some code they worked out in years past. Mom got up and started toward the kitchen. "Where are you going?" Pops asked.

"I don't work for you," she said. "And you don't give me orders. If Rocco is coming over, I need to make some food." Mom turned and went into the kitchen. She put Pops in his place, as she always had.

"Pops," Terry said quietly. "When did Mom kill someone?"

"How do you think we met?" Pops said as he sat back down. He was whispering, so Mom didn't hear. "You know her. She lived in the old Italian neighborhood. Some dago wannabe gangster was beating the shit out of her little brother. She did what she could. She went and got her dad's gun."

"She shot him?" Terry was shocked. Pops nodded and drank some coffee. "So, how did you get involved?"

"Ha!" Pops said with a smile. "I was the one who arrested her." Terry sat back in his chair. "They let her go. It was a different time."

"How have I never heard this before?" Terry asked. Pops didn't answer. "Sonofabitch," he said to no one in particular. Mary came back from calling Rocco. Pops gave her an expectant look.

"He said he can't come over," Mary said, "and the liquor store is closed." Terry thought it must be another code. Mary had a confused look.

"Mom!" Pops yelled. "You can stop cooking. Rocco isn't coming." Mary and Terry looked at each other and then at Pops. "After all these years, I can't believe he just cut me off like that." Mary and Terry shared another glance. "Beer is information. And if the liquor store is closed, that means he isn't sharing anything."

"Maybe he just doesn't have anything," Terry said. Pops shook his head.

"If he didn't have anything," Pops said, "he would have said they were out, not that the store was closed." The big man slammed his hand on the table. Pops looked at Terry. "What do you think we should do?" Terry was floored. The old man had never asked his opinion on anything, ever. Terry looked at Mary. She gave him a subtle shrug.

"Pops," Terry said, "I think you and Mom need to take Jimmy and Dana and get out of here. Pack up and go. Mary and I will take care of this." Pops looked at him, listening. "Truthfully, I'd like you to take Mary too, but I know she won't go."

"She'll go if I tell her to," Pops said as if Mary wasn't even in the room.

"The hell I will," Mary said. Pops never even looked at her. His eyes remained locked on Terry.

"Whether she goes or not," Pops said, "we can figure out in a minute." Mary tried to interrupt. Terry stopped her with a stare. "But we will go. I agree with you. I'll pack them up, and we can head north." Terry knew exactly what 'north' meant. The family bought a small cottage in Wisconsin shortly after Mom and Pops adopted Jim and Mary. It was supposed to be a vacation place where they could be a family and do family things. Pops couldn't have kids after a car accident when he was a teenager. He and Mom tried for years before a doctor broke the bad news, so Mom decided they would adopt a child.

The couple was introduced to Seamus, who had only been in the foster system for about a month, mainly because Pops wanted a son. Jim refused to go with them the first time they met, but he wouldn't say why. Mom and Pops came back two days later to give it another try, only to find out from the nun at the orphanage that they were being forced to close by the Illinois Department of Family Services.

Sister Alice Marie wanted desperately to place as many of the children as she could before she had to hand them over to the state. Mom and Pops were more than willing to take Jimmy, but he didn't want to go with them. That's when the nun told them about Mary. Mary was Jimmy's birth sister, and he didn't want to leave her. Without even asking Pops, Mom said they would adopt Mary, too. There was no argument from the big man, and they took both kids home that day.

A few summers later, they bought the place in Wisconsin. Pops went up there and fished and drank beer while Mom went for walks with the kids in the woods and down to the river. Terry was twelve the first time he went with them to the cottage in the woods, which became a repeat trip every summer until they graduated from high school. Once Mary graduated and went to college, Mom and Pops spent less time there until he retired, then it became a summer place where they would spend weeks at a time. It was in the middle of nowhere and a great location for the family to hide out until Terry could figure out what to do next.

"That's a good idea, Pops," Terry said. "It shouldn't take you more than a few hours to get there. If you leave now, you'll be there well before sunrise."

"Mom!" Pops yelled into the kitchen. "Get packed. We are heading up north." He looked at Mary. "Go tell your brother and the nurse to get ready to go." Mary nodded and headed upstairs. "What are you two going to do?"

"We are going to go meet those guys tomorrow morning," Terry said. Pops frowned. "I know what I'm doing, Pops. We won't walk in there empty-handed. And I won't let anything happen to her."

"You better not," Pops said, "or you'll have to deal with Mom."

"Your car in the garage?" Terry asked. "I'm going to give you some firepower just in case." Pops nodded. "Still the Buick?"

"Hell no," Pops said. "I bought a Cadillac." He smiled. Terry smiled back before heading to the garage with his bag full of guns. Inside, the car keys were hanging on a nail by the door. Pop never worried about his car being stolen. He thought of himself as a cop, and he still believed no one would be dumb enough to steal from a cop. Terry popped the trunk and pulled the sterile AK-47 and Colt 1911 from the bag. He knew Pop could handle the pistol for sure, and Jimmy could likely fire the rifle if needed. He put the weapons and some spare magazines in the trunk and shut it. Terry hoped they wouldn't need the guns.

"Hope is not a course of action," he said as he turned out the lights in the garage, hanging the keys back on the nail, and headed back into the house. Mom was wrapping up sandwiches in the kitchen when he came in. There was an old metal thermos on the counter, which Terry assumed was filled with coffee. She was getting ready to leave, just like Pops told her to. Terry leaned down and kissed his second mother on the head before heading back into the living room.

Jimmy and Dana were in the living room as he came out of the kitchen. He could tell they were both pissed. Jimmy stood there with a red face. Dana was tapping her foot with her arms folded. Jimmy fired the first shot.

"I'm going with you and Mary," he said.

"Brother," Terry responded, "stop being a dumbass. What are you going to do with your arm in a sling if this goes bad? You need to go north and take care of Mom and Pops." Jimmy didn't have a real argument, but he felt like he was being left out. Terry had reached his limit for taking feelings into account. "You'd be more of a liability than an asset."

"You can't make me go," Dana said. She was right, and he wasn't in the mood to argue with her.

"Then don't," Terry said. He was tired, and his patience was thin. "Take an Uber. Go back home. These guys know where you live, but whatever. If you don't want to go, then go home." She was hurt, and he could see it in her eyes. He turned away from her and stepped toward the kitchen, intent on grabbing the remaining guns from the back porch.

Terry could feel himself transitioning mentally. He was moving into mission execution mode. He became focused, but with that came irritability and tension. Near the end of his tour in Baghdad, the Operations NCO came into his office. The battalion was getting ready for their last big operation before the unit replacing them arrived, and Terry spent two days in a bad mood. Sergeant First Class Gonzales sat down in the chair in front of Major Terry Davis's desk and put his feet up. Terry was immediately irritated.

"Can I help you, Gonzo?" Terry said.

"You can probably help everyone, Sir," the senior noncommissioned officer said, "if you'd just stop being a grumpy bastard all the time." Terry stopped what he was doing and looked at the old infantryman. He could smell the cigarettes coming off his uniform.

"I'm not grumpy," Terry said.

"Sir," Gonzales said, "you get like this before every operation. I've known you since you were a Captain, and I was a Staff Sergeant. You were like that back then, too. You're still like that. Before a big op, you get grumpy as fuck. Everyone avoids you like the plague. Hell, even the battalion commander walks on eggshells around you." Sergeant Gonzales was talking about Lieutenant Colonel Kolowski, who was Terry's immediate boss.

Most officers would have been self-conscious about being called out like that and tried to change their behavior. A few would have completely ignored it, but would let it fester in the back of their brain somewhere. Terry acknowledged it and embraced it. It was who he was, and it was who he needed to be to ensure as many young soldiers made it home as possible. If his being a grumpy bastard accomplished that one thing, then so be it.

"Thanks for that, Gonzo," Terry said. "I'm not changing anything. Someone around here needs to be an asshole at times like this. Now get the fuck out of my office."

"Yes, Sir," Gonzales said, standing up with a smile.

Terry Davis, Lieutenant Colonel retired, could feel that same tension coming. The same irritability. He didn't care. His focus now was to take care of this family, just like he took care of those soldiers. He needed to get them out of here and off to relative safety in Wisconsin. He also needed to get Mary prepared for tomorrow. He didn't have time to massage egos or make people feel good about themselves.

Terry didn't even realize he had made his way onto the porch; he had been lost in the memory of Baghdad while he moved through the house. Suddenly, he was standing in the dark alone. He didn't even know how long he had been standing there. Terry grabbed a couple of the bags and turned to find Mary standing there, leaning against the doorframe.

"You don't always need to be an asshole, you know," she said. Terry felt like he was about to have the same conversation with Mary that he had just replayed in his head with Gonzales. He opened his mouth to return fire, but Mary turned and walked back into the house. Terry followed her, carrying the bags, setting them on the floor in the living room.

Pops was fully dressed, in blue jeans and a flannel shirt with work boots. Jimmy was standing behind him, ready to go as well. Mom was wearing a wool coat and old rubber boots, and she was tying a scarf over her head. Dana was on the couch, sulking. He could see she had been crying. *I don't have time for this shit.* Terry walked over and hugged Jimmy. The SWAT officer grimaced from the pain in his shoulder after the embrace. Pops put his hand out, and Terry took it. The two men headed toward the kitchen. Terry hugged Mom, and she kissed him on the cheek. Dana never moved as Mom followed her husband and son.

"You don't have to go home," Terry said, "but you can't stay here."

"What are you," Dana said to him, "a fucking bartender?" She stood and faced him, her eyes still red. "I saved your life. You'd be dead if it weren't for me." Terry stood quietly but was aching to get this over with. "Why can't I stay?" she asked. Terry screamed inside his head.

"Because," Terry said flatly, "I don't need you here. Jimmy needs you. Take care of him. Or go home."

"You needed me when he got hurt," she started counting on her fingers, "you needed me when those people were chasing us, you needed me in that parking lot when I *killed someone* to save *your ass*, but now you suddenly don't need me anymore." Terry stood there staring at her, completely unmoved. "You know, when I apologized for telling you to go fuck yourself? I'm not apologizing this time. Go fuck yourself." She snatched her coat off the couch and went out through the kitchen. Terry turned to find Mary standing on the bottom stair leading to the second floor.

"You really suck with women," she said. "No wonder you've been married three times." She turned and headed up the stairs.

"Twice," he said out loud. "It's only been twice."

Terry was exhausted. He didn't know what time it was. He wouldn't even know what day it was if it weren't for Mary's planned meeting in the morning. There was work to be done, though, and preparations made. He was running on adrenaline and anger, but he knew those would soon run out. Terry looked at his watch; 0133. Both he and Mary would need to be moving in less than four hours. His kit was spread out on the living room floor, including a rifle and a pistol, with spare magazines in pouches on his body armor and war belt. First aid kit. Helmet. Night vision. It was all ready to go.

Terry went upstairs to talk to Mary, to plan, to prep for the meeting in a few hours. She was on her bed, asleep. He was tempted to crawl in next to her, not for any reason other than a warm body to sleep next to. He decided against it and went into Jimmy's room to lie down, setting the alarm on his watch.

Three hours. You've done more on less sleep. Three hours.

CHAPTER 10

Terry Davis woke in a haze to the beeping coming from his Garmin watch. He didn't know what time it was, or even where he was sleeping, but he knew he needed to get up. Rubbing his eyes and his face, he realized he was in Jimmy's room at Mom and Pops. His body was sore and slow to move as he stood, still feeling tired from the activities of the last three days and lack of sleep; he desperately needed to recover at his age. He could hear the line from Raiders of the Lost Ark in his head, "It ain't the years, *honey, it's the mileage.*" Terry had a lot of miles on his body and even more on his soul. Today was one of those days he could feel those miles, but there were more important issues to deal with. He walked across the hall to make sure Mary was awake.

Terry slept in his clothes and his hiking boots. He was ready to leave as soon as he grabbed his gear from the living room. He pushed Mary's door open without knocking to find her pulling up a pair of blue jeans over a black thong. Mary had always been fit, and she maintained that by being a cop. She worked out every day, and it showed.

"Going to a gunfight in a thong," he said, "interesting choice." Mary didn't even flinch; she just kept getting dressed. "Nice ass, by the way."

"Your charm is amazing," she said, dripping with sarcasm. Terry wondered if she was still pissed at him for how he talked to Dana the night before. He didn't have time to worry about that now; he turned away to head down the stairs. "She will keep you in line," Mary called from her room. Terry turned and looked at her. "Dana. She will keep you in line. She is exactly what you need. Quit being an asshole and find out." Terry just turned and walked down the stairs.

Today was going to be a life-or-death day. People were most likely going to die, so Terry wasn't particularly concerned about his love life. He stood in the living room and surveyed his kit; everything was at his disposal, he just needed to decide what tools were required. Terry was a planner without a plan. He knew the shape of the building, the streets surrounding it, and even the closest hospitals, but he didn't know what or who was going to be inside. The two of them walking in there was ludicrous in the first place, but he knew Mary was going with or without him, so he took ownership of the whole thing. It was the only way Terry knew how to protect Mary in all of this, short of putting her in zip ties and meeting the rest of the family in Wisconsin.

The only thing Terry could plan for was the worst-case scenario. In his mind, it would be the two of them walking into the building and finding a bunch of special ops guys all geared up and ready to fight. The chances of that were pretty low by Terry's estimation, but he couldn't just discount it either. Mary came walking down the stairs with her department-issued bulletproof vest on, pulling a sweatshirt over the top.

"I'm guessing," Terry said, "there is no way for me to talk you out of this."

"These guys threatened my career," she said with venom, "and my brother's career. I'm pretty sure they shot him and tried to kill you. And Dana, too." Dana stopped and looked at Terry's kit lying in the living room. "What the fuck is all this?"

"We aren't going to the fucking prom, Mary," Terry said. "This has a high probability of turning into a gunfight. A real gunfight. Not some shithead on the street that you trade bullets with. Like guys who know what they are doing. Guys who will move *toward* gunfire and not away from it. If you think this is going to turn out any different than that, you're kidding yourself."

"So, what are we going to do?" she responded. "Breach the door and start shooting everyone inside? That's your plan?"

"I don't have a fucking plan, Mary," Terry could feel the anger rising. "I don't have a plan because I have been running all over the Chicagoland area for the last seventy-two hours trying not to get killed. And trying to keep your brother from getting killed. And even Dana." Terry reached down and grabbed his plate carrier, tossing it over his head and strapping it on. Mary noticed very quickly that what he was wearing was combat gear and not cop gear. His plates were made to stop high-velocity rifle rounds, not pistol rounds, off the shelf at the sporting goods store. Terry wasn't kidding; he expected a gunfight, and she suddenly felt underdressed. Mary went to the basement and returned carrying her big, black tactical carry bag.

"They told me I had to bring this with me, so everything is packed," she said, dropping it on the floor. Terry opened it up. Standard issue gear: black vest, helmet, boots, and various other gear. All of it immaculately clean.

"You ever use any of this stuff?" Terry asked, already knowing the answer. Mary had a guilty look on her face. Knowing he didn't have time to reconfigure anything for her, he pulled the pieces out and made sure her department gear was at least combat functional. "Any chance the department gave you a rifle?"

"I haven't been to the carbine course yet," Mary said. "They don't send detectives."

"So that means 'no'," Terry said. "Do you know how to use one?"

"Of course," Mary said. "We train with them every year." Terry reached down and grabbed the suppressed rifle and handed it to her, then handed her five thirty-round magazines. "What are you going to use?" Terry grabbed the case with the other AR-15. It was the one he set up like his service rifles, the one he was most comfortable with. He planned to use the suppressed rifle specifically because of the noise, but sending Mary in with only a pistol was out of the question. Terry strapped on his war belt and took the suppressor off the FNX-45, then slipped it into its holster. He had experimented with various holsters that would allow him to keep the suppressor on, but he found out at Peggy's farm that what he thought was a viable solution wasn't.

Mary was trying to figure out how to carry the rifle magazines Terry gave her when he walked over and turned on the television. It was already tuned to the local news, which was precisely what he was looking for. There was 'breaking news' about another gang fight that left fourteen dead. Terry looked at Mary and grabbed the back of her vest, dragging her in front of Pops' old tube television. Her eyes got wide.

"That's what we are up against this morning," he said. "These are the same kinds of guys that used to bang targets in Baghdad every night when I was there. These guys are professional pipe hitters. Look at that," he said, pointing at the television screen. "No holes in the front of the house. No broken windows. That's not amateurs and damn sure isn't accidental."

"Yeah, I can see that," Mary said. Her eyes were steely. It wasn't fear, and it wasn't anger. She did look like she was ready to take this on.

"Mary, listen to me," Terry said as he stepped in front of her. "I'm not going to try to talk you out of this. I've known you most of your life, and I know that is a waste of time." Her green eyes were focused on him. "If this turns bad and the shooting starts, just keep moving and keep shooting."

Those words were Terry's mantra in combat and life. *Keep Moving, Keep Shooting*. Terry Davis had uttered those words out loud and inside his head more than anything he could remember, and he was convinced they had kept him alive more than once. Mary had her kit ready to go, or at least as close as it was going to get. Terry loaded the rifle he was giving to Mary and set it next to her bag. She was about to take off her vest when Terry heard the door to the porch open. The two lifelong friends shared a look. Mary grabbed the rifle from the floor and shouldered it, orienting toward the back of the house. Terry grabbed his empty rifle and moved to the side, giving Mary a clear shot at the doorway separating the dining room from the kitchen.

There were two sets of feet coming in. Terry could tell by the shifts in the linoleum floor that there was more than one person. He and

Jimmy had been caught either sneaking out or sneaking back in multiple times as teenagers, trying to walk across that same floor. Terry wished he hadn't taken the suppressor off his pistol just a minute before, and now it was out of reach. Trying to be as quiet as possible, he put a magazine in the well of his rifle. He knew as soon as he pulled the bolt back to chamber a round, the whole house would explode into a firefight.

Terry heard the supersonic crack of two rounds coming from the kitchen and looked at Mary as she fell backward. He pulled the charging handle back on his AR-15 and flipped the selector lever from 'SAFE' to 'FIRE' as the first man came through the kitchen doorway. His eyes only had enough time to register that the man was Caucasian before Terry exploded his face with a round of 5.56mm. The man behind him made a tragic mistake and was caught in what the Army called the 'fatal funnel' when the lead man went down; he was stuck in the doorway.

Clearing rooms is dependent on decisive and swift action. Hesitation will get someone killed, but so will poor technique. This was a combination of both. Terry moved forward and rotated into the doorway, firing twice. The second man in the stack was caught with a falling body in front of him, the doorframe on both sides, and a third man behind him. With nowhere to move, he took the first round in the chest and the second through the neck, splitting his spine. Terry could see at least two more men in the kitchen and closed the distance. Firing another pair of rounds, Terry hit the third man in the chest and shoulder. The fourth man smartly moved to the side and snapped off two shots. The first hit the doorframe, and the second hit Terry in the plate carrier, knocking him backward.

Terry could hardly breathe as the impact of the 9mm round was absorbed across his chest. The plate stopped the round, but when travelling almost twelve hundred feet per second, the energy from the round must be absorbed by something. It was like getting hit in the chest with a baseball bat. Terry was trying to regain his balance when he was hit with another round, probably within a few inches of the first. He felt his ribs crack and saw a white flash behind his eyes as he fell to the floor. *Fuck.*

He was blind, could barely breathe, and was deaf from the half dozen rounds he fired from his rifle. There was at least one bad guy left alive, and Terry was trying to regain his senses before the man killed him. The dining room table partially shielded Terry, so the last man needed to move closer to finish him off. Mary fired two rounds, the first splitting the man's skull and putting him down. She moved to Terry to help him up as he cringed in pain and tried to breathe.

"We need to go," he hissed as air returned to his lungs. Mary was too short to carry the older man. She was probably strong enough, even with all his kit, but she didn't have the leverage to get underneath him. He would have to suck it up and move through the pain. "Where is your car?"

"Out the door and to the left, two houses down," she said. Terry was leaning against the stair railing leading to the second floor. He had his breath back, but the broken ribs were killing him. He nodded. Mary grabbed as much of Terry's kit as she could and headed out the door. Everyone in the neighborhood knew it was a house full of cops, and they all knew Mary. When she came out the front door, there was a half dozen people on the street wondering what was going on. The sun was starting to come up.

"Please, everyone," Mary said in her best cop voice, "go back inside. This is a police matter, and officers will be here shortly." She shuffled to her car and dumped what she was carrying into the back-seat. Terry had made it as far as the front steps by the time she made it back to the house. He was breathing better but moving slowly; every step vibrated his broken ribs. Mary dashed past him into the house to grab whatever was left. She was out again before Terry got to the bottom of the steps. The crowd hadn't dispersed at all.

"EVERYONE," Mary said much louder, "GO BACK INSIDE YOUR HOUSES!" This time, she had her badge in her hand, holding it above her head. Terry moved slowly from tree to tree as they lined the sidewalk until he reached Mary's car. She opened the passenger door for him, and he fell in with an audible moan. Police lights were coming down the block. Mary was standing in the street.

"Get in the car!" Terry yelled and winced.

"I need to talk to the police," she told him.

"Mary, the police will not help you," he said. The pain was severe. He was wondering if the bullet had done more than break his ribs. "They will arrest you. They will take you in. And these guys will kill you. Kill both of us. We need to go."

Mary quickly realized he was right. She remembered that Rocco wouldn't share information with Pops. There were at least some cops who were in on this. Hoping the ones who showed up at the house weren't involved wasn't an option. She opened the door and got into the driver's seat. Terry pulled his legs into the car and shut the door. Mary looked at him. He had blood on his face, which she knew wasn't his, but he was in pain. She loved and respected Pops and Jimmy, but Terry was the toughest man she knew, and she had never seen him like this. She pulled away from the curb.

"Where do we go?" she said as she turned onto a side street, avoiding the incoming police cars.

"North," Terry said. "Go north." He passed out.

CHAPTER 11

When Terry woke, they were somewhere just across the state line into Wisconsin on Interstate 90. With the pain, the exhaustion, and the stress, his body had shut down. His plate carrier was still wrapped around his body, but he could feel his face burning. He was disoriented and fighting to gain situational awareness. Mary put her hand on his shoulder.

"Hey," she said softly. "You OK?" Terry shook his head and immediately felt the pain in his chest. The sun was rising through the clouds. He looked over at her. The clouds were lifting inside his head, and he began to remember what had happened at Mom and Pops about two hours before.

"We need to get off the highway," he said as he leaned the seat back, hoping to relieve some of the pain in his chest. "Why does my face feel like it is on fire?"

"Because I had to scrub the blood off," she said as she drove. "And the only thing I could find was the alcohol swabs in your little med kit. People were starting to stare as we drove. You had your face pressed against the glass like a kid at the zoo."

"We need to get off the highway," Terry repeated.

"I'd love to," Mary said, "but without GPS, I have no idea how to get to the cottage without taking the highway." Terry opened his mouth to speak, but she cut him off. "And no, I don't have a map." Terry closed his mouth. Other than stopping for a map of some kind, he didn't have another suggestion. His eyes were barely open, but he could see that Mary wasn't wearing her vest.

"I thought you got shot," he said. "What the hell happened?"

"I did get shot," Mary said, keeping her eyes on the road. "It was a nine-mil round. I still had my tac vest on with the ceramic plates and trauma pads underneath. It barely hurt." Terry closed his eyes all the way. "You should probably get some. That steel shit you were wearing didn't do a great job."

"I'm alive, aren't I?" he said with his eyes closed.

"Barely," she was keeping right above the speed limit and staying in the right lane. "It's alright, I am sure Dana will be more than willing to patch you up." She smiled. He couldn't see it with his eyes closed, but he knew. He held up his middle finger. "Who do you think those guys were?" she asked.

"They weren't what I thought they were," Terry said, breathing slowly. "We got lucky. We both had armor on and had guns ready before they tried to sneak in," he winced as he spoke. "They probably assumed we would be sleeping or just standing around, maybe with a pistol close by, but that's it."

"Who did you think they were?" she asked with a confused tone.

"I thought those guys were going to be pros. Delta, SEALs, Rangers, something. Those guys tried to be sneaky, but they hesitated when bullets started flying. What did I tell you?"

"Keep moving and keep shooting," she responded.

"Right," Terry said. "As soon as they spotted you, especially with gear on, they should have closed in quickly. When that guy fired, he should have been moving forward. He fucked the guys behind him. They all got stuck in the doorway, falling all over each other because he hesitated. That was rookie work. Those guys weren't pros."

"Yeah, but that raises a new question," she said. "If they weren't pros, who were they?" Terry was fading a little, but this exchange felt like something he would have done with Peggy. Something he *had* done with Peggy, multiple times.

"Did any of them look familiar?" Terry asked.

"You mean like cops?" she asked. She was looking for clarity. Terry was asking a leading question.

"Or criminals," he added. She was more confused. "Look, I can train anyone to do a four-man stack and clear a house. Anyone. Especially if the folks inside aren't expecting it. Those guys could have been cops, criminals, or anyone else who could have been manipulated to do it. They could be using right-wing nutjobs, fringe groups, militias, anyone."

"Why do you think they would be criminals?" she asked. "It could have been any of those other groups, but you keyed on criminals."

"Because if anyone died inside that house," he said, still breathing slowly, "it would be easy to blame it on someone with a long record. Especially your house. A house that cops live in." It was making more sense to him even as he said it out loud. "They wouldn't use cops because there would be a chance someone would know you, or Jimmy, or Pops. I guess they could get some fringe group to do it. Neo-Nazis or someone like that, but criminals are just easier." The vest was uncomfortable because the back plate was digging into him, but he knew keeping it tight on his torso was probably the best option for broken ribs. He was fading again.

Terry fell asleep, and Mary kept on driving. It was mid-morning, and they were within twenty miles of the summer place when he started to stir. Mary was keeping one eye on him and the other on the road. He was dreaming about something Mary had no idea about. She could only imagine what he had been through over the years, deployment after deployment. She looked at him with a mix of pride and pity. He was the love of her life, but not in the way everyone thought. Nothing would ever happen between them because he was much more of a brother than he was anything else, but he was exactly the type of man she wanted. Terry sat up suddenly and scared the shit out of her. He also hurt himself and groaned in pain.

"Where are we?" he asked.

"About twenty minutes or so," she said. He looked around and adjusted the seat, bringing it back upright again. He breathed slowly as his body absorbed the pain. He nodded.

"Have you noticed anyone following us?" he winced.

"No," she said. They were on a Wisconsin state road with only two lanes. "We would easily see anyone. There is no one else out here." Terry looked out the window and saw the snow-covered landscape: pine trees and farm fields, everything covered in snow.

"Unless they are watching us from above," he said. Terry mentioned drones when he told her the story about what happened in Nebraska and Florida, and that awful woman, Peggy. "Not much we can do about that unless you have a Stinger missile lying around. If they want to find us, they will find us." He sounded like he was resigned to the fact that they hadn't escaped anything.

"This is just us buying some time, isn't it?" Mary asked.

"Time and space," Terry replied. "I tried to tell you these people can do whatever they want. They seem to have any asset they choose available to them. Ditching the phones was trying to buy time. Living like a Spartan in my apartment was buying time. That's all any of this is."

"So, we are just stuck with this?" she said after a lengthy pause. It wasn't as much a question as a statement. "This is how things are, and we just have to take it? You. I know you. You don't believe that for a second."

"Mary," he said with a wince. "I'm in fucking pain. How about you get me to the summer place, and then we can figure out how to defeat the evil empire? Let's do that first, OK?" Mary turned left off the pavement and onto rock. Terry felt the change and sat up.

"You'd better start thinking about that evil empire plan because we are here," she said. Terry could see the trees passing by on either side and knew the A-Frame house was just up the road. Mary slowed the car and turned left again into the small drive that led to the cottage. She could see Pops' Cadillac parked on the right side of the structure and parked behind him. Mary stepped out of the car and into the cold. It was much colder here than it was in Chicago when they stumbled out of the house a few hours ago, even with the sun shining through a cloudless sky.

Pops came through the sliding glass door and onto the wooden deck, holding his revolver. Mary thought it a bit odd because they were in her car, so it wasn't like a stranger pulled up. *Times are definitely different.* Terry pulled himself out of the passenger seat and into the cold. He saw Pops turn and walk back into the small house. There was smoke coming out of the chimney, but the smell of pine was strong in Terry's nose. He loved it up here. Dana came out of the house and moved to Mary, hugging her. She gave Terry an evil look over her shoulder as the two women walked inside.

"I'll take care of myself, thanks," Terry said to the forest. He moved slowly around the nose of the car and up the steps. He was two paces from the door when Mary reemerged, intending to help him from the car to the house. "I got it," he said and brushed past her. Mom had something that smelled like stew cooking on the stove. Pops was in a chair, facing an old color television. It was even older than his tube TV back home. The news was on. Jimmy sat upright on the couch, his arm still in a sling. The small house was warm, and Terry took a second to look around.

Much like stepping into Mom and Pops just a few days ago, Terry was overwhelmed with nostalgia. This place hadn't changed except for the carpeting. He could hear Mary and Dana up in the loft that covered the back two-thirds of the cottage. Mom emerged from the bedroom that was furnished only with two double beds and a nightstand. She was wiping her hands with her apron again.

"Hey brother," Jimmy said, "drop your gear and have a seat."

"I'm not positive," Terry said, "but I think if I take this vest off, my insides might fall out."

"Stop being so goddam dramatic," Pops said from his chair. For whatever reason, there was no rule about foul language up here in Wisconsin. Even as a kid, Terry noticed that Pops' language was worse up here, and it just seemed to be allowed. Dana was coming down the stairs with Mary behind her.

The little nurse stopped in front of Terry and pointed to the kitchen table without saying a word. The kitchen table was a set, and to some hipster furniture fan, it was probably worth a fortune. The legs and trim were all steel and chrome with a tabletop that was a pattern with different shades of grey that always reminded Terry of metal flakes. The chairs matched the table, including the vinyl backs and seats matching the tabletop; some of the chair edges were held together with silver duct tape. Terry walked over to the table and turned around, and Mary moved quickly to help him take the vest off.

"Sooooo, baby nuts," Dana said with her arms folded, "where does it hurt?"

"Baby nuts?" Terry questioned. "Your bedside manner could use some work."

"Yeah, baby nuts," she said with a sarcastic smile. "I learned that from Jimmy on the way up here." Terry looked at his best friend, who just smiled. "Now, where does it hurt?" Mary pulled the vest off him and set it on the table; the metal plates made a 'clank' when they hit the tabletop. Terry touched his right ribcage below his pectoral muscle, drawing a line with his finger that moved around his ribs from the front to the side.

"It's broken ribs," he said.

"Are you a medical professional?" Dana snapped at Terry. Dana and Mary helped Terry out of his flannel shirt and then pulled his t-shirt over his head. Terry winced more than once. There was a large bruise right where Terry had traced his finger. Dana looked over at the front of his vest and could see the thumb-sized dent where the bullet had hit the plate. "Isn't there supposed to be some sort of padding behind those plates?"

"Yeah," Jimmy said as he stood up. "They are called trauma pads, and they are designed to prevent shit like that from happening."

"You don't have any of those?" Dana asked, looking up from the bruise to Terry's bearded face. Terry didn't answer because he obviously didn't. "Not smart," Mary said. "You are right, there are broken ribs, but I am worried about liver lac." She pronounced it 'lack' even though it was short for laceration.

"His liver?" Mary asked.

"Energy transference is weird," Terry said. "Depending on the angle, the round, the plate, all of that energy has to go somewhere. I know the ribs are broken. My liver is fine."

"Is it?" Dana poked Terry in the upper right abdomen, below the ribs, with her finger. Terry grabbed his side and leaned back against the table.

"Fuck!" he said in pain. Dana immediately felt bad, but she wouldn't let him know. Mary snickered into her hand. Jimmy outright laughed. Pops looked over his shoulder.

"It's not fine, tough guy," Dana said. "On a good note, I don't think it is lacerated." Mary leaned in as Dana spoke. "There isn't a bulge or anything that feels firm under the skin. I won't know for sure without blood tests or a CT scan." She looked up at him. "We will keep an eye on it, but you need to rest." It was the first time she noticed some of his other scars, but her professional curiosity was kept to herself, and she didn't ask about them.

"Just like I thought," Jimmy said, "you're all soft. Must be getting old, brother."

"Eat a dick," Terry shot back at Jimmy and then looked at Dana. "What's the recovery time?"

"Well, assuming it is just a bruise," she rang her fingers over the skin again, "and it isn't severe, the liver is probably three to four weeks. The ribs are about six weeks."

"Bullshit," Terry said, "we don't have three weeks. We are going to be lucky to have three hours before they get to us." Suddenly, Mom pushed her way through the group and grabbed Terry's arm.

"Bed, now," she said. "I'll get you some ice and medicine for that." The little woman led him back into the bedroom, returning to get some ice from the freezer. "Mary, go into the linen closet and get him one of your dad's old t-shirts." Mary scurried off quickly to retrieve a shirt. "Dana, you need to keep an eye on that boy. I will take care of Jimmy, but Terry won't sit still for a second. He never could."

"No way," Pops said. "Those two aren't going to be alone back there. No shenanigans. Jimmy, go with her. Or bring him out here, but no kids alone in the bedroom." Dana turned red, and Jimmy laughed.

"I'll go back there, Pops," Jimmy said. "That way Dana can keep an eye on both of us." Mom reluctantly nodded in agreement. Mary came back from the linen closet with a white T-shirt. The three of them went back into the bedroom to find Terry sitting on the bed.

"Lie down," Dana said as she gently pushed on Terry's left shoulder. He looked up at her and reluctantly followed orders. Jimmy plopped down on the edge of the bed, knowing it would cause his best friend needless pain. Terry winced.

"You're such an asshole," Mary said to her brother, tossing the shirt onto the nightstand. Mom came walking in with a Ziploc bag full of ice and gave Mary a stern look for her language, but didn't comment. Mom handed the bag to Dana and walked back out.

"Why don't you go get us a beer?" Terry said to Jimmy from his back. "We can split it." Jimmy and Mary began to laugh. Terry smiled and then winced. Dana looked confused; it was an inside joke she wasn't part of. Mary started to clarify.

"We were up here one summer and these two got drunk..." Mary started.

"Wait, wait, wait," Jimmy interrupted. "This is *our* story. Let me tell it. You'll screw it up anyway." Mary just shrugged and sat on the other bed. Dana looked at Jimmy as he started to tell the story. "There is a campground down the road. We would come up here, and Terry and I would always find a couple of girls to hang out with."

"And make out with," Mary added.

"Anyway," Jimmy continued, "this one time we stole a cooler full of beer from one of the campsites. Terry and I meet up with these girls, and we are heroes because we have all this beer to drink."

"How old were you guys?" Dana asked.

"Fifteen," Terry said from his back, holding the ice in place on his ribs.

"Right," Jimmy kept going, "fifteen. So, we start drinking down by the river. Terry and I get shithouse drunk. We probably drank most of two cases. We stumbled our way back here and sneaked into the house, or at least we thought we did. Pops was in his chair, and Mom was at the kitchen table, in the dark." Dana looked at Terry, and he was smiling, even through the pain. "So, Pops turns on the lamp and dipshit over here stops to say hi to Mom and kisses her. We think everything is cool."

"But Mom and Pops knew," Mary said.

"They knew we were drinking," Terry said, "because *you* ratted us out." Mary nodded and smiled.

"So, we went upstairs to the loft, and I fell flat on my face," Jimmy said and started to laugh. "Terry grabs me and drags me upstairs. Mom is pissed and storms off to the bedroom."

"This bedroom," Terry interrupted. Dana looked at him, and he continued the story, never opening his eyes. "We get upstairs, and I think that Jimmy is passed out, face down with his head under the pillow. Pops finally comes upstairs and asks if we've been drinking. I know we are busted, so lying about drinking wasn't going to work." Dana started to smile. She could very much picture these two men getting into this kind of trouble as kids. "Pops says, 'You two been drinking?' and I said yes."

Jimmy was trying to contain his laughter as Terry continued. "And Pops says, 'How much did you have to drink?' and I was trying to act as sober as possible. So, I said, 'I swear, Pops, we only had one. '" Jimmy was outright laughing now, sitting next to Terry on the bed. "This dumbass pipes up from under the pillow and says to Pops, 'And we split it!' Even Pops couldn't keep from laughing." Jimmy was dying laughing now. Even Mary was giggling out loud. Dana had a smile on her face.

"And that's the story," Mary said, "of these two *splitting* a beer. Do you know they never got into trouble for that? Mom even made them breakfast the next morning." Everyone but Terry laughed, mostly because he was trying not to inflict any more pain on himself. It was the first touch of normalcy since the night after Thanksgiving at Mom and Pops. It was only three days prior, but it seemed like a lifetime before. Terry was drifting off to sleep again, and he needed his rest. Dana stood up and waved Jimmy and Mary out of the room. The nurse gave the wounded soldier one last look as she followed them out, then closed the door behind her.

Mom was in the kitchen spooning stew into bowls, and Mary moved to help her. Jimmy reoccupied the couch, and Pops was watching the news in his chair. It was a very cozy feeling, even for Dana, who had never been here before. She saw Pops lean forward in his chair to look closer at the television.

"Mary Anne," he called and waved his hand, never taking his eyes off the screen.

CHAPTER 12

Dana stepped closer to the television as Mary walked past her. Pops was now pointing at the screen. The television was still on an aerial antenna mounted on the roof. Sitting on top of the television itself was a box that allowed Pops to control the direction of the arrow-shaped antenna to get better reception. It was antiquated, but that was the point. Pops didn't want a television in his getaway spot to begin with, so when they installed this in the mid-1980's Pops swore he wouldn't spend another penny on it. At this moment, they all wished they had a big screen and digital cable.

"Is that our house?" Pops asked, pointing at the screen. It was. Mary suddenly realized only she and Terry knew the details of what had happened right before sunrise. Mary suddenly felt guilty. She looked intently at the screen.

"Pops, turn that up," Mary said. Jimmy stood up from the couch and moved closer. Dana closed in as well. The scroll at the bottom of the screen read: *"Historic Police Family Targeted by Gangs."* The live footage of Mom and Pops' house was replaced with photos of Mary, Jimmy, and Pops. The picture of Pops was black and white.

"Jesus, Pops," Jimmy said with a laugh, "what year was that picture taken?" Pops was less than amused.

"Now is not the time, smartass," Pops said. Jimmy felt like Pops had just taken his belt to him. They all turned back to the TV. The on-scene reporter was back and speaking into a microphone.

"In an early morning shooting, this multigenerational police family was attacked," the young Hispanic woman said from the sidewalk in front of the house. *"Police have identified three of the men as repeat felons with long records of criminal gang activity. A fourth man survived but is under police guard at Cook County Hospital. Police have not released details about who the fourth man is or why this attack happened."*

"Nurse girl," Pops spat out, "Don't you work at Cook County?"

"Yes, Pops," she said quietly. She had a feeling she knew what was coming. "I do. And the name is Dana."

"You need to get back there and talk to that guy," Pops said, referring to the mysterious 'fourth man.' "You can get into the hospital, and you can get to him."

"Not really," Dana said. She was making excuses, and she knew it. "He's probably in ICU and I work in the PICU..."

"I thought you said you were an ER nurse," Jimmy said.

"Well, I was," Dana was stumbling over her words, "but I got tired of asshole adults, so I went back and got certified..." Pops cut her off.

"Nurse girl!" he shouted. "Do you remember shooting someone just last night?" It hit Dana like a brick. She nodded. "Do you want to have to do that again?" Dana shook her head 'no.' "Then you need to get your skinny ass down there and find out who this guy is." Jimmy looked down and checked out Dana's butt. He didn't realize Mom had joined the conversation, and she smacked him in the back of the head.

"I'll go with her," Jimmy volunteered.

"Um, no," Pops said. He was irritable and in no mood to waste time. "You're less than useful right now, and someone needs to be able to protect her. Mary, get cleaned up, and go with her." Mary just nodded. Pops was in police sergeant mode. Jimmy looked like a kicked puppy. "Quit being a baby," Pops said to him. "Mary, make sure you take your badge and gun. You go into the hospital, find out who this guy is, and then call here. Then out of the hospital. Got it?" Mary nodded again. "Nurse girl, you got it? In and out." Dana nodded too.

"Good, now go check on Terry while she gets cleaned up." Pops turned back to the television.

Dana and Mom both went in to check on Terry. He was still asleep, and the bag of ice slid off his chest and onto the bed. Mom gently lifted the bag, somehow not waking up the old warrior. Dana was impressed. Terry seemed to be breathing normally and not in enough pain to keep him awake. The two women walked back out of the room, stopping in the kitchen.

"I'll take care of him, dear," Mom said. "Don't you worry." Dana looked the little Italian woman in the eye. Mom winked at her, and Dana blushed. "I love him like my own son. Give him some time. Life has been hard on him, and he is even harder on himself. He lives with some demons, dear, but all he wants to do is protect people. That's who he is. That's his cross to bear." Dana instinctively touched the cross hanging around her neck that Terry had been obsessing over. She couldn't help herself and hugged Mom.

Mary came out of the bathroom, her face still wet from the sink, and pulled her hair back into a fresh ponytail. Dana grabbed her coat, and the two women headed for the sliding glass door. Pops was glued to the television, and Jimmy was sulking on the couch. Mary paused at the door.

"We will call when we know something," Mary said, seemingly speaking to the house in general. Pops waved his hand to acknowledge he heard his daughter. The old man was acting like this was business as usual.

"Be safe, Sis," Jimmy called to her as she opened the door. The two women walked out, climbed into Mary's car, and headed back to Chicago. A few minutes later, Terry emerged from the bedroom, holding his ribs. He looked around and wandered into the family room. Jimmy looked up at him.

"Where are the girls?" Terry asked.

"You left one alive," Pops said. "He's at the county hospital. I sent Mary and Nurse Girl to go find out who he is." Terry immediately felt sick.

"What?" he said. Pops turned and looked at him. "Why did you do that?" Terry looked at Jimmy. "And why did you let him?" Pops stood up. Terry could see the anger in his face.

"He didn't *let* me do anything," the old man said. "You two fucking mopes went and got shot, and neither of you is worth a shit right now. Someone had to be in charge, and we need information." The big German's face was red. "I made a command decision," Pops added.

"Who is going to protect them?" Terry shot back.

"Protect them?" Pops said. "Mary is a Chicago Police Detective. That girl puts her ass on the line daily. She isn't a big bad SWAT guy," he looked at Jimmy, "or some Airborne Ranger," he looked back at Terry. "But she isn't laid up here either. She didn't get shot like you two. If anyone should be watching over that nurse girl, it's probably her. I know she hasn't been unfortunate enough to have to kill someone like the rest of us…" Terry cut him off.

"She did," Terry said. Pops stopped. "This morning. At your house. She killed one of those men. She saved my ass. And she did get shot. Right in the vest."

"Even more reason to send her then," Pops said quietly. He sat down. "If she has to do it again, it will be easier. And getting shot didn't hurt her as much as it did you two fucking babies." The old man was on the verge of tears. As proud as he was that his adopted kids followed in his footsteps, he never wanted them to have to carry that burden.

"What happened this morning?" Jimmy asked. Terry exhaled and leaned against the kitchen table.

"Four guys came in through the back door. We were getting ready to leave for the meeting, so we had our gear on and our guns loaded when they came in. Mary took a round in the plate." Pops turned and looked at him. Hers are better than mine. I killed two for sure. I don't know about number three. Number four is the one that shot me. He was coming to finish me off, and she killed him."

"She never said a word," Jimmy said. "She came in and said hi, and then you came in and they took care of you and got you to bed. Never said a word."

"Pops," Terry said. "This isn't cop work. The guys from this morning, those weren't the professionals. Those guys were cannon-fodder."

"We know," Pops said. "The news said the three dead guys were all shitbag criminals, but wouldn't say anything about the guy who was alive at the county. That's why I sent the two of them to find out who he was." It wasn't a terrible decision by Pops. Terry was coming to grips with the fact that this organization, whoever or whatever they were, could reach out and get to you whenever they wanted. Thinking about it a little harder, coming up here to Wisconsin probably wasn't a great decision. There were so many 'what ifs' that it was making Terry's head spin.

Terry Davis had spent his entire adult life being in charge—almost every duty position he was ever assigned to put him in charge of soldiers. Even the ones where he wasn't in charge, like when he was a student at the Army Staff College, he always ended up as an informal leader. It never failed. It is the kind of burden that wears on everyone. For people like Terry, it was better to bear the burden than to relinquish that leadership role. He hated not being in charge, but as he looked at the people in this room, he knew he wasn't in the best shape to lead, and he would need their help.

"I apologize, Pops," Terry said. "She is your daughter, and you made the decision. I won't question it. You've been protecting this family for decades, and I know how hard it is to let that go."

"You know that includes you," Mom said from behind him. "We are all doing this to protect you, too." She handed him a bowl of stew.

The rifle round came through the sliding glass door and was meant to hit Terry, but the glass changed the trajectory just enough to move the point of impact four inches, landing the round in Mom's chest. She died instantly. Terry dove onto the floor as a reflex, and so did Pops. Jimmy sat on the couch, staring at the shattered glass door. The glass didn't fall out of the frame, keeping the shooter from getting an accurate second shot off as Jimmy sat dumbfounded.

The screen provided by the shattered glass lasted only until the second round hit it, knocking it all to the floor. The round impacted the back of the couch about eighteen inches from Jimmy, and only then did the wounded SWAT officer dive to the floor. The front wall of the house was shielding Pops. Terry crawled back into the bedroom, his ribs screaming with pain. He could see Mom lying on the kitchen floor in a pool of blood.

"Terry!" It was Pops yelling from the floor next to his chair. "Under the bed!" Terry crawled on his elbows to the bed and looked underneath. The AK-47 originally given to him by George the moonshiner was stashed under the bed frame with two spare magazines. Terry heard shooting from the living room. No rounds were impacting inside, so Terry assumed it was either Pops or Jimmy firing blind.

Terry never heard the shot that killed Mom. The shattering glass must have masked it. He did hear the second one, so the shooter wasn't using a suppressed rifle. It came from across the road; the shooter was probably using the trees for concealment. That wouldn't last long. Now that shots had been fired, Terry expected bad guys to make an entry into the house at any second. He got to his feet and shoved the spare magazines in his back pockets.

"Save your ammo!" Terry called out to Pops and Jimmy. It hurt to yell, but he had no choice. "Prepare for assault!" Terry had no idea what guns Pops or Jimmy had, or how much ammo they had available, but he knew they would need as much as they had in the next few minutes. He took a knee and poked the barrel of the Soviet battle rifle out the bedroom door. The easiest entry point into the cottage was the shattered front door. There was a back porch, which would require any assault team to breach the solid core door that led into the house. Terry could see the front door as he looked out of the bedroom. The back door was to his right.

Against his training, Terry flipped the selector lever to 'AUTO', putting the AK into fully automatic. Terry was always trained to fire a controlled pair of two rounds into targets as he cleared rooms, but firing fully automatic on the first burst might give any follow-on attackers something to think about before they came in. Terry waited, listening. He hoped Jimmy and Pops were doing the same.

Terry saw the flashbang grenade come through what used to be the sliding glass door. He ducked back inside the bedroom until it went off and then stepped back out. The first silhouette that came through the door went left, hard. Terry pulled the trigger on the AK and killed the man, hitting him with four of the seven rounds of 7.62mm. He saw the second man make a hard right. These guys were trained, which meant the third man would come in following the first, going left. Terry held the front sight just to the side of the door and fired, letting the third man run into the burst of automatic fire and going down.

Terry had fired more than half the magazine out of the AK, so he ducked back into the bedroom and fed a full magazine into the weapon. He heard two rounds fired in the living room, then another two. Controlled pairs. *Shit.* There was an explosion at the back door; a second team was making entry. Terry shifted inside the bedroom and stepped halfway into the hallway. The first man came through, and Terry pulled the trigger of the AK, pumping fully automatic fire into the doorway. The second man dove into the bathroom to his right, exposing the third man in the stack to Terry's AK fire. Terry heard two more shots from the living room. At least Jimmy or Pops was still alive and fighting. Terry assumed there was a fourth man out on the porch, and there was still the number two man in the bathroom.

Terry fed his last full magazine into the AK and prepared to close on the two men in the back of the house. He knew he couldn't fight in both directions, so he chose the back. His ribs were aching, but adrenaline was his friend right now. Terry stepped into the hallway and fired through the thin interior walls that enclosed the bathroom. He didn't know if he had hit the man inside, but it was at least keeping him pinned down. *Keep Moving, Keep Shooting.* The combat veteran moved quickly toward the back door, preparing to climb over the two dead bodies blocking the entryway, when the last man fired blindly into the hallway from outside. Terry was forced to dive into the bathroom, colliding with the bad guy inside.

The two men were chest to chest. Terry grabbed the smaller man and shoved his head downward, shattering the tank behind the toilet. The man collapsed in a pool of cold water. Terry was fighting to recover his AK from the corner when he heard a single shot. Terry turned to see the last man collapse dead in the hallway. He grabbed his rifle and waited. After about five seconds, Terry poked his head out of the bathroom. Jimmy was standing in the kitchen over his dead mother, holding his Glock. Terry walked out and surveyed the carnage.

The carpet was smoldering from the flashbang grenade. The front wall of the house was riddled with bullet holes. There were four dead men, dressed in Army-issued camouflage from head to toe. Only then did Terry realize the men who came through the back door were in uniform as well. As he crept into the living room, Terry saw Pops dead on the floor, holding his Smith and Wesson. He went down fighting, and at least he didn't have to live without Mom.

Terry went back to Jimmy; both their eyes filled with tears. Terry hugged his brother, the two of them crying in the kitchen.

CHAPTER 13

Terry Davis was a planner. It was wired into him as a kid by a father who truly believed the Vince Lombardi mantra, "if you're five minutes early, you're already ten minutes late." He learned as a young man to plan ahead, find efficiencies, backward plan so you are never late, and build in contingencies. The Army honed those abilities through organization and learned planning processes, and Terry was very good at it. When he arrived at the 82nd Airborne Division, he was forced to learn a new way of thinking. Paratroopers inherently understood that even the best plans went to shit as soon as the first man exited the aircraft, the enemy always gets a vote, and no plan survives first contact with the enemy. Planning in the Airborne community was a matter of course; it took a lot to alert a three-thousand-man brigade and get them loaded onto airplanes with combat gear packed and parachutes on, especially on short or no-notice.

Plans, he learned quickly, gave the commander the ability to call an audible from the playbook. The late General Dawson, a college football player himself, told Terry 'You can't call an audible if you don't have a playbook.' Davis adapted himself so he could live, and even flourish, in the unknowns of combat. He learned to adapt and 'call audibles' on the fly, even when in direct fire contact with the enemy. The lessons he learned from his father ensured he knew what assets he had available and how to apply them, even if it wasn't in the plan. From attack helicopters to artillery to fast-moving close air support aircraft, Terry Davis always knew what he had to turn the battle in his favor. In the end, it was as much about preparation as it was about planning.

Terry stood there in the kitchen with his best friend, feeling like he had been behind the curve since he showed up at their house on the day after Thanksgiving. He never thought through what might happen when he surfaced. He didn't think through the possible repercussions of his actions. As a result, his 'second parents' were dead, both he and Jimmy were wounded, and Mary and Dana were off to Chicago and in distinct danger. The feeling of failure was like a gorilla on his back. It didn't matter that the man in the suit and his organization had every asset at their disposal or that they could track Terry's every move as he was making it. He needed to get ahead of them.

"Brother," Terry said to Jimmy. "You don't want to hear this, but we need to move."

"What about Mom?" Jimmy replied with tears in his eyes. "And Pops?"

"Jim," Terry said as he grabbed Jimmy's shoulder, "I think I know these guys well enough by now. The local cops are already on the way. And probably the media too." Jimmy sniffed and looked Terry in the eyes. "But Mary and Dana are on their way to Cook County, and these assholes are probably waiting for them. If we don't get there quickly, those two are going to be in a world of hurt." Jimmy nodded in agreement. Terry gave him a minute to settle himself. The adrenaline was wearing off, and his ribs were starting to ache again, but Terry busied himself gathering a couple of weapons from the assault team strewn all over the little cottage.

Terry had two AR-15s and a couple of Glocks from the guys at the back of the house and set them on the kitchen counter. He could see Jimmy leaning over Pops' body, pulling the old Smith and Wesson from his hand. Whether Jimmy wanted it as a keepsake or as another gun to fight with, it didn't matter; Terry wasn't going to stop him. Terry was going to use the over three-hour car ride back to Chicago to develop a plan. Right now, they needed to get themselves moving. Terry opened his mouth to say something to Jimmy when the landline rang. The two men looked at each other. It couldn't be Mary and Dana already. Terry picked up the handset.

"Mr. Davis?" the voice on the other end asked. Terry knew the voice; it was the man in the suit.

"You know," Terry said into the phone. "I just realized that you know my name, but I don't know yours."

"Names are merely a formality, Mr. Davis," the man replied. "But you can call me Mr. Smith if you'd like."

"Somehow," Terry said dryly, "I don't think you're being entirely honest with me, Mr. Smith. Usually, after a few conversations, I at least know someone's name, especially after we've tried to kill each other."

"Mr. Davis," Smith said. "I've been several people with several names over the years. Smith is just easy for both of us to remember." Terry's brain started to spin. *This guy is a spook, or at least he was.*

"Fine," Terry said. "What can I do for you, Mr. Smith?" Jimmy came closer, and Terry pulled the handset away from his ear so Jimmy could listen.

"Mr. Davis," Smith started again, "these repeated incidents need to stop, for your sake."

"My sake?" Terry asked.

"Yes. You see, Mr. Davis, for us, they are a no-lose proposition. If we kill you, then you are out of our way. If we don't, then we spin the story to help achieve our goals. Either way, we win. You, on the other hand, lose regardless of the outcome," Smith said. There was a smug tone in his voice. "Either you die, or someone close to you does."

"What if I kill you?" Terry said, mimicking the smug tone. "That sounds like a win-win for me."

"You fail to realize, Mr. Davis," Smith said, "this is much bigger than you and me. Even if you kill me, this effort continues."

"Not for you it doesn't," Terry interrupted. "You ran like a little bitch the other night. Off into the darkness. Scared. That tells me you have something invested in this. It tells me you are full of shit."

"Mr. Davis, I signed away my life before you were born," Smith said. Terry smiled as he seemed to get a reaction out of the mystery man for the first time. "My sacrifices on behalf of this country are deeper than even yours, and I know what you've given up: two marriages, your health, Ms. Baron, and now even friends close enough to be family." Jimmy looked at Terry and then around at the house. Smith seemed to already know about Mom and Pops.

"Mr. Smith," Terry continued to push. He knew their time was running short, so he went all-in, "I don't think you are as courageous as you portray. I think you are a fucking coward. But I can promise you, we are going to find out." It was a ploy. Terry wanted to see how far he could push the man.

"Mr. Davis," Smith said. There was confidence in his voice. "That's not a fight you want to take on, is it?"

"Let's find out," Terry said. "Come see me, Mr. Smith. Bring your boss. I know you are someone's bitch. So, come find me and bring your boss, and we will see who is willing to sacrifice more." Terry waited. He rarely used this kind of bluster, even when playing poker. It wasn't his style, but he was goading the man into a reaction.

"Soon, Mr. Davis," Smith said. "We will have that opportunity soon enough." The line went dead.

"What the fuck was all that?" Jimmy said.

"We can talk about it in the car," Terry said, grabbing the weapons off the counter. "We need to go." Terry headed out through the broken sliding glass door to Pops' Cadillac. Jimmy paused for a moment, looking at his adopted parents on the floor, then followed Terry to the car.

Terry knew Pops always left the keys in the car when they were up here. 'Who the hell is going to steal a car out here?' he used to say. He popped the trunk and dumped the rifles and magazines in the cavernous compartment. He could feel the pain in his ribs as he reached for the trunk lid. He winced.

"You want me to drive?" Jimmy asked.

"You're a shitty driver with two good hands," Terry said, moving to the driver's door. "I'll drive." Jimmy went in the passenger side as Terry put the car in reverse. They were out on the two-lane highway, heading back to the interstate, when Jimmy turned on the radio. He needed something to break the silence. Pops only listened to the news while he drove. The local station was giving a national news update, so Jimmy turned up the volume.

"*Today, the Mayor of Chicago joined with several governors to ask Congress to suspend the Posse Comitatus Act of 1878, which prohibits the use of active duty military to act in a law enforcement capacity on US soil.*" Terry looked at the radio. "*Suspension of the Posse Comitatus Act would allow the city mayor, and other state and local officials, to request active forces, including special operations forces, to assist them as violent crime continues to rise.*"

"Holy shit," Jimmy said. Terry listened as the Chicago Mayor spoke at a press conference.

"*We have seen a significant rise in organized and violent gang activities here in the Windy City. These gangs are no longer a threat we have the capacity to combat without help. I am formally requesting Congress and the President to allow military forces to work with the Chicago Police Department to combat this threat.*" Her voice was squeaky and annoying. It was like a Muppet asking for help. "*These gangs have become militarized. They are organized and trained like a military force. I do not want to take officers away from their normal duties to deal with this threat. I also do not want to convert our Chicago Police Department into a paramilitary organization. This is a request for temporary assistance only.*" The radio announcer cut in to announce a commercial break, followed by a sports and weather update.

"There is no way this gets approved," Jimmy said.

"It will," Terry said with steel in his voice. "It will because this is what they want. Smith and whoever he works for. It's Pandora's box. They get it approved once for Chicago, and you can't go back. You can't put it back in the box." Terry was on the overpass, getting ready to turn left onto the onramp for the interstate, when two police cars passed heading in the opposite direction, lights and sirens blaring. The two men watched them go by, then shared a look. The cops were headed for the cottage, just like Terry said.

"Why didn't they pull us over and haul us in?" Jimmy asked.

"Because Smith wants me to keep fighting," Terry said. "You heard him, it's a win-win for them." Terry turned left and headed down the ramp.

"So, what do we do?" Jimmy asked. That was what Terry needed to figure out. Jimmy was a good cop, but he was muscle. Jimmy was a door kicker on the SWAT Team for a reason. He wasn't a planner and probably wasn't going to be much help. This was where Peggy and Terry excelled as a team. He wished Mary were here. She was the smart one and would have been a great partner to plan with. For the first time, Terry thought of Dana, the cute little nurse who had caused him so much grief over the last few days. He didn't know if she was worth a shit as a planner, but they certainly worked well together. Terry shook his head and snapped out of the haze.

"Let's work from small to big," Terry said. Jimmy was already confused; he could see it on the man's face. "We need to get Mary and Dana out of the Cook County hospital. That's first. Then we need to find out how Smith is pulling strings with the mayor, who convinced her that bringing the military in was a good idea. Once we cut that string, whoever or whatever it is, then Smith will come find me," Jimmy was taking all this in. It wasn't over his head, but it was certainly over his normal operating level. "I poked that guy in the eye hard enough that he won't let me walk away again."

"So, we get the girls," Jimmy said, as if that was his entire plan. Terry had to restrain his facial expressions.

"Yeah," Terry said. "That's step one. It should be pretty easy for the two of us to get into the hospital between your shoulder and my ribs. We look like shit, so no one will question us walking in the door." Terry was feeling lively as he was settling into his comfort zone. "We need to keep it public. Big areas of the hospital only. The emergency room, waiting rooms, and hallways. We can't get pulled into any exam rooms or offices." Jimmy was looking confused again. *This is going to be a long ride.* "You have your badge?"

"Yep," Jimmy said and fished it out of his pocket. "We can go to the desk and ask for my sister. She will have to sign in when she gets there. If they ask why we are so beat up, we can say we are working the gang case with her. They will buy that. Desk nurses generally don't ask a lot of questions when cops come in."

"Good," Terry said, happy his best friend was contributing. "If Dana sneaks her in, we just ask for Dana. Either way, it's simple and it should work." Jimmy nodded in agreement. "Then we get them out of there."

"What about the mayor?" Jimmy asked. "How do we figure that part out?"

"Your boss," Terry said. "What's his name? Moriarty?" Jimmy nodded. "He was pretty close-mouthed with Pops. He knows something he didn't want to share. I say we go see him."

"He's going to be fucking pissed when he sees me," Jimmy said. "They have probably been looking for me for two days."

"Or he is in on it," Terry offered, "and he will be shocked when you knock on his door and not dead. I am confident he knows something or can at least get us pointed in the right direction." A plan was formulated, and it made Terry much more comfortable. "We will take both cars. It would be better if you and Mary went in hers. I'll take Dana with me." Terry was thinking in terms of able-bodied individuals being split between the two vehicles, maintaining mobility with two vehicles, spreading out the firepower, and about ten other contingencies. Still, Jimmy assumed otherwise and had a shit-eating grin on his face. "What?"

"Nothing," Jimmy laughed. "You go ahead and take the hot little nurse with you. I'll ride with my sister." Terry shook his head.

"Anyway," Terry resumed, "You and I will go talk to him. Mary and Dana can stay with the vehicles. Once we find out what he knows, we will figure out our next move." Jimmy was still smiling like an idiot. Terry punched him in the chest, making Jimmy grab his shoulder in pain and simultaneously laugh. Terry's rib pain exploded from swinging his arm. He grabbed his ribs instinctively and looked at Jimmy. He couldn't help but laugh.

CHAPTER 14

Jimmy slept for most of an hour, allowing Terry to think through more details in their planning. He was listening to the news as he drove, changing stations as reception faded in and out. It didn't take him long to figure out Pops had every news station between Chicago and the cottage set up in the presets on the radio. As one station faded, Terry just pushed buttons until he found the next one. He heard the recap of the mayor's press conference more than once, each time hearing the same sound bite. After hearing the mayor screech and squeal for the third time, Terry was getting ready to change the station when he heard an update from the Superintendent of Police for the City of Chicago. Terry shrugged because he had always heard Pops refer to that position as 'The Chief,' but times change.

"I didn't originally agree with the mayor," the Superintendent began, *"but after multiple gang-executed shootings in the last three days, I am convinced she is doing the right thing. These gangs are now targeting police and their families, both inside and outside of Chicago."* Terry knew he was referring to the shootout at Mom and Pops and, probably, the one at the cottage just a few hours before. Terry looked, and Jimmy was still sleeping. He was thankful Jimmy wasn't awake to hear this. *"These*

attacks are planned. They are rehearsed. And they are being executed with military-like precision. While Federal Agencies are normally requested for this type of violence, the mayor and I believe that we need to fight fire with fire. There is no one better at combating these types of operations than our own US military, and specifically special operations forces." Terry was impressed; this guy was polished and well spoken. He quietly wondered how long the Superintendent had been in office.

"I support her request to bring in the military and every asset they have at their disposal. The Chicago Police Department is not a war-fighting organization. That's not what we are here for. Make no mistake, there is a war going on in these streets. I am concerned for the safety of our citizens and for the officers who are being targeted." Terry looked over, and Jimmy was awake and upright in his seat.

"Who is the Superintendent of Police?" Terry asked.

"The chief? Um, Gorgonzola. No. Garragiola. No. I don't know. Italian name that starts with a G."

"You don't know the name of the chief?" Terry said in shock. "How the fuck is that possible?" He didn't let Jimmy answer. "Is he CPD? Or did he come from somewhere?"

"He came from Virginia somewhere," Jimmy said. "About ten months ago. He showed up after New Year's."

"Last guy get fired?" Terry asked.

"No," Jimmy replied. "Dropped dead. The job killed him. Heart attack."

"Heart attack, my ass," Terry proclaimed. "I would bet you my disability check the last guy got killed and Smith and his cronies put this new guy in, for exactly this reason." Terry's brain was spinning again. They were still going to see the SWAT Commander, but Terry knew they would end up talking to the Superintendent.

"For what reason?" Jimmy was lost again. "The mayor picked this guy. It wasn't Smith or whoever."

"I call bullshit," Terry said, rubbing his beard. "These guys are playing the long game. They are moving chess pieces, and that's what this was: a chess move." Jimmy was still confused, but Terry was thinking too quickly to explain it to him. They were getting into the city now, probably less than twenty minutes from the hospital. "Do me a favor and keep your eyes open." Jimmy understood this. He may not have been a brilliant mind, but he was a damn good cop, and he grew up running the city streets with Terry.

The hospital was located in what the locals referred to as the 'Near West Side.' It wasn't far, just a few blocks south of the United Center, where the Bulls and the Blackhawks played, and it sat in a cluster of medical facilities. The two men navigated to a parking garage, parked the Cadillac, and hobbled inside the front doors of the hospital. There was an elderly woman at the front desk in an all-white uniform, complete with a name badge and about thirty different pins on a lanyard around her neck. Terry nodded Jimmy forward.

"Excuse me, ma'am," Jimmy said as he pulled his badge out. "I'm looking for another police officer. My sister, actually," he let out a charming laugh. Mary always said Terry was dangerous, but Jimmy was the charmer. "She is working a case and was supposed to come here." Jimmy threw a smile on at the end. The desk nurse wasn't impressed.

"She is here as a patient? Or just as a cop?" the woman asked.

"No, just to question someone," Jimmy said. "I know we are supposed to sign in here. Can you tell me if she is here?" There was suspicion in the woman's eyes. She looked over Jimmy's shoulder at Terry.

"Who's he?" she asked, throwing a nod at Terry.

"He's my partner," Jimmy was just bullshitting now, making things up as he went. "We've been undercover. He doesn't have his badge on him." The nurse looked Jimmy up and down. He had a badge, and he looked like hell.

"Well, see if she is here," the woman said. "But if she is, he can't go with you. No badge, I can't let him through. You can check the sign-in roster." She handed Jimmy a clipboard. He scanned it quickly but didn't find her name. *Shit.*

"She isn't on here," Jimmy said. "She may have come in with her friend, who is a nurse here. Dana. Do you know her?"

"Little bitty thing. She came through here about a half hour ago with another woman," the nurse said. "Said she was escorting her upstairs. I guess that was your sister."

"Yes, ma'am," Jimmy said, trying the charming smile again.

"Well, I can't tell you where they went," the nurse said plainly. "I can page her if you want, but I can't let you go wandering around the hospital."

"Wait," Jimmy said. "Don't page her. My sister is working undercover, too. I don't want to blow her cover." Jimmy was tap dancing now.

"Sonny," the nurse leaned on the counter, "if you got the hots for that little nurse, just say so. Quit the bullshit."

"Well," Jimmy shrugged and smiled, "you caught me. That really is my sister with her, though."

"Sure, it is," the nurse said, rolling her eyes. "They did go up to where that suspect is being treated. Fourth floor. You'll see all the rest of the cops in the hallway." She pointed at Terry. "But he still stays here. No badge, no go."

"Yes, ma'am," Jimmy said. "Thank you." He turned and walked back to Terry.

"You get a hot date out of all that?" Terry asked cynically.

"Eat a dick," Jimmy shot back. "I can go up there, but you can't. They are up on the fourth floor. I'll go get them and be right back."

"What do you mean I can't go?" Terry asked.

"No badge," Jimmy said plainly. "I swear, I'll be right back."

"No closed spaces. I'll be right here in the lobby," Terry reiterated to his best friend. "Make this quick."

Jimmy turned and walked quickly through the double doors and into the elevator. He was immediately paranoid because Terry told him no closed spaces, and the elevator was definitely a closed space. Jimmy hit the button for the fourth floor, and the doors closed, letting him breathe a sigh of relief. When the doors opened on the fourth floor, four cops were waiting for the elevator. Jimmy didn't recognize any of them, so he stepped out onto the floor, ensuring his badge was showing as he did.

He wandered the halls, looking for Mary or Dana as he moved. There were several uniformed police on the floor, but none with familiar faces. He saw Dana talking to a woman in scrubs at the nurses' station. He could see it wasn't a pleasant conversation by the look on Dana's face. He walked straight to her and interrupted.

"You OK?" he asked Dana.

"Holy shit," Dana said. "Can you please tell my supervisor that I cannot work today?" she pointed at the woman in scrubs.

"Where is Mary?" Jimmy acted like he didn't hear her.

"What?" Dana said, a little pissed that Jimmy wasn't helping. "She is in there, talking to a cop." She pointed to a room over her shoulder.

"I'm going to get her," Jimmy said, "and then we are leaving." He looked at Dana's supervisor. "She can't work. Police business." Dana smiled smugly at her supervisor and turned on her heel. Jimmy walked to the room Dana directed him to, finding Mary inside talking to a uniformed Sergeant. There was a man restrained to the hospital bed. He was unconscious and had more tubes sticking out of him than Jimmy could process.

Jimmy was dreading telling Mary about Mom and Pops. It was one of the few things he and Terry hadn't talked about in all of this. He knew he needed to be the one to tell her, but he wasn't sure how or when. She would be devastated. Mom and Pops had been so good to them, taking them in and adopting both of them, never keeping it a secret of any kind, but never treating them like they were anything but their own children. He was afraid she would blame herself, that her involvement with the two guys who tried to recruit her brought all of this on, or maybe that she would blame Terry for dragging them into it just by being around. He knew Terry would let her blame him if that was what she needed. He would let her be mad at him, or even hate him, as long as she needed to if it would help her get beyond this tragedy.

The uniformed Sergeant caught Jimmy's eye as he walked in and looked at him. Mary turned to see who was coming in the door to find her brother standing there, looking like hell. Dana was only two steps behind him. Suddenly, the room was full of people, and she felt very crowded. The sergeant had no idea who Jimmy was.

"You can't be in here," said the tall Hispanic man with a manicured mustache.

"He's my brother," Mary said plainly, "and he's a cop."

"Who's she?" the officer asked.

"I'm a nurse," Dana said, flipping her ID badge at him sarcastically. "I work here."

"Mary," Jimmy said, "we need to talk in private." There was a seriousness to him that Mary rarely saw. Her brother had always been the joker, the funny and charming guy that women loved for about a week and then got rid of. She instantly knew something was wrong.

"What's wrong?" she asked. "Where's Terry?" Her thoughts went immediately to him. Terry was her rock for a long time; even when he was away on Army business, he was always the person she reached out to. She also knew that Jimmy wouldn't voluntarily be running around without him at a time like this.

"Terry is fine," Jimmy said. "He's downstairs in the lobby. Can we go somewhere?" Mary never considered that something had happened to Mom and Pops. She assumed Jimmy needed to tell her something regarding the mess they were in, something he didn't want to share with the uniformed cop in the room.

"The nurses' break room is around the corner," Dana said. "Follow me." The trio walked out of the hospital room, Jimmy's heart in his throat. Dana pushed the door open and shooed two nurses out of the room in a not-so-nice manner.

"Hey," she said, "you two. We need the room. Go chart or something." The male nurse started to scurry, but his female counterpart gave Dana a 'go fuck yourself' look. "Seriously, police business. Get out." Dana wasn't in the mood to tolerate any bullshit. After they both left the room, Jimmy looked at his sister. His eyes welled up with tears; he couldn't help it.

"Jimmy," Mary said, "what is it?"

"After you left, they came to the cottage," Jimmy said, folding his arms. "They blew through the door. Mom and Pops..." he openly began to weep.

"Oh my God," Dana said in a whisper.

"What?" Mary said as she covered her mouth. "What happened?" She wasn't crying. As much as Jimmy was her big brother, she mothered the hell out of him. "Jimmy, you have to tell me what happened."

"They shot mom through the front door," Jimmy said between sniffles. "Then four men came in the front. Terry shot two of them as they came in. Pops got one. But, but the last guy…" he started to cry again.

"Jimmy," Mary said with some ice in her tone. She looked over to see Dana sitting in an orange plastic chair, crying into her hands. "What happened with the last guy?" she urged him to continue.

"He shot Pops," Jimmy said. "I shot him, but I wasn't fast enough. I didn't…" his emotions were pouring out now.

"OK," she hugged him, but she felt the anger building in her. "What happened with Terry?"

"There were four more that came in the back," Jimmy said. "Terry got three of them. And, and I got the last one."

Her parents were gone. The only parents she ever knew. Jimmy said he had very faint memories of their birth mother. She was neglectful and abusive, but her addiction killed her and landed the two of them in the orphanage. Mary was beyond mad at this point. It wasn't anger anymore; it was building into rage. The last time she felt this way was a few years ago when her last boyfriend beat the shit out of her. The anger she felt that day was with herself. She saw all the signs of an abuser but ignored them until he almost killed her. He was lucky he packed up and was gone before she got home from the hospital, or she would have killed him. That's exactly what she felt now; the urge to make someone pay.

"Jimmy," she could hear the anger in her voice. "We need to go get Terry. I need to talk to him." Her brother gave her an incredulous look.

"Did you hear what I just said?" Jimmy asked. "Mom and Pops are dead." Dana looked up at the two of them. She couldn't decide what to make of all this.

"I heard you," Mary said, "but I can't change that, and neither can you. We need to get to Terry." She looked at Dana. "Are you coming?"

"Of course," Dana said. She was shocked at her friend and how little emotion she was showing. She just found out her parents were dead, and she was acting like a robot.

"OK," Mary said and grabbed her brother's shoulders. "Jimmy. Look at me." Jimmy wiped his eyes and looked at his little sister. "We have to go, now." Mary turned and headed for the door. "Because I'm going to kill a motherfucker," she said to no one in particular.

CHAPTER 15

Terry stood in the lobby for what seemed like an eternity. The crabby old nurse who was unimpressed with Jimmy's charm kept an eye on him, occasionally looking out from behind the frosted glass around her desk to see if Terry was still in her lobby. He counted a total of five uniformed officers who left through the sliding doors and another six who came in—lots of cops moving through the hospital. In a moment of introspection, Terry wondered if his paranoia had risen to an unreasonable level because he started to doubt if these were cops at all. *It's hard to be overly paranoid when people keep trying to kill you,* he justified to himself.

Two police officers were beginning to give him a few too many looks when the elevator door opened and Mary, Dana, and Jimmy came pouring out. Mary got to him first, but Terry could see Jimmy and Dana with telltale red eyes; they had been crying. Jimmy had obviously told Mary about Mom and Pops. He looked down at Mary, and there was anger in her eyes. She hadn't been crying, but she was pissed.

"Where are you parked?" she asked.

"Out in the parking garage," Terry was conflicted between worry and admiration at her reaction to the news of her dead parents. She was all business.

"Let's go," she said. Without a word, the four went out the door and followed Terry's quick pace to the parking garage and the Cadillac. "Jimmy told me what happened," Mary said plainly.

"You OK?" Terry asked. Jimmy and Dana were both somewhat emotional and not engaged in the conversation.

"Yeah," Mary said, "I'll deal with all that later. I talked to some uniforms about the guy inside that tried to kill us at Mom and Pops," she didn't even flinch when she mentioned them. "He's a John Doe. No marks, no tattoos, no prints on file anywhere."

"So, he's not a gang banger," Terry surmised. "Not even a criminal."

"No," Mary said. "But he was the only one. The rest were shit heads with long rap sheets. All gang-affiliated. Two were on parole, and the other was out on bail for a high-end misdemeanor. Did you find anything out?"

"Didn't find anything out," Terry said. He watched Mary's face drop with disappointment. "But I did put some pieces together. At least the framework of a plan." A car came around the corner of the parking garage, and Terry stopped talking long enough to let it pass. "We need to go talk to Pop's buddy Moriarty. Did you hear the shit on the news about the Mayor and the Superintendent asking for help from the military?"

"I overheard some cops talking about it," Mary said, "but that's it."

"We heard it on the news while we were driving," Terry went on. "Press conferences from both of them. They are asking for Congress to suspend Posse Comitatus and allow the military to help the CPD. The Superintendent asked for special operations guys to come in here and fight this gang war."

"That seems a little heavy-handed," Mary said. Terry could see that Jimmy and Dana were freezing in the cold air passing through the concrete structure. He tossed Jimmy the keys to the Cadillac so they could get out of the cold.

"That's the play by Smith and his organization," Terry said. Mary looked confused. "The guy in the suit. I talked to him on the phone. He called the summer place, after…" Terry paused. "Anyway, I think the guy used to be a spook, like CIA or another organization like that. This is part of their larger plan. Once they get Congress to do this once, it's over. You can't put the toothpaste back in the tube. They will be able to put the military anywhere they want on US soil. *Legally*."

"Jesus Christ," Mary said. "So why do we need to talk to Moriarty?"

"Because someone is pulling the strings behind the Mayor," Terry said. "He told you on the phone he wasn't sharing any information, which means he has some. I think it is the new Superintendent. Your dumbass brother couldn't even remember his name."

"Gagliardi," Mary said quickly. Of course, she knew. "He isn't CPD. He came from Alexandria and was connected in the DC area." That made Terry even more suspicious.

"Exactly," Terry said. "He fits the profile of a plant by Smith and his people."

"So, what do we do then?" Mary asked. "Once we figure that piece out. If he is tied to these people, what do we do then?"

"We are stirring the pot," Terry said. "Sometimes you have to create activity to gain intelligence. We talk to Moriarty, and then we talk to Gagliardi. Then we watch what happens."

"What do you think happens after that?" Mary asked. "I mean, if we talk to those two, one of them is going to go to the Mayor, or this Smith guy. Then they will know we are on to them." Terry looked at her for a second. He missed this. He and Peggy used to go back and forth like this constantly. As much as it helped flesh out the plan itself, just the teamwork was what Terry missed.

"Mary," Terry said, "you should have been a soldier." She smiled and turned a little red. "After that, we will see movement. I'm not entirely convinced the Mayor is in on this. They may be moving behind her and just propping her up, but we will find out. If she is just a prop and she doesn't know she is being used, maybe we will see her change directions. That would help.

"Regardless of all that," Terry continued, "Smith is going to be pissed that I keep pushing. That *we* keep pushing. He told me that no matter what I do, it is a win-win for them. They need to lose and lose big." He paused as another car passed by. "When I killed Dawson, I thought that would slow them down, but it didn't. I was wrong."

"They need to lose something or someone they can't replace at the drop of a hat," Mary added. "Smith? Is he that person?"

"I don't know if he is," Terry said. "He says he isn't, but I'm not sure. Let's head over to see Moriarty and get that ball rolling." Mary nodded. "I'll take Dana with me; you take your brother." Mary gave him a suspicious look. Terry frowned in return. "Your brother gave me shit over this, too. I'm beat up, but I can fight. So can you. You and I need to be in separate cars, but what we don't need is the two wounded guys in the same car." She let her suspicious look linger for a second, long enough to make Terry uncomfortable.

"OK," Mary said, "I'll buy that. My car is one level up." The pair turned and went to the Cadillac. Jimmy was in the front passenger seat with Dana sitting behind him. "Get in the back with me, big brother. Dana, get in front with Terry." It was direct, not a request. Terry quietly smiled to himself as he climbed in.

Terry started the engine and waited for everyone to switch places and close all the doors before putting the car in reverse. He negotiated the parking garage and, after the soft squeal of tires turning slowly on concrete, they found Mary's car. The brother and sister pair jumped out, and Mary leaned back inside.

"Follow us," she said. "I'll lead." Terry nodded. The car was desperately quiet as he and Dana waited for Mary to back out of the parking space.

"Answer one thing," Dana said, staring out the windshield. "Why are we doing this?" Terry gave her a confused look. "I mean, what do we all gain out of this? Mom and Pops are gone. Jimmy got shot. *You* got shot. Mary and Jimmy's careers are probably destroyed. What is the value in what we are doing?"

For Terry, it was simple. This was about right and wrong and about the country he spent his life defending. It was probably the same for Jimmy and Mary, too, even for Mom and Pops. They had all spent their lives defending right versus wrong, and that is what this was. It sounded somewhat corny, even to him. Terry wasn't sure if that would sit well with Dana. He didn't know anything about her, really, other than she was a nurse.

"You ever disagreed with a doctor or another nurse about a patient?" Terry asked. He put the Cadillac into gear and began following Mary's car through the garage.

"Of course," Dana said.

"Have you ever had a patient that was in really bad shape and the decisions the doctor was making...you just knew it was the wrong thing for the patient?" Terry was trying to put their situation in a context Dana could relate to. She listened quietly. "In those situations, what do you do?"

"I fight for the patient," Dana said. "That's part of my job."

"And at some point," Terry continued his questions, "you have to decide how wrong you think the doctor's decision is and how hard you want to fight, right?" Terry looked at her, and he could see her processing. "And you do that because it is your job, and that patient deserves the best care possible. That's what this is. It's a matter of doing what's right. And Mary, Jimmy, and I decided a long time ago that we would fight for what's right, no matter the consequences. Pops did too." She paused.

"OK," Dana said. "I get it. I'm in."

"Dana," Terry said cautiously, "This is probably going to get worse. Before you commit to this, you deserve to know that." They were pulling out onto the street, still following Mary. Dana turned and looked at him.

"You don't know me," Dana said, "really, at all. I mean, we've spent the last few days riding around together, trying not to get killed, but you don't know anything about me." Terry sat quietly and listened as he drove. "I became a nurse in my late twenties, and I wanted to become an emergency room nurse. You know why?" Of course, he didn't know, but he was playing along.

"I would imagine there was a good reason," he said encouragingly.

"I did it because I was in a car accident," she said. "My dad was driving, and my mom was in the backseat. A drunk driver hit us on the driver's side. Dad died of a massive heart attack. Mom bled out in the snow. I couldn't do anything to help them because I didn't know how.

I didn't know much of anything, really. I just sat there in the snow, helpless and crying, holding onto this cross hanging around my neck." Terry looked at her and could see in her glassy eyes that she was reliving the accident as she talked. "I never wanted to feel like that again. You have your cross to bear. That's my cross."

"So, you became a nurse," Terry completed her thought.

"Not just a nurse," she corrected him, "but an ER nurse. I didn't want to be an EMT, but I wanted to be as close to the point of injury as possible. To help save people."

"But now you work with kids," Terry was looking for confirmation. He turned right as he followed Mary. "How did that happen?"

"In the ER, you just get whatever patient comes in next," she said plainly. "I got a little jaded trying to keep criminals and assholes alive. Kids are innocent. Even the ones who are little assholes are innocent." Terry chuckled.

"It's admirable," Terry said. "What you do. I couldn't do it."

"Yes, you could," Dana said flatly. "According to Mary, you can do anything." Terry snapped a look at her. "She talks about you like you're the second coming. It took me a long time to realize she isn't *actually* in love with you." Terry squirmed behind the steering wheel. He had never been comfortable with compliments.

"Well, Mary never had good taste in men," Terry said, trying to downplay.

"Agreed," Dana said. "The last one was a nightmare. The one that beat the shit out of her. I tried to warn her about him." Terry showed no surprise and no reaction. "Amazing how he took off before she made it home from the hospital. Total blessing." Dana was dragging it out, trying to get a reaction out of Terry. "Very uncharacteristic of him. He thought he was a tough guy, but something must have scared him off." She looked at Terry.

"What?" he said, feigning innocence.

"I thought so," Dana said. "From the minute I met you, it made sense. What did you do? Is he dead in a ditch? You dump his body in a lake?" Terry said nothing. "That's what he deserved. I think Mary suspects it, too, but she would never say it out loud because it might get you into trouble." She was staring at him now. Terry looked at her and then back at the road. There was a pause.

"He's not dead," Terry said. She laughed out loud.

"I knew it!" Dana exclaimed. "Who told you? Did you hurt him? You should have hurt him." She was smiling now.

"Mom called me, actually," Terry said quietly. "She didn't ask me to do anything or even get involved. She just said that she wanted me to know and that she just hoped it didn't happen again." Dana looked intently at him. "It was right after I retired. Before all of ... this," he waved his hand in the air. "I was a few hours away, so I drove. I woke him up in the middle of the night. In his own bed. With a knife at his throat." Dana's face went a little pale. "I told him to pack his shit and never come back. Then I sat in the parking lot and watched him leave."

"Ever the protector," Dana said as she sat back in her seat. "That's what mom said about you, what I said before. Your cross to bear. You're the protector. You protect everyone." They were turning again.

"No one else knows about that," Terry said. "So, keep your mouth shut." He looked at her intently. She put her fingers to her mouth and motioned like she was locking her mouth shut.

"My lips are sealed," she said. There was admiration and a bit of triumph in her voice. She had gotten the man of stone to reveal a secret to her. Dana had never met a man who would do the things Terry would do for other people. The lengths he would go to protect his friends and his family were something she had never seen before.

Mary pulled into a parking place in a neighborhood. There was a huge park on the side of the street where they parked. Across the street was a row of large, old houses. Whether the wealth was still in the same families or not, this neighborhood was built with old money. As Terry opened his door and got out, he looked back inside at Dana.

"You stay here," he told her. She frowned but sat back in her seat. "Get in the driver's seat, just in case." Terry looked up to see both Jimmy and Mary getting out of Mary's car. He closed the door. "Jimmy, stay with the car. Mary and I will go in." He pointed at Mary's car. "In the driver's seat, ready to go." Jimmy began to protest.

"But it's *my boss*," he said. Terry and Mary gave him a look. He stopped whining and started pouting, but he dutifully got into the driver's seat. Terry didn't know which house they were going to, so he let Mary lead. He followed her through a wrought iron gate and up stone steps to a massive brick house.

"Since when do cops make this much money?" Terry asked. He felt inside his waistband to ensure the Glock was still somewhat concealed. Mary banged on the door.

"Cops don't," Mary said. "But his wife's family is loaded. He can quit anytime he wants." She shook her head. Mary lifted her hand to knock again. Terry was looking around the portico as the door opened.

CHAPTER 16

"Mary!" the tall, thin woman said from the open doorway. Mrs. Moriarty was absolutely stunning. She was extremely tall for a Korean woman and impeccably dressed. Her smile was genuine and inviting, and she reached out to hug Mary. Mary reciprocated and stepped back. "It's so good to see you. It's been forever," she looked at Terry. "Who's this?"

"This is Terry," Mary said. Terry was suddenly very self-conscious about how he looked. Less than twelve hours ago, he was in a firefight trying to stay alive and hadn't cleaned up since. The woman was genuinely unfazed by his appearance. "Is your husband home?"

"Yes! Please come in," she said. "Rocco is back in the kitchen." Mrs. Moriarty turned, and Mary followed her. Terry closed the door behind him and fell in step with the two women. "Rocco!" she called to her husband. The house was cavernous. Terry looked around and was impressed with its size, but also how comfortable it all looked. As he came into the kitchen, Terry felt massive guilt about his preconception of this man. Never in a million years did he consider that Rocco Moriarty would be a massive black man with a Korean wife.

"Mary!" the man said as he came around the bar that divided the kitchen from a small eating area. He enveloped the much younger officer in a hug. "What are you doing here? Where is your brother? His ass is in some trouble with me." It was all said with the warmth and feeling of family. Terry had heard Pops mention Rocco often over the years, but had never met the man. Pops always classified Rocco as 'a really good cop' and 'a guy who could climb the ladder.'

"Can we talk?" Mary asked. She looked at Mrs. Moriarty. "Somewhere private?" The lifelong wife of a cop didn't need any other hints. She smiled and threw up her hands.

"I guess that's my cue to leave," she said. "I've been down this road before. It was nice meeting you, Terry." She touched Terry's arm as she said it and walked out of the room. *She may be the nicest person I've ever met,* Terry thought to himself. The SWAT Commander's eyes got wide.

"Terry?" he said out loud and then looked at Mary. "Is this *the* Terry? The legendary Airborne Ranger that your dad always talks about?" Terry was at a loss. This wasn't going at all how he thought it would. He was going to have to change tactics on the fly.

"Yeah," Mary said with a touch of envy. "Two kids as cops, and he brags about this one. Sir, I need to tell you something," Mary said. She was taking the lead. Terry fell into a supporting role. "Mom and Pops are dead."

"What?" Rocco said. His face dropped. There was genuine surprise in his voice. Terry decided to focus on the man's body language rather than his words. "What the hell happened?"

"It's complicated," Mary started. Terry was impressed with Mary and the story she was weaving. She told Moriarty about getting recruited and Jimmy getting shot, the attack at Mom and Pops, and then finally about Mom and Pops getting killed. Tactfully, she left out any reference to Mr. Smith and the growing threat of his organization.

"I heard about what happened at your parents' house. Or at least one version of it. Where is Jimmy now?" Rocco asked. There was genuine concern in his voice, not just as Jimmy's commander but as a family friend. Terry was doubting any suspicion he had about the man. Mary hesitated.

"When I called," she changed the subject, "you said the liquor store was closed. Pops said that meant you had information you couldn't share." She looked intently at the large man. "Sir, you can see what is going on. What information did you have?" The big man stood to his full height. He was every bit of six feet, four inches. Terry suddenly had an image of Rocco and Pops in their prime riding around in a squad car together. They must have been an intimidating pair to any punks on the street.

"Mary," he said. "This is a deep pool that you don't want to go wading in." Terry stepped in.

"Sir," he said flatly, "I've waded into deeper pools than this. Much deeper." Terry looked the man in the eyes. Most men cowered from Rocco's stare, but Terry remained unintimidated. Rocco flinched first; he looked at Mary.

"Listen, you two," he said, tucking his hands into the pockets of his green tactical pants. Terry just realized the SWAT Officer was still dressed for work. "Something is going on that is above me, above the City itself." Mary nodded. Terry leaped to the conclusion that when he referred to the City, the big man meant the mayor's office. "I don't like the new Superintendent. I don't trust him. And the mayor is an idiot." Terry was more confident that Moriarty was shooting straight with them. "That woman couldn't run a doughnut shop, let alone the whole city. The Supe told me a few weeks ago that SWAT was going to be cut out of anything having to do with gang violence." Mary turned and looked at Terry.

"Sir, he just announced today that he was supporting the Mayor to bring in active military to fight that fight," Terry said. The big man nodded his head. "But he said he didn't agree with her until recently."

"I saw that, too," Rocco said. "Initially, I thought he was just turning it all over to the gang crime unit, but after today, I'm not so sure."

"Sir," Mary broke in, "the guys at Mom and Pops' house and the guys that killed my parents were not just gang bangers. I mean, some of them were, but some weren't. Have you seen or heard of anyone hanging around, maybe whispering in the Superintendent's ear?"

"Like whom?" Moriarty asked.

"Like anyone who doesn't fit in," Terry said. "Someone who is always around but never in meetings. Never anywhere there are cameras." Moriarty went to the refrigerator and pulled out a beer, waving one at Mary and then Terry. Both politely refused with a silent wave. The big cop opened the bottle and drank half as he thought.

"Not anyone I can think of," Rocco said. "What do you think is going on?" Mary looked at Terry. It was his decision how much he wanted to tell the SWAT Commander, not hers.

"Sir," Terry stepped in, "you've been up front and honest with us. I'm going to extend you the same courtesy." Mary tried to hide her shock. She assumed Terry was about to tell one of the highest-ranking officers in the City of Chicago a conspiracy story about domestic terrorism. She assumed wrong. "This is something you don't need to know about. It is for your protection and for that of your family." Moriarty looked insulted. "I know Pops told you all about me, or at least what he knew. I'm going to ask you to take this on faith, based solely on that." It hit the big man hard.

"Well," Moriarty said after he finished his beer, "I can't argue with Pops' judgment. He taught me everything, and I never had reason to question it. So, what are you two going to do next?" Terry and Mary stood there quietly. He looked from one to the other. "OK, I get it. Better that I don't know, but if I don't know anything, I can't help you much either." He walked around to the backside of the bar and pulled open a drawer. After extracting a pen, he pulled two business cards out of his pocket and scribbled on the back of them. He handed them to Mary. "That's my direct number on the back. If you two get pulled over, harassed, or even questioned by a cop in this city, you hand them that." Mary handed one to Terry, and he put it in his pocket. "I can at least stop someone from locking you up for carrying a concealed weapon in the city."

"What?" Terry asked.

"Son," Moriarty said, "I've been a cop for a long time. I saw that pistol under your shirt before I saw your face." Terry smiled in admiration. "If you two need anything, call me."

"Thank you, Sir," Terry said as he reached out his hand. The big cop shook it with a grip to break steel. Mary leaned in and hugged him. Terry led the way out the front door, Mary close on his heels. When they got across the street, Mary stopped him.

"Where to now?" she asked. Terry thought for a minute.

"Do you know where the Superintendent lives?" he asked.

"I do," Mary replied, "but he has security at his house all the time. Cops on detail. We will never get in." Terry thought about trying to sneak in, but he knew that wasn't going to do them any good. Going back to Mom and Pops was a waste; it was probably still surrounded by crime scene tape and may even have some officers hanging around. Hotel? His apartment? He was thinking through the options.

"Hey," Dana said, standing in the open door of the Cadillac. "Let's go back to my place." She had been listening to the conversation. Terry didn't think it was the best option, but there were no good options, so they may as well be comfortable.

"Why not," Mary said. Terry nodded in agreement. He went back to the Cadillac and walked to the passenger door. Dana looked at him with confusion.

"It's your house," he said. "You drive." He climbed in and closed the door. Terry was starving. He hadn't had anything to eat in what seemed like an eternity. "You got any chow at your place?"

"Chow?" Dana responded. "You mean food? You know, you're not in the Army anymore." He gave her an exasperated look. "Yes, I have food." She pulled out of the parking space, letting Mary and Jimmy fall in behind her.

"Do you enjoy busting my balls?" Terry asked her. He could feel the exhaustion crashing over him like waves. The pain in his ribs was throbbing.

"Actually," Mary said, "I do. Somebody has to. You need it. I have a feeling you haven't had anyone busting your balls enough."

"That's what you think, huh?" Terry said. His eyes were getting heavy.

"Hey," Dana said, "You need to stay awake. I'll poke you in the fucking ribs again." She was trying to keep things light, but she knew it was a losing battle. Terry sat up in his seat, but his eyes closed again. Dana turned her focus to the road.

In a matter of minutes, Dana could hear a soft snoring coming from Terry as he slept in the passenger seat. She took a long look at him, longer than she should have. Mary had talked about him for years. He became almost a mythical creature that Dana never thought existed.

Before she met him, Dana pictured Terry as a tall, suave man who was charming, gorgeous, and looked like he was chiseled out of granite. The man snoring next to her wasn't that. He was a fractured man with more baggage than anyone she knew. His hair was shaggy, and his beard was worse. Dana had gotten a closer look at his body when she checked his broken ribs, and it was far from granite.

In the few days since they met, Dana got a good look at who Terry was. She had seen him angry, thoughtful, protective, caring, challenging, and even funny. While his outside didn't live up to what she expected, his inside was much more than advertised. If anything, Mary undersold who he was. Her mind started to wander, trying to decide if there was ever the possibility of a relationship with a man like this. Dana hadn't had a man in her life in almost a decade. There had been more than a few that chased her, and she had been on her fair share of dates, but no one grabbed her imagination. All the guys she met could fit in the same box she referred to as 'Chicago-typical.' She wasn't a die-hard Cubs or White Sox girl. She didn't care about the Bears or the Blackhawks, and she hadn't watched a Bulls game since Jordan left the second time. Hanging out in bars or playing golf didn't interest her, but she wasn't much of a museum or long walks in Grant Park person either.

Dana didn't know what she wanted. The only thing she knew was that she had never met a man like Terry in her life, even with all the faults that came with him. Her mind kept coming back to what Mom said to her about Terry: *"Life has been hard on him, and he is even harder on himself. He lives with some demons, dear, but all he wants to do is protect people. That's who he is. That's his cross to bear."* Dana realized that what she knew about Terry was all from Mary and not from Terry himself. She was curious about the demons Mom talked about and why he was so hard on himself, but she wanted to hear it from him. She wondered if she ever would.

Before Dana realized it, they were just a few minutes from her house. Terry startled awake in the passenger seat and scared the shit out of her. She didn't jump or even shriek, but she gasped and grabbed the steering wheel tight with both hands. Terry rubbed his eyes and realized what had happened.

"Where are we?" he asked casually. There was no attempt at an apology. He adjusted himself in the seat.

"Are you even going to say you're sorry?" Dana snapped back at him. "You scared me to death." Terry just shook his head. He promised himself years ago that he would never apologize for who he was. "Do you always wake up like that?"

"No," Terry said. "Sometimes, but not always. Just don't ever shake me awake, it never turns out well."

"Are you OK?" Dana asked. Terry looked at her. "Like really OK? I mean…"

"Let me save you the trouble," Terry said. "The short answer is no. The VA determined me to be broken. Like a hundred percent disabled. I have all my parts, but nothing works well." Dana unintentionally gave him a look of pity. "Don't look at me like that. I'm not a fucking invalid. My life was hard, and it took a toll, that's all."

Dana turned onto her street and headed for her house. Mary and Jimmy were still right behind her, and they followed her up the driveway, parking both cars next to the house. Terry started to open the door, but Dana stopped him.

"Listen," she said softly, "I didn't mean to offend you. I'm a nurse and I naturally try to help people."

"Thanks," Terry said, "but I'm good." He got out of the car. Dana hesitated and wondered if he was worth the effort. Hopefully, Mom was right, and he would eventually come around.

CHAPTER 17

I t was dark by the time they got inside, and the house was cold. Dana was annoyed when she unlocked the kitchen door, and Terry held her aside to go in first with his pistol drawn. As crazy as things had been, it was still difficult for Dana to accept that someone would be waiting for them inside her own house. Once Terry was satisfied the home was safe, he started laying down some ground rules.

"Listen," Terry said, "no lights on if you can help it. Someone is awake all the time. I will get the rest of the stuff out of the cars, so we know what we have. I've kind of lost track. We all need some sleep so that we can sleep in shifts. Dana, see what food you have. Mary, put together a sleep schedule. Jimmy, you go shower first so we can get that wound cleaned up."

"Hey," Dana cut him off. "You want to take a breath for a minute? My fucking house, OK?" Terry stopped himself from snapping back at her. She was right, they weren't soldiers. "We are *all* in danger, not just you. So, give it a rest." Terry turned and walked outside before he lost his temper, closing the door with a thud.

"Damn," Jimmy said. "I haven't seen that in a long time."

"What?" Mary asked.

"Terry get shut down like that," Jimmy said. "Last time I saw that was when his first wife gave him the 'It's me or the Army' ultimatum.' I was standing there when she said it. He was speechless." Dana immediately felt bad about talking to Terry like she did.

"He will be fine," Mary said. "He's been through much worse."

"Hey, Sis," Jimmy said, "I know he is your hero, but no one on Earth knows him better than I do. Has he been through worse? Sure, he has. But for a twenty-three-year-old kid, that wrecked him." Just then, Terry came back through the door carrying a pile of weapons and gear. Dana and the two siblings stopped talking and stared at him.

"What?" Terry asked. He looked at Dana. "Where can I lay this stuff out so I can see everything?"

"Plenty of space in the basement," she said, pointing at a door to his left. Mary reached over and opened the door for him. Terry maneuvered down the staircase with all the gear. As much as Dana protested, they all fell in line with Terry's instructions. Dana was pulling a couple of frozen pizzas out of the freezer when Jimmy asked where the towels were. Mary grabbed a pencil and a pad from a wooden holder mounted on the side of a kitchen cabinet. Terry came up the stairs and returned to the cars to get any remaining gear they had outside. Dana preheated the oven while Jimmy went upstairs to shower. She didn't know he came back inside when she heard his voice.

"I'm sorry," Terry said to Mary and Dana. "I've never *not* been in charge. Tough to turn it off sometimes." He ducked his head and returned to the basement to take inventory. He set Dana's medical bag aside, knowing he would have her dig through and see what was in there. He knew both Jimmy and Mary had their CPD Glocks, and Jimmy still had Pops' Smith and Wesson. He took stock of the rest.

He had the FNX-45 and the two additional Glocks he picked up off the dead guys in Wisconsin. There was his AR-15 with the ACOG and his suppressed short-barreled AR that he handed off to Mary at Mom and Pops. They left both the AK-47 and the Colt 1911, which George the moonshiner had given him in Nebraska, in Wisconsin. The two ARs he picked up in Wisconsin were set up with red dot sights. Six

pistols and four rifles. There was enough ammunition and spare magazines for five full mags for each rifle and three mags for each of the
four Glocks. He had two full magazines for the FNX. There was no
spare ammunition for the Smith and Wesson.

Dana's med bag was leaning against the wall with both his dented
plate carrier and Mary's body armor with the round still stuck in the
ceramic front plate. Lying on the ground was his assault pack with his
bump helmet, night vision, and war belt. It wasn't bad for four people
and only three trained fighters. Dana had proven she would pull the
trigger if she needed to, but Terry wasn't prepared to count on her in a
real fight. She did have significantly more medical experience than he
did or the siblings, so that was a bonus. Hopefully, she wouldn't need
to use it.

Terry looked at his watch; 2035. They would go to see the Superintendent in the morning, and he needed to talk to Mary and Jimmy
about when and where. *They needed to lose and lose big.* His own words
were circling in his head. Killing Smith was almost an imperative at
this point, but he still wasn't convinced that would stop this moving
train. *Lose big. How do they lose big?* It was nagging at him.

"Terry," he heard Mary call down the stairs to him. "Pizza is ready."
He grabbed one of the Glocks and headed upstairs. He was famished,
and even frozen pizza sounded amazing right now. It was almost blas-
phemy in Chicago to talk about frozen pizza like that, but he didn't
care.

Jimmy was out of the shower, and Dana was bandaging his
shoulder back up when Terry emerged from the basement. Mary was
shoving pieces of pizza in her face. It was square cut, not in big slices,
another very Chicago thing. He grabbed a piece and stuffed it in his
mouth, burning the roof.

"You have any more medical stuff lying around here?" Terry asked
Dana. "I need you to inventory the med bag and add whatever you
can." Everyone looked at him. "Please," he added sheepishly. Dana
resumed bandaging. Mary rolled her eyes at him, and Jimmy just
chuckled. Terry realized this is what he missed when he was living
alone for four months: being around real people. He was never alone

in his military career. There were days when he thought of it as a curse, never having a minute to himself. This was certainly not that.

Terry laid the Glock on the kitchen counter and grabbed two more pieces of pizza. He walked over and shoved one of them into Jimmy's mouth, then stood eating while he watched Dana work. The wound was already covered, so he couldn't see how well it was healing, but Jimmy had more mobility already, so that was a good sign.

"No pizza for me?" Dana said. "You're a real gentleman." Jimmy laughed, almost choking on his pizza. "Hold still, dammit." Terry just shook his head.

"My turn to shower," Mary said, finishing another piece. "You didn't leave anything in the shower drain like when we were teenagers, did you, big brother?" Jimmy's face turned red as Terry took his turn to laugh.

"Ewwww," Dana said. "That's nasty." Mary headed upstairs. Terry grabbed two more pieces as Dana finished up. He shoved one in his mouth and held the other out as Dana turned around. She smiled.

"Where's mine?" Jimmy said.

"She's done," Terry said to his best friend. "Get your own fucking pizza." Terry started rummaging through the cabinets for a glass to get water from the sink. Dana opened the refrigerator and grabbed a beer for him. "Thanks, but I'll stick with water."

"Suit yourself," Dana said. She popped the top off and downed half the beer. Jimmy and Terry shared a look of surprise. Dana finished her pizza and grabbed another piece. "I'll go check out the medical bag...as ordered," she said, flashing a sarcastic smile at Terry. She headed downstairs with Terry close behind. Jimmy stood alone in the kitchen and grabbed three more pieces of pizza for himself.

Dana set her beer on the floor and held the piece of pizza in her mouth as she pulled the bag open. Terry stood over her while she dug through the various pockets sewn into the backpack. He didn't know what she was looking at or what she was looking for. He was used to med bags that had everything labeled, so you knew what was in each pocket. This was her personal bag, and she never considered anyone else using it; she just knew where everything was.

"Gunshot wounds," he said. She looked up at him and took the piece of pizza out of her mouth. "That's what we need to prep for."

"No shit," the nurse said and dug back into the bag. He should have just trusted her professional judgment and let her be, but he couldn't help himself. "I have some more stuff upstairs—gauze and bandages. How many tourniquets do you have?" she asked him. She caught him off guard. He hadn't inventoried his own med gear. "Seriously?" Terry scurried over to his plate carrier and war belt to verify what he thought to be true.

"Three," he said. She kept digging. "Plus, a full individual first aid kit."

"IFAK," she said. "Got it." Terry was impressed again. She used the military acronym as a noun, like any soldier who had been issued one before heading to Iraq or Afghanistan. She stood up and looked him in the eye. "Listen, there are probably only a few things in this world that I am better than you at, but this is one of them. I'm sure you've had plenty of basic medical training, but all that is predicated on keeping someone alive long enough for a helicopter to come get them." Terry reeled back. She wasn't yelling, but her voice was firm. "But what I do, what I am trained to do, is much more than that."

"I asked you to come inventory this stuff for *exactly* that reason," Terry responded. "You're right. I don't know as much as you and don't have as much experience with this stuff as you do. Hell, on my first deployment, they were still telling us to stuff tampons into bullet wounds." She shook her head. "Yeah, it was dumb, but we didn't know that back then." The whole interaction felt weird to Terry, like they were arguing over something they actually agreed on.

"I just don't want you doubting me," Dana said. "I know all these guns and stuff aren't for me. That's what *you* do. But this?" she kicked the med bag with her toes. "*This* is what *I* do. And I am as good at patching holes in people as you are at making them. That's all."

"Is this a fight?" Terry asked. "Are we fighting about this? You patched Jimmy up. You sort of patched me up. I know what you are capable of. I'm not doubting you."

"Yes, you are," she countered. "You doubt everyone because they aren't *you*." She poked him lightly in the chest for emphasis.

"Where the hell is all this coming from?" Terry asked. His voice was getting louder.

"You know," Dana said, folding her arms, "I've been hearing stories about you for about ten years now. But, what I've seen over the last few days, you're not who people think you are."

"Yeah?" Terry responded. "You're so damn smart, who am I?"

"You're scared," she said softly. "You're broken, physically. You said it yourself." Terry stood there, staring. "But you carry demons, mentally. Too much loss and too much stress and too many what-ifs.' And right now, you're scared to death that there is more of all of that headed your way." Terry opened his mouth, then closed it. "You know, Mary told me once that you were like a force of nature. You could change things and make things happen, almost at will. Newsflash, Terry, you can't. No one can."

Terry had no response. Nothing he could say to her would change what she thought or how she felt. He could feel the anger building in him. He wasn't angry because she was wrong; he was angry because she was right. This little woman had sized him up and figured him out in what, four or five days? People who knew him his entire life hadn't figured out what she had in less than a week. And even if they had, no one had ever said it to his face, not even Peggy.

"PTSD?" she said. It was a half-question. She already knew the answer. He looked up at her. "I'm not saying all this to bust your balls or break you down. I'm saying all this because *we need you*. Mary, Jimmy, and I. We all need you right now. But we are here to help, too. You can't do this alone, but we can't do it without you, either."

"I..." Terry said. He let out a deep breath. "I do trust you. But being an asshole...in times like this..."

"It's what has kept you alive this long," she finished for him. "I understand. But we don't need an asshole right now. We need the guy that Mary has been bragging about since literally the day she and I met."

"Yes, ma'am," he said quietly. Dana reached up and put her hands on his beard and kissed him. It took him by surprise. He kissed her back.

"It's about damn time," Jimmy said from behind her. He and Mary had come down the stairs at some point in the discussion. Terry and Dana were so focused on their conversation that neither one noticed. Dana turned red. Terry gave Jimmy the finger and then kissed Dana again.

"So, now what?" Jimmy asked.

CHAPTER 18

The four of them were back in the kitchen, standing over the crumbs of two frozen pizzas. Dana was standing close to Terry, both leaning back on the kitchen counter. Jimmy sat at the small table sipping a beer while Mary stood in the middle of the room.

"Neither of you has an idea of how we can talk to the Superintendent, alone?" Terry asked the cop siblings.

"We know his house is a no-go," Mary said. "Too much security."

"What about the police headquarters, or whatever you guys call it?" Dana said. "Like his office."

"Possible," Jimmy said, "but difficult. Mary and I can get in there, but getting either of you two in, especially up to his office, isn't easy. And no way Terry is carrying a gun in there."

"So, we either need to get him in transit," Terry said, "or at an event somewhere."

"He travels in an armored vehicle," Jimmy said. "Like something you were running around in when you worked for that General in Afghanistan," he said to Terry.

"Then vehicle interdiction won't work," Terry said flatly.

"Seriously?" Mary asked. "You were thinking about running him off the road or something? Then we, what, pull him out of the backseat and stick a gun in his face?" Terry just shrugged.

"What about Moriarty?" Jimmy asked. "Maybe he can help?"

"Do you think he would be willing to risk his career?" Terry said. "Because that's what this is. If he invites the Superintendent somewhere and we hijack him, ol' Rocco pays the price." Terry was starting to get antsy. All this back and forth was getting to him. He was overly conscious of Dana and what she said, so he was biting his tongue, but they were getting nowhere.

"Any high-profile events coming up?" Dana asked. "In the movies, they always have some big fundraiser or a ball or something when they plan stuff like this." Terry raised his eyebrows. It wasn't a bad idea.

"Nothing that I can think of," Jimmy said. "Mary would have her dress blues at the cleaners if there were." Mary stuck her tongue out at him like they were still kids.

"Let's drag that out a little bit," Terry said. They all looked at him. "He has a personal assistant, right?"

"You mean like an aide to a general?" Jimmy said with a smartass look.

"Boy," Mary said, "you're on a roll tonight."

"Yeah," Terry responded, "something like that. Someone who keeps his calendar or runs his daily schedule."

"Diane," Mary and Jimmy said in unison.

"OK, Diane," Terry said. "Bear with me on this. Mary, why don't you see Diane tomorrow? Tell her you and Jimmy are planning a funeral for Pops, and you want to make sure the Superintendent is available." Jimmy looked down at the floor. Mary just stared at him. "I know this sounds bad, but something as sensitive as that, she will probably share the whole calendar with you."

"You want me to use my dead father as bait?" Mary snapped. Dana dropped her head.

"Frankly, yes," Terry said. There was no way to sugarcoat it. Dana touched his arm.

"You are *unbelievable*," Mary said. "I'm going to bed. I have to be up in four hours for my guard shift anyway." She turned and walked out of the room. Terry could hear her shoes stomping up the stairs. Jimmy stood and walked out without a word.

"You need a filter," Dana said as she turned and stood in front of him.

"I know it wasn't the best idea," Terry said, "but we didn't have anything else." He put his head in his hands and rubbed his face. She stepped closer and kissed him.

"So, is this a thing now?" Terry asked. He was kidding.

"I haven't decided yet," Dana returned, smiling. "But as long as you're here, I may as well take advantage."

"How do you think Mary feels about this?" Terry asked her as they stood very close.

"I think she is just pissed at you right now," Dana said, "so it's fine."

"She's been pissed at me before," Terry said.

"Really?" Dana pretended to be shocked. "I would have thought you walked on water the way she always talked about you."

"When I left for the Army, I didn't say goodbye," Terry said. "She didn't see me or hear from me for almost three years. She was pretty pissed." Dana stepped back. She had never heard this story from Mary. "I spent a year going through a bunch of different schools, then went to my first duty station and ended up divorced. I came back a year after that and was already dating my second wife. I think she was mad because I never gave her a chance. She was barely out of high school at the time."

"Terry!" Jimmy yelled from the second floor. "Incoming!" Terry grabbed Dana and dragged her to the floor as a hail of bullets came through the picture window and the front of the house. It was a classic drive-by shooting, like something out of a 1990s gang movie set in South Central Los Angeles. Terry heard two shots come from the second story, followed by silence.

His brain was in reaction mode now. He grabbed Dana and shoved her toward the basement stairs. She didn't need more instruction and flew down the wooden steps. Footsteps were coming from the second floor. Terry reached up and grabbed the Glock he had put on the counter, taking a knee and readying himself to fight. Mary was first down the stairs with Jimmy close behind, both of them carrying their CPD pistols in their hands.

"What the fuck was that?" Terry asked.

"Drive by," Jimmy said.

"Good thing we were upstairs, and you guys were back here," Mary said. "Where's Dana?" she asked, looking around.

"Basement," Terry said. "We need to get our shit and go."

"So much for a comfortable night's sleep," Jimmy said.

"Mary," Terry directed, "go check the cars, make sure they can drive. Jimmy, let's get the stuff out of the basement." Mary turned in a squat and went out the back door, clearing the area with her pistol as she moved. Jimmy led the way into the basement. Terry almost knocked him over at the bottom of the steps.

"What the f…" Terry said as he bumped into Jimmy's back. He saw Dana standing there with a gun to her head. A man was standing behind her, using her as a shield. Terry looked around, seeing the basement door open but no other enemies in sight. He wasn't a burglar, and it wasn't a coincidence that he appeared at the same time as the drive-by. It's probably why they didn't hear him kick the basement door in. Jimmy was standing there holding his pistol over his head.

The man opened his mouth to speak, and Terry shot him right below the eye, killing him instantly. It was the same shot he made when he killed the would-be suicide bomber as an aide in Afghanistan. The man slumped behind Dana, and she started shaking. Terry moved to her.

"Get some of that shit outside and be alert!" Terry told Jimmy. He looked at Dana, her eyes wide. "Hey. Hey. Look at me." She slowed her breathing and made eye contact with him. Jimmy was heading upstairs with a load of guns and gear. "Can you move? We need to go." Dana nodded her head slowly and stopped shaking. Terry turned and grabbed his plate carrier, then turned to Dana. He strapped the heavy body armor onto her as she stared at him.

Terry put on his war belt and holstered the FNX. Bending over, he grabbed the rest of the guns and gear and started up the steps, making sure Dana was following him. As he made it through the kitchen door, he heard rifle fire from the driveway, then a pause, more firing coming from the street. He dropped all the gear in his hands except his AR-15 with the ACOG scope and gave Dana the stop sign, with a flat hand to her face. Terry dashed to the broken-out picture window. The car was driving slowly from left to right, and the shooter hanging out the passenger window was concentrating on Jimmy and Mary in the driveway. The assholes were making a second pass.

Terry calmly looked through the four-power magnification of the optic on his rifle and waited. The car was less than fifty yards away, and the scope made the shooter look bigger than life. The car was passing under a streetlight when Terry pulled the trigger. He watched the shooter's head snap back and his body go limp in the window frame of the dark colored Dodge Charger. Terry fired a second shot, shattering the back window and hitting the silhouette sitting in the back seat. The Dodge began to accelerate when Terry fired his third round, striking the lid of the trunk.

Terry stood for a second in the vacant window frame, watching the taillights disappear up the block. If this were Baghdad or Kandahar, Terry would have kept firing until his magazine was empty, but people lived here. Families lived here. It was bad enough that whoever was in that car sprayed bullets into a suburban neighborhood; Terry certainly didn't want to contribute to the potential damage or loss of innocent lives.

It was a discretion he learned over countless encounters with civilians while deployed. Commonly referred to as EOF, or Escalation Of Force, soldiers were trained to use only the minimum amount of force required to reduce the threat. Sometimes that force was no more than pointing a weapon; other times, it meant firing a belt-fed machine gun. Every situation was different, so you had to train your brain to think independently of bias based on experience.

Terry stepped back into the house, only then realizing he had leaned into broken glass with his left forearm. He was so focused on assuming a good, stable firing position and accurately engaging his target that he didn't notice the glass cutting through his skin and into the muscle. The glass came from the window frame Terry braced himself against, providing both cover and stability that would ensure he fired as accurately as possible in the dense neighborhood.

Terry moved back to Dana in the kitchen. She was huddled in a ball at the top of the basement steps. She wasn't in shock and didn't appear to be overly frightened; she was doing what she needed to survive.

"You OK?" he asked the little nurse. She nodded. "Alright, let's move then." Dana got to her feet and started grabbing some of the gear. For a woman who just had her house shot to hell, followed by having a gun pointed at her head, Terry was impressed with her response. Jimmy and Mary were outside using Mary's car as cover; rifles still pointed at the street. Terry could see in the ambient light of the suburban neighborhood that Mary's car was shot up.

"Where do you want this stuff?" Dana asked him.

"Throw it in the back of the Cadillac," he told her. He looked at Mary. "The good news is the Cadillac is fine. The bad news is your car is fucked." Mary dropped her head. She bought the Altima less than six months ago and paid cash. It was the nicest car she had ever owned, and now it was destroyed. Terry could feel the adrenaline wearing off again, this time quicker than the last. His body could only do so much at his age, and it was losing the fight. His ribs were screaming, and he could feel the pain from the cut in his left arm. No time for that now. *Keep moving, keep shooting.*

"Jimmy," Terry called to his friend, "get the Cadillac started. Dana, get in the driver's seat," he pointed to Mary's car. "Put it in neutral, and Mary and I will push it down the drive." They needed to get the Altima out of the way; it was blocking the Caddy. Terry could smell gas coming from somewhere under the black Nissan, so he didn't want to start the engine and risk a fire. Terry was back in soldier mode again and didn't care about any backlash from Dana. Shit needed to get done, and this was the only way he knew how to do it. There was no backlash; Dana jumped in the driver's seat, and Mary joined him at the front bumper to start pushing.

"Hey," Jimmy said, "get out of the way, and I will push it with the Caddy." Mary and Terry stared at each other, marveling at the practicality of Jimmy's solution.

"Damn," Terry said, stepping aside, "I should have thought of that. Dana," he said. She poked her head out of the broken window. "Jimmy is going to push you." She nodded. Jimmy put the big luxury car in reverse, the white backup lights illuminating the front of the Altima. He backed up slowly until he made contact with the bumpers and pushed slowly. Mary sighed heavily as she heard the plastic bumper cover of her Nissan crack. The Altima began to move backward down the drive. Jimmy saw it gain momentum as it went down the ever-so-slight decline in the driveway toward the street. He stopped the Cadillac. Dana got to the street and cut the wheel hard, backing it into a spot mostly parallel to the curb.

Terry went back into the house before Dana got out of the car. Mary watched her run up the drive, and the two got into the backseat, assuming Terry would be back out in a second or two. They waited. Jimmy tapped his fingers on the steering wheel. Dana looked anxiously at the door to the house, waiting for Terry to reemerge. Mary looked out the back window, waiting for the police sirens she knew were coming. Terry finally went out the door, carrying the body of the man from the basement.

"Open the trunk," he said to Jimmy. The SWAT officer reached under the dash and pushed a button, opening the rear deck lid. Terry dumped the body inside, then slammed the trunk shut. When he climbed into the front passenger seat, the other three were staring at him. "What?" he asked the stunned faces.

"What the fuck are we going to do with him?" Mary asked from the back seat.

"We never had evidence before," Terry said. They all stared at him. "Before this, every dead body was picked up by the cops or someone else. We only knew who they were because the news told us." The police sirens could be heard at a distance now. "Drive to the train station."

"The train station?" Jimmy asked.

"Yeah," Terry said. "We need another vehicle, and your truck is still there. Now drive."

CHAPTER 19

J immy wound the big Cadillac through the suburban streets, navigating easily through Terry's old neck of the woods. They never saw a police car as they drove, but sirens could be heard on nearby streets as the foursome sat in the luxury car, maneuvering through the neighborhood. When they were about two blocks from the train station, Jimmy asked the question Terry had been worrying about since they started moving.

"What if the truck is gone?" he asked. "That's a permit lot. Always was, anyway. So, if it sat there long enough, they might have towed it."

"We will deal with that if we have to," Terry responded. He had been running other options in his head. The 4Runner was left at Mom and Pops; they might be able to pick that up. If not, they would be stuck with one car. He was still skeptical that Smith and his organization would be monitoring the internet, and if they rented a car, it would immediately be known from where and what kind. Jimmy pulled the Cadillac into the lot at the train station and saw his truck sitting there.

"Jesus," Jimmy said. "There's about fifty tickets waiting for me." He could see the stack of papers under the windshield wiper, flapping in the night air. "Someone else is going to have to drive it." Terry looked at him. "It's a stick. I only have one good arm."

"Jesus," Terry said and looked into the backseat. "Can either of you drive a stick?" Dana shook her head. Mary did the same. "Mary? Seriously?"

"I never needed to learn," she said sheepishly. "Cruisers are all automatics, and..." Terry turned and faced forward in disgust.

"Well, I guess I am driving your truck," Terry said. "Dana, you're with me. Mary, drive the Cadillac." He held out his hand, and Jimmy handed him the keys after fishing them out of his pocket.

"Where are we going?" Mary asked as she climbed out. All four of them were moving around the Cadillac to assume their new seats and vehicles. It was like an old Chinese fire drill at a stoplight you would see in fifties movies.

"Back to see Moriarty," Terry said as he walked to Jimmy's truck, Dana moving quickly to join him under the weight of the body armor. Mary and Jimmy looked at each other. "He said he would help if he could. He can run this guy's prints for us."

"Do you know how many laws we are breaking?" Mary asked, suddenly sounding like a cop again. "He could arrest you on the spot. We tampered with evidence. Tampered with a crime scene..."

"I know," Terry said. "My read on Moriarty is that he wouldn't want to be party to all this. If he knew half of what was going on, he would intercede. If we can get an ID on this guy, without anyone interfering, I think we have a better picture of what is going on." Mary stared at him.

"This is a huge risk, Terry," Mary said to him. Dana stood listening. "What happens if Rocco puts you in cuffs?"

"He's not going to put me in cuffs," Terry said. He turned and walked toward Jimmy's truck. Dana hesitated, looked at Mary, and then walked to the truck herself.

"I hope you're right," Mary called out. She got into the driver's seat of the Cadillac and looked at her brother. "What do you think?"

"I think he is sticking his neck out awfully far," Jimmy said. "But I think he is right about Moriarty. He won't arrest him. And he will help." Mary put the big car in gear and led Terry out of the parking lot.

He had only been to Moriarty's house once, so she knew she would have to lead. Jimmy had his pistol in his hand, casually resting it on his thigh. A lot had changed in the last four or five days. Here they were, brother and sister cops, in the middle of some national-level conspiracy. Their parents had been killed, and Jimmy had been wounded. Mary didn't know if Jimmy was even aware that she had 'busted her cherry' and killed someone.

"I never thought I would say this," Mary said, staring out the windshield, "but I almost wish Terry hadn't come home." She was somber. Jimmy looked at her with wide eyes.

"Are you kidding me?" he said. "Do you realize if he hadn't come back when he did, that you would've gone to that meeting on Monday and you'd either be running around doing all these illegal gang raids, or you'd be dead."

"I know," she said, still somber. "But Mom and Pops would still be alive."

"Jesus," Jimmy said. "Stop with all this sacrificial lamb bullshit."

"What?" Mary responded. She sounded offended, but deep down she wasn't.

"You know what I'm talking about," Jimmy said. "This is the same bullshit you started when we were younger. 'You should have just left me at the orphanage.' The first time you said that you were twelve years old," he was on the verge of shouting. "Mom and Pops were trying to figure out how to send me to college and how they were going to pay for it, and that was your input. 'You should have left me at the orphanage.' Like that was the solution to their money problems. Give me a fucking break, Mary."

She drove quietly. Her brother was right. It was almost a reflex; she wanted people to pity her. It was the genesis for her poor taste in men and probably why she never considered getting married. It was easier for her to tolerate people whispering behind her back, saying 'poor Mary,' than it was to take honest criticism. She didn't have many weaknesses, but that was one of them.

Terry and Dana were following close behind in Jimmy's truck. Terry was trying to drive while Dana patched up his left arm. It was an almost impossible task in the small truck, especially while Terry was trying to steer and shift gears. Usually, Dana would have thoroughly cleaned the wound, and then a doctor would have put stitches in it. That wasn't an option tonight. The little nurse was leaning over the center console, wrapping athletic tape over some sterile gauze and Terry's bare arm. It was the best they could do to stop the dripping blood, at least for now.

"That's going to be fun to take off," Terry said after she finished, looking down at the tape sticking to his arm hair. His blue jeans had a rapidly drying pool of blood on them.

"I'll certainly enjoy it," Dana said as she sat back in her seat and put her seatbelt back on. The dinging alarm in the truck stopped. "Can I take this thing off?" she asked, referring to Terry's plate carrier still wrapped around her torso.

"No," Terry said flatly. She looked at him. He changed his tone, "At least wait until we get to Moriarty's. You can take it off then."

"So, what happens if *you* get shot?" Dana said, counterpunching.

"Listen," Terry said, "if we had another vest, I would have it on. You're the one capable of patching up the rest of us. If anyone needs to stay alive, it's you. That means, you get the vest."

"You really are the protector," Dana said, "aren't you. I know nurses have that reputation, and I know soldiers do, too. Policemen, firemen. But I've never met anyone who is protective of *everyone*." Terry kept driving in silence. The neighborhood was starting to look familiar. They weren't far from Moriarty's place. "Where does that come from?" she asked him. Terry just looked at her. He didn't know how to verbalize what he knew was true, especially to this woman he had only known for a few days. It was impossible to say it without sounding arrogant; *It's just who I am and who I have always been.* Even inside his head, it sounded absurd, even though he knew it was the truth. He just let the question hang in the air.

They pulled into the same two parking spaces across from the SWAT Commander's house that they had parked in earlier in the day. Terry looked at his watch: 2342—almost midnight. The wealthy neighborhood was dark, except for the streetlights that resembled old gaslights. Terry climbed out of the truck and looked at Dana.

"Stay here," he said. She immediately nodded and began to remove the heavy plate carrier.

"You stay here," Mary said to Terry as she and Jimmy walked across the street. Terry looked at her; she was pointing at him. Terry left the door open and stood watching the street. He looked inside at the perfect time to see Dana pulling the vest over her head, exposing a black lace bra as her shirt rode up with the vest. She caught him looking and smiled as she pulled the shirt back down.

"Cheap thrills, soldier-boy," Dana said to him.

"I'll take what I can get," Terry said, trying to be funny.

"They match," she said. Terry looked at her, confused. "The bottoms," she said, clearing it up for him. "They match. In case you were wondering." Terry didn't answer, but in his head, he *was* wondering. He just shook his head and smiled.

Davis could hear voices from the portico across the street, but couldn't make out what was being said. He could see Mary and Jimmy on the porch, standing in front of the open door to the house. Moriarty stepped out onto the stone in a pair of Chicago Bears pajama pants and a white t-shirt that showed how huge the man was. The three of them came down the steps toward the cars, Mary walking and talking next to Moriarty, with Jimmy trailing behind. They walked straight to Terry.

"Open the trunk," Moriarty said, waving a hand at the Cadillac. He was staring intently at Terry. He wasn't happy. Jimmy reached in the driver's door and hit the button. Terry went to open the trunk when Rocco stopped him. "You know, as soon as I see this, I can't unsee it." Terry stared at him, unafraid. "OK then. Open it up." Terry lifted the trunk lid, and the light inside illuminated the corpse with a bullet hole in his cheekbone.

The SWAT Commander looked inside and let out a long breath. He reached down and grabbed the man's hand, turning it over and looking at it, then pulling up his sleeve. He reached deeper into the trunk and did the same with the other hand. He looked the man up and down, pulled back his collar, and looked at the man's neck. Terry assumed he was checking for tattoos or any distinguishing marks of any kind. The big man stood up from the trunk and looked at Terry, then Jimmy, then Mary, and back to Terry.

"Tell me, Mister Airborne Ranger," Moriarty said, "what do you think this is?"

"I don't think he is a gang banger," Terry said. "I am willing to bet he's not even a criminal."

"So, what, or who, is he?" The big man shoved his hands into the pockets of his pajama pants. It was cold out, and he seemed unfazed.

"Maybe DoD. Maybe CIA," Terry said. "Not exactly sure yet, but he ain't a thug."

"He's not inked up like a gang member," Mary said, adding to Terry's assumption.

"And he doesn't smell like shit, like most gang members," Jimmy said. His boss turned and scowled at him. "He doesn't, boss. No cigarette smell. No pot smell. No body odor. This guy is abnormally clean."

"If he is DoD or CIA, getting prints from him won't matter," Moriarty said. "We won't get anything back."

"Most likely," Terry agreed. "But we will know that is the case instead of the media giving us a made-up name."

"Are you going to tell me what the hell is going on?" Moriarty was starting to get frustrated. "You've got me out here in the middle of the night, looking at a dead body of someone you *think* might be in the CIA or something. The least you can do is tell me what this is all about." Terry sighed. Jimmy looked at the ground.

"It's a plot," Dana said from behind Terry. No one even knew she was there. "Sir, I got dragged into this by accident, but I can promise you it is all real."

"Who the hell are you?" Rocco asked.

"Dana," the nurse responded. "I'm Mary's friend. I got caught in the middle of this, too. I didn't want to believe it, but I've almost been killed about five times in the last couple of days. This is real. These aren't gang guys doing random shit, these are real bad guys."

"I like you," Moriarty said. "You're the only one here not trying to blow sunshine up my ass." Dana smiled. "Let's go inside and talk about this."

CHAPTER 20

The five of them stood in Moriarty's kitchen as Terry once again told his story. Moriarty showed no surprise, no shock, no real reaction at all. Terry Davis stood there and admitted a long list of crimes to one of the senior ranking officers in the Chicago Police Department, including what would be multiple counts of murder. Rocco consumed three beers in the time it took Terry to tell his story, and only once had to tell his wife to go back to bed when she wandered into the kitchen full of people.

"Alright, Mr. Airborne Ranger," Moriarty said after Terry brought him up to date, "you've admitted murder, theft, and a shitload of other crimes to me, including what could possibly be construed as treason. If I were a lawyer, I would tell you never to repeat that story, to anyone… ever." Terry stood there staring at the huge man, expressionless. "And if I were a lawyer, I could make an argument for self-defense in many of those cases. Not all of them, but most. What you've presented is filled with assumptions and conjecture, with no known evidence to prove any of it. So, why should I believe you? And better yet, why shouldn't I arrest you?"

"Because Pops trusted you and he believed me," Terry said. "And because I am standing here with his family. A family full of cops, including one who works for you. Because I think you're a man of principle who believes in right versus wrong. And mostly because I have three other people standing here that can attest to most of what I am telling you."

"And because it's all fucking true," Dana said. Moriarty looked at her. "And we need your help."

"Sir," Mary said, "I believe honestly that what Terry is saying is true. And I think the best way to find out is to run that guy's prints." Jimmy stood there nodding.

"Seamus," Rocco looked directly at his subordinate SWAT officer. "You've never been this quiet since the day you were born. Where do you sit in all this?"

"They shot me, Sir," Jimmy said. "Sitting on the roof of a train station, they shot me. And they tried to kill Mary. And they killed Mom and Pops. They shot Terry. All of this in a matter of days isn't an accident, and it isn't a coincidence. This is coordinated. I believe all of it." Moriarty looked around the room at each of them, one by one. He let out a long breath.

"I should be pissed," he said finally. "If these people are as dangerous as you made them out to be, I should be pissed you dragged me into it and put my family at risk."

"But you're not," Terry said.

"You're right," the SWAT Commander replied, "I'm not. I knew when they cut SWAT out of this whole thing and started asking for military help that something was up. It was just plain wrong. We don't need soldiers on the streets of my city, killing people." He opened another beer. "And that stupid fucking mayor let herself get manipulated by my boss, the Superintendent. Motherfucker."

"What do we do?" Mary asked.

"The short answer is we go see him," Moriarty said, "but we may be too late." Terry had a feeling he knew what was coming next, and Rocco was about to confirm it. "The military is arriving in the morning. I have to be there to get them integrated into our operations center." Terry hung his head.

"What about the guys who are already here?" Mary asked. "The guys that recruited me, that I was supposed to meet with. The guys who have been orchestrating all these gang operations. What about them?"

"Let's take a breath and get ourselves organized," Terry said. All these good ideas without a clear structure were making his planner's brain hurt. "First, we need to pull that guy's prints. Sir, can you run those, or whatever you cops say?" Moriarty nodded. "Then we need to go talk to the Superintendent. I think that is me and Mary and you, Sir." Moriarty nodded again.

"What about me?" Jimmy asked, looking like a kicked puppy.

"I need you and Dana to go put eyes on that building Mary was supposed to go to," Terry said. "See if you can spot any activity at all. If people are moving around, we can at least narrow in on that."

"I'll do you one better," Rocco said. "Jimmy, you and this one," he threw his thumb at Dana, "go check that place out. I'll have Ferguson and Benton around the corner. If you see anything, they can go knock on the door." Terry assumed those were two SWAT guys that Moriarty and Jimmy both knew. Jimmy nodded.

"Sir," Terry said. He was reflexively calling Moriarty 'Sir' as he would have any superior officer when he was still in uniform. "You still need to meet with whatever military contingent is coming to town. We all know there is a connection between them, the Superintendent, and that body in the trunk. Chances are, only the most senior guy on the ground will have any connection to Smith and his organization. The rest of them are just here to kick in doors." Moriarty was visibly impressed with how quickly Terry was putting all this together. "So, you can't deviate from whatever role you're supposed to be playing. He can't know you suspect anything."

"It might even be better," Dana said, leaning against the wall, "if you told him that you didn't like him being there." Everyone looked at her. "If you're too nice, especially if you wouldn't normally be, that would be a tip off, too." She was right. Terry smiled in appreciation.

"I have to be at the EOC at eleven when they show up," Moriarty said. Terry could hear a touch of excitement in the older man's voice. Terry knew the feeling. The thing he hated most about getting promoted in the Army was that you got further and further away from soldiers, and further away from the fight itself. It had probably been a while since the SWAT Commander had last done something this involved. "If we are going to surprise the big boss before then, we need to get some sleep."

"How are we going to get in to go see him?" Mary asked. Moriarty winked at her.

"Young lady," Rocco said with a smile, "I have the keys to the kingdom. As the SWAT Commander, I can go see him anytime I want."

"Good," Mary said. "Then I don't have to make up some funeral story for Diane." Moriarty was confused, and you could see it on his face.

"It was a bad plan," Terry said. "We can explain later, but it was my idea. So, we need to get the prints off the dead guy. Then, Jimmy and Dana will check out the bad guy's building. Sir, you submit the prints, then the three of us see the Superintendent." He pointed at Mary and Moriarty. "Then, Sir, you go to the Emergency Ops Center to meet the DoD guys."

"All before lunch," Jimmy added.

"We do more before nine in the morning," Terry was paraphrasing an old Army recruiting commercial, "than most people do all day." He slapped his hand lightly on the counter.

"We've got spare rooms enough for everyone upstairs," Moriarty said with a wave of his hand. "Go ahead and pick one. I'll make sure everyone is awake when they need to be." He turned and walked out of the kitchen; the four guests fell in line behind him. At the top of the stairs, the big man just waved his hand down the hallway as if to say, 'down that way.' Mary turned right into the first room, with Jimmy taking the one directly across the hall from her and closing the door behind him. Mary paused long enough to watch Dana follow Terry into the room next to Jimmy's. She shook her head and closed the door.

Terry was startled to find Dana following him into the spare room when he turned to close the door behind him. She didn't ask, and he didn't offer, but there they were. She stood on her toes and kissed his bearded face. Neither one of them said a word. It didn't take long before they were both standing shirtless and kissing. Terry could feel the lace from her bra against his chest. He grabbed her ass, making her moan softly in his ear. She was hungry for him. She wanted him more than she cared to admit. The little nurse undid Terry's belt and pants, but he slowed her down. One of those uncomfortable moments where he knew his hiking boots were going to be an issue.

Terry sat down on the bed and untied his boots, tossing them aside. He looked up to see Dana in her bra and thong, eyeing him. *She wasn't lying, they do match.* He stood and took his jeans off while Dana moved slowly to him, playfully pushing him back onto the bed and climbing on top of him. Dana didn't even take off her thong; she just pushed it out of the way. It didn't take long, but it was intense. Terry could feel her reach orgasm, and then she looked at him with a dirty smile and did her best to make sure he finished quickly, too. She collapsed on top of him, resting on his chest and listening to his heartbeat. The nurse in her took over for a second, realizing that his heart rate was impressively low for a man his age after that kind of physical activity.

She was about to get up when he wrapped his arms around her. Dana hadn't anticipated that from him. Really, she hadn't anticipated anything from him except what she had already gotten. It was nice and comfortable. She felt warm and safe for the first time in longer than she could remember. In an instant, Terry was snoring. Probably any other man, under any other circumstances, and Dana would have been embarrassed and angry, but not him and not now. She knew he was exhausted and injured, and he fell asleep. She lay there smiling and was asleep within minutes.

CHAPTER 21

T erry woke slowly. He was aching, seemingly in every muscle and bone in his body. He needed to rest, but today was not that day. As he blinked his eyes open, he looked at the Garmin watch strapped to his wrist: 0747. *Shit.* It was later than he thought and later than he wanted to get moving. He remembered Dana and the night before and looked around the room for her. The room was bigger than he realized, masked by the darkness and his exhaustion just a few hours ago. His clothes were clean and folded on a chair against the wall, with his hiking boots on the floor under the chair. There was a bathroom with a shower attached to the big bedroom, and he took advantage. Moving was slow, and even the bottoms of his feet hurt.

As the hot water hit his body, he could see the dirt, grime, and blood rinsing off him and down the drain of the shower. He couldn't even remember when he showered last. *My memory is getting worse.* The last few days had been fast-paced, even hectic, but the aging warrior honestly couldn't remember his last shower. Terry had more than his share of concussions throughout his life; probably a dozen all counted. Some had been officially diagnosed, and equally as many were undiagnosed and ignored at the time. When Terry went through his medical screenings prior to retirement, he had been diagnosed with both PTSD and Traumatic Brain Injury. The symptoms were so similar and so many veterans were suffering from one or both, the VA doctors were lumping them together and giving a significant disability rating as a result. Terry financially benefited from the abuse his head had taken while he was in uniform, but it wouldn't fix his increasingly poor memory.

Terry Davis had proved his bravery in combat more than once. He had exited a 'perfectly good aircraft' over seventy-five times in his career. Terry wasn't scared of much, but the idea of him suffering from Alzheimer's, dementia, or chronic traumatic encephalopathy scared the living shit out of him. CTE was the condition so many professional football players were dealing with. Most of the cases he read about included incidents of uncharacteristic violence and angry outbursts. That worried him. He stood in the shower and realized this fight with Smith and his people was going to kill him, either by a bullet or by wrecking what was left of his body.

He turned off the shower and dried off, grabbed his clean clothes, and got dressed. Walking down the stairs, he could smell coffee and hear voices from the kitchen. He followed the sounds and smells to find everyone, including Mrs. Moriarty, eating breakfast at various places in the kitchen. There was a mocking round as he walked into the room.

"Sleeping beauty," Jimmy said. "Welcome to the world of the living." Terry gave him an evil look, half kidding and half not.

"Thanks for washing my disgusting clothes," Terry said to Mrs. Moriarty. Sun-Hee Moriarty laughed at Terry and touched his arm.

"You're cute, dear," she said. "I don't do laundry. Rocco does that." Terry looked apologetic. "And he does the cooking, too. I make all the money so he can play police officer." Terry was sensing another unanticipated dynamic from this house. Dana handed him a mug of black coffee that he raised toward Rocco in salute.

"Yeah," the huge black man said, "I didn't need her walking in to find you butt-naked either." Terry turned red.

"I'll let you all do whatever it is you are going to do," Sun-Hee said. Terry noticed she was dressed for business, wearing a full grey suit that fit her slim build like a glove, heels, and her hair up in a tight bun. She walked over to her husband and kissed him. "Be safe." Terry admired the woman as she commanded the room; everyone was watching every move she made. She walked out of the room, and Terry heard the front door close a few seconds later.

"You were right," Rocco said, speaking up. Terry had a mouth full of eggs and stopped chewing to look up at the big man. "Your dead guy is a nobody. No record on file. No name associated with the prints. Nothing." It was exactly what Terry assumed they would get back, but now it was confirmed and unaltered by Smith and his media influences. Terry nodded and resumed chewing.

"One task down," Mary said.

"Dana and I are leaving in a bit to go sit on that building," Jimmy said. Terry nodded again. "The boss gave me a spare radio so I can contact you guys if needed." Dana leaned in next to Terry, and it surprised him how comfortable it was.

"Officer Moriarty even gave me a class on the radio," Dana said, "so I know how to use it, too." Terry gave her a grin. She was invested in all this and picking up on things quickly.

"You've got those other two guys standing by?" Terry asked.

"Benton and Ferguson," Dana stepped in. "They will be on channel nine." She smiled proudly. Terry gave her an approving pat on the ass.

"These guys are reliable?" Terry asked Rocco and Jimmy.

"Definitely," Rocco said.

"I know both of them well," Jimmy said. "Ferguson has a thing for Mary, so he won't fuck this up." Terry watched Mary turn red.

"Good," Terry said, stuffing bacon into his mouth. "Body armor for both of you. No exceptions." He could see the look of dread on Dana's face, but it washed away quickly.

"We will go see Gagliardi when they take off," Rocco said, referring to the CPD Superintendent. "Terry, you can carry a pistol. I'll tell everyone you're with the military contingent, and if you're with me, no one will question it." That was a huge relief to Terry. With everything going on, moving around unarmed was not on the list of things he wanted to do.

"What are you going to say to him?" Mary asked Terry.

"I'm going to call him out," Terry said flatly. Mary looked

surprised. "We don't have time to play Tom Cruise and Jack Nicholson," Terry said, referring to the movie *A Few Good Men*. "He isn't going to jump up and admit he ordered the Code Red."

"That's the plan?" Mary was incredulous.

"That's the only way," Rocco agreed with Terry. "This guy is cancer to the PD, and he needs to be dealt with as such." Terry nodded. He liked Rocco more and more.

"It's more than just the PD and more than just Chicago," Jimmy said. Everyone looked at him. Jimmy was far from stupid, but he wasn't prone to deep thinking either. "You've been saying it the whole time, Terry. This is about right and wrong. Smith and Garragiola…"

"Gagliardi," the room corrected him in unison.

"Whatever," Jimmy continued. "What they are doing is illegal and un-American. We can't let this go. If it happens in Chicago, it will happen everywhere, just like you said." Terry raised his coffee mug again.

"You know," Terry said to Rocco, "this could be the end for you. After today, you may be out of a job."

"I am pretty sure," Moriarty said, raising his hands to the massive house surrounding him, "I'll be fine."

"It's more than that, though," Terry said. "You're putting yourself and your wife at risk. These people have power. They could come after you, after her, after her business."

"Listen, Mr. Airborne Ranger," Moriarty said, "I appreciate the concern, but I'm a big boy. And my wife and her business are global, international. These people, at least according to what you've been saying, are American. We will be fine." Terry just shrugged. The man knew the risks, and he was making a call. Far be it from Terry to second-guess him.

"It's about time to go," Jimmy said, standing up.

"How's your shoulder?" Terry asked. "Can you drive?"

"I'm good," Jimmy said, moving his arm slowly in a circle, showing his range of movement. Terry turned and looked at Dana.

"Body armor," he said. It wasn't a request. She nodded. "Do what Jimmy says. Anything looks bad, you get a bad feeling, whatever, you leave. Keep that radio close and keep your head on a swivel." He leaned down and kissed her.

"Why are you telling me this?" she asked him. "Jimmy is driving."

"Yeah," Terry said, loud enough for Jimmy to hear. "He may be driving, but you're the grown-up in the car."

"What the..." Jimmy said, mocking offense. Terry smiled. Dana kissed him and followed Jimmy out the front door. Terry followed them and watched Dana check over her shoulder a half dozen times to make sure he was there. Terry came back into the house and met Moriarty and Mary in the kitchen.

"So, we just walk right in?" Terry asked Rocco.

"Yep," the big man said. "Like I told you, I have access at any time." Terry nodded, then looked at Mary.

"I'm not even going to ask," he said, "if you're ready for this."

"These assholes killed my parents," Mary said, frankly.

"That ends that," Terry said. "When do we leave?"

"Ready when you are," Rocco said. "We will take my unit. It's parked out back." Moriarty turned on his heel, and Mary and Terry fell in step and followed him through the house and out the back door. There was a detached, three-car garage in the back, and the trio went in through the side door. Terry's eyes got wide. In the first stall of the garage was a full gym. You didn't maintain Rocco's level of fitness at his age without regular exercise. The third stall of the garage held Moriarty's cruiser, a flat black, unmarked Ford Expedition.

Between the gym and the police SUV was what caught Terry's eye and made him stop in his tracks. Even obscured by a grey, cloth car cover, Terry recognized the outline of a late sixties Camaro. He leaned down and pulled up the corner of the cover, revealing the front right headlight and bumper. The white paint was gleaming, and the headlight cover with three slots looked brand new. Moriarty stopped as Terry pulled back more of the car cover. The SWAT Commander smiled. Terry could see the orange racing stripes on the hood. He looked up at the big man.

"Is this what I think this is?" Terry asked.

"Tell me what you think it is," Rocco replied. He wanted to see if Terry knew what he was looking at.

"A nineteen sixty-nine Camaro. The Indy-500 pace car," Terry said.

"Yep," Rocco said. "All original. Numbers matching. There are benefits to having a wealthy wife." Terry put the car cover back in place and shook his head.

"That's my dream car," Terry said and began moving toward the cruiser.

"Mine too," Rocco said. "After this is over, we can take it for a drive."

"I will never understand," Mary said, climbing into the front seat of the SUV, "men and cars." She closed the door. Terry climbed into the back and began to speak. Mary just held up her hand. "And I don't want to understand." He stopped. Rocco climbed into the driver's seat and hit the garage door opener.

The ride to the Public Safety Headquarters building was relatively quiet. Terry resisted the urge to tell stories about the number of times he and Jimmy had ridden in the backseat of a police car when they were kids. Rocco cut the silence by turning on the radio to a local news station. Terry didn't know if all cops did this, or if it was something Rocco learned from Pops. The newscaster came in after a commercial.

"The Army is arriving in Chicago today, to do a job the Chicago Police Department can't do on its own: rid the city of violent gangs. At the request of the Mayor and the Police Superintendent, the military is sending in a group of special operations soldiers to wage war against the gangs that have taken over city streets. In a recent interview, the head of the Chicago Police Department said he was initially reluctant to support the Mayor's request for military assistance. Still, now he is on board with the Mayor and agrees with her request for the Army to provide expertise and manpower to defeat the gangs that plague the city."

"Don't we look incompetent?" Moriarty said from behind the steering wheel. There was a scowl on his face, and Terry didn't blame him. Rocco dedicated his entire adult life to the city and the police department, only now to have all that degraded by Gagliardi and the Mayor was a tough hit to take.

The rest of the ride was silent. Only the radio station providing updates on sports, traffic, and weather kept the police cruiser from replicating a hearse. Officer Moriarty shut off the radio as he wheeled the Ford into the parking lot and pulled into his reserved parking spot marked 'SWAT Commander.' The trio climbed out of the vehicle and headed to the front doors, Rocco in the lead. Moriarty was in his tactical uniform, and Mary was walking with her badge on her belt. Terry suddenly felt self-conscious, walking into police headquarters carrying an exposed pistol.

"Excuse me, Sir," the security officer manning the metal detectors inside the front door held his hand up to Terry. "No weapons allowed…" Rocco cut him off.

"He's with me," Rocco said. The officer began to protest, but Moriarty cut him off. "He's the advance party for the military contingent coming in today." The young security officer opened his mouth, then quickly closed it when the huge SWAT Officer glared at him. They were waved through security. Terry nodded, playing along.

"I can't believe that worked," Moriarty said. Terry and Mary looked at him with shock.

"What?" Terry said. They were walking toward the elevators.

"I mean," Rocco said, "I assumed it would work, but you never know." Terry lifted his ballcap and ran his hand through his hair. The bell for the elevator in front of them went 'ding.' Terry followed the two police officers inside and waited for the door to close. Moriarty pushed the button for the fifth floor, and they watched the doors close.

"Here we go," Mary said quietly.

CHAPTER 22

Jimmy pulled into a space across the street from the building Mary was supposed to walk into on Monday. It would have been just a few days ago, but it seemed like a lifetime. He could only imagine the shit she would be in if she had made that meeting. The building itself was innocuous, grey, and very plain on the outside. It was surrounded by an eight-foot chain-link fence, with portions having green strips of plastic woven through to provide some privacy. Off to the right, as Jimmy looked at it, there was a large opening in the fence that led into the parking lot. The two gates that would have closed off access were both hanging open, giving Jimmy a view through his sideview mirror into the lot and a good look at the front door. He took the truck out of gear and put on the parking brake.

"That's the building?" Dana asked.

"Yep," Jimmy said. "Hand me the radio." Dana had the radio in her hand and gave it to Jimmy, a little disappointed that he didn't allow her to use it. He pushed the button on the side of the black handheld radio. "This is unit one, in position." There was a pause and then a chirp from the radio.

"*Copy. Unit one in position. Unit two in position,*" the voice on the other end of the radio transmitted.

"Copy. Unit two in position," Jimmy sent back. It all seemed very redundant to Dana. She looked over Jimmy's shoulder at the grey building. The second-story windows were mainly painted over, but she could see the lights on inside.

"I hate stakeouts," Jimmy said. "So, fucking boring."

"But this is important," Dana said to him, trying to understand. She understood that sitting and waiting, especially after you've done it a few hundred times, could be boring, but to her, this was exciting. "Exactly what are we looking for?"

"Signs of life," Jimmy said, looking back into the sideview mirror at the building. "Movement, people, vehicles in and out. Anything that looks out of place."

"Give me an example," she said. "Like, what would be something out of place?"

"OK," Jimmy said, trying to hide the condescension in his voice. "A building like that, you'd expect guys in dirty clothes to be in and out. Maybe hard hats and safety vests. Vehicles in the parking lot would be work trucks and industrial equipment. Around lunch, you'd see people coming in and out for lunch break. Maybe see some guys standing outside smoking off and on during the day." Dana was listening to him but looking at the building for any of those things.

"I don't see any of that," she said.

"Right," Jimmy said. His tone started to change. He was teaching her, and she was responding. "So, if those are the normal things, the abnormal things would be the opposite. Guys in clean clothes. Nice cars in the parking lot, more than one or two. Or a fleet of vehicles all the same, but not work trucks. No movement at all, no activity around a building like that isn't normal." She was nodding.

"So, seeing the lights on inside," she said as she was putting puzzle pieces together, "but no movement is out of place."

"It can be, sure," he said. Jimmy looked up and down the street along both sidewalks. "Once you get a read on the building, you start looking around the building, too."

"What do you mean?" Dana took her eyes off the building and looked at Jimmy.

"Places like this," Jimmy said, "neighborhoods like this, people around here know things. If you see people avoiding the place or pointing or staring, those are indicators, too."

"This is like diagnosing a patient," Dana said. "Someone comes in, and all you know is what you see and what the chart says or what the EMTs tell you. That isn't the whole story, though. You have to look for more. That's what this seems like." Jimmy nodded in appreciation. "Speaking of which, how's your shoulder?"

"I'm good," he responded. It was achy, but he could move it, and it wasn't bleeding.

"You two are so much alike," Dana said, continuing to look at the building. "You and Terry. I know you two are close, but you really are a lot alike."

"I appreciate that," Jimmy said, "but Terry is special. He is the smartest person I know. Mary used to call him a force of nature. You should have seen him in his prime, like in his late twenties. He came home a couple of months before his first time in Afghanistan. He was like a fucking rock. He could run for miles, stay awake for days. Super intense..." Jimmy trailed off.

"What?" Dana asked, looking at Jimmy.

"There's been a slow change," he said. "I don't see him all the time, but I know him better than anyone, so I see the changes, like in chunks. He's beat up. I know we aren't kids anymore, but his body is broken. Too much abuse over the years."

Dana was looking at the grey building, but she was thinking about Terry, wishing she had met him twenty years ago. He was still in great shape for someone his age, at least on the surface. He had a sharp edge to who he was and how he acted; she almost couldn't imagine him being more intense than the man she had seen over the last few days. There was something about him, though, that she couldn't shake.

"Look," Jimmy said, interrupting Dana's daydreaming. "Can you see the garage doors?"

"No," Dana said, trying to adjust herself inside the cab of his truck to get a better view.

"One of the garage doors just opened," Jimmy said, looking at the sideview mirror. He could see headlights inside the depths of the garage, but that was it. "At least one vehicle inside. Sit down so you don't look so suspicious." He grabbed her and pulled her back into her seat. "Just look forward. If they go that way, try to get a license plate."

"*Unit one, this is unit two,*" the radio crackled. "*You seeing this? I got two vehicles exiting the garage.*" Jimmy was curious about where his SWAT teammates were. All Rocco said was that they were around the corner. He never took that literally, but he wasn't clear where they were.

"I see it," Jimmy said into the radio. Two Ford F-150 pickup trucks pulled up to the gate and paused to check traffic before turning left. Dana tried to pick up as many details as she could as the two trucks drove away; one red, one white, both crew cabs, each truck had two men, both clean, both with Illinois plates.

"*Unit one, this is unit two. We are going to follow them just long enough to get a good look. Be right back.*" Dana still didn't know if it was Benton or Ferguson talking into the radio. A silver Chevy Suburban pulled out three parking spots in front of them.

"Copy, unit two," Jimmy transmitted into the radio. "That's them," he said, pointing with the radio antenna. Dana looked back at the building.

"Jimmy," she said, tapping him on the shoulder. There was another truck pulling out of the lot. This one was a Nissan full-sized truck, and it turned in the opposite direction from the other two. Jimmy looked over his shoulder at the white truck pulling out of the fenced-in parking lot. "Should we go?" Dana asked.

"No," Jimmy said, looking back into the mirror. The garage door was closing, and he grabbed the radio. "Unit two, we just had a third vehicle, a white Nissan truck, depart the target location."

"*Copy unit one,*" the radio crackled back.

"Did you see anything?" Jimmy asked.

"Only the color," Dana said. "The windows were tinted. I couldn't see inside."

"So," Jimmy said, looking at Dana, "three trucks. At least five people. Different makes and models. All clean."

"And going in opposite directions," Dana added.

"Yeah," Jimmy said. "And all came from *inside* the building. Nothing from the parking lot." Jimmy grabbed the radio. "Unit two, this is unit one." Dana was looking back at the building. There was a pause, and no answer from Benton and Ferguson. "Unit two, this is unit one," Jimmy said again into the radio.

"Unit one, this is unit two!" the voice on the radio was excited. Dana tensed up. *"They just flipped a U-turn, both vehicles. They are heading back toward you at a high rate of speed!"* Dana looked over her shoulder at oncoming traffic; she could see the Nissan coming. He turned around, too. Jimmy popped the emergency brake and put the truck into gear.

"Jimmy!" Dana yelled. "The other truck!" Jimmy hit the gas and pulled into traffic. The Nissan was behind him with a car in between.

"Shit," Jimmy said. "There are the other two." Dana turned and looked out the windshield. The Fords were coming at them. Jimmy turned hard right onto a side street. Dana grabbed the radio. She watched through the rear window as the Nissan and then both Fords followed them.

"Unit two," Dana said into the radio. "All three trucks are following us!" Jimmy accelerated and shifted gears. The white Nissan Titan was closing the distance on them, with both Fords keeping pace.

"This is Unit Two. Copy."

"Hold on," Jimmy said as he jammed the brakes, downshifted, and whipped the truck around a corner. He accelerated again as the back end straightened itself out. The truck behind them barely made the turn, allowing Jimmy to gain some distance. "Get that rifle out of the backseat." Jimmy winced as the pain in his shoulder reemerged. Dana unhooked her seatbelt and reached behind them, dragging the black rifle forward and resting it between her leg and the center console. "Get your pistol out and put your seatbelt back on." Dana did as she was told.

"Unit two," Dana said into the radio. "Where are you?"

"We are on your six, behind the white Ford," the voice came back. Jimmy had to slam on the brakes to avoid hitting cross traffic. They had been lucky so far, blowing through two stop signs along the way. Their luck ran out. Jimmy shifted into first and hit the gas, turning right and trying to get into traffic. The white Nissan closed too

quickly and hit them in the rear bumper, pushing them into oncoming traffic.

Jimmy's door was hit at an angle by a rusted old Chrysler. It was a blessing. The car that hit them was an old Aries K-series station wagon from the early eighties. Chrysler designed the cars to crumple on impact to absorb most of the energy. It knocked him unconscious but probably saved Jimmy's life.

The truck Dana and Jimmy were driving spun and was facing the big Nissan Titan when it stopped. Two men got out of the car, both armed. During the impact and the spin, Jimmy's rifle came out from between Dana's leg and the console, the buttstock hitting her in the cheek, just under her left eye. She was stunned but regaining her senses as the two men approached. Both men paused and turned as gunfire erupted behind them. It gave Dana the second she needed. Undoing the seatbelt, she opened the door and pointed the Glock at the back of the man closest to her and fired twice, hitting the man in the back and killing him instantly.

The second man turned and raised his gun, pointing it at Dana. She fired again, missing the man but making him dive to the ground. She kept firing, hitting the man in the leg, then the torso, as he lay on the city street. She could hear more gunfire coming from behind the white Nissan, but couldn't see anything. Dana's nurse instincts took over, and she dove into the truck to check on Jimmy. He had a pulse and was breathing steadily.

Satisfied that Jimmy wasn't going to die in the next few seconds, Dana stepped outside the truck with the pistol in her hands. There were two more shots in the distance, and she ducked out of reflex. From behind the door, Dana could hear sirens coming. All she had to do was survive long enough for help to arrive. People were gathering in the street, pointing at her and the accident. She looked at the rusted Chrysler as the driver climbed out of his door. The sirens were getting closer—two more shots from behind the other trucks. A man ran from the sidewalk to help Dana, and she almost shot him.

"You alright, lady?" the man asked with his hands in the air. Dana just nodded, still hiding behind the door of Jimmy's truck. "C'mon, put that gun down. The police are almost here." The little nurse, who had performed so heroically under pressure, started to shake. Suddenly, another man was standing there dressed in olive drab fatigues and holding a rifle.

"Jimmy!" he called into the truck. Dana barely heard him over the ringing in her ears. She couldn't even hear the sirens anymore. Her vision faded, and she passed out on the cold pavement.

CHAPTER 23

Coming out of the elevator, Terry could sense an 'ivory tower' feel to the floor. It was immaculate. Paneling on the walls was real wood. The floors were buffed and shiny. There were no fingerprints on the glass doors leading into the Superintendent's office area. Inside the doors was a waiting area with modern furniture and fresh flowers. A young receptionist was sitting behind a circular desk. She looked like she came out of a fashion magazine and not out of the City of Chicago general employment pool.

"I'll let Diane know you are here," the young woman said without any prompting from Moriarty. *I guess he does have the keys to the castle,* Terry thought to himself. The young woman picked up a desk phone and pressed a button. "Commander Moriarty is here. No. Plus two others." Terry assumed Diane was on the other end of the phone, asking if Moriarty was alone and how many people he had with him. "You can go ahead, Sir." The young woman waved a hand toward a large wooden door.

Terry heard a buzzer and a mechanical click, unlocking the massive door. The trio passed into a second waiting area, this one smaller but just as clean and well decorated. An elderly woman stood up from behind her large, traditional desk. Mary stepped forward and walked around the desk to hug her. *That must be the 'famous' Diane.*

"Hello, dear," Diane said. The woman came out of the embrace and turned her attention to Rocco. "Hello, Commander," she offered her hand. Her smile was genuine. Rocco took her hand and shook it. Diane looked at Terry and then at Rocco.

"Pardon me, Diane," Moriarty said. "This is Terry." Diane gave Mary an inquisitive look and then squinted her eyes at Terry.

"If you are the man I think you are," Diane said, "then it is an absolute pleasure to meet you." Terry was genuinely taken aback. The plan was for Moriarty to tell everyone he was part of the incoming Army contingent. Diane was a trusted agent and had heard about him from Pops over the years. If Rocco trusted her, Terry certainly would. She offered Terry her hand, and he took it. "The Superintendent is on the phone. If you three would take a seat, I will take you in when he is done." She pointed to the four leather chairs in the center of the room. Mary quickly took a seat, followed by Moriarty. Terry took his cues from the two officers and followed suit.

"She reminds me of all the civilians that actually run the Army," Terry said in a low tone. "We used to call them the 'little ladies in tennis shoes.' They were there, day in and day out. New commanders come and go, but those ladies remained."

"She has been here for over forty years," Rocco said. "She could probably tell you how many, but I have no idea how many Superintendents she has worked for."

"Pops got her this job," Mary said. "She was an old-school meter maid, and Pops put in a word for her and got her into the front office. I've known her my whole life." Mary's eyes started to water. "She is going to be devastated." There was an intercom beep from behind Diane's desk. She stood up and walked from behind her desk to the door.

"The Superintendent will see you now," Diane said. Terry admired her professionalism. In a room filled with people she knew well, and no one else watching, it would have been easy to take the shortcut and say something from her chair. Diane wasn't that sort, making it a point to do what she knew was right even when no one was looking. They stood and walked to the door, Diane pushing it open, so they didn't even break stride. Her timing was impeccable. She smiled at Terry as he passed by.

The office was huge, and Terry tried to take it all in as he followed Rocco and Mary through the door. There was an American flag, an Illinois flag, and a Chicago flag arranged behind the glass-topped, oak desk. Superintendent Gagliardi sat behind the desk in his full dress blue uniform, barely raising an eye as the three entered the room. Terry had seen this type of leadership before. It was a snap assessment, but Terry had learned those were generally the most accurate.

"Commander," Gagliardi said, looking at his computer screen. Terry could feel the anger boiling inside him. This man's lack of deference for another high-ranking officer stunk of something sinister. His attitude reeked of the perfumed princes that ran rampant in the general officer corps of the Army. "What can I do for you?" Moriarty looked at Terry and gave him a nod.

"You can start," Terry said in a firm tone, "by explaining why the Army is coming in here." Gagliardi looked up from his computer.

"And who the hell are you?" the head of the CPD said. "I was told you were the lead from the military contingent." Terry could hear the Washington, DC beltway tone in his voice. He wasn't Chicago, that was for damn sure. If he were, he wouldn't have tipped his hand. The only person Moriarty told about Terry and the Army was the security guy at the front door. Obviously, Gagliardi had spies throughout the building.

"Let's be clear," Terry said, returning fire, "that's not how this conversation is going to work. Now answer the question. Why did you bring the Army in here?" Gagliardi stood up behind his desk, trying to project power. Terry closed the distance, keeping only the corner of the desk between them. The Superintendent's power play failed, so he tried a different tactic.

"Commander," Gagliardi said, removing his glasses, "get this man out of my office."

"I don't think so, Bob," Moriarty said flatly. "You see, what you are doing, and the people you are doing it with, well...I think it's all illegal." Gagliardi looked at the SWAT Commander and then back at Davis.

"You're Terry Davis," the Superintendent said. He tipped his hand again. "I was told you were in the city."

"Yeah?" Terry countered. "Who told you? Old guy in a suit? Maybe the guys running fake gang attacks here in the city? Who was it?" Terry had him cornered and grinned. Gagliardi seemed unfazed.

"You've got a reputation," the Superintendent said. "A real tough guy. Career Army. Awards and decorations. But you don't know your limits. And you don't know when to keep your nose out of other people's business."

"That sounds like me," Terry said, leaning in. "Sounds like they left a few things out, though."

"Really?" the Superintendent chuckled. "And what did they leave out?"

"That I'm the motherfucker that will throw you out that fifth-floor window," Terry pointed to the wall of windows at the back of the office. Gagliardi's eyes got wide. "I'm also the one they have tried to kill a half dozen times, but I'm still here. And if you're half as smart as I think you are, that should concern you." Gagliardi stepped back, creating some space between himself and Terry. The Superintendent looked at Rocco and then at Mary.

"Don't look at us," Mary said.

"I recommend you answer the man's question," Moriarty added. Terry knew he had Gagliardi on the defensive.

"Let me guess," Terry said, changing his tone, "they promised you something. Maybe a job back in DC. Or in Federal law enforcement somewhere? You got put into this job with that promise, but they needed you to help them get the military in here, right?"

"You think you have it all figured out," Gagliardi said. It surprised Terry; he wasn't expecting a counterattack. "I'll have you arrested before you leave the building. All of you. You can't come in here and intimidate me."

"Seems to be working so far," Terry said sarcastically. "But, shit, if you're going to arrest me, I might as well earn it." Terry's hand fell to the FNX-45 on his hip. His eyes turned cold. Gagliardi was a cop in name only; he hadn't been on the street in decades. He was used to dealing with politicians who would smile and stab you in the back, not a man who threatened to kill him face-to-face. The Superintendent looked at his two subordinate officers again; both Mary and Rocco remained expressionless. Gagliardi tried to call Terry's bluff. He reached for his desk phone and spoke into the handset.

"Diane," the Superintendent said. "Can you please have security come up here?" Terry pulled the pistol from his holster and held it casually at his side. Gagliardi looked at the black plastic telephone in his hand as if it were a snake. "What do you mean the phones are down?" Mary and Rocco exchanged a look. "Get security up here now!" Terry stepped around the desk. He was inside Gagliardi's personal space, still holding the pistol.

"Looks like help is a long way off," Terry said, taking the phone from the CPD boss and placing it back on the receiver. "You've got a choice to make. Right now, you need to decide what is most important to you. I would put 'breathing' at the very top of that list." Terry adjusted his grip on the big pistol for emphasis.

"Sir," Mary interrupted. She felt like Terry was boxed in. "We know you are working with someone. And we know who that someone is and what their plans are." Gagliardi looked at her. "You can either tell us what you know, or Commander Moriarty and I can step out of this office and let Terry do what he does best."

"Either way," Rocco added, "today is your last day as the Superintendent." Mary snapped a look at her dad's protégé. Gagliardi looked back at Terry, who hadn't moved a muscle, his cold eyes staring back at the policeman. He knew he was out of options.

"They only tell me what I need to know," Gagliardi started to spill the beans. "It was about a year and a half ago. A man came to me in DC. He asked if I wanted to be a police chief in a big city, and that it could be arranged." Terry looked at Mary. His hunch about the former Superintendent dying of a heart attack was true. "But, I had to be willing to help them when the time came." Gagliardi took a breath, hoping that would be enough to satisfy Terry. It wasn't. "They came to collect about three months ago. All they told me was that they were going to bring the Army in here to help fight the gangs and that they were going to recruit some officers from the department to help." Terry looked at Mary again.

"You realize they created the spike in gang violence," Terry said. It wasn't a question, but he was looking for confirmation from Gagliardi. "Specifically, as an excuse to bring in the Army." Gagliardi nodded.

"I didn't agree at first. I even said so in public," the Superintendent said, trying to build a position that he wasn't a horrible guy. "But they came back to me and told me I had to support the mayor."

"Did they call you," Terry interrupted, "or did they come see you in person?"

"He came in person," Gagliardi said. "The same man from DC. Older guy…"

"In a grey suit," Terry finished the sentence for him. "What else?"

"That's it," the Superintendent said. "That's all I know." He began to grow bold. "Now get out of my office."

"I don't think so, Bob," Moriarty said. "You're resigning. Today. And you're going to keep your fucking mouth shut about all of this. These people, us, all of it. Not a word."

"I'm not resigning anything," Gagliardi continued in his bold tone. "You can't make me…"

"Terry," Mary said abruptly. He didn't need more than that. Terry raised the pistol and put the barrel to the CPD Chief's forehead.

"Wait!" Gagliardi shouted. Terry hesitated, but the pistol didn't waver. "Just wait. I'll resign. And I won't say anything. But they aren't going to like it. They are going to come after you. They know you. You can't beat them."

"You let me worry about that," Terry said as he lowered the pistol.

"Today, Bob," Moriarty said, turning on his heel. "Resign today." Mary fell in line behind the big man. Terry let his stare last for an extra second and then followed them out. Once the door was closed, he looked at Diane.

"The phones are down?" Terry said with a wry smile.

"I don't like that sonofabitch," she said quietly. "Not even a little." Terry couldn't help but laugh.

"Pleasure meeting you, Diane." He followed Moriarty through the outer door and into the waiting area, heading for the elevators. Terry was nervous as they stood, waiting for an elevator. "You know they are going to kill him, right? When he resigns. He's a dead man."

"I don't care," Moriarty said. "Fuck 'em." Mary concealed a smile behind her hand. The elevator went ding, and the three of them stepped inside when Diane came through the outer doors.

"Commander! Commander!" she called to Moriarty. "The call just came in. Seamus is hurt. They are taking him to the hospital. They've been looking for you."

CHAPTER 24

Terry ran through the lobby of the Chicago Public Safety Headquarters expecting to be tackled at any moment. He was moving with Moriarty and Mary, but he knew he was the outlier, and if anyone were going to get arrested, it would be him. The big man moved well, considering his size and age. Mary was keeping up with him as they weaved through the clusters of people, Terry doing his best to keep pace. The cold air hit Terry's lungs as they burst through the doors, heading for Rocco's unmarked cruiser.

"I forgot how fucking cold it is here," Terry said as he pulled open the rear door. Once inside the cruiser, Mary grabbed the radio mic. Moriarty fired the engine, hit the lights and sirens, and then put the Ford into drive. Mary pushed the transmit button.

"That's my internal SWAT Channel," Moriarty said before Mary could speak. Mary reached for the dial to change the frequency. "Stay on that one. Call my guys. Benton and Ferguson are whiskey-four-four. Get them on the radio." He weaved through the lot to get to the street.

"Whiskey-Four-Four, this is command," Mary said into the radio. Terry was bouncing between a feeling of absolute comfort and familiarity and a distinctly different feeling of dread. Mary hesitated before transmitting again. "Whiskey-four-four, this is command. Do you copy?"

"*Command, this is four-four. I copy. Who is this?*" the voice came through the radio. Rocco grabbed the radio hand mic.

"Four-four, this is command actual. I want SWAT officers guarding four-one and his passenger. No one else. SWAT officers only." Terry assumed that four-one was Jimmy, and the passenger was Dana. "I want two outside the room and one inside. I am en route to your location. ETA is ten minutes." Moriarty pressed hard on the gas.

"*Command, this is four-four. I copy.*" Terry winced every time the cops used 'copy' on the radio. Rocco handed the mic back to Mary and continued to weave through traffic.

"You don't want a report on what happened?" Mary asked.

"Don't want it broadcasted," Terry said from the back. "If Smith and his people are listening, they don't need to know what happened. We will find out when we get there."

Terry was trying as hard as he could to remain focused. Focus was what this situation required, and he couldn't let emotions get in the way. He almost felt guilty because his mind kept going to Dana and not his best friend and brother. They only knew Jimmy was hurt and he was going to the hospital. Diane told them he was being taken to Cook County, but when they asked about Dana, she had no idea who Dana was or her status. Not knowing was driving Terry crazy. If he were driving or running the radios, at least he would have that to keep him focused. Riding in the backseat as a passenger was making it worse. *Focus. What did we learn from Gagliardi?*

Terry tried to replay what happened in the Superintendent's office. Smith put him in the Chief's chair on an open-ended promise. Smith and his people probably knew Chicago was a city they could exploit, and they wanted someone in there ahead of time. Gagliardi was that person. What about the mayor? Is she in on this, too? In reality, Gagliardi only confirmed what they already assumed and provided no new information. Terry took solace in the fact that his instincts were all correct. The gang war, the death of the former Superintendent, Gagliardi's role; all correct.

"You know you still have to meet with the Army, right?" Terry said to Rocco from the back seat.

"I will, but that shit can wait," the SWAT Commander came back. "If these guys are soldiers, they will understand dealing with a wounded officer." Rocco pulled into the hospital lot and parked in a spot marked 'Emergency Vehicles ONLY.' The trio jumped out and ran for the door. Terry was hoping the crabby nurse wasn't behind the desk again, barring him from going up and into the hospital without a police badge. He doubted Moriarty could bully him past that lady like he did those security guards at CPD headquarters. Two SWAT officers were standing in the lobby when they came through the doors.

"Boss," one of them called out to Moriarty. When they got closer, Terry could see the name tape on his olive drab uniform that said FERGUSON.

"What happened?" Moriarty asked.

"It was a setup," the second officer replied. Terry couldn't see his name tape, but he assumed it was Benton. "They drew us away. Two trucks pulled out of the lot. We tailed them, trying to get a plate number, but they flipped a U-turn in the middle of the road."

"Jimmy reported a third truck left and went in the opposite direction," Ferguson said. He was talking with his hands like a fighter pilot recreating a dogfight. "They all turned back toward Jimmy and the woman." Terry wanted so badly to interrupt and ask about Dana, but he resisted. "Jimmy pulled out and we got into a pursuit; Jimmy in front, then their three trucks, then us in trail."

"Their lead truck rear-ended Jimmy and pushed him into traffic," Benton jumped in. "He got hit broadside—driver's door. We pulled up behind the rear truck, and two men exited the vehicle and began firing at us. We engaged and killed them both." Moriarty was standing patiently with his arms folded as his officers debriefed. "We heard gunfire to our front and began to move forward. The two men from the second truck were already on the street and armed with assault style weapons."

"I gave a verbal command for them to drop their weapons," Ferguson continued. "Both men turned and attempted to engage. Benton fired and killed one. I fired and wounded the man to my front.

He returned fire. I fired again, striking and killing him." Terry had a great professional appreciation for these two officers. He had been in his share of firefights, and he knew how confusing it could all be, but these two had their shit together.

"Once we reduced both threats, I moved forward while Ferguson covered me," Benton added. "I finally made my way to Jimmy's truck. He was in the driver's seat and unconscious. A citizen had moved to help the woman with Jimmy. It seems like she engaged the two men in the first truck and killed them both." Terry's eyes got wide. He looked at Mary, who returned his shocked expression. "The ambulance was already on its way. Someone on the scene called it. We secured the area and helped the EMTs treat and evacuate the injured. CPD uniforms showed up, and we handed the scene off to them."

"Thanks for that," Moriarty said. "What is Jimmy's condition? And what about Dana, the woman with him?"

"Sir," Ferguson said, "they are both upstairs. Jimmy is in room three-thirty-one. The guys from Team Two are securing him. The woman…Dana? She is up there, too. Three-thirty-four. The guys from Team One are with her. Preliminary word from the docs is that Jimmy caught a head injury and may have broken his pelvis. The woman had a head injury, like a concussion, and they were treating her for shock."

"Well done," Moriarty said. "Thanks again. You two go home." Terry stepped in and shook both of their hands. "Let's head upstairs."

Moriarty led the way, Terry using his huge frame to block the view of the nurse's station as they moved through the lobby. Once inside the elevator, Mary started to sniffle. Terry looked at her and put his arm around her shoulder. It had been an extremely rough couple of days for her; she had lost both her parents, she had been shot in the body armor and killed someone for the first time, and now her brother had been wounded for the second time. He was impressed that she held it together for as long as she had. He kissed her on the top of her head.

The doors opened on the third floor, and all Terry could see was a sea of olive drab fatigues. It looked like the entire Chicago SWAT team was on the third floor. Looking down one hallway, he could see officers standing guard outside two of the rooms, all of them in full kit, including helmets and body armor. Moriarty ran a tight ship, and it was on full display in Cook County Hospital. An officer wearing stripes on his fatigues walked up to Moriarty. Terry had no idea what the rank was in the Chicago PD, but in the Army, he would have been a staff sergeant; three stripes on top with a single curved rocker underneath.

"Sergeant O'Donnell," Moriarty said, "what's the update?" O'Donnell wasn't as tall as Moriarty, but just as broad. Terry guessed he was either a team leader or Moriarty's second in command. He almost chuckled at the two huge black men standing in front of him with deeply Irish names. Only in Chicago.

"Sir," O'Donnell began, "Jimmy is in there." He pointed at the room closest to the group. "Concussion, minor brain swelling, some fractured ribs, and a broken femur. All left side. Did you know he was shot recently?" Moriarty looked at Mary and Terry. "Regardless, he is busted up pretty good, but he is going to be alright. He is sedated right now." Rocco nodded.

"What about Dana?" Mary asked. O'Donnell looked at her; clearly, they knew each other.

"She's in the other room," O'Donnell said. "Looks like she took a rifle butt to the face, right below her eye. I think it was during the accident, not from one of the assailants. She is pretty tough. She took that shot to the face but came out and killed two with a pistol. She was out of it for a while, but she started to come around just a little bit ago."

"Start setting up a guard rotation," Moriarty directed. "No bullshit. Only SWAT or these two are allowed into the rooms. Hospital staff are monitored, and none of them come in alone." O'Donnell nodded his head.

"Let's go see my favorite little nurse," Rocco said. Mary and Terry smiled. The big man had taken a liking to Dana from the first time they met. He led them past the officers standing guard outside her room. There was a third officer inside, just as the SWAT Commander directed. He was standing next to Dana's bed, talking to her. Terry felt an uncomfortable level of jealousy that he hadn't felt in years. "Look at this little badass," Moriarty said as he walked in. The SWAT officer quickly backed off like a kicked puppy.

Mary moved to her and hugged her. Moriarty positioned himself at the foot of her bed. Terry walked around the far side and leaned in to kiss her as Mary cleared out of the way. She kissed him back but recoiled a little when he touched her face. His thumb grazed the bruise on her cheek from the rifle butt.

"So, you shot two more bad guys," Rocco said. "I ought to give you a badge and put you on the streets." He was trying to be light, even jovial, to take some of the sting out of the day.

"I'll pass, thanks," Dana said with a forced smile. "You all can have this. I'm done with all of it." Her voice turned sour. Terry's heart sank. Dana wasn't wired for this type of life, and it was already too much for her. He touched her arm, but she wouldn't look at him.

"Well, you are safe here," Moriarty said. "I've got SWAT officers on guard for both you and Jimmy, inside and outside the rooms. You did well, though. You saved your life…and his." Dana sat quietly, not even acknowledging what Moriarty said. The big man looked at Mary, then Terry. "I'm going to check on Jimmy." He could feel the tension and looked at the officer posted as security inside the room. "Step outside for a minute. Give them some privacy." The SWAT officer followed his boss out of the room and closed the door.

"Are you OK?" Mary asked quietly.

"OK?" Dana snapped back. "I am far from OK. Nothing about this is OK. I just *killed* two more people. Do you know how absurd that is? The fact that I had to say 'two *more*' people is insane. I've killed three people in the last couple of days. I'm a fucking nurse!" Her voice was getting louder. "I'm not a cop and I'm not a soldier. I don't do this. This isn't me." Terry felt sick to his stomach. He brought this on, him and no one else.

"I'm sorry," Terry said softly.

"Sorry?" Dana yelled at him. "You're not sorry for any of this. You *love* this. People are dead, Terry. Lots of them. Mom and Pops. Jimmy is sedated. He almost died twice. Twice! But you keep going. You're addicted to this shit." She was crying. "I can't do this anymore." Terry stood quietly.

"Dana," Mary said in a stern tone. "That's not fair. Terry didn't do this. He is caught in the middle, just like the rest of us."

"Bullshit," Dana said. "He attracts it. It follows him everywhere, like some dark cloud over everything."

"An apology is all I have to offer," Terry said. His voice and his heart were turning cold.

"Well, I don't want it," Dana snapped back at him. Terry stood straight and walked out of the room without another word.

"You're a bitch," Mary said to her. "You may be my best friend, but that was shitty. You forget that these fucking people were recruiting *me,* and I asked for *his* help. This shit started *before* we even knew he was in town, and it would be going on with or without him." Dana kept staring into nothing. "I'm going to check on my brother." Mary turned and walked out.

Terry was standing outside Jimmy's room when Mary walked into the hallway. He was looking off into space. It was the 'thousand-yard stare' she knew many veterans brought home with them. She didn't know if it was a coping mechanism or a byproduct of all the killing. Mary felt awful. However, they found themselves in the middle of all of this, all of them; it wasn't Terry's fault.

"Hey," she said as she walked up to him. "Sorry about that."

"No," Terry said quietly. "Nothing to be sorry about. She's right. I did this."

"You didn't do this, Terry," she said, touching his arm. "*They* did this." She hugged him, but he stood there like a statue. She backed away. "You're still the love of my life," she said with a smile.

"You keep an eye on Jimmy," Terry said. He started to walk away, but she grabbed his arm.

"Where are you going?" she asked. Mary had a bad feeling.

"I'm going to fix this," Terry said. He turned and walked away. Mary stood there for a long second, staring at his back as he moved through the corridor.

"Shit," Mary said to no one in particular.

CHAPTER 25

Terry Davis was about three steps from the elevator doors when a huge hand grabbed his arm. His blood was up after the words from Dana, and he went into fight mode. Terry spun quickly, twisting his arm as he moved to break the unknown attacker's grip. He failed miserably. Rocco Moriarty had hold of him and wasn't letting go. Had Terry taken a swing at Rocco in his turn, it probably would have ended badly for the combat veteran; he had little doubt that Rocco would have been more than he could handle.

"Where are you going?" Rocco asked Terry.

"I need a ride to Mom and Pops' house," Terry said. The big man loosened his grip.

"For what?" Rocco asked.

"Sir," Terry said in the calmest voice he could muster, "this shit needs to end. Jimmy is fucked up. Dana is fucked up. Two of your guys got shot at today…" Moriarty cut him off.

"So, what? You're just going to go start killing folks, Mr. Airborne Ranger?" Rocco was leaning in close. "And then what? What happens when these JSOC guys show up today? You going to kill them, too?"

"If I have to," Terry said. Moriarty gave him an exasperated look. "Listen, these people do what they can to manipulate the system, but it all boils down to violence. They understand that. They understand violence."

"Listen to yourself," the big SWAT Commander said. "Terry, I've heard stories about you for years, even before you were in the Army. Pops always said you were too smart and too strong for your own good, and he was right. I've been watching you and listening to you for the last day or so. I can see what you are capable of but running off and getting yourself killed isn't going to stop any of this. Use your brain, Ranger."

Terry squinted. Moriarty had been calling him 'Mr. Airborne Ranger' since they met and assumed it came from Pops or watching movies. Calling Terry 'Ranger' was something that came too easily for the SWAT Commander. Students at the US Army Ranger School are commonly referred to as 'Ranger' since students do not wear rank. Members of the elite 75th Ranger Regiment are also referred to as 'Ranger' just like members of the 82nd Airborne Division are referred to as 'Paratrooper'. Those monikers are used within elite organizations to build esprit de corps; instead of just being a 'soldier,' they are something different, better. Moriarty said it with too much familiarity.

"This isn't a wristwatch that you can smash with a hammer," Moriarty continued. "This is like a locomotive. You can't stop it with a hammer, you have to derail it." Terry's blood was still boiling, but he got Rocco's point. He knew what he needed to do.

"I get it," Terry said. "But I still need a ride."

"I'll get you a ride," Moriarty said. "But what's your plan?"

"I'll fill you in when I can," Terry said. Moriarty gave a concerned look. "I swear. But this is just me. I can't have you, or anyone else, involved."

"You need anything besides a ride?" Moriarty asked.

"Yeah," Terry said. "Keep the Army off the streets as long as you can. Who am I riding with?"

"Let's go downstairs," Rocco said as the elevator opened. "I think I have a solution. I have to go meet the Army guys anyway." He held the door open as Terry stepped inside. "O'Donnell!" Moriarty called down the corridor. The SWAT Sergeant came jogging down to the elevator. "I'm going to meet the Army contingent. You're here until I say otherwise. Give me your keys, I need your cruiser." O'Donnell handed off his keys without question, and Moriarty let the doors close.

"When were you in?" Terry asked.

"Ha!" Rocco said. "I guess you caught me. Seventy-five to eighty-three. Air Force pararescue. I went to Ranger School in eighty-one." Terry smiled. "I missed all the big stuff. Vietnam was over when I went in. I missed Lebanon and Grenada and got out. Nothing like what you did." The doors opened, and Terry followed Moriarty through the lobby and out the front doors. They walked to a cruiser that looked exactly like Rocco's, parked a few spaces away. Moriarty unlocked it and opened the back hatch. Outside, it looked like the SWAT Commander's vehicle, but inside it was a normal cruiser, including the metal fencing between the cargo compartment and the backseat, and the backseat and the front seats.

"Thanks for letting me have this," Terry said.

"Oh, no, Ranger," Moriarty chuckled. "I'm giving you mine. I can't have you busting up O'Donnell's ride. I know I am not going to stop you from doing whatever you are going to do, but I can help. Grab that bag and follow me." Moriarty pointed to a large, black duffel bag in the cargo compartment. Terry hoisted the bag out of the back and closed the liftgate. Over at Moriarty's cruiser, he opened the back and held out the keys.

"You're welcome to whatever is in that bag," Rocco said. "I had O'Donnell put your body armor in the backseat. They took it off Dana when they put her in the ambulance. Benton and Ferguson didn't know what to do with it." Terry dumped the bag in the cargo compartment and took the keys from Moriarty. The big man went around to the driver's door, opened it, and came out with a handful of stuff.

"Channel nine is SWAT internal," he said, handing a radio over to Terry.

"I think they are monitoring your comms," Terry said.

"They are, but if you need help, we will still hear you," Rocco said. He handed him a cellphone with a small antenna attached. "That is a secure messaging phone. There is only one app on it, so message over that. We have repeaters all over the city. Eventually, the Army will figure that out, too, but in the meantime, you can message me on that.

I'll send you a test message in a little bit. Respond to that, and we will be connected." Terry nodded. "Do *not* call from it." Terry nodded again.

"Lastly," Rocco handed him a worn, leather billfold. He flipped it open to reveal a badge as worn as the leather it was protected by. "That's Pops' extra badge. He gave it to me when he retired. It doesn't make you a cop, but if you have that and my cruiser, someone will at least call me before they put you into cuffs. Anyone else won't know the difference." Terry was stunned and even a little choked up.

"Thanks again," Terry said. "For all of this."

"Don't thank me yet," Rocco said. "But you'd better keep me informed, or I'll arrest you myself." Terry put the handful of items into the front seat of the blacked-out cruiser.

"Let me ask you something," Terry said. "Why the ultimatum to Gagliardi? The whole last day as the Superintendent thing."

"Because that guy needs to go," Rocco said. "And that job should have been mine in the first place," he added with a chuckle. Terry held his hand out, and Moriarty shook it. "Good luck, Ranger."

"Thanks, Sir," Terry said. He climbed into the cruiser and fired the engine. He watched Moriarty walk back to the other cruiser before he backed out of the parking spot. Terry's brain immediately started shifting gears. *You have to derail it.* Rocco's words were ringing in his ears. The concept was forming in his head as he drove. He knew he needed to draw out Smith, and it had to be big and public.

Killing Smith was definitely on the agenda, but it wasn't *the goal.* The goal was to take this whole operation off the rails. Terry knew working the plan from the end to the start was probably optimal, but he also knew he needed to do a few things first. He wanted to inventory whatever it was in the black bag he got from O'Donnell's ride. He assumed it was a bunch of SWAT gear, but he needed to find out what assets he had at his disposal. There was going to have to be a trip to Moriarty's. His AR-15 with the ACOG scope was still in Pops' Cadillac parked out front with the dead body in the trunk, and he definitely wanted *his* rifle. The war belt and his night vision were in the assault pack in the Caddy as well. He got most everything out of his apartment, but he wanted to grab his grandfather's Winchester Model 12 shotgun. There wasn't a weapon in his personal arsenal that he felt more comfortable with.

"They don't know I'm in this vehicle," he said out loud. "They aren't looking for it, but as soon as they know I have it, that cover is blown." Terry spent most of the year going back and forth with Peggy before things went to hell. She was always a good sounding board and helped him through his planning. He had been doing it with Mary over the last few days, with small inputs from Jimmy and even Dana. Now, he was alone and had to work through this by himself.

"At some point, I want them to find me. To come after me," he kept thinking out loud. "If I go to Rocco's first, that won't draw any attention. This is his car. They probably have eyes on my apartment. And Dana's place. And Mom and Pops'." The secure messaging phone vibrated and was flashing red. Terry picked it up and saw a message icon over the single app on the phone. Terry stopped at a red light and swiped the phone open. He touched the app, and the message popped up.

W65: TEST. RLTW.

Terry smiled. The acronym 'RLTW' was shorthand for 'Rangers Lead The Way.' It was the motto of the 75th Ranger Regiment and known to anyone who wore a Ranger Tab on their uniform. That message was definitely from Moriarty. He messaged back.

W66: RGR. ACK.

Terry messaged back using radio terminology he knew Moriarty would recognize; it was short for 'Roger. Acknowledge.' The most secure comms he was going to have were established. He assumed neither the radio nor the secure messaging phone would work outside the city, so he would be cut off from any help once he left downtown.

"Moriarty's first," he said to himself. "Then the apartment. I want them to pick me up. But when? And then what?" Terry turned on the radio, and it went to Rocco's news station.

"Today, the star running back of the Bears, the General Manager of the Blackhawks, and the first baseman of the White Sox all spoke out in support of the Mayor's effort to bring in the military to defeat the violent gangs plaguing Chicago."

"Jesus," Terry said. "They even have the sports world involved in this shit."

"They joined a long list of powerful Chicagoans who support the mayor, including the Presidents of Loyola University and the University of Chicago, as well as the board Presidents who control the Chicago Museum Campus, which includes the Adler Planetarium, Shedd Aquarium, and the Field Museum."

"The whole city is in on this," Terry said. His heart sank. Maybe this is too big, too far gone. If they have all those people on board, how do I stop this? His mind was racing as he moved through the streets heading for Moriarty's. *You have to derail it.* He was fighting the negative thoughts in his head. There had to be a way. "OK, so lots of big-name, public support. How do you change public support? What's the opposite of public support?" He turned off the radio.

"I was right!" he said as he slammed his hand on the steering wheel. "The opposite of public support is public outcry. This has to be big and public, just like I thought." He was gaining traction now. "But where? Sports stadium?" He caught himself wishing Peggy were there to listen. "Stadiums are too big. Too many corridors, skyboxes, entrances, and exits." He shook off any idea of Wrigley Field or the United Center. "Where?"

Terry drove with his hand on his chin, thinking. He pulled up in front of Moriarty's house and parked directly behind the Cadillac. He knew the answer would come to him, but he couldn't wait much longer. Terry climbed out of the unmarked cruiser and walked up to the Cadillac, opening the door and thanking God whoever pulled the prints off the dead guy had left the doors unlocked. His green assault pack was in the backseat, and he grabbed it. *Shit, no rifle.* He thought to himself. Terry opened the driver's door, pushed the trunk button, and walked to the back. He could almost taste the stench of the body before he opened the trunk itself. There was his rifle, underneath the dead John Doe in the trunk. Terry closed up the Caddy and locked the doors —*no need for anyone to find a corpse in front of Moriarty's house.*

Terry put the assault pack and his rifle into the passenger seat and stood in the street. Every house on one side had a brick or wrought iron fence in front of it. The park was on the other side of the street, the curb lined with massive hardwoods that had probably been there for decades. *Nice place for a vehicular ambush. Nowhere to escape.* Terry was half ashamed of himself for not noticing the restrictive terrain before now, especially since it was the third time he had been parked in front of the house. *You're slipping.*

Terry looked up and down the street again, and then it hit him. *Vehicular ambush. Restrictive terrain. That's what I need. Somewhere, I can control the terrain.* He climbed back into the cruiser and put it in gear. *Where is there restrictive terrain in the city? City streets. Alleys. The parks are open, just like the stadiums. The lake is a big barrier, but the beaches are open.* Terry stopped at a stop sign and messaged Moriarty.

W66: MOVING OUT OF COMMS RANGE. WILL MESSAGE WHEN ABLE.

Terry pulled away from the stop sign and headed for the highway. He was off to his apartment in the suburbs to pick up the shotgun. He still needed to find out what was in the bag in the back, but that could come later. Rocco messaged back.

W65: COPY

No matter what, Moriarty was still a cop. Terry shook his head as he turned the radio back on. The news had gone a full cycle because it was the same twenty-second bit about Chicago celebrities supporting the Mayor. Terry reached to change the station when he paused to listen again.

"...*as well as the board Presidents that control the Chicago Museum Campus, which includes the Adler Planetarium, Shedd Aquarium, and the Field Museum.*"

Terry thought about the cluster of attractions on the lakefront of Lake Michigan that were collectively known as the Museum Campus. Starting in the south was the Arie Crown Theater with the harbor on the lakeside and McCormick Place convention center across the street to the west. North of the Arie Crown were a couple of parking lots, then Soldier Field, where the Bears played. North of that was the Field Museum. Off to the one o'clock of the Field Museum was the Shedd Aquarium, which sat on a point that stuck out into Lake Michigan. East of the aquarium, at the end of a narrow strip of land, was the Adler Planetarium. Heading back south, on a peninsula, is where the old Meigs Field airport used to be, across the harbor from Soldier Field and the Arie Crown.

"That's got to be the most restrictive piece of terrain in the city," Terry said to himself. The layout of the campus had changed in small bits and pieces over the years, but the physical terrain was the same. Thanks to multiple Catholic School and high school field trips, as well as plenty of bored summer afternoons wandering the city with Jimmy, Terry knew the area reasonably well. The old Meigs Field was shut down in the early two thousand's, fifteen years after Jimmy and Terry ended up in the back of a squad car for hopping the fence that surrounded the runway and tarmac.

Terry was cruising down the highway and smiled at the memory of him freaking out in the back of that CPD cruiser while Jimmy just smiled. Terry knew they were in trouble and couldn't understand why Jimmy was smiling. Eventually, the cop dropped them off at Mom and Pops and just drove away. Terry never understood why the cop just let them go. *Holy shit.* Terry realized as he drove that the cop in the front seat was Moriarty. His smile grew. *I guess we have met before.*

CHAPTER 26

SWAT Commander Rocco Moriarty walked into the Chicago Emergency Operations Center and was immediately unhappy. Typically, the EOC was buzzing, but controlled. People were on headsets, talking on radios or phones. The noise was minimal, and the shift leader sat at the front of the room in case the EOC had to coordinate a major event. It was a controlled environment by design.

What Rocco saw was the opposite. There were about a dozen people not in a CPD uniform that he didn't recognize. They were huddled around the desk that on any other day oversaw operations in what was known as 'The South Side.' He recognized the dispatcher who usually sat at that desk; he was now standing off to the side with his laptop in his hands, trying to find a new place to sit. The shift leader was a good officer who had been in the department for about a dozen years but had taken a bullet in the leg during a foot pursuit and couldn't run anymore. He was standing in front of the group of intruders, being ignored.

"What the fuck is going on here?" Moriarty's bass tone echoed through the big room. Everyone in a CPD uniform turned and looked at Rocco. The dozen unknowns just kept on working and talking. The shift leader moved to Moriarty.

"Commander," he said. "The Army is here. They just took over."

"I got this, Baker," Moriarty reassured the shift leader. Rocco walked into the middle of what he knew was the Army contingent. "Who the fuck is in charge of you people?"

"I am," a muscular white guy with a beard said as he stepped forward. "And since we are being confrontational...who the fuck are you?"

"Commander Moriarty," Rocco said, standing fully erect. He was a full four inches taller than the man in front of him. "Who authorized you to take over this space? I know it wasn't the shift leader." Moriarty stepped closer to the man.

"The fucking mayor did," said the Army leader in a cocky tone, "when she invited us in. And so did the police chief. I assume that's not you."

"Baker!" Moriarty said, calling for the shift leader. The red-haired man appeared by his side. "Did the Superintendent announce his resignation yet?"

"About fifteen minutes ago, Sir," Baker replied.

"Get the mayor on the phone for me," Rocco said to Baker. The shift leader moved to another desk and picked up a phone. "We will get this settled shortly," Moriarty said to the Army commander. "In the meantime, what's your name?"

"Dave Boyd," he replied, not offering a hand to shake. "I'm the detachment commander."

"Well," Moriarty fired back with sarcasm, "Dave Boyd, detachment commander, do you have a rank?"

"That's not relevant," Boyd responded. "What is relevant is that you are slowing my operation down." Moriarty opened his mouth to return fire when he heard Officer Baker behind him.

"Sir, the Mayor is on the phone," Moriarty said, seeing him holding the phone in his outstretched hand. Rocco turned and walked to the desk, taking the phone from the shift leader. *Just keep them off the streets as long as you can.*

"Ms. Mayor," Moriarty spoke into the receiver.

"*Commander Moriarty,*" the mayor said from the other end of the line. "*I understand the Army has arrived.*"

"Yes, ma'am," Rocco said. "Ma'am, I understand the Superintendent resigned."

"That's correct, Commander. If you are calling to politic..." Moriarty cut her off.

"No ma'am," he said. "His chair isn't even cold yet. That's a discussion for another time. I am just wondering about the chain of command for the Army. They were supposed to report directly to the Superintendent for all operations. I'm here in the EOC with the Army, and we all need to know who they are reporting to. Is there an acting Superintendent?" Rocco was testing the waters. If the mayor said she wanted the Army to report to her, she was probably as guilty in all this as Gagliardi was. If she pushes it off to someone else, she was likely as clueless as Moriarty thought she was. There was a pause from the mayor.

"Since you're there," the mayor said, *"it's probably easiest to have them report to you, at least for now."* Moriarty smiled. The mayor didn't realize it, but she just bought Terry some time. Rocco didn't know how long it would last.

"Thank you, Ms. Mayor," Rocco said loud enough for the Boyd to hear. "I'll let the Army know they have to clear everything through me until you say otherwise." He hung up the receiver and walked back to Dave Boyd with a smile on his face. "You guys report to me now."

"Well played," Boyd said. "We will see how long that lasts. In the meantime, what do you want us to do? The mayor didn't ask us here to sit on our asses."

"The first thing you can do," Rocco said smugly, "is pack that shit up and give my dispatcher his desk back. Then, you can give me everyone's name and social security number, as well as the serial numbers and types of all your weapons. Once you're done with that, and we run everyone's background, we will talk. In the meantime, there's coffee in the breakroom."

"I'm not giving you that information," Boyd said. "No fucking way. All these guys have Top Secret clearances, and all our weapons belong to DoD."

"Enjoy the coffee then," Moriarty said. "Be sure to put some money in the coffee fund. We don't have DoD money here, and that shit ain't free. And don't let me catch you guys on the street with weapons. You *will* be arrested."

"I get it," Boyd said. "I'll call my boss and get this straightened out."

"Who *is* your boss, by the way?" Rocco asked.

"Also not relevant," Boyd responded. "At least not until you're getting your ass chewed by the mayor, and possibly getting fired." Moriarty realized the entire room was watching and listening. He stepped in close to Boyd, leaning over the smaller man.

"You're not from Chicago, are you?" Moriarty said.

"No," Boyd responded, not giving an inch.

"Didn't think so," Rocco said, "because if you were, you'd know that people who make threats like that...in this city...end up at the bottom of Lake Michigan."

"Wow," Boyd said. "I knew Chicago cops were corrupt, but murder? That's a bit of a shock."

"Fuck around," Moriarty replied, "and find out." He turned and walked back to Baker, who was standing by his chair at the front of the room. "Get that dispatcher back on his desk," he gave instructions in a low tone only Baker could hear. "Get these guys out of the EOC, but don't let them leave the building. I am sure the Mayor is going to call back within the next hour or so. I'll be in my office downstairs, but make sure you can't find me when she calls. Hold her off as long as you can."

"Yes, Sir," Baker said with a smile.

"I'll send some of my guys up here to secure their weapons in our gun cage," Rocco added. "Maybe we will lose the keys after we take the time to inventory everything by serial number." Baker smiled again.

"What are you up to, Commander?" Baker asked.

"Son," Rocco tapped him on the chest with the back of his hand, "you don't want to know." Moriarty turned and walked out of the EOC. In the lobby, he pulled out O'Donnell's secure messaging phone and sent a text to Terry Davis.

W65: VISITORS ON SITE. BOUGHT MAYBE TWO HOURS.

"Secure messaging," Dave Boyd said from behind Moriarty. "We have that, too." Boyd was smiling. Moriarty walked away without acknowledging him.

In his office in the basement, Moriarty picked up the phone and called Cook County Hospital, asking to be connected to the nurse's station on the third floor. When the nurse answered the phone, he asked her to get O'Donnell for him.

"*Sergeant O'Donnell speaking,*" the voice of Moriarty's most trusted officer came from the other end of the phone.

"Everything good there?" Moriarty asked.

"*Yes, Sir,*" O'Donnell replied. "*No visitors. Guards are in place. Med staff are being monitored. Can I ask what is going on, Sir?*"

"Better you don't know," Moriarty said. *I seem to be saying that a lot lately.* "Is Mary still there?"

"*Right here, Sir,*" O'Donnell replied. Moriarty heard the rustling of the phone being handed off.

"*Sir?*" Mary's voice came through the phone.

"Mary, I'm at the EOC, in my office in the basement," Rocco told her. "Your boy is out moving around. He is going to keep me informed. I will share what I know whenever I can. Do not leave the hospital. Our guests are here, and they have to answer to me because I don't have a boss right now. I don't know if you heard that or not."

"*I'm on a hospital floor full of cops,*" Mary said. "*Of course, I heard.*"

"Is Jimmy OK? What about the little nurse?" Moriarty asked.

"*Jimmy is still out of it. I don't know about her. I haven't spoken to her since you left,*" Mary replied. Rocco could hear the tension in her voice when Mary spoke about Dana.

"Just keep an eye on them," he told her. "No one leaves the hospital unless I come to get you."

"*Yes, Sir,*" Mary replied. Moriarty hung up the phone. He picked up the secure messaging phone and began to text Terry.

W65: SECURE COMMS MAY BE VULNERABLE. USE CAUTION.

Terry never got the message.

CHAPTER 27

Terry pulled into the parking lot of his apartment building and scanned each vehicle. He recognized every one of them—nothing out of place. There was a car parked in the street, across from the lot, but no one was in it. No foot traffic anywhere. Terry's spidey-senses weren't tingling, but he wasn't fool enough to believe the apartment wasn't being watched somehow. Smith and his people had assets available to them that he would never see. Terry knew that as soon as he stepped out of the blacked-out cruiser, there was no turning back.

There were a lot of variables Terry didn't know and had to be comfortable with not knowing. He didn't know how close Smith's assets were and how quickly they could respond. He didn't know if they would follow him or engage him directly. All he knew was they would know he was at the apartment and probably what he was driving. Terry checked the FNX in the holster on his hip and stepped out of the vehicle. He moved to the building at a jog, through the outer door into the hallway that led to his apartment door, feeling his broken ribs with every step. Terry paused and inspected the doorway. There were no marks in the frame or around the knob or deadbolt. That didn't mean much; many special operators were trained to pick locks with a set of picks, but he knew no one had forced their way in.

Terry put the key into the deadbolt and turned it, pushing on the door as he turned the knob. Nothing inside seemed out of place, and the door swung freely. Terry looked around the apartment slowly. It had only been a few days since he was here last, so there was no stagnant smell or layer of dust on everything. Terry moved quickly into his room and grabbed the only thing he needed: Grandpa's Model 12. He slid the old shotgun into a padded canvas case and went out the door, locking it behind him and jogging back out to the cruiser. Terry usually made it a point not to move guns in and out of his apartment during daylight, but he didn't have time to wait.

Terry put the shotgun into the backseat and got out of the parking lot as quickly as he could. Whether anyone was following him or not, he had to assume they knew he was in the apartment. Thinking otherwise was being naïve. Terry drove through the familiar residential streets, and his mind wandered to Dana, but he quickly shook those thoughts away. No time for that now, no time for her. Terry could only afford to focus on the task at hand: getting Smith's people to follow him out to the Museum Campus. The fight had to happen there, but there was a fight Terry wanted to pick before that. He was heading for the building in the city that Jimmy and Dana had staked out when they were attacked. That couldn't go unpunished, and he knew it would force Smith and his people out of hiding.

The sun was starting to go down, fading more quickly as they approached the winter solstice. This was all going to happen tonight in the increasingly cold weather. Terry knew it would escalate swiftly and would culminate within the next few hours. He only hoped Moriarty could keep the Army off the streets until morning. *Hope is not a course of action.*

Terry pulled up to a stoplight not far from the apartment complex and grabbed the secure phone. He knew he was outside the coverage area, but would be driving almost directly to the stakeout building, and wanted to send a message to Moriarty before that. Terry picked up the phone and tapped on the app; as expected, there were no unread messages. He began to type quickly.

W66: EN ROUTE TO SEAMUS BUILDING. GOING TO PECK A FIGHT.

He was trying to be somewhat secure and not reveal the address or exact location where he was headed. Terry thought that by using Jimmy's given name, Moriarty would know what he meant. The second sentence was a reference to the movie Braveheart. Warriors are the same, no matter what. It was a classic quote he had heard thousands of times during his time in the Army. Terry was confident Rocco would get the quote and understand what he was about to do. He tossed the secure phone into the cup holder in the console and started looking for a place to inventory the bag in the cargo compartment with a bit of privacy.

It didn't take long for Terry to find what he was looking for, an industrial area just before the on-ramp for the highway. It was a cluster of distribution warehouses, all with large parking lots and tons of traffic in and out. The first one he came to had a gate with a guard-house, so he drove on.

Terry turned left into a big lot and weaved his way between parked cars and slow-moving tractor-trailers pulling in and out of the loading docks. He backed the cruiser into a spot at the end of the lot, so there was nothing and no one behind him. It was already dark, and, as much as he didn't like it, Terry would be forced to use the interior lights of the vehicle to dig through the bag. He knew it risked attracting attention, but he didn't have a choice.

Terry walked to the back of the vehicle and opened the rear hatch. He peeled open the dual zipper in the top of the black nylon bag to reveal its contents. The duffle was like a Halloween trick-or-treat bag for a professional door kicker. Terry pulled out each item and set it aside in the cramped space. He found a half dozen, loaded, thirty-round magazines for his AR-15. Next came four flashbang grenades. They weren't designed to be lethal, but to be used entering buildings and rooms. When the toilet paper tube-sized grenade detonated, it produced a loud noise and a bright flash designed to deafen and blind anyone inside. There was a small tactical breeching tool jammed in the back of the bag. The wicked-looking device looked like a hammer, a crowbar, and a pickaxe had a baby. Terry hoped he wouldn't be forced to mechanically breech any doors, but if he needed to, this was the tool to do it.

Off to one end of the bag was a full SWAT uniform and a pair of boots, all sized for O'Donnell and all clearly too big for Terry. Those were immediately returned inside the black bag. In the opposite end of the bag was a ballistic helmet with a night vision mount. This one offered protection against actual bullets, unlike the plastic 'bump helmet' Terry had in the assault pack in the backseat, but it was also sized for O'Donnell's much larger cranium and would likely be more of a hindrance than some help. Back in the bag it went. At the bottom of the bag was a tactical vest with various pouches attached to it, but that wasn't what caused Terry to smile. The vest was equipped with much higher quality ceramic plates, like the one that saved Mary at Mom and Pops.' He was going to happily replace his steel plates, especially the one dented in that same gunfight, with ceramic.

Terry was rifling through the pouches attached to the vest, generally finding smaller items that O'Donnell determined he needed to do his job. Terry left the Gerber multi-tool, a bevy of colored markers, more first aid gear, a seatbelt cutter, and a small flashlight in the pouches where the SWAT Officer kept them; he either had no use for them or already had a similar item in his own kit. He almost tossed O'Donnell's gloves aside, but decided to try them on. They were military issue, flyer's gloves made out of fireproof Nomex. Terry wore out countless pairs of these in his career; they were the best mix of protection and dexterity a shooter could ever find. Surprisingly, they fit, so he set them next to the magazines and flashbangs. The last thing he grabbed was four sets of flex-cuffs; the industrial strength zip-tie handcuffs that the military and police began using with increased frequency. *Those may come in handy.*

Terry stepped away from the rear of the vehicle, intending to grab his plate carrier out of the backseat and swap out the plates, steel for ceramic. He was met with a flashlight in his eyes. *Security Guard.* It was the only logical answer. If it were one of Smith's guys, Terry knew he would already be dead.

"Excuse me, Sir," the man said. Terry couldn't even see the silhouette because the light was so bright. "Do you mind telling me what you're doing here?"

"Yeah," Terry said. "Chicago PD. SWAT actually. I just got a call and have to go in."

"Can I see a badge or ID?" the man said as he lowered the flashlight. Terry's eyes adjusted as he moved to the driver's door. He knew the old badge Moriarty gave him was in the driver's compartment; he just hoped it worked on the rent-a-cop. Terry produced the worn, leather billfold with the badge inside. As he handed it off, Terry's eyes fell to the man's hip...no gun. At a minimum, if this guy gave Terry an issue, he could subdue him and take off. Definite sigh of relief. "Aren't you guys supposed to live in the city? Like, are actual Chicago residents to be on the force?" He closed the billfold and handed it back to Terry.

"Um, yeah, we are," Terry lied. "My girlfriend lives out here. I grew up out here. I was on my way back to my place in the city and got the call, so I pulled in to square my gear away." The man in front of him was enthralled—a total wannabe cop.

"Is it another gang thing?" the security guard asked like a little kid. "That shit is all over the news, man. Like every day. You ever kill any of those fuckers?" Terry gave him a confused look.

"Look, man, I really need to get going. I have to take care of a couple of things, and then I'll be out of your lot and on the road," Terry said, both trying to get done what he stopped here to do, but also to get rid of this weirdo.

"Yeah, yeah. Of course," the man sounded dejected. Terry was wary that he would sound an alarm or something, elevating the situation unnecessarily.

"Hey, man," Terry said. "You have a card or something? We are always looking for good people. Maybe I can put in a good word for you."

"Really?" The man's eyes lit up with excitement. "You know, I've taken the test twice and haven't gotten a call back." he was fumbling in his pocket for a card when Terry heard the tires squeal near the entrance to the parking lot. The security guard looked in that direction.

"Get down!" Terry commanded. The man ducked down next to him as Terry produced the FNX-45 from his hip holster. "Do you have a gun on you?" Terry could tell by the confused look on the man's face that the answer was 'no.' "Shit."

The headlights were approaching, faster than anyone should be driving in a busy parking lot. The distance was closing, but Terry knew he had enough time to get the AR out of the backseat. *I guess the clock is ticking faster than I thought.* He holstered the pistol and grabbed his rifle from the passenger area of the cruiser, yanking a magazine from the pouch attached to the front of his body armor sitting uselessly in the seat. He slapped the plastic magazine in place and racked a round into the chamber. The security guard was completely confused.

"Behind the vehicle, now!" Terry moved, and the younger man followed him. Whoever was in that SUV knew Terry was here, and it was only a matter of time before they found him. Terry tried to get a glimpse of the vehicle and how it moved. If it was armored like the one from the apartment parking lot, he was probably fucked. He could only see the top half of the vehicle as it weaved its way through the parking lot. By the outline, Terry could tell it was a Ford Expedition, and as it moved between obstacles, Terry thought it looked too nimble to be armored. *Maybe I have a chance.*

"What's your name?" Terry said.

"My name? I'm Frank," the security guard said with a quiver in his voice.

"OK, Frank," Terry was peeking around the rear fender at the Expedition. "When I get a clear shot, I am going to kill the driver." Frank's eyes got wide. "Hey, listen, Frank. Trust me." Frank nodded. "When I kill the driver, I need you to make a break for that dumpster over there."

"What?" Frank was scared.

"Seriously," Terry was calm, which was making Frank even more nervous. "You'll have enough time to get there. But when the vehicle stops, those guys are going to shoot at the dumpster," Terry peeked at the Ford again. "The dumpster will stop the bullets. Just stay behind it. I'll take care of the rest." Frank swallowed hard and nodded. Terry got to take a knee and braced the rifle against the taillight, waiting for the driver of the Expedition to expose himself.

Terry moved his weapon from 'SAFE' to 'FIRE' and looked through the ACOG. When Terry bought the scope, there were several options for the reticle inside. Almost all of them had the reticle illuminated by a fiber optic element mounted on top of the scope. Any light in the area would be pulled in and projected into the scope to 'light up' the center of the reticle. You could buy them in various colors, including green, amber, and red. You could also choose many different reticle images, from a horseshoe to a traditional crosshair. Terry stuck with what he knew, a red chevron. The lights coming from the building and the light posts scattered throughout the parking lot provided just enough illumination to light up the red chevron inside his ACOG, giving him an excellent sight picture when the dark SUV finally showed itself. Then it accelerated toward them.

Terry fired a single round, hesitating long enough to see it impact and penetrate the windshield. *Definitely not armored.* He fired again, striking the windshield in front of the driver. He looked over his shoulder, and Frank was still there.

"GO!" he yelled to his impromptu partner. Frank got up and ran. Terry was using him as bait, so he tucked himself behind the police cruiser, hoping whoever was in the Expedition focused on Frank as he moved. It worked. The SUV swerved and came to a stop, the nose pointing at Frank's hiding spot, the blue dumpster. It worked better than Terry anticipated. When the Ford stopped, the doors on the passenger side were at the perfect angle to offer the bad guys tons of protection from unarmed Larry hiding behind the dumpster, but zero protection from Terry's firing position behind the cruiser.

Terry switched to the right rear taillight of the cruiser and watched as both passenger doors opened. The distance to the target was less than twenty yards. Terry concentrated on the front passenger door first. Once he was down, the man at the rear door had nowhere to hide. *Bang, Bang.* The first man went down in a spray of blood and brains. Terry switched targets. *Bang, Bang.* The guy in the backseat went down in a heap. He had to verify the driver was dead or dying and if there was another guy in the backseat. He didn't hear any firing, and he didn't see any feet under the vehicle.

Terry came out from behind the cruiser, weapon to his shoulder, and pointed at the SUV. As soon as his body was exposed, the right rear window of the Expedition exploded. Someone fired at Terry from the backseat, and he was caught in no man's land: two steps in front of the cruiser and seven steps from the back of the Expedition. *I'm dead.*

CHAPTER 28

"Are you avoiding me, Commander?" a female voice said. It was the Mayor of the City of Chicago, and she was standing in the doorway of Moriarty's basement office at the Emergency Operations Center. The EOC hadn't been around that long, so most people weren't familiar with the building itself, let alone the basement where the SWAT Commander had set up an office. Rocco Moriarty knew his role as the senior officer for all tactical operations would require him to spend a lot of time at the EOC, so he found an unoccupied space in the basement and built himself a second office complete with desk, phone, coffee maker, and even a folding cot he could sleep on, if needed. The big man rose to address the mayor.

"No, Ms. Mayor," Rocco said. "I've been on the go, to and from the hospital. I just got back here," he lied. He had been avoiding her. Less than two hours ago, he put a spike in the military operations that the mayor not only supported but requested. He was trying to buy Terry Davis as much time as he could before the special operations team was let loose on the city.

"You're a shitty liar, Rocco," the mayor said. She stepped into his tiny office and sat in a metal chair older than she was. "I asked for the

Army to come in here for a reason, not to sit in hotel rooms on the city's dime. Why aren't they getting set up?"

"Ma'am," Rocco started. The mayor gave him a look of disapproval. "Sorry. Ms. Mayor, I know you wanted this, and I know the former Superintendent supported it, but I don't."

"You afraid someone is going to come here and piss in your pool?" the mayor asked. She had a foul mouth in private.

"Actually," Moriarty said, "that is exactly what I'm afraid of." The mayor squinted at him. "This isn't me worried about my job or worried about my team. This is me worried about any city in America bringing the military in to do law enforcement."

"It's not up for discussion," the mayor said. "So, get off your ass and get them operating." She stood. "You know, Rocco, if that is really what you are worried about, I can accept it. But don't let me find out this is a dick measuring contest between you and the Army."

"Yes, ma'am." That time, he said it to piss her off. She turned and looked at him.

"Just so you know," the mayor said with ice in her voice, "I already have another Superintendent picked. And it isn't you." She paused. "People in this city think I'm clueless," the mayor continued. "Just some dumb woman who got elected because I have long legs and a nice ass. I fit all the stereotypes: female, pretty, fit, black. I was even a college cheerleader. You probably knew that." Moriarty stood motionless and expressionless. "But you know what, Commander? I graduated from an Ivy League school with a degree in political science. I have two master's degrees and a doctorate. You probably knew that, too. You don't get where I am just by having a nice ass, Commander."

"I never assumed you did," Moriarty said and folded his arms.

"Sure, you did," the mayor said, standing in the doorway. "Everyone does. They make all kinds of assumptions. Do you know how many times I've been called a lesbian because I'm not married?" There was no animosity in her voice; she stated everything as fact. "I'm an expert at playing the game. That's how I ended up behind the Mayor's desk. But I'm not staying there forever. Be careful which fights you pick, Commander, and who you pick them with." She turned and began walking out of the tiny office. "Did you know the Army is bringing helicopters, too?" she said over her shoulder. "They should be landing any minute." The mayor walked out of the tiny office. "Get moving, Commander!" she yelled from down the hall.

Helicopters. You've got to be fucking kidding me. His first thought went to AH-64 Apache attack helicopters. He knew no one would authorize that, and there was no use for their weaponry on this type of mission. Moriarty stopped himself from jumping to conclusions. He picked up the phone, thought better of it, and put the handset back on the receiver. *Might as well go to the source.* He got up from his desk and headed to the main floor of the EOC. He bought Terry a couple of hours, and he would try to buy him a few more.

Walking into the operations center was like déjà vu. The dispatcher covering the South Side was standing in an aisle with his laptop in his hands, and the same cluster of people in civilian clothes was setting up equipment on his desk. Dave Boyd saw Moriarty walk in and moved directly to him.

"Your boss just told us to get to work," Boyd said with a smug look. "I guess you got outranked."

"It happens," Moriarty said. "Everyone has a boss, even you." Moriarty made eye contact with Officer Baker, the shift leader, and waved him over. "I heard you guys have some helicopters coming. I wasn't aware. Care to fill me in?" Baker heard the tail end of Moriarty's question.

"It's a pair of Little Birds," Boyd said, offering no detail and making the mistake that Rocco wasn't familiar with the airframe.

"MH-6's?" Moriarty asked. Boyd didn't hide his surprise well. "Not armed, correct? Just the pods on the sides for your guys?"

"Yeah," Boyd said. "That's right. Infil and exfil birds. We are connecting with the FAA and will run our A2C2 from here." He spat the acronym out, again testing what Moriarty knew.

"What airfield are they operating out of?" Moriarty asked and didn't wait for an answer. "And I assume you'll coordinate for any other helipads in the city? Any flights between buildings or below one hundred feet will have to be coordinated with our air team. They are over there." Moriarty was pummeling him with information. "There are no landings inside the city unless the area is secured by CPD or at an authorized helipad. You'll be responsible for any FOD damage caused by your aircraft, and everyone in the city will be filing claims with CPD when they see you guys flying around. I send all those directly to you. Your aircraft will be required to operate on our frequency. You can get that from the air team as well." Boyd tried to break in, but Moriarty cut him off.

"I'll need your frequencies for all your internal communications," Rocco said. "And I am sure you have some restriction about giving us one of your radios, so I'll post one of my guys here at your station to keep us all updated. I'll call maintenance to help you get an antenna on the roof. Baker, call them. Shouldn't take more than an hour." Boyd kept trying to get a word in, but Moriarty was ahead of him. "I hope you have about four hundred feet of cable. And I'm the only one authorized to use a cell phone in here. There are no weapons in the EOC and no tobacco use. And no open drink containers. I think you found the break room with the coffee earlier? Good. Anything I can help you with, I'll be right down there with the shift leader." Moriarty turned to walk away, and Boyd grabbed the big man's arm.

"I don't know who you're used to dealing with, but we ain't them," Boyd said. "And we already established that I'm not working for you, I'm working for the mayor, and she is a phone call away. So, quit playing fuck around and just give me what I need."

"First things first," Moriarty said, "if you fucking touch me again, you're going to get a one-way trip to the fucking hospital. And I can promise not a single officer in this room will side with you, so don't make that mistake again. Second, the mayor already told me she isn't promoting me, so I've got nothing to fucking lose. Call her. I don't give a shit." Moriarty outmaneuvered the Army officer. Unlike him, Moriarty wasn't bound to his job by anything other than personal duty. If he got fired, so be it; he was trying to buy Terry a little more time.

Rocco Moriarty walked down to Officer Baker, who was standing at his desk, phone in hand. Baker looked at the SWAT Commander with a grin.

"Sir," Baker said. "What the hell was all that? A2C2? FOD? I don't even know what that shit means."

"A2C2 is Army Airspace Command and Control. Two A's and two C's. It's air traffic control. FOD is short for Foreign Object Damage. If they get too low, the rotors from those helos are going to blow rocks and trash and shit all over the place. Tends to break windows and cause other damage." Baker had a curious look on his face. "He was trying to play 'Who's smarter than who' with me. And he lost." Baker laughed. Moriarty turned around to watch what was going on. The Army contingent had their systems set up on the desk and were now busy running cables. One of their guys was talking to the people at the air team desk. Boyd just decided to put his head down and make progress for now. Moriarty looked around and didn't see the Detachment Commander.

"I've been standing here holding this phone, pretending to call maintenance for those antennas for five minutes," Baker said. "Sooner or later, they are going to catch on. I know you said it was better if I don't know what is going on, but I have to ask again."

"And I stand by my previous statement, Baker," Moriarty said. "I'm going to find that Boyd guy." The big SWAT Commander walked back up the aisle toward the back of the room and then walked out into the lobby. He saw Boyd standing in a corner, facing the windows, and talking on a cell phone. It was getting dark. Moriarty walked toward the man slowly. He could hear Boyd's voice echoing off the glass.

"Yes, Sir," Boyd said into the phone. "We are on the ground and setting up...No, Sir...only minor complications from the locals...we haven't connected with them yet...No, Sir. No intel on him yet...No, nothing. We should be operational in a couple of hours. Yes, Sir, I understand...See you then." Boyd turned to find Moriarty staring at him. The Army commander hung up the cell phone. "Is there a problem?"

"Just curious who you're talking to if you work for the mayor," Rocco said. "They didn't put a federal umbrella over you. No FBI or anything, so you're working for the city and the mayor. So, who are you reporting to?" Rocco was playing a dangerous game. He knew the old Superintendent was out of the loop now that he had resigned. It wasn't the mayor because Boyd kept saying 'Sir.' It could easily have been Boyd's boss at Fort Bragg or wherever he came from, but Moriarty wanted to see his reaction more than anything.

"What?" Boyd feigned innocence. "That's none of your business." Moriarty went all in.

"I know who it was," Rocco said. "It was Smith. The guy in the grey suit." Boyd fought hard to hide his surprise and failed, but he quickly regained his composure. The Army officer stood erect and walked past Moriarty and back into the EOC.

"Thought so," Rocco said quietly. He moved quickly down to his basement office and grabbed the secure messaging phone. There was no bubble over the app. No word yet from Terry. He hesitated for a moment, trying to decide how to send a message to Terry, assuming the Army would have hacked into their secure network if they hadn't already. He typed as quickly as his sausage-sized fingers would allow.

W65: TIME IS SHORT. CASPER ON HIS WAY. CHUCK NORRIS CONNECTED.

It was the best Rocco could think of. Casper was a reference to Smith being a spook of some sort. Chuck Norris played a team leader in the movie Delta Force. All Moriarty could do was hope Terry understood. The big man locked the phone inside his desk—no sense giving anyone snooping around a free opportunity to get hold of it. Moriarty closed the office door behind him and walked up the stairs and back into the EOC. The normally quiet atmosphere was buzzing with activity. *What kind of trouble can I cause now?* he thought to himself.

CHAPTER 29

Terry dove onto the ground as a reflex. He thought for sure that when the glass broke in the rear passenger window of the big SUV, he was dead. The aging combat veteran scrambled on his hands and knees to the Ford Expedition. He knew if he tried to go back behind the cruiser, he was giving the shooter another opportunity to engage him. Crawling forward, while somewhat counterintuitive, gave him the best chance at survival. He stayed low, out of the shooter's line of sight, and stopped behind the right rear tire.

Terry used to have a speech that he gave new lieutenants when they arrived at his battalion about what it was like in a firefight. Terry used to tell them that the first time you got shot at was like the first time you got punched in the face; you'd see that bright flash behind your eyes and lose situational awareness, and all you were trying to do was survive. The more times you got into a fight and the more times you took that punch, the quicker you could regain your senses and fight back. When you were fighting in a bar or on the street, you were worried about yourself, or maybe you and your buddy. When you were a platoon leader and a firefight started, you had thirty-five guys you had to worry about, and their lives depended on how quickly you could regain your senses and fight back.

He was amazed during his two years in command how few of the young officers had ever been in a real fistfight when they were teenagers. He couldn't count how many he and Jimmy had gotten into, and how many more he had gotten into while in college. For the younger generation, it just wasn't common to settle things with your fists like when he was young. It was discouraging to find out how few officers had that kind of experience growing up. He always closed the discussion about realistic training, training hard, and that the Army was a full-contact sport. It was better to get punched in the face in training, so you learned how to fight back when it counted most. The last thing he would tell the young officer was, 'When in doubt, *keep moving, keep shooting.*'

Terry had that in the back of his mind as he got his feet under him, leaning against the tire of the big Ford. Terry laid his rifle on the pavement, drew the big FN pistol from its holster, and moved around the back of the vehicle in a crouch. Terry held the pistol close to his chest, keeping the smallest silhouette possible. Looking around the left rear corner, Terry could see the side mirror, but couldn't see the condition of the driver inside. He assumed the man was dead from the two rifle rounds that shattered the windshield, but he wasn't positive. As Terry cleared the back corner and started to move along the rear fender, he saw Frank come out from behind the dumpster and start jogging toward the SUV.

Terry held up a hand, giving Frank the 'stop' sign. The security guard froze in the open ground. Just as Terry started to stand, the rear passenger door opened, and the fourth man came out with a Heckler and Koch MP5 submachine gun in his hands. It was an iconic piece of hardware, carried by someone in every nineties action movie from Bruce Willis to Mel Gibson. The man set one foot on the ground and raised the German weapon to his shoulder, focused solely on Frank. Terry probably could have taken the man prisoner, but he chose not to. Instead, he put a forty-five caliber round through the back of the man's head, dropping him to the concrete.

The man was careless, or inexperienced, or probably both. Just a few seconds before, he shot at Terry through the window of the vehicle and then lost track of him. When he got out of the vehicle, he never checked behind him; he just got out and focused on Frank, allowing Terry to kill him easily. *Maybe they are running out of professionals.* Terry carefully cleared the back of the Ford, ensuring there was no one else hiding or still breathing. The driver was missing his face. Terry guessed the bullet started to tumble after it broke through the double-layered windshield glass and hit the man's face while turning end over end.

Terry heard Frank's footsteps and turned, aiming the pistol at the pale-faced security guard. As soon as Frank saw the two men on the driver's side, and the mess Terry's handiwork had made of their heads, he puked on the parking lot pavement. Terry did a quick check of the four men around the vehicle while Frank regained his composure and what was left of his dignity. All had various tattoos on their arms, necks, and faces. These were straight gangbangers, no pros here.

"You OK?" Terry asked Frank, the security guard.

"You're not a cop, are you?" Frank said with some puke still on his chin. "Cops don't fire first like that. You didn't try to arrest them or anything."

"You saw my badge, right?" Terry asked in a futile attempt to convince Frank he was a cop. Frank just stared at him. "Listen, I'm working with the police. These are gang members, and I knew if I didn't kill them, they would kill us. They would have killed you, Frank."

"I know," Frank said quietly.

"I need you to wait before you tell anyone about this," Terry said, "before you call anyone, OK?" Frank looked resigned to whatever Terry wanted.

"Sure," Frank said, fighting another dry heave. "And you don't have to put in a good word for me. I don't think I'm cut out to be a cop." Terry chuckled.

"A man's got to know his limitations," Terry said, quoting Clint Eastwood. Frank didn't show any sign of recognizing the infamous line from Magnum Force. "Are there cameras that point out here?"

"Yeah, one. On the corner of the building," Frank said.

"Do me a favor," Terry said. "I'm going to take off. Take your time and erase that camera footage. Then wait about half an hour. Then call the cops. Tell them you heard shooting and just found these guys out here." Frank nodded. Terry walked over to the man. "I'd shake your hand, but I don't want any puke on me. You're a good man, Frank."

Terry jogged back to the cruiser, stopping to pick up his AR from behind the Expedition. He closed all the doors and drove back through the lot. Terry's adrenaline was up, but he could feel the aches in his body coming back as he drove. He added his right knee to the list of aches and pains after diving on the ground between the two vehicles. In a bit of gallows humor, Terry thought by the end of the night, he would either have time to recover or he wouldn't have to worry about aches and pains ever again. A grim smile came over his face.

After ten minutes of driving, Terry reached into the console and grabbed the secure messaging phone. Driving with one hand and manipulating the phone with the other, Terry could see he was back inside the repeater coverage area for the secure messaging app. The little bubble over the app icon had a small '3' indicating three messages were waiting for him. He touched the app with his thumb, glancing up to keep the police vehicle between the lane lines. The app opened, and Terry could see the three messages in the inbox.

W65: SECURE COMMS MAY BE VULNERABLE. USE CAUTION.

W65: TIME IS SHORT. CASPER ON HIS WAY. CHUCK NORRIS CONNECTED.

UNK: SHOULD BE MORE CAREFUL. YOU WERE WARNED. SEE YOU SOON – SMITH.

"Fuck!" Terry said, slamming his hand on the steering wheel. He reread the messages. The first message was valid based on the third message from Smith. Terry knew the secure phone was useless at this point. His only communication with Moriarty now was the handheld radio that he knew everyone was monitoring, including Smith and his people. The second message took Terry a minute to decipher. The 'received' times for all three messages were all from six minutes ago, when he got back into repeater range. He had no idea when they were sent.

Terry didn't know how much time he had because he didn't know when the message was sent. He could only assume he needed to hurry.

The 'Casper' reference was pretty easy. He had referred to Smith as a spook, so Moriarty was warning him that Smith was on his way to Chicago and might already be there. Chuck Norris took him a few minutes to understand. Terry wracked his brain for every movie reference he could.

"Missing in Action. No. Lone Wolf McQuade. No. Enter the Dragon? Not that either," Terry was tapping the steering wheel and thinking. "Dammit. C'mon, Terry. Think." It came to him. "Delta Force. Of course." Moriarty was telling him the Army special ops commander was connected to Smith, as they had assumed. Terry had a decision to make: Hit the stakeout building or not?

The ultimate goal was to get the Army engaged on the piece of terrain he knew was best for him, that strip of land between the aquarium and the planetarium. He could drive there and send a message to Smith saying, 'Come and get me.' That would allow them to plan and set the conditions they wanted on the timeline they wanted. He needed them to chase him to that piece of terrain. They didn't know it as well as he did, and he didn't want to allow them to analyze it. They started following his trail of breadcrumbs; the attempted ambush in the parking lot with Frank the security guard proved that. His apartment, the parking lot. There had to be another breadcrumb for them to follow.

Deep down in Terry's soul, he wanted to kill anyone and everyone inside that building. They tried to kill Jimmy and Dana. It was a weak moment, but he succumbed and talked himself into hitting the building, but not killing everyone as he felt they deserved. It was the last breadcrumb that would get them to follow him the rest of the way into the city and out onto that little strip of land. He made the decision. Good or bad, he justified it in his head.

"Now, I'm Hansel and fucking Gretel," he said out loud. The metaphor wasn't exactly accurate. The German kids wandering through the woods left a trail of breadcrumbs to find their way home. Terry was leaving a trail to be followed by Smith's people, the Army, and hopefully Smith himself. This was going to turn into a movie car chase like Bullitt, The French Connection, or Ronin. Terry intended to dish out some payback to the folks in the stakeout building; unfortunately, killing them all was counterproductive. He needed some of them to survive and alert the rest, then follow him to the lakefront. Somewhere along the way, he would make the frantic call over the SWAT radio that he needed help. It would be monitored, he knew, by Rocco and his team, but also by the Army and whoever Smith had in the area.

When to make the radio call wasn't something Davis had time to plan, which was against his instincts. If Terry were sitting in a sterile or protected planning environment, he would have timed this out to the minute if he had the correct data. Even that type of planning needed some gut instinct when it came to application. Terry used to refer to it as 'where the science of warfare meets the art.' He remembered an exercise when he was a captain, coordinating direct fires while attacking a fixed position. He and his lieutenants analyzed the terrain on topographic maps, estimated their rate of march, how long it would take to call on the radio and request fires, how long it would take the artillery to process the request and fire, and even the time of flight for the artillery rounds.

They did all this in planning. Artillery rounds from two different cannons: 155mm. and 105mm. Mortars from two different tubes: 81mm and 60mm. The idea was to coordinate their movement with the use of the gradually shrinking fires hitting the enemy, the burst radius of the impacting rounds getting progressively smaller as they approached to initiate a ground assault. Fire big rounds until you couldn't get any closer, then smaller rounds to get closer, then again, and again, with the intent being the ground force never actually stopped moving, and the enemy was constantly bombarded while they approached. One of Terry's lieutenants was brilliant, a math major who graduated from an Ivy League school. He made most of the calculations in his head. The young officer understood the science of what they were planning.

While the planning required data, timing, and precision, Terry could not convince the young math wizard, or any of the other lieu-tenants, that it was never as simple as drawing timing lines and trig-gers on a map. This wasn't a pool table, flat and clean; this was undulating terrain that would change and shift their speed and even their route to the objective. Terry and his team ran through a daytime rehearsal of the exercise, no real artillery rounds being shot; basically, it was a walk in the woods while talking on the radio. As expected, that rehearsal went smooth as silk. The young Stanford lieutenant could hardly contain his smug attitude, feeling he had proved his boss wrong.

Later the same day, Terry's leadership team walked through the exercise with real artillery landing in front of them. Anticipating this iteration wouldn't go as smoothly as the first, Terry kept his radio close at hand. He could see the lead lieutenant calling and adjusting the artillery as they moved through the woods. Still, Terry was listening to the radio and paying attention to the rhythm of the artillery. There were slight delays in the timing it took the artillery unit to process their data and adjust their firing. Terry's planning estimates were based on inaccurate times given to them by the artillery unit; he knew he would have to make adjustments on the fly. If they strictly followed their execution times, without paying attention to what was happening, the delays in processing firing data would eventually have them walking into incoming artillery rounds.

Terry let the art meet the science in his head and adjusted while they were moving, adjusting fires earlier than scheduled to account for the delay. His Stanford lieutenant protested on the radio to the point Terry had to break procedure and tell him to shut up and get off the net. After the exercise was over, the Major who was overseeing the artillery fires told Terry and his team they had been the best company to execute the exercise. Their timing was as close to perfect as possible. Terry just thanked the higher-ranking officer and, once he had his team alone, reiterated the necessity of using your experience to adjust to a well-laid-out plan. 'The world is not a pool table,' he reminded them, and nothing ever goes as planned.

Terry rapidly went through the variables in his head: response time by Rocco and his guys, traffic leading to the University campus, the response time from the Army, and how many of Smith's 'gangbangers' would be following him. The list was too extensive even to make a base plan to adjust from. Terry would have to make the call and stay alive as long as he could.

"Hell of a plan, Terry," he said to himself.

CHAPTER 30

Dana sat quietly in her hospital room, watching the world outside grow slowly darker as the sun went down. The hospital staff had been in and out of her room, regularly checking on her, but she hadn't seen Mary since she walked out a few hours ago. She quietly wondered how long it would be before her best friend returned. Dana replayed Mary's words in her head over and over; *You're a bitch.* She wasn't wrong. Whether all this was Terry's fault or not was arguable, but he didn't deserve the treatment Dana gave him. Dana looked at the SWAT officer sitting in a chair against the wall, directly opposite the foot of her hospital bed.

"Can you find Mary for me?" she asked. The young man looked up at her, then rose from his chair and stuck his head out the heavy hospital room door. He spoke to the two men standing outside the door, then returned to his seat. It was over fifteen minutes before Mary came into the room. Dana could tell by the look on her face that all was not forgiven. "Can you give us a minute?" Dana said to the SWAT Officer.

"Ma'am," he responded, "I'm supposed to stay here…"

"I'm here," Mary cut him off. "I'll get you before I leave." The

SWAT Officer nodded and walked out. She turned to Dana. "What is it?"

"You're not going to make this easy," Dana said. Mary stared at her. "I was wrong. I shouldn't have said that to Terry."

"He is the one that needs to hear that," Mary said, "not me."

"I know," Dana admitted. "Where is he?"

"Gone," Mary said flatly. Dana looked confused. "He went to *fix this.* Those are his words, and I have a pretty good idea what he has in mind."

"Fix what?" Dana asked.

"*This!* All of this," Mary said, holding her hands to her sides. "He is going to find Smith and whoever else he can find, or thinks is responsible."

"And what is that going to do?" Dana asked. She was being incredibly naïve after everything they had been through.

"He's going to kill them, Dana," Mary said, connecting the dots for her. "That's what Terry does. Smith and his people tried to kill all of us. And they killed my parents. For Terry, there is only one solution to that problem."

"Can't you just go arrest him?" Dana asked.

"Smith?" Mary responded. It wasn't a real question. "For what? And even if we did, then what? He is connected Dana, to people we probably don't even know about. You don't arrest someone like him."

"But Terry killed that General in Florida, and that didn't change anything," Dana said. "So how does this change anything? And how does this all end?"

"I don't know," Mary said in a softer tone. Dana looked at her for more. "Even if Terry kills Smith, I don't know how this all ends. All I know is that he is doing this for all of us. To protect us."

"*The Great Protector,*" Dana said, quoting herself. Mary shook her head. "He doesn't care what happens to himself, does he?"

"Not even a little," Mary said. "If he thinks it is the right thing to do, there is no changing his mind, damn the consequences. That's why he is so beat up, his body. And his head."

"That's what Mom said to me," Dana said. Mary looked at her.

"She said life has been hard on him, and he has been even harder on himself. That was his cross to bear. She told me to be patient and that he would come around. Do you think he will ever come around? Forget whatever demons he is fighting?"

"No," Mary said. "Terry isn't a man who can be changed. And he damn sure can't be fixed. You either love him for who he is or get as far away from him as you can." Dana looked out the window. The sky was dark. Dana knew Mary was begging a decision out of her.

"Then what do we do?" Dana asked, still looking out the window.

"Well, I am going to help him in any way I can," Mary said. "Right after I figure out how to get out of here without Moriarty's guys finding out. What are you going to do?"

"Come see me before you go," Dana said. Mary knew her friend was struggling internally, trying to decide what to do. She chose not to push Dana too hard.

"I will," Mary said as she walked toward the door.

"Mary," Dana called out as her friend reached for the doorknob. Mary turned back. "How's Jimmy?" Mary paused for a second.

"He's going to be OK," Mary said.

"Good," Dana said. There were a thousand other things she wanted to tell her best friend, but she didn't. Mary walked out and was quickly replaced by the SWAT Officer, who resumed his position in the chair across from her bed.

Dana stared quietly out the window and thought about Terry. She didn't even know how she felt about him, whether she was falling in love with him or not. There was an obvious physical attraction, and he was more intelligent than any man she had met in the last ten years. She would admit, although only to herself, that her track record with men was unquestionably bad. Dana never had a man hit her like Mary did, but she had never been with a man like Terry, who would go to the ends of the earth to protect her, either. She never considered herself to be a woman who needed protecting, but the idea of having someone willing to do it was certainly appealing. She made a decision.

"I'm sorry," she said to the SWAT Officer. "Can you please go get Mary again?" The man exhaled deeply in frustration but hauled his frame out of the chair and went to the door. A few moments later, Mary reappeared. This time, the SWAT Officer didn't need to be asked; he just left the two women alone in the hospital room. Mary stood in front of Dana and crossed her arms.

"Have you figured out how to get out of here?" the nurse asked her police detective friend.

"Not yet," Mary said.

"Have you heard anything?" Dana asked. "About Terry, I mean."

"Nothing yet," Mary said. She knew Dana wanted to say something, but was stalling.

"And you said Jimmy is going to be OK?" Dana asked.

"Jesus Christ, Dana," Mary said. "What is it? You've got something on your mind. Just say it."

"Can you stop being his biggest fan for five minutes?" Dana said. "And just be my best friend?" Mary hadn't realized the predicament this was putting both her and Dana in. To Mary, it was a no-brainer; Terry wasn't a man you had to 'think about.'

"I'm sorry," Mary said. "You're right."

"Mary, he is a good man. I know he is. Watching him with you and your family, who've known him all his life, I can see it," Dana said. "But all of this…"

"It's a lot, I know," Mary said, comforting her friend.

"You know your boyfriend? The one that hit you?" Dana said. She was breaking Terry's confidence, but she needed to work all this out. Mary nodded. "It was Terry who scared him off. He didn't leave. Terry threatened him with a knife in the middle of the night."

"I don't understand," Mary said. "I mean, I understand it was Terry. I always assumed he had something to do with it, but I don't understand how that relates to all of this."

"That's not normal, Mary," Dana said. "There is something admirable in it, sure. But you don't threaten people like that. Normal people don't do that." Mary smiled.

"Dana," she said. "Terry is far from normal. What he did for me, he would do for anyone he loves. That isn't me being a fangirl. That is the truth. Terry isn't perfect. He is broken, physically and mentally. But, honestly, he is extraordinary. You have to decide if you want normal or extraordinary." Dana's eyes were filling with tears. She sniffled and wiped her eyes.

"Thank you," she said. Mary nodded and walked toward the door.

"Mary," Dana said. Mary paused and looked at her friend lying in the hospital bed. "Find me some clothes and a medical bag."

CHAPTER 31

Terry stopped a few blocks from the stakeout building and got his gear settled. He swapped the steel plates for ceramic, strapped on his war belt with his Ek combat knife, and put his bump helmet with the PVS-14 night vision monocular attached on the passenger seat. He was carrying six full magazines for his AR-15 spread between the body armor and war belt, along with two spare magazines for the FNX-45 and the four flashbang grenades. On the floor of the passenger side was the breeching tool; he would grab that last. The last two things Terry did were to throw on his dog tags with his Saint Michael's medal and slip his Benchmade mechanical knife into his pants pocket. Terry didn't consider himself superstitious about anything but those two items. He had them with him for every combat operation he had ever been on, and he was still alive, so why tempt fate?

Terry knew his only entry point without climbing the fence was the large gate in front. He wasn't trying to be particularly stealthy; this operation was meant to attract attention, so he opted for the most direct approach. Terry parked the police cruiser outside the front gate, set up for a quick getaway, and climbed out. The sidewalk was empty on this cold night, so a man dressed in body armor and strapping on a variety of weapons and tactical gear wasn't drawing any attention. He put on his helmet, grabbed his rifle and the breeching tool, and steadied himself for the havoc he was about to wreak.

Terry came through the big gates and could see lights on inside the building. He approached quickly from the road and set himself next to the door. In a perfect world, Terry would be part of a four or eight-man stack, with a platoon ready to come in behind him. Not tonight, though. He was on his own. Terry paused for a second, listening for any commotion that would let him know if the people inside had been alerted to his presence. He heard music. At first, it was tough to make out; it sounded like a symphony, but he quickly realized someone inside was blaring Kashmir by Led Zeppelin.

"They're playing my song," Terry said with an evil smile.

He jammed the teeth of the breeching tool between the metal door and frame and yanked. The door pried open with the sound of twisting metal. Terry dropped the tool and, putting his rifle to his shoulder, entered the building. The music was louder than he antici-pated when he was outside; he doubted anyone heard the door open. The exterior door led into what used to be a foyer. There was a service desk and a couple of office spaces, one on each side. Everything he saw was bare of any paperwork or other evidence of being used. He kept moving toward the music.

The next door he came to was already open and led into the garage area of the building. Terry paused and looked into the cavernous space. It was big enough to fit a half dozen tractor-trailers, with garage doors on both sides. He could see the roofs of five different pickup trucks, each in a different color and manufacturer. He caught himself singing along with Robert Plant as he wailed away. He moved quickly in a crouch, bracing for contact with the enemy as he did. He could see open space behind the pickups and moved toward it as the most likely location for any people in the building.

Terry paused at the bumper of the last truck, a white Ford, and peered around the fender. Four men were sitting on garage sale couches and drinking beer like they were at a college party, except they all had weapons within arm's reach. Terry readied a flashbang and tossed it sidearm right in the middle of the four men, ducking back behind the truck.

BOOM.

Terry came out shooting. Three of the men dove when the grenade came in, but one froze on the couch. He was the first to catch two rounds from Terry's rifle. Terry shifted quickly to the man closest to him. The rifle barked again. Terry transitioned to the only other man still in view, blowing his head apart. Stepping sideways and trying to find the fourth man, Terry saw three more men. They had been shielded from his view by the trucks, but all three were close enough to feel the effects of the flashbang—b*ang, bang.* Terry's shots were in rapid succession and always in pairs, just like he had been trained.

Keep moving, keep shooting. Terry was still trying to find the last man from the group on the couch when he heard a burst of automatic fire coming from his left. Terry looked straight across the five truck beds to see a man firing an AK-47 wildly on full automatic. Terry moved to the fender of the white Ford and fired over the bedrail. *Bang, bang.* The man with the AK went down. Moving again, Terry spied movement out of his peripheral vision. The man running away from him went down in a heap, two shots to the back—*Bang, bang.*

Terry's blood was up, and he could feel the fear permeating the building. Six men down and two unaccounted for. He didn't know how many more were in the building, but he felt he had accomplished his mission. *Time to go.* Terry turned and moved around the front of the Ford, ending up chest to chest with a big man in a red shirt. Terry's momentum beat the bigger man's mass, knocking him to the ground and the rifle out of Terry's hands. The AR was spinning on its sling while Terry stood over the bigger man, empty-handed. Davis drew his pistol and pumped two rounds of forty-five caliber into the big man's torso, then a third into his head.

Keep moving, keep shooting. Terry pinned the rifle to his body armor with one hand, holding his pistol in the other. He moved quickly toward the door. Gunfire from behind the trucks shattered one of the windshields. Terry fired five rounds blindly from his pistol as he went through the door and into the empty office area. He shoved the pistol back in its holster and untangled his rifle, pausing briefly to listen. It was impossible to hear over the music, so Terry fired two more shots through the open door, striking the truck with the shattered windshield. He turned and ran through the exterior door, almost tripping over his breeching tool. *No time for that now.*

Terry ran toward the gate, taking his helmet off as he ran. He knew he couldn't get in the police cruiser with it on, let alone drive. As he rounded the corner of the gate, he could hear one of the garage doors opening, the music getting louder as it did. Terry grabbed the handle of the driver's door and yanked it open, tossing his helmet into the passenger seat and flipping the sling from the AR over his head, freeing it from his body. The rifle went into the floor on the other side of the console, barrel pointed down. Terry climbed in, starting the engine and putting the black SUV into gear as he closed the door. He squealed the tires as he pulled out from the parking spot, watching two pickup trucks come out of the lot behind him. *Bingo.*

Terry knew he could use the lights and sirens to make time through traffic, but that wasn't the point, at least for now. He wanted these guys chasing him, and it was working. He was weaving through traffic, heading toward the city. Keeping the two trucks in his rearview, never getting too far ahead or losing visual contact with them. He just hoped to God they didn't pass any real police cars that might scare these guys off. *Hope is not a course of action.*

Terry reached into the console and pulled out the secure messaging phone. The app had a '1' on it; there was an incoming message. Terry tapped the screen with his thumb, briefly looking up at the road in front of him, into his rearview to make sure the trucks were still there, then back at the phone. The message had loaded onto the screen.

W65: READY WHEN YOU ARE.

It was Rocco. It sounded to Terry like the cavalry was ready whenever he gave the call. Terry dumped the phone onto the passenger seat and grabbed the radio, putting it into the cupholder. He looked back; the trucks were still following him. He turned hard left across traffic and guided the SUV onto the ramp for the interstate that took him into the city. Interstate Fifty-Five, or I-55, as the locals called it, essentially dead-ended into Highway 41, better known as Lake Shore Drive when you were heading east into the city. The interstate would fade, either right or left, as it reached McCormick Place, the large convention center that was south of the Museum Campus cluster. It was a straight shot.

CHAPTER 32

SWAT Commander Rocco Moriarty walked onto the main floor of the Emergency Operations Center and into a flurry of activity. The west side desk officer was chattering away into her headset. The south side desk had been relocated with her after the Army contingent kicked him out of his workspace. He was also chattering away, but leaning over and peeking at her screen as he talked. Something was going on that was crossing boundaries. Rocco looked at the soldiers, off to the right of the operations center floor. They were chattering away as well. Rocco walked straight to Officer Baker, the shift leader who had less than an hour left in his twelve-hour shift before he changed out with the next person on duty.

"Officer Baker!" Moriarty called out as he moved closer. The watch officer turned and saw the big man coming.

"Sir, I was just trying to call your office downstairs," Baker said.

"What the hell is going on?" Moriarty asked.

"Reports of a shootout in the southwest," Baker said, putting the phone down. "Three vehicles moving into the city." Moriarty nodded. "Sir, you need to fill me in on what is going on."

"And why is that, Officer Baker?" Moriarty was getting irritated with the repeated question.

"Because one of the vehicles is yours," Baker said quietly. Moriarty cringed. At least he knew where Terry was and what he was up to. Rocco knew if the plates came over the radio, there was no way to keep this quiet. It was only a matter of time before the mayor showed up asking 'What the fuck?.' Moriarty determined quickly that he could use this to Terry's advantage.

"I've got this," Moriarty said to Officer Baker. "I'll get my guys together and we will intercept. Keep me posted on the vehicle location."

"Did someone steal your vehicle?" Baker said.

"Must have," Moriarty said with zero innocence in his voice. "What's the Army up to?"

"They got clearance from the mayor to do something they called V-I," Baker said. "So, they are getting their folks spun up. What's V-I?"

"Vehicle Interdiction," Rocco said. "Are they coordinating with our Air Team?"

"Yes, Sir," Baker replied. "Looks like they are planning on using their helicopters."

"Lovely," Rocco replied with sarcasm. "Call the hospital and get O'Donnell on the phone." Baker grabbed the black handset and dialed. Moriarty was thinking while he was waiting for Baker to get his second in command on the line. The SWAT Commander surveyed the room. There were only two people left at the Army desk, and a third was over talking to his Air Team. The rest were gone, probably gearing up somewhere. Baker handed him the phone.

"O'Donnell," Moriarty said into the receiver. "Get everyone loaded up. Leave three to watch over Jimmy...bring them too...yes, both of them. Rally at Public Safety Headquarters." Rocco hung up the phone and looked at Officer Baker. "You're not going home. Stay on shift until I say otherwise. When your replacement gets here, keep her on as well. I have a feeling shit is going to be crazy tonight, and it will take both of you to manage."

"Yes, Sir," Baker said without a flinch.

"Call the Mayor," Moriarty said. "Tell her I need to meet her at Public Safety. Don't let her say no." Baker nodded. Rocco walked out of the room and down to his office. He grabbed the secure messaging phone and his bag full of gear. He didn't anticipate putting on his kit tonight, but better safe than sorry. He was in the lobby and on his way out of the building when Baker caught him.

"Sir!" Baker yelled. Moriarty turned. "Two things. First, the Mayor said she will meet you at Public Safety. She was already home, but she would come in," Moriarty smiled. "Second, the report states that there are now four vehicles heading into the city. Your cruiser and three more. Heading east on I-55."

"Thanks," Moriarty said and walked out to the cruiser he took from O'Donnell. He tossed the gear bag into the back and climbed into the driver's seat. "Where are you going, Airborne Ranger?" he asked out loud. He pulled the secure messaging phone from his shirt pocket. The last message he sent to Terry was unanswered. He began to type.

W65: WHAT DZ ARE YOU HEADED TO?

Rocco knew the phone was probably being monitored, secure or not. Special Operations had much better communications capability than the Chicago PD did, and they likely had intercept capability. This was a long shot, but he needed some idea of where Terry was heading. Moriarty put the phone in the cupholder and drove the blacked-out SWAT cruiser out of the parking lot.

The drive to Public Safety Headquarters was short. He would likely beat his team to the building. He knew Terry was headed east on the Interstate and into the city. Public Safety headquarters was south of the intersection where the highway met Lake Shore Drive. There were dozens of places where Terry could get off the highway before he got to Lake Shore Drive. Moriarty had no idea Terry was planning on staging this performance just north of where the SWAT Team would assemble.

The Mayor's reserved parking spot was empty, so Moriarty stood and waited. The first few members of the SWAT Team started to arrive at the mostly empty parking lot. A blacked-out SUV like O'Donnell's pulled up next to him and rolled down the window. It was the leader of Team 3.

"Hey, boss," the mustached man said. "What the hell's going on?"

"I'll brief you when everyone gets here," Moriarty said, having no idea what he was going to tell everyone when they did. "Until O'Donnell gets here, take control of everyone and have them park at the back of the lot. Tell the Heavy Vehicle team to prepare the two armored cars. Thanks, Three-Six." The team leader nodded and drove to the back of the lot, waving his arm out the window for the few others to follow him. Moriarty watched as more SWAT Officers arrived, clustering together. He felt a touch of melancholy as the big man realized this may be the last operation he runs with these amazing men and women under his command. He hoped it was all worth it.

Rocco squinted as headlights flashed across his eyes. It was the Mayor in her Mercedes. It was her personal car, not the city car, that drove her to official functions. That meant no security and no other CPD with her; she was coming alone. He stepped back, allowing her a clear path into her parking spot. He saw her talking on her phone as she put the vehicle in park and shut off the engine. The mayor stepped out wearing blue jeans, a sweater, and an insulated jacket.

"You know that's illegal, right?" Moriarty said, referencing the mayor driving and using her cell phone.

"I know some judges," she quipped back, "and the district attorney. So, what's so important that the entire SWAT unit is here, and I had to come in?" Moriarty was suspicious. There was little chance the mayor hadn't heard about his vehicle being involved in a shooting and a car chase, and he knew she had authorized the Army to get involved.

"There was a shooting," Rocco said. "Southwest. Suspects are heading into the city."

"What does that have to do with me?" she snapped back.

"Well, you authorized the Army to get involved. I have my folks on standby in case anything happens. I thought you might want to see what you're paying for."

"That's what you called me for? You're fucking kidding me, right?" She lit a cigarette, something she never did in public.

"You nervous about something?" Rocco said, pointing at the cigarette. She stared daggers at him. "Who was on the phone?" She blew smoke into the cold night. "Ms. Mayor, I think we both know what is going on here, and no matter how this goes, you're going to be held responsible. Now, you're coming with me, or I'll be standing in front of the press at sunrise tendering my resignation and blaming you for whatever happens tonight."

"Let's get one thing straight," the mayor said with venom, "come sunrise, you're going to be out of the department, whether you resign or I fire you."

"I can agree to that," Moriarty said. The mayor flicked her cigarette into the night. "That's a two-hundred fifty dollar fine." Moriarty looked at his troops assembled at the back of the parking lot as the two military-style armored vehicles pulled up. O'Donnell was walking toward him.

"Everyone is accounted for," the deputy SWAT Commander called out from about fifteen yards. He had been around long enough to stay away from conversations between his boss and the mayor.

"Thanks," Moriarty replied. "I'll be there in a minute." O'Donnell turned without a word and jogged back to the cops decked out in olive drab uniforms and tactical gear. Moriarty walked past the mayor and grabbed the secure phone from his cup holder. There was a message waiting for him.

W66: WHERE THE STARS AND SEA AND ANIMALS MEET. ETA 10 MINS.

The message was only two minutes old. He thought about Terry's encoded message. He said, 'the sea' and not 'the Lake'. Stars. Animals. *The Museum Campus.* Terry was referring to the Aquarium, Planetarium, and the Field Museum. It was minutes away, and so was he. Moriarty threw the phone down and grabbed his radio.

"EOC, this is Whiskey Six Six," Rocco transmitted.

"Whiskey Six Six, this is EOC. Go ahead." It was Baker.

"I need an update on the inbound vehicles," Moriarty said on the radio.

"Copy Six Six," Baker's voice came through the speaker. "Air Team reports they are about to hit Lake Shore Drive."

"Copy EOC," the SWAT Commander responded. He was standing outside his vehicle, ensuring the mayor could hear. "Let me know if they go north or south. Also, what's the status of the DoD assets?" Moriarty knew Terry was heading north, but he couldn't tip his hand.

"DoD assets have coordinated with Air Team and are ready to

respond," Baker said. He was letting Moriarty know the Army contingent was going to move using their helicopters. "Update on the inbound vehicles. There are now six vehicles moving east." Rocco stood there, staring at the mayor.

"You've got the Army spinning up two helicopters with six shooters each," Commander Moriarty said to his boss. "These guys are planning to do vehicle interdiction in the middle of your city under *your* orders. Do you know what that means?" She didn't say a word; she just lit another cigarette. "That means, this is on *you*. Now, do you want to tell me who was on the phone?" The mayor hesitated. The radio crackled.

"Whiskey Six Six, this is EOC," a female voice called through the radio. It was Baker's replacement as shift leader, Officer Maureen Hanrahan. Moriarty had no personal experience working with her, but her reputation was exceptional. He just hoped she had the same level of discretion and loyalty Baker had been displaying throughout all this.

"This is Whiskey Six Six. Go ahead," Rocco said. He held the radio up in the air, so it was very clear to the mayor.

"Six vehicles went north on Lake Shore Drive," Hanrahan transmitted. "I say again, they are heading north. DoD air assets are launching now. CPD Air Team will come off station to clear airspace for DoD."

"Copy," Moriarty said into the radio. He looked at the mayor. "You see, this is what happens when you get in the middle of this shit. We are losing *our* eye in the sky because you let the Army off its leash. These guys aren't going to follow any police procedures, and they are going to shoot first. The only person held responsible for all this is going to be *you*. Last time I'm going to ask, *who was on the phone?*"

"If you're asking me," the mayor said, "you already know."

"I thought so," Rocco said. "I'm going to brief my people. I suggest you think through how you're going to survive this, both professionally and personally." Moriarty headed toward the back of the parking lot. He heard the mayor flick her cigarette butt into the night. "That's another two-fifty," he called back without looking.

CHAPTER 33

Terry heard the radio traffic between Moriarty and the Emergency Operations Center. He knew they were tracking him as he approached the city using the CPD helicopter. He didn't know there were five vehicles behind him until the EOC said so on the radio. He also didn't know the Army Special Operators had helicopters of their own.

Davis was confident they weren't using CH-47 Chinooks. The big, twin-rotor beasts required a football field to land in, so unless they were setting down in Soldier Field, those were out of the question. They might have been using Blackhawks. The medium lift utility helicopter was the 'do everything' airframe for the military, but even it had some limitations. The main rotor had a fairly wide footprint and would limit where they could land inside the city. If the 160th Special Operations Aviation Regiment were flying them, they would be using special operations variants of the helicopter. Terry had flown a handful of times with the Nightstalkers of the 160th SOAR and was always impressed by their ability and courage to put helicopters into places other pilots wouldn't try. They were the best in the world, without question.

As he weaved through traffic, keeping one eye in his rearview mirror, Terry concluded they were using MH-6s. The tiny helos were affectionately known as 'Little Birds' because they were, in fact, small. Flown exclusively by the Nightstalkers, there were multiple configurations of MH-6, including gunships armed with rockets or miniguns. Terry didn't see the Army conducting 'gun-runs' inside the city, so these aircraft were most likely outfitted with seats on the outside for door-kickers from Delta, the SEALs, or Rangers to ride on. It wasn't something Terry had done himself, but he had seen it more than once in training and combat. He gave those guys credit for huge balls for riding on the *outside* of a helo.

The use of helicopters wasn't something Terry had planned for and may present something of a problem. The MH-6s were small enough that they could land almost anywhere, including rooftops and small parking lots. Terry knew he would be able to gain some separation from the now five cars chasing him into the city once he hit traffic on Lake Shore Drive. He'd be able to use the cruiser's lights and sirens to clear traffic in front of him. He was confident he could reach the restricted terrain as planned. The goal was to get to the far end of that strip of land and use the Adler Planetarium as a backdrop. He could engage the trailing vehicles while they were trapped on the strip of land. Any rounds they fired would hit the planetarium, which would give this whole operation a black eye.

In Terry's planning, he assessed that the Army would be in vehicles, coming across the same narrow strip of land, and he would be able to hold them off while they caused even more damage to the Planetarium. He didn't plan for the helicopters. With the helos, the Army was going to be able to outflank him, possibly landing and coming from the south. It is hard enough to fight in two directions for any unit. For one man, it was impossible. Terry was going to need help. He grabbed the radio.

"Whiskey Six Six, Whiskey Six Six. Ranger, Ranger, Ranger," Terry transmitted over the SWAT channel. It was what the Army referred to as a 'running password.' If you were getting shot at and approaching a friendly unit, soldiers were supposed to yell a pre-coordinated word to let everyone know they were friendly. Use of 'Ranger, Ranger, Ranger' was the standard operating procedure for students at the Ranger School. The radio crackled back.

"This is Whiskey Six Six, Copy," Moriarty said. Terry cringed. He saw brake lights in front of him as he made the sweeping left turn onto northbound Lake Shore Drive. He didn't know which buttons to push to activate the lights and sirens, so he pushed them all and began to accelerate. Cars on the big thoroughfare began to move out of his way. The vehicles in his mirror were falling back. The traffic light in front of him was yellow, so Terry moved left into the empty turn lane and blew through the intersection as the light turned red. Cross traffic didn't wait and began to fill in behind him. He left the lights and sirens on so the cars behind him didn't lose him in traffic. The goal was still to get them onto that narrow strip of land.

Terry reduced his speed but continued to move through traffic. Soldier Field was big and ominous as it passed to Terry's right. He knew the traffic pattern had changed over the years, but this upcoming right turn was the one he needed. The street sign said E. McFetridge Dr., but Terry only cared that this was the road passing between the football stadium and the Field Museum. He slowed and turned right, heading east toward Lake Michigan. Terry was keeping an eye in the mirror, taking his foot off the gas until he knew Smith's people were back on his tail. He watched a pickup truck slam on its brakes and make an erratic right turn behind him. *There you are.* Terry accelerated again.

At this point, the roads dead-ended at the planetarium. Terry knew the convoy of Smith's people would follow him because they had no other option. He turned left across divided traffic onto Museum Campus Drive and then faded right, pointing the nose of the cruiser directly at the planetarium. The original Adler Planetarium building was somewhat unimpressive. It was round and built of very bland stone with a few windows, but it did have a large copper dome for a roof. Behind the old building was a different story.

The modern structure that sat between the old building and Lake Michigan was gorgeous. The exterior was completely glass and provided a visually stunning backdrop to the old building. The foundation of the new building arced to match the curvature of the stone structure it backed, and the roof peaked in a glass triangular point. It was almost a linear pyramid. Most important to Terry was the glass. It was late, nearly midnight, and although Chicago was far from sleeping, the planetarium would be closed. As much as Terry wanted this to go badly for the Mayor and the Army, he didn't want any innocent bystanders to be injured or killed.

Terry saw the Lake to his left and the harbor to his right. This was the spot he wanted. He whipped the cruiser into a skid, completely blocking the lane heading out to the planetarium. He knew the single vehicle wouldn't be able to stop everything from coming through, but he gave himself a clear lane to fire if anyone tried to shoot the gap between him and the lake to the north. Terry jumped out of the driver's seat, grabbed the radio, and rested it on the driver's seat. The aging warrior stood erect, slinging his rifle across his chest and donning his helmet. *Here we go.*

When the first set of headlights came around the corner, Terry crouched behind the cruiser, resting the rifle on the hood. He peered carefully through the four-power magnification of the ACOG and aimed at the base of the windshield in front of the driver. As if he were on an Army rifle range, he calmly flipped the weapon from 'SAFE' to 'SEMI' and squeezed the trigger. The shot was about two hundred yards, putting the round near the peak of its ballistic arc when it struck the glass. The 5.56mm round stuck four inches above Terry's point of aim, just clearing the top of the dashboard and the steering wheel. It hit the driver directly in the sternum and killed him instantly. The truck swerved and struck a decorative tree in the median. Terry let out a breath and waited.

The Nissan truck was a crew cab, so Terry was watching the two doors he could see on the passenger side. The rear door opened, and a man fell out onto the pavement. The impact with the tree rattled his cage. *Wait.* The man tried to stand but stopped halfway up, dizzy from the crash. Terry fired, dropping the man next to the truck. A second set of headlights came around the corner. Now a third.

Terry lined up his scope on the lead vehicle, just like he had done with the Nissan, and squeezed the trigger. The glass broke, but the truck kept coming. *Shit.* Terry shifted, aiming at the pavement in front of the driver's tire, and fired three rounds. The tire blew on the big Chevy truck, making it slide out of control, nearly missing the Nissan embedded in the tree. Terry quickly fired two rounds into the passenger window. The third vehicle was coming. Davis unleashed fury on the front of the vehicle, emptying the magazine into the grill, front bumper, and windshield. The dark colored SUV was one hundred yards away when it finally stopped. Terry dropped down behind the nose of the police cruiser and inserted a fresh magazine into his rifle.

Slapping the bolt release on the left side of the rifle's receiver, Terry resumed his firing position. He could still see the Chevy truck, but lost sight of the Nissan behind it. He put two more rounds into the cab of the Chevy to let anyone still alive inside know they weren't safe. Men began to pile out of the SUV in front of him. It was an interesting bunch; some in jeans and flannel shirts, others in functional tactical-style clothing like hard fleece jackets and cargo pants. They used the doors for cover as the men moved to the back of the vehicle for cover. *C'mon motherfuckers, start shooting back.*

Terry knew he had the cruiser's engine block and his body armor to protect him. He was confident he wouldn't get shot, but he needed these guys to start firing at him. It didn't take but a second or two, and Terry got his wish. One of the windows on the passenger side exploded, and he heard gunfire coming from his one o'clock, the general direction of the Chevy truck he could see, and the Nissan behind it that he couldn't. Using the vehicle to screen his movement, Terry moved to the rear of the SUV Moriarty lent him. He poked the barrel around the taillight and fired two rounds at the red Chevy Silverado, both impacting the side of the truck. He couldn't see anyone moving and didn't see any muzzle flashes to target, but he needed these guys to know he was still here and, if they wanted to survive, they were going to have to shoot back.

Suddenly, a fourth vehicle came speeding in Terry's direction. It was a black Suburban, and it was in the westbound lanes, heading east. Somewhere behind the three disabled vehicles in front of Terry, the Suburban must have jumped the median between the series of monuments, statues, and concrete planters attempting to close the distance with him. Davis opened fire on the SUV, breaking every window in the vehicle as it approached. He couldn't let them get behind him, or he was fucked. After firing the remaining twenty-eight rounds in his rifle, the bolt locked to the rear. *Empty. Shit.*

The black behemoth was less than thirty yards from him when it came to a screeching halt. Terry hit the magazine release with his trigger finger, dropping the empty plastic magazine onto the pavement. He was reaching for one of the full magazines in a pouch on his war belt when a bloodied man climbed out of the backseat of the Suburban and fired at him. Instinctively, Terry let his rifle fall slack on its sling and yanked the FNX-45 from its holster on his right hip. *Bang, bang. Bang, bang.* The man went down. Terry looked beyond the man, checking for targets around the Suburban, then holstered his pistol and jammed a fresh magazine into the AR-15.

Sporadic fire started to come from the vicinity of the other vehicles. Terry hit the bolt release on his rifle, loading a round into the chamber. He needed to move. There was one more vehicle out there, and the bad guys were getting their shit together. He knew it wouldn't do any damage, but Terry pulled one of the flashbangs from his kit and heaved it toward the cluster of disabled vehicles. *Boom.* Terry ran diagonally away from the SWAT cruiser and toward the median. He was moving closer to the planetarium and purposely exposing himself, hoping to draw more fire. *Hope is not a course of action.*

The grass-covered median was decorated with various trees and shrubbery between the statues and monuments. If it were warmer out, earlier in the year, these would have provided Terry some decent concealment as he moved closer to the stone building. In Chicago, on the cusp of winter, there were no leaves or flowers to hide behind. Terry would have to rely on speed and accurate fire to reach the staircase in front of the building. He was playing a dangerous game with these men. All it would take was for one of them to keep his cool, and Terry was likely to take a bullet. He got to the first mound of landscaping and took a knee. Davis looked behind him to see men advancing. They began shooting at him from behind the disabled SUV closest to his cruiser. Terry fired quickly. *Bang, bang.* He moved again. Found more cover. *Bang, bang.*

The firing directed at Terry increased every time he moved. He could hear bullets zipping by him. Firefights in real life are seldom like they are in the movies. More often than not, people shoot about as poorly as the Storm Troopers in Star Wars. Firing accurately wasn't an easy thing to do in the best of conditions; add adrenaline, heavy breathing, nerves, and fear, and it becomes infinitely more difficult. For better or worse, Terry had been shot at enough that he could keep his cool and accurately engage the enemy in times like this. He fired two more rounds and turned to make the last dash toward the stairs.

Facing the building as he ran, he could see the rounds from Smith's people impacting the stone building. *That's better.* The first pane of glass shattered and fell inside the new addition behind the old, stone planetarium. Terry smiled right as an incoming round hit the ceramic plate in the back of his body armor. The kinetic energy from the 7.62mm round knocked him down, face-first into the concrete. His forward momentum and the push from the bullet travelling at over two thousand feet per second drove his face into the cold ground when he fell. Terry saw a flash of white behind his eyes and heard his jaw crack as the left side of his face was the first thing to make contact with Mother Earth.

Fuck. Terry knew he had to get up or he was going to get killed. He felt a wave of pain through his face as he pushed himself off the ground. Rounds continued to whiz by as he dragged himself behind a concrete planter. The glass in the front doors of the old planetarium building shattered as bullets passed far over Terry's head. He could hear voices now, getting closer. There was at least one AK-47 firing at him; he knew that sound well. Putting the AR-15 up onto the concrete rim of the planter, Terry fired again. *Bang, bang. Bang, bang. Bang, bang.*

A man firing an AR-15 from the hip went down. Whoever was carrying the AK must have put it on full auto because Terry's fire was countered with a barrage—three more of the huge pieces of glass shattered behind him. The pain in Terry's face was excruciating; he could feel it every time he pulled the trigger on his rifle. Looking beyond the handful of baddies trying to kill him, Terry could see a set of headlights stopped in the road next to the Suburban. It was the fifth vehicle that followed him into the city.

Terry looked over his shoulder to find the next piece of cover. Directly behind him, about thirty yards away, was a statue. Somewhere in the back of his brain, he remembered from a grammar school field trip that it was Nicolaus Copernicus. He fired off four rounds in rapid succession and ran back to the statue. *Keep moving, keep shooting.* Every footstep shot pain through his jaw. When he got behind the statue, Terry threw up from the pain, making his jaw throb even more. A round impacted the statue above him as he hid behind the concrete base. Now a second. The bad guys were getting closer and more accurate.

Terry turned when he heard rounds ricochet off the metal tiles on the rotunda of the Planetarium. Another burst from the AK drew his attention back to the fight. He could see two men in the open in front of him. *Bang, bang.* The guy with the AK went down. Terry shifted his attention to the second man. His face was screaming in pain. The man's torso filled the glass inside the ACOG. *Bang, bang.* The man went down. Terry exhaled softly, trying hard not to push too much air through his mouth. Breathing slowly, he watched for movement in front of him. Five seconds. Ten seconds. No firing. No movement. Terry allowed himself a bit of relief.

Then he heard the helicopters.

CHAPTER 34

"Saddle up!" Moriarty yelled to his people. He briefed his team a few minutes prior that the car chase had entered the museum campus on the lakefront, which was likely their target area. In his head, he guessed Terry was baiting Smith's people into a fight on terrain he could control, but he hoped the retired Army officer wasn't boxing himself in at the same time.

Moriarty looked over at the mayor. She had an anxious look on her face, hoping she could extricate herself from the situation, but Rocco wasn't going to let that happen. It was vital for her to own this, good or bad. He viewed the outcome as a win, either way. If she took responsibility for whatever happened in the city tonight, she would probably face political repercussions. If she pushed back against the Army and let them take the blame, she would probably stay in office, but everything Smith put into getting the Army into the city would be a failure and wouldn't be replicated across the country. That would likely get her killed.

As the crowd of SWAT Officers broke up and began loading into the various vehicles, there were two small figures left standing. Two women. Both dressed in full SWAT gear that blended them into the crowd until now. The big man smiled and walked through the moving mass of humanity until he was standing in front of them.

"How are you feeling?" he said to the woman on the right.

"Better," Dana said. "I want to help."

"I guessed as much since you're dressed like one of my officers," Rocco responded. "Is that a medbag on your back?" The little nurse nodded. "Good, then you can help." He turned his attention to the other woman. "How about you?"

"This needs to end tonight," Mary said sternly. Rocco nodded. The mayor walked up to the trio.

"Ms. Mayor," the SWAT Commander said in a grandiose tone, "allow me to introduce you to Mary and Dana. Mary is a detective, and her father was my training officer. Her brother Jimmy is one of my officers. He's lying in a hospital bed right now because these assholes tried to kill him." He waved a hand at Dana. "Dana is a nurse at Cook County Hospital. She was with Jimmy when they tried to kill him. They tried to kill her, too."

"And they fucking killed my parents," Mary said. The mayor recoiled, not because of the cursing but because of the venom in Mary's voice.

"And they are trying to kill my boyfriend," Dana snapped. Mary turned and smiled at her.

"They aren't SWAT Officers?" The mayor asked. No one answered. "Then they aren't authorized to go on this operation."

"Did you not hear me?" Mary shot back. Ever the professional police officer, Mary's temper reached its boiling point. Her hand fell to her hip, resting on the butt of the CPD Glock. "They killed my parents. I'm fucking going." The mayor stepped close to Mary.

"This isn't *your* decision, Detective," the mayor said. It was a feeble attempt to intimidate Mary, and it failed miserably.

"She's right," Rocco said. "It's *my* decision." The mayor snapped a look at him. "The senior sworn officer has the authority and responsibility to determine who participates in police operations. You're not a sworn officer, are you, Ms. Mayor?" She just looked at him. "And we don't have a Superintendent at the moment, so I guess that means I'm the senior sworn officer. And I say they are going. So are you."

"I'm not going anywhere," the mayor said to him.

"Bullshit," Mary said. "You're going."

"Get in the fucking car," Dana said. The mayor found herself standing in the center of the trio. She wasn't being given a choice, and her face showed resignation.

"Let's go," Rocco said and led them back across the parking lot to his borrowed cruiser. In a gesture of sarcastic fealty, Rocco opened the front door for the Mayor. He bowed and swept his hand like a valet at a pricy hotel. Dana and Mary climbed in the back. Rocco grabbed the radio.

"Whiskey Six Five, this is Whiskey Six Six. Let me know when everyone is loaded up," Moriarty transmitted.

"Copy, Six Six," O'Donnell sent back.

"Do we even know where we are going?" the mayor asked from the passenger seat.

"The museum campus," Moriarty said. The mayor gave him a quizzical look. "Call it a hunch." The radio crackled again. Moriarty was expecting to hear O'Donnell's voice, but he was wrong.

"Whiskey Six Six, Whiskey Six Six. Ranger, Ranger, Ranger," came the call over the SWAT channel. The voice was calm, and the transmission crisp. Moriarty smiled.

"That's our queue," Rocco said. He pushed the transmit button on the radio. "This is Whiskey Six Six, Copy."

"What was that?" the mayor asked, genuinely confused. Moriarty ignored her; he was waiting to hear back from O'Donnell. "Dammit, I asked you a question!" the mayor demanded. She wasn't used to being put off like this. Mary was tempted to jump in, but held her tongue. She had known Moriarty her whole life, and as much as she wanted to say something, he certainly didn't need her help. Dana was a different story.

"That was Terry Davis," the nurse said. She was sitting behind Moriarty, the Mayor turned to look at her through the cage between the seats. "And these guys who have been pretending to be gang members are the ones chasing him." The mayor looked at Moriarty, who remained silent and unmoved. Mary figured the cat was out of the bag, so she piled on.

"They tried to recruit me into this, too," she told the mayor. "Those are cops who have been threatened and bullied into working with criminals to wage this gang war. Probably some ex-military, too. This whole thing is fabricated. It's total bullshit."

"But you knew that already," Moriarty said. "Maybe not all of it, but you knew. All of this to get the Army in here, so they can *help*." The mayor looked out the window. "Now we have the Army flying in, loaded up like they are going into combat. They are *all* going after Terry Davis. All of them."

"Whiskey Six Six," O'Donnell's voice came over the radio. "We are set. Six vehicles. Four light and two heavy. Twenty personnel."

"Copy," Moriarty said into the radio.

"Whiskey Six Six, this is EOC." It was Officer Hanrahan again. "We have reports of vehicles inside the museum campus, heading for the Planetarium."

"Whiskey Six Six, I copy," Moriarty said. He took a breath. "Whiskey Six Five, I'll lead. Put two light vehicles at the intersection of McFetridge and Museum Campus. The rest of us will move up to Solidarity."

"This is Whiskey Six Five. Copy," O'Donnell's voice came across the radio. Moriarty knew that was all the guidance he needed to give his second-in-command. O'Donnell was his inevitable replacement, and Rocco trusted him implicitly. He knew the two cruisers would be precisely where he wanted them, stopping any traffic from wandering into the fight Terry was starting. The other five vehicles, including the two armored cars and Moriarty's vehicle, would continue north and wade into the fray.

Rocco backed the Ford Explorer out of the parking space and headed toward the parking lot exit. He could see in the sideview mirrors that the rest of the vehicles were falling in line behind him. There was no coordination necessary and no orders he needed to give; everyone on his team heard the radio traffic between him and O'Donnell and knew what to do. He was proud of his team. He paused briefly to let everyone get set when the radio crackled.

"Whiskey Six Six, this is EOC." It was Baker this time. He stayed on shift as Moriarty ordered. "We have multiple reports of shots fired in the vicinity of Solidarity, north of the harbor." Rocco grabbed the radio.

"EOC, this is Whiskey Six Six. I copy." He put the radio into the cupholder. "Looks like our boy got what he wanted," he said to Dana and Mary in the back. The tension was palpable inside the vehicle, a mixture of excitement and dread. Moriarty turned on the lights and sirens in the cruiser, watching the other vehicles follow suit in the side-view mirror.

Rocco led the convoy of SWAT vehicles through the city streets and onto Lake Shore Drive, heading north. They weren't far away from the museum campus, but the two lumbering armored vehicles weren't built for speed. This was going to take much longer than if Moriarty were weaving through traffic on his own. In the back of his head, Rocco knew Terry had a plan of some sort, but every minute it took his team to get on site was a minute Davis was on his own.

The seven-vehicle column was moving north as quickly as Moriarty thought they could go. The intersection with I-55 passed on their left, then the McCormick Place convention center. Slowly, the well-known Chicago landmarks came into view. Moriarty could see the dark outline of Soldier Field against the night sky when the radio crackled again.

"Whiskey Six Six, this is One Six." It was the leader of Team One. "Two helos inbound at your eleven o'clock. Maybe two hundred feet." Moriarty looked out his window. It took him a second to find them. The red and white flashing aviation lights blended into the backdrop of smattering office and apartment lights, high in the skyscraper windows. Once he found them, they were easy to track; two MH-6s flying low through the night.

"This is Whiskey Six Six, I copy," Moriarty said. He turned right onto McFetridge, hoping they weren't too late.

CHAPTER 35

Terry scanned the night sky. He knew the acoustics of the buildings and the lake were going to play hell with his ears if he tried to pinpoint their approach from the sound of the rotors. He could feel his face burning as the sweat dripped down and into the scrape on his cheek he took when he faceplanted. Despite the cold night, the excitement of the firefight and his movement from cover to cover got his heart rate up, and he was sweating. Out of reflex, he reached up to wipe the sweat away. Before he could stop himself, Terry touched his cheek to wipe the sweat out of his beard. It was all he could do not to pass out from the pain in his broken jaw.

The helicopters were getting louder. *There.* He could see the aviation safety lights flashing. In a combat environment, those would be turned off, and the pilots would be flying completely blacked out, using night vision goggles. As much as the Army contingent wanted this to be combat, it was still Chicago, and those helicopters had to follow FAA rules. The two Little Birds were flying straight toward him and directly over the top of the Field Museum when Terry spotted them. Once the two helos cleared the roof of the museum, they dropped low, just clearing the streetlights as they headed east toward the planetarium, using the street as their approach vector.

As they got closer, Terry could see the shooters riding on the pods outside the fuselage. *I bet that's fucking cold.* Terry waited and watched, hidden behind the statue of Copernicus. The lead helo faded to Terry's left and began to flare, slowing to land and offload the six passengers riding along like baby opossums on their mother. He couldn't let them land here, not this close. He fired four rounds at the rotor, seeing two impact sparks. The helo banked hard to the south, and his wingman followed. Terry made a break for it, trying to cover as much open ground as he could. He ran toward the north side of the building, up the stone steps and across the grass terrace, stopping once he had the glass structure to his back. He knew the aircraft pair would likely make a second pass, trying to identify his location.

The rotor noise faded and then grew louder. They were coming back to find him. He could still see old Nicolas Copernicus standing on his pedestal in front of the stone steps. The helos made a sweeping pass less than fifty feet off the ground, coming from the south. Terry felt as if he was at head height with the pilots as they whizzed by. The three shooters riding on the right pod of the lead helicopter were closest to the statue, and all of them had their eyes trained on the sculpture, as if Copernicus had personally shot at them. Tucked in a dark corner, Terry fired four more rounds and then hit the ground.

Terry could hear the whine of the rotors change as they banked hard left, away from the building. The second aircraft was trailing behind but didn't make the turn. The special operators fired their rifles at him from their exposed positions. The glass above and behind Terry sounded like a plane crash as it shattered over his head. *Holy Shit.* Terry fired his rifle from the prone, hitting one of the operators and knocking him off the pod.

The big man fell from the pod for less than a second. His four-foot safety line caught him and kept him from smashing into the concrete. Each of the men riding on the pods had a safety line made of nylon webbing that was attached to their belt at one end and the helicopter at the other. In the event of turbulence, evasive maneuvers by the pilots, or any number of reasons, falling off the pod didn't mean certain death. It did, however, make the helo more challenging to fly. The pilot of aircraft number two had to make a quick correction to keep his beloved Little Bird from colliding with a streetlight.

As the rotor noise faded, Terry tried to listen hard for the other helicopter. He could hear his own heart pounding inside his head and felt every beat in his jaw. The helos were off in the distance, but Terry couldn't see them. Lake Michigan was to the north and east, and the city to the west. They had to be south, toward the old Meigs Field. Terry Davis lifted himself off the ground and began jogging back toward the front of the building, trying to find the helicopters while using the building as cover. Out of the corner of his eye, Terry could see that the fifth vehicle that followed him into the city had crept closer. It was a brand new, black Chevy Suburban sitting alone on Solidarity Drive. No one was standing outside the vehicle, and it wasn't moving. He was so preoccupied with the helicopters that he hadn't noticed the SUV slowly moving forward. *No time to deal with that now.*

Terry Davis reached the edge of the building. Peering around the stone façade, he could see that the large parking lot to the southeast of the Planetarium was empty, except for the two MH-6s parked next to each other. Terry could see five of the men facing outward, pulling immediate security for the aircraft while they were on the ground. The rest of the team was treating and tying the injured man to the pod of one of the aircraft. Terry assumed he would be evacuated to the nearest hospital with a helipad.

Terry looked back at the black Suburban; it was still in the same spot. Terry's eyes flicked into the distance, and he could see red and blue lights reflecting off the side of the Field Museum. *The Cavalry is here. Just hold out a little longer.*

He turned his attention back to the special operators. Their patient was secured to the pod, and he watched as one man moved around the nose of the black helo and climbed onto the opposite side. The rest of the men moved outside the rotor wash and fell in amongst the four already pulling security. Terry admired the pilots as they executed a synchronized left pivot turn and then flew away in unison. As the remaining ten men stood, looking for revenge on Terry Davis, he noticed for the first time that they were wearing mostly civilian-style clothing and not uniforms.

Davis knew he needed to continue to delay their advance. There was no way he could stand up to these ten men with malice in their hearts. He had to keep them at bay long enough for Moriarty and his troops to arrive. Terry was still using the curvature of the building to shield himself from view. The men were about one hundred fifty yards away, some of them partially masked by trees and dumpsters and even a hotdog stand, but they were mostly in the open. He braced the rifle against the stone exterior of the Planetarium and fired. *Bang, bang.* The man he was aiming at went down, and the other nine dove for cover or just made themselves flat on the asphalt. *Bang, bang.* Terry knew he had to move. In the darkness, his muzzle flashes were giving away his firing position. *Keep moving, keep shooting.*

As he moved backward, keeping the building between him and the shooters, Terry heard them return fire. There was anger in it. While he assumed some of the shots were well aimed and well placed, the sheer volume of lead and copper aimed in his direction told him the enemy was trying to pin him down and keep him from firing again. Terry assumed another protected position and quickly glanced to the left. The Suburban hadn't moved, but the police lights in the distance were distinct now, no longer just colored reflections. The return fire from the special operators stopped. *They are reloading, treating the casualty, and splitting up.*

Terry had done exactly what Moriarty hoped he wouldn't do; he boxed himself in. He was standing on a point with Lake Michigan to his back and one side. To his front was the enemy. The Delta Force boys would know this and wouldn't let him take his only avenue of escape, back up Solidarity toward his borrowed cruiser. They would send one element around the back of the building and another one to maneuver west, pinning him against the lake. Terry knew he hit one man, that would take two of them out of the fight at least temporarily. Their fighting strength at this point would be eight. He needed to even the odds as much as he could.

The element moving to the west would have to put themselves in open ground at some point, crossing Solidarity and using the median and landscaping as cover. The guys moving around to the lakeside had nothing. There was a single row of bare trees between the glass building and the lake. Terry poked his nose out, looking for movement of any kind. *There.* One man moving, making a mad dash across the pavement. *Bang, bang.*

The man went down in the middle of the street. He wasn't dead and began dragging himself behind a concrete planter exactly like the one Terry used just minutes before. Another barrage of fire answered Terry's two rounds. Terry saw the Suburban idling in the street. *Bang, bang. Bang, bang.* Three of the four rounds Terry fired hit the windshield; the other hit the roof. The windshield didn't shatter like the other vehicles. *It's armored. That's Smith.*

Terry Davis had run out of curve to hide behind. He had to make a run through the broken glass he was lying in earlier to get around the corner of the building. Behind the Suburban, he could see the police lights getting closer. He had to look twice, but he swore there were two armored vehicles in the lead. Terry snatched his second-to-last flash-bang from his vest and pulled the pin. He threw it as hard as he could in the general direction of the element moving in front of him. *Boom.* As soon as it went off, he turned and ran, leaping over a metal railing. The smell of the lake filled his nostrils as he breathed in the night air. Bullets from the Delta team chased him around the corner of the building. The long prairie grass was covered in ice, making Terry's feet slide out from underneath him.

The decline leading away from the building was only about fifteen feet, but Terry covered all of it on his ass. Only the concrete sidewalk at the bottom stopped his slide. The hill stopped abruptly at a marble wall to his left. Terry used it for cover, peering over the top. He could see another man running across Solidarity. *Bang, bang. Bang, bang. Bang, bang.* The man dove for cover. Terry might have hit him, but he wasn't sure. The police lights were getting closer, and he could see men in tactical gear moving on foot with the vehicles. It wouldn't be long before the element Terry was confident was moving around the building would be on him. It was basic fire and maneuver that every lieutenant learned in their earliest days of training. He dropped down below the concrete wall and turned his focus east toward the rear of the building.

Knowing he had only a few rounds left in his magazine, Terry dropped it and jammed a full one into the magazine well. Fire ripped into the wall behind him, covering him with dust and debris. Terry knew he was safe but ducked out of reflex. Whether it was adrenaline or the cold Chicago air, he could no longer feel the pain in his jaw. Sitting here, he could feel the wind coming off the lake; it was biting cold.

In front of him, across the sidewalk, there was another strip of grass with knee-high stacks of stone spaced about ten feet apart, then concrete steps that led down to a platform where the lake waves crashed. Terry considered moving down to the platform, hoping to use the stairs to mask his movement, but he knew it would be covered in ice on this cold night like the prairie grass next to the building. He could quite possibly end up in the lake, drowning or dying of hypothermia. *Fuck that. Keep moving, keep shooting.*

About twenty yards in front of him, he could see the dark outline of a railing. He moved to it quickly, staying as low as he could. Another burst of fire hit the concrete wall as he departed. The railing marked a doorway set into a concrete hallway, leading into the Planetarium itself through the hill he just navigated on his ass. It provided great cover but almost zero visibility. The attackers would be on him almost before he could see them, but he didn't have any other options other than the low piles of stone across the sidewalk. Terry could hear more firing coming from the parking lot. It sounded like Moriarty's men were getting into the fight. That should keep the Delta guys to the west occupied.

Terry backed himself into the concrete cave and peered into the darkness. He could see the top of the small observatory building between the planetarium's glass back and Lake Michigan. The prairie grass on the backside of the building was weighed down with ice, much more than the slope Terry had slid down a few moments before, giving him a much clearer field of view than he would have otherwise.

Terry watched for movement. He saw the first man moving in the darkness, quietly stepping heel to toe, rifle at his shoulder. Without the ambient light of the city to wash out his night vision, Terry flipped the AN/PVS-14 down in front of his eyes and turned it on. With the naked eye, Terry only saw one of the four men. With his night vision monocular, he saw them all. Two were moving between the observatory building and the lake, while the other two were moving between the observatory and the planetarium. None of them was wearing helmets or night vision goggles. He smiled.

Terry didn't want to lose sight of the two men out by the lake. It would be easy for them to get behind the concrete stairs and maneuver on him. The two closest to him had nowhere to hide. Davis shouldered his rifle and squeezed the pressure switch attached to the PEQ-15 infrared aiming laser mounted on the front rails of his rifle. The slope of the ground and the icy grass concealed all but the head and shoulders of the man to the left. It was enough for Terry to aim his laser at. *Bang, bang.* Terry transitioned to the next man. *Bang, bang.* Both men were down. It looked like they were both still moving.

The men closer to the lake returned fire, hitting the concrete in front of him and the railing over his head. Terry ducked back and then heard a splash. One of the men hit the icy platform and found himself in the icy waters of Lake Michigan. Davis poked his head out and fired again as one of the near men closed on him. *Bang, bang. Bang, bang.* The man went down in a heap. Terry scanned the open terrain in front of him through his night vision. One of the pair nearest the water was lying still on the ground. The other was out of sight. *Where is number four?*

CHAPTER 36

Moriarty got out of the cruiser and opened the door behind him. The interior handles of the door had been disabled, like all police cars, making sure criminals in the back couldn't escape. Dana got out and slung her med bag over her back. The mayor got out of the passenger seat but didn't have the situational awareness to let Mary out. Rocco ran around to the other side and opened her door. The mayor looked embarrassed as Mary glared at her.

"You stay right next to me," Moriarty called out to Dana. The foursome met at the nose of the cruiser. The SWAT Officers were getting out of the backs of the two armored vehicles in front of them. "Mary, keep an eye on that Suburban. Ms. Mayor, you stay here with the cruiser." Moriarty went to the back of the Explorer and grabbed his rifle. The police and military model Colt M4 rifle looked tiny strapped across the big man. The fourteen-and-a-half-inch barrel looked stubby and barely poked outside his massive silhouette. "Let's go!" he called out to the SWAT Team.

Dana moved behind him, Mary to his right with her pistol in hand. The big diesel engines of the armored vehicles belched smoke as they rolled forward. The MH-6s took off and flew toward the city to their right. Moriarty could see muzzle flashes coming from the planetarium, but couldn't hear the gunfire over the vehicle noise.

"No one fires until I say so," Moriarty said, activating the throat mic wrapped around his big neck. The cluster of officers moved forward slowly, using the armored vehicles as cover. Moriarty knew Terry was up there somewhere, and the last thing he wanted was one of his officers shooting the combat veteran. They moved slowly toward the disabled vehicles in the road, bodies strewn around them on the concrete. "I'm glad I'm not fighting him," Rocco said to Mary. Dana tried to hide a proud smile.

Once they reached the shot-up trucks, Moriarty could see the Delta Force element emerging from the south parking lot, exchanging fire with whoever was up at the planetarium. He watched a man go down in the street and then drag himself to cover. Dana started to run forward, but Moriarty grabbed her by the drag handle on top of the medbag.

"Where are you going?" he asked as she regained her balance.

"That might be Terry!" Dana exclaimed. He realized quickly that her untrained eye hadn't picked up on the fighting that was going on. Four more shots came from the planetarium.

"That ain't him," Moriarty said. Terry's flashbang went off in the street. Moriarty watched the operators dive for cover. He pointed up toward the big stone building. "That's him."

"How do you know?" Dana asked, visibly confused.

"Trust me," Moriarty said. He activated his throat mic. "All stations do not fire at the planetarium. Suspects to the south are cleared to engage if they pose a threat. Watch your background." The vehicles continued to move forward. Six shots came from Terry up at the Planetarium, spurring the Army to return fire. They didn't realize they had identified their positions for Moriarty's men, who began to engage them. Rocco grabbed Dana again and pushed her close behind the armored vehicle in front of them. Mary moved next to her, both peeking around the armored skin of the green vehicle.

Once the Delta team realized the police were shooting at them, they instinctively returned fire. This only brought more fire back in their direction. The two or three that were left were outgunned five times over. The exchange of bullets didn't last long. Moriarty spurred his people forward.

"Let's go," he said into his throat mic. "Close in on them." He looked at Mary. "You go straight to that Suburban. Me and you." She nodded, waiting for the go-ahead from the SWAT Commander. Moriarty looked over his shoulder, the mayor standing back at the cruiser as directed.

Moriarty saw his cruiser out of the corner of his eye. A few of the windows were shot out, and it had more than a handful of bullet holes in the body panels. *No way that guy is driving my Camaro.* They were closing on the Suburban. There was no more fire coming from the special operators in front of them; they were dead, wounded, or had given up the ship. He grabbed Dana.

"You stay behind the vehicle," he yelled over the engine noise. "Let's go," he tapped Mary on the shoulder. The pair peeled off from behind the vehicle and moved at a run. Mary couldn't keep up with the big man, no matter how much older he was than she was. He stopped ten yards from the back of the vehicle. The engine was running, and the lights were still on. Moriarty raised his rifle, orienting it at the driver's window as he moved. Mary slipped off to the right of the vehicle, her pistol aimed at the passenger side.

"Get out of the vehicle," Moriarty bellowed. There was no movement.

"Out of the vehicle, now!" Mary yelled from her side. The armored vehicles had stopped behind them. SWAT Officers were moving forward on foot to clear the area. Moriarty grabbed the handle on the driver's door, but it was locked. He tapped the muzzle of his rifle on the glass. Mary tried the rear passenger door, but it was locked, too.

Moriarty could see where Terry's rounds impacted the windshield, identifying that it was bulletproof glass. *They'd better come out, or we'll have to pry it open.* Moriarty banged his barrel on the glass again, this time with more force. The rear passenger door on Mary's side opened. She stepped back. An older man in a suit and overcoat stepped out confidently.

"Get on the ground! Now!" Mary yelled at the man. He stood there looking at her.

"Young lady," he said, buttoning his coat. "I've done nothing wrong. We merely drove out here to look at the planetarium and got caught in the middle of all this." Moriarty came around the back of the vehicle, aiming his rifle at the older man's head.

"Turn around and put your hands on the vehicle!" Mary commanded. He continued to stare at her. Moriarty grabbed the man, picking him up off the ground, spinning him, and pinning him against the vehicle. The front passenger door flew open, and a man started to emerge with a submachine gun. Mary shot him in the face.

"That was a mistake," Rocco said. The man didn't struggle. Gunfire came from behind the planetarium.

"Commander Moriarty," the older man said. "It is Commander, correct?" Rocco looked at Mary. "I think the mayor is with you, probably somewhere back by those police vehicles. I want to speak to her, please." The corpse without a face fell to the ground after a moment of hesitation. Mary looked through the open door, pointing her pistol at the driver.

"Get out!" she yelled at the man. More shots from behind the stone and glass building. "If I see a gun, you're a dead man." Mary moved slowly around the nose of the Suburban as the driver got out. She cuffed him and walked him back to the passenger side, sweeping his legs so he landed face down and staring at his dead compatriot.

"Commander Moriarty," the old man said again, calmly. "The mayor, please." Moriarty and Mary looked at each other.

"Whiskey Six Five," Moriarty said, touching his throat. "Bring the Mayor up here to my location." Rocco spun the old man around again. "Let me guess. You're Smith." Moriarty said as the old man straightened his expensive overcoat.

"I've been known by lots of names, Commander," Smith said. "But you can call me Mr. Smith." Mary looked down Solidarity to see O'Donnell walking toward them with the mayor in tow. "And very soon, you'll no longer be known as Commander." He looked at Mary. "And you'll no longer be known as Detective."

"I should fucking shoot you right now," Mary said.

"And what do you think that would achieve?" the old man chuckled. "Killing me stops nothing. All of this," he held his hands up, "continues with or without me. Your friend Mr. Davis fails to understand that."

O'Donnell and the Mayor walked up, stopping about three yards away from the vehicle. The mayor reached into her pocket, fishing out a box of Marlboros and a Bic lighter. She lit the cigarette and stood there expectantly. O'Donnell traded looks with Moriarty, taking the hint to turn and leave them alone.

"Ms. Mayor," Smith said. "It's a pleasure seeing you again. I want to be released." The mayor exhaled smoke into the night sky. "And I would like these two fired."

"I don't think I can do that," The Mayor said.

"Suit yourself," Smith replied, seemingly unfazed. "You know, the violence in this town has gotten out of hand. Look at your poor planetarium. Terrible. I doubt your career will survive all this. It could be worse, I guess."

"What do you mean by 'it could be worse'?" Moriarty asked.

"For the Mayor," Smith said. "She won't get reelected, but it could be worse. Haven't you heard? Former Superintendent Gagliardi was killed this evening. Not even out of the office for twelve hours and killed by gang violence. It's a tragedy, really." Moriarty, Mary, and the mayor exchanged looks.

"Did you just threaten me?" the mayor asked. Smith just shrugged. "I should have the Commander arrest you."

"He'll be released before we get him processed," Moriarty said. "If these people have the power, Davis says they do, arresting him is futile." Smith stood quietly. The mayor had nothing left in her bag of tricks. Smith wasn't afraid of being arrested or killed. Her tenure as mayor seemed to be falling apart on this cold Chicago night. She agreed to do business with Smith and his organization on the promise of a long political future, and it was evident by Gagliardi's fate that she didn't have any options.

"Commander, Detective," the mayor said, clearing her voice, "release Mr. Smith. You're both fired." Moriarty began to laugh. Mary was dumbfounded.

CHAPTER 37

T erry felt his broken ribs give way as the weight of the fourth
man landed on him. Amid the fight, Major David Boyd had
maneuvered up the icy hill toward the building instead of
down, along the path of least resistance. It is counterintuitive to move
uphill when you're getting shot at; it's slower, and you're generally
more exposed. His move was brilliant. From Terry's position inside the
concrete hallway, he couldn't see the man moving. The structure that
gave him great protection and a stable firing position also blocked his
vision.

The AN/PVS-14 night vision device Terry had mounted to his
bump helmet actually made things worse. The night vision goggle was
a monocular, only covering one eye. In Terry's case, it was his left eye.
As a young officer, Terry found out that as much as people wanted to
wear it over their dominant eye, it prevented them from being able to
shoulder their rifle into a good firing position. Every time he tried to
fire, the monocular would bang into the optic mounted on top of the
rifle.

Terry tried everything before that first deployment: firing the rifle
canted, lifting his head high to prevent the night vision-optic collision,
and even relying on the infrared laser in concert with the night vision.

Terry's muscle memory built from shooting thousands of clay targets on trap and skeet fields with his father and grandfather was unbreakable; he couldn't fire unless the rifle was in that pocket in his shoulder and his cheek welded to the stock. Wearing it over his left eye allowed him to look through his night vision, shoulder his rifle, and fire reliably.

Tonight, that tried-and-true method bit him in the ass. His right side was a blind spot, and Dave Boyd moved through it without being seen. It would have been incredibly easy for the Delta Force team commander to fire down and kill Terry Davis, but he was under direct orders to capture the man alive. Boyd landed on Terry, knocking him to the ground. Terry lay in agony, trying to breathe. One of the ribs he fractured a few days ago broke and splintered, puncturing his lung. Terry clawed for his pistol; the AR-15 was tangled on its sling underneath his body.

"I don't think so," Boyd said as he kicked the pistol away as soon as Terry got it out of the holster. Dave Boyd stood over him. He was younger and bigger than Terry. Davis knew there was no fight here to be won, but if the man wanted him dead, he would have killed him already. He needed to look for an opportunity. Boyd pushed the button on his chest, keying the boom microphone built into his Peltor headset. "Any station, this is Six. I have a jackpot." There was a pause in the night air. No one answered. "Any station, this is Six. I say again, jackpot." Nothing.

Boyd grabbed Terry Davis and lifted him to his feet. Terry let out a weak moan from the pain in his ribs and tried to catch his breath. The special operations officer whipped a set of flex cuffs from his body armor. He knew he couldn't carry Davis by himself, and he didn't know the status of the rest of his team. He'd have to walk the old man out under his own power, back to the helos to link up with his guys and fly out. Dave Boyd knew he wasn't taking his prisoner to the police. He was going to be handed over to the old man in the grey suit. Whatever they did with him didn't matter to Boyd, but he was told to bring him in alive.

"You're in bad shape, old man," Boyd hissed at him. "You're lucky this isn't a kill mission, or you'd be dead already." Terry knew he was right. "Now, I'm going to take you back and hand you off to Smith, and you're going to cooperate or I'll fucking shoot you and dump you in the fucking lake." Boyd grabbed Terry's left wrist and began to slip the flexcuffs over it. Davis knew if those plastic restraints were put on his wrists, the game was over. Summoning whatever strength he had left, Terry pulled his Ek fighting knife from the custom Kydex sheath on his warbelt and plunged it into Boyd's side avoiding his body armor, just below his left armpit. The blade slid between the big man's ribs and into his heart.

Boyd had been careless. He should have kept Terry on the ground, his knee in his back, just like a cop would do, while he put the zip ties on his hands. He should have searched him, removing all weapons from his body, including Terry's long-bladed dagger. Now he was paying the price. The wasp-waisted blade was long and thin, designed to do just what Terry had just done; slip between bones to reach vital organs. Terry buried the blade up to the brass hilt inside the man's torso, and at just over six-and-a-half inches, the steel tip punctured Boyd's heart.

The younger man gasped and recoiled from the pain in his chest, then fell backward. Terry watched as the special operator collapsed. He knew the stab wound itself wouldn't kill the man lying in front of him, and it would take him minutes to bleed out, but Terry knew the shock to the man's heart was as lethal as a gunshot wound and that would probably kill the man before anything else. Boyd scratched and clawed at the knife under his arm until he went limp.

Terry felt lightheaded and fell to his knees. The pain in his ribs and jaw was ensuring his body kept pumping adrenaline through his system, but the lack of oxygen from his punctured lung made him feel like he was going to pass out. He could feel his body getting cold. *Am I fucking dying?*

Terry fought to catch his breath, every inhale jarring his broken jaw. He knew what it was. He knew his lung had collapsed, and someone needed to stick a needle into his chest cavity, allowing the lung to reinflate. Like an airplane operating on one engine, Terry knew he could survive in the short term on only one lung, but he wasn't going to be able to fight, and he sure wasn't going to be able to run like this. In his medkit, he had a decompression needle, but he knew for damn sure he couldn't successfully stick himself and allow the lung to inflate. *I need a doctor…or a nurse. I need Dana.*

She was the first person who came to mind. He knew Moriarty and his people were out front, and they likely had a trained medic who could do the job, but he thought of the little nurse who was so pissed at him just hours ago. Terry fought to his feet, using his rifle and the concrete wall to brace himself. He trudged forward, trying to breathe and keep his balance, all while not throwing up or passing out.

As Terry came around the rounded glass edge of the Adler Planetarium, he could see the police and ambulance lights. There were dozens of people strewn across Solidarity Drive, from police to EMTs to special operators. He could see the black Suburban sitting in the same place it was when he fired four rounds at it, except now he could see Moriarty and Mary standing next to it, with a woman, and…Smith. *Motherfucker.*

Terry hit the magazine release and dropped the magazine from his rifle. He couldn't remember how many rounds were left in it, but he knew he had one full magazine left. He pulled the black plastic magazine from the pouch mounted on the chest of his body armor and pushed it into the magazine well. Every move he made was painful, but anger ruled him now. His hand dropped to the holster on his hip, empty. The FNX and his Ek knife were in the concrete corridor. Terry walked out of the darkness and into plain sight. His movements were slow, his speed governed by the pain and shortness of breath.

Davis was less than thirty yards from the Suburban when two SWAT Officers ran toward him, pointing their rifles. They were covered in Olive Drab, black M4 rifles pointed at him, yelling at him to drop the weapon and put his hands up. Terry let the rifle fall on its sling and raised his hands as high as he could, which wasn't even as high as his shoulders. One of the officers kept his rifle trained on Terry while the other approached, hitting the quick-release on Terry's sling and taking control of his rifle. They should have had him face down on the concrete, spread-eagled, but their actions were halfhearted.

It took Terry a second to realize, but the two officers were Benton and Ferguson. They knew him, or at least had met him and knew who he was. These were the two guys who were watching over Jimmy and Dana on the stakeout. Terry felt relieved he wasn't going to be thrown to the ground and handcuffed.

"I need to talk to Moriarty," Terry said through his broken jaw.

"I kinda figured," Ferguson said. "Dude, you need to see a medic."

"That shit can wait," Terry wheezed. He followed the two officers over to the crowd outside the Suburban.

"Mr. Davis," Smith said. "We meet again. Ms. Mayor, this man needs to be arrested. He killed those Soldiers."

"Fuck that," Mary said.

"No one here is going to arrest him," Moriarty said.

"You're no longer in command, Rocco," the mayor said. "Sergeant O'Donnell!" she called into the night air. O'Donnell came jogging up. "Sergeant, arrest this man." O'Donnell looked at Moriarty, who stood silently. O'Donnell had been extremely loyal to him for several years. Moriarty didn't think it was fair to pit the officer's personal loyalty against his duty.

"What am I arresting him for?" O'Donnell asked.

"For shooting all these soldiers, destruction of property..." Smith started talking. O'Donnell cut him off.

"I don't know who you are, but I don't work for you," O'Donnell said. Smith gave the mayor an expectant look.

"What he said," she said impatiently. "Just arrest him." At that moment, Terry collapsed on the concrete.

"Terry!" Mary yelled. She knelt beside him. Smith shook his head and smiled.

"Terry!" Dana yelled from twenty yards away. She had been helping with some of the wounded soldiers and hadn't seen the old warrior limp up to the Suburban. Mary's scream caught her attention. She rushed over to him. "Oh my God." Dana went straight into nurse mode.

"Punctured...lung..." Terry hissed to her, saliva coming out of his mouth. She went to dump her med bag on the ground, but he grabbed her arm. "Rocco's cruiser," he said.

"What did he say?" O'Donnell asked.

"He has a pneumothorax," Dana said. Everyone looked at her. "A punctured lung. Jesus, you fucking people..." Dana was worried about her patient and missed the second statement, but Mary didn't. He specifically said, 'Rocco's cruiser.'

"We need to get him inside a vehicle and off the concrete," Mary said. Dana opened her mouth to protest, but Mary cut her off. "Let's get him over to the cruiser," she pointed to the shot-up vehicle, "it doesn't have a cage in the back, we can lay him down." O'Donnell and Moriarty leaned in and helped get Terry to his feet. The big men carried him over to the cruiser and held him long enough for Mary to open the back hatch.

"You all need to leave," Terry said through his broken jaw. "Except you," he looked at Dana. Mary and O'Donnell looked at Moriarty, who never took his eyes off Terry.

"What are you up to, Ranger?" Rocco asked him. Terry managed a weak smile and tapped his fingers. They were resting on Grandpa's Model 12, still lying in the back of the cruiser.

"Don't let him leave," Terry said. Rocco nodded.

"Sergeant O'Donnell, get as far away from this vehicle as you can," Moriarty said. "Mary, what you do at this point is up to you." Rocco turned on his heel and walked back to the Mayor and Smith. O'Donnell jogged off into the night. Mary stood where she was.

"If I have a punctured lung..." Terry said to Dana.

"Pneumothorax," she interrupted. He looked at her as if to say 'Really?' "Sorry," she said.

"How long will it stay inflated after you stick me with that needle?" Terry asked. Dana was confused. "How long?"

"Um, I don't know. I, um, it depends," she said.

"Just fucking do it then," Terry said. He was watching Rocco with Smith and the Mayor.

"Mary, help me get this off," Dana said. Mary grabbed the quick-release built into Terry's vest and pulled. The cable holding the vest together came free, and the front and back panels fell away from Terry's body. He felt the broken rib shift and yelled in pain. Smith looked at him.

"Hurry," Terry said. Dana ripped open his shirt and grabbed the fourteen-gauge needle from his medkit, popping off the red cap. Smith began walking toward the cruiser.

"This is going to hurt…" Dana said.

"Just do it," Terry winced. Smith was getting closer. Dana pushed the hollow needle into his chest cavity, immediately hearing air escaping and allowing Terry's lung to inflate slowly. The pressure in his chest was decreasing, but the pain in his rib was getting worse. His hand slid back to the wood pistol grip of the old shotgun.

"Mr. Davis," Smith called as he approached. "We had an agreement, and you broke it. I warned you, and you didn't listen. Now, look at you…"

Terry stood, his hands wrapping around the stock and fore end of the seventy-something-year-old shotgun. The metallic click of the safety coming off was as loud as an artillery round. Smith had a look of surprise on his face as Terry shouldered the weapon, the big black hole at the end of the barrel aimed right at him. With a broken jaw, broken ribs, and a needle sticking out of his chest, Terry pulled the trigger and shot Smith in the chest from six feet away and then passed out.

CHAPTER 38

When Terry Davis woke up in the hospital, he didn't know how long he had been unconscious. He didn't even know what day it was. Faint orange rays of light from the setting sun, poking through an overcast sky, were shining into the empty room. He looked around slowly. There was no doctor in the room, just the faint beeping of monitors near his bedside and a television mounted on the wall. There weren't even any pictures in the room, no tacky hospital decorations bought in bulk, like hotels.

He tried to open his mouth and felt immediate pain. *My jaw is wired shut.* His mind cycled quickly. His jaw was broken. The fight at the planetarium. His ribs. Smith. Davis tried to get out of bed, only then realizing his hand was cuffed to the bedrail. *Shit.* His bedside monitors started to make all kinds of noise. He could feel the broken ribs, but the pain wasn't as sharp as he expected. *How long have I been here?* Then he realized the same arm that was cuffed to the rail had an IV tube in it, probably giving him something for the pain.

Dana was the first one in the room, with Mary pushing Jimmy in a wheelchair right behind her. He tried to speak again, not thinking. Dana came to him and kissed him softly on the forehead. Moriarty went into the room behind Mary. Terry had a million questions running through his head. Being unable to verbalize was already driving him crazy. Dana started first.

"Your ribs are going to take some time to heal," she said. "They were broken and displaced, but not bad enough to require surgery. Your pneumothorax..." Terry looked at her. "Sorry. Your collapsed lung is healing nicely. We have to keep an eye on both that and the ribs to make sure you don't develop pneumonia or something else. And your jaw is fractured, so they had to wire it shut."

"Pussy," Jimmy said with a laugh. Dana shot him an evil look. Jimmy mockingly recoiled in defense. Terry pointed to his cuffed hand and looked at Moriarty.

"That's just for show," Moriarty said. "I have officers standing by outside your door, and we told everyone you are a dangerous criminal." The big man smiled at him. "It keeps people out who don't need to be here." Rocco leaned down and took the handcuff off Terry and the bedrail. Terry tried to speak again.

"*Smfh,*" he said through the wiring. Jimmy laughed at him again.

"Oh, you killed him," Mary said. "No question about that." Terry looked confused. "On paper, it was one of the gangbangers who killed him. And his two bodyguards." Terry's confused look got worse. He vaguely remembered one with his face missing and one lying on the ground, very much alive, when he walked up to the Suburban.

"When you shot Smith," Moriarty said, "the other one made a break for it. Didn't turn out so good for him." As much relief as he felt that Smith was dead, Terry didn't like this at all. These were all honest, good people, and he had turned them into killers. He decided then and there that he was leaving as soon as he was able.

"OK," Dana said, back in nurse mode. "He needs some rest. Time for everyone to go." She began shooing them out of the room. Mary walked up and kissed him on the forehead.

"Love of my life," she whispered.

"Catch you later, brother," Jimmy said as he gave him the finger. Terry started to laugh, but the pain was too much. He returned the gesture to his brother.

"My guys are on the door until you leave," Moriarty said. Terry made a gesture as if steering a car. "My Camaro? I saw what you did to my cruiser. Not a fucking chance, Mr. Airborne Ranger." Terry feigned disappointment. "Besides, the new Superintendent of the Chicago Police Department can't be seen hanging around with a troublemaker like you." Terry's eyes opened wide. He was happy for Rocco, but his mind went to Pops. *Troublemaker. I guess some things never change.*

The trio left the room, leaving him alone with Dana. She sat down on the bed facing him, holding his hand. There was no pity or animosity in her eyes. It wasn't even the same look from the night they spent together in Moriarty's guest room. It was the same look she gave him the morning he drove up to her house with coffee, a look of undetermined expectation.

"You're going to be here for a few days," she said. "And I'll be here the whole time." Terry's mind started to wander back to the million questions he had. *What about the Mayor? What happened to the Army guys? How long have I been here?* He caught himself. He looked at her and nodded. "You get some rest. I'll turn on the news for you." She stood and turned on the television to the local ABC channel. There was a commercial for Empire Carpets when the TV came into focus. She leaned in and kissed his forehead again. "Then we need to figure out where we are going once you get out of here."

Terry didn't know what she meant. He pointed at her and then motioned his hands around, indicating the whole hospital. She smiled at him and handed him the call button and the TV remote.

"Have you ever seen Tombstone?" she asked him. Terry nodded. "Do you remember at the end when Wyatt tells Josephine he has no money and nothing to give her?" Terry nodded again. "Well, Wyatt, my family is rich." Terry was shocked. He wouldn't have known what to say even if he didn't have his jaw wired shut. *That's how she could afford her house on a nurse's salary.* She blew him a kiss and walked out. Terry was sitting in stunned silence when the newscaster came on.

"At a news conference earlier today, the city Mayor named former SWAT Commander, Rocco Moriarty, as the new Superintendent of the Chicago Police Department." Terry smiled as he saw the Mayor with Rocco standing next to her. *"The Mayor also walked back her support of the Army operating inside Chicago after the firefight that caused over five million dollars in damage to the Adler Planetarium. Many business owners, celebrities, and*

athletes across the city echoed her sentiments." Terry smiled again. It worked. *"The Secretary of Defense admitted it was a mistake for the military to act in a law enforcement capacity and said the suspension of Posse Comitatus should never happen again."*

Terry was taking it all in. Smith was dead, and his organization was on its heels. The Secretary of Defense they put into office was backpedaling. The Army was out of Chicago. Rocco was the new Superintendent. The Mayor was still in office. That answered some of the questions rolling around inside his head. He shut his eyes for a second. The phone rang. Terry looked around the room, then picked up the phone.

"Mr. Davis," it was a woman's voice. "Mr. Davis, I know your jaw is wired shut, so I won't expect a response." Terry's blood ran cold. "Killing Mr. Smith was unfortunate, Mr. Davis. We wished you hadn't done that, but it cannot be undone." Her voice had an accent, a touch of British snobbery maybe. "I am confident that Mr. Smith informed you that our efforts would continue with or without him. I can assure you that they shall." Scottish. A watered-down Scottish accent. "I do not conduct business as Mr. Smith did, Mr. Davis. I will not waste time or energy chasing you. You are merely not worth the effort." There was a very matter-of-fact tone to her voice, unlike the smug undertones of her predecessor. Dana walked into the room and saw him on the phone; he frantically waved her over. She held her head next to his so she could hear into the receiver.

"Mr. Davis," the woman resumed. "I do not like messes. Mr. Smith created a mess with your help. I suggest you do not create any more of them. Since I know you have a fascination with names, you may call me Ms. Crawford. She is the mother of all patriots where I come from. And that's what we are, Mr. Davis, patriots. I hope this is the last time we speak, Mr. Davis. Good luck with that lovely nurse." The line went dead.

ACKNOWLEDGMENTS

To my family and friends, thank you for your continued support of my journey as a storyteller. To my partner, Elsa, thank you for the friendship and invaluable exposure.

Thank you to all the fans and friends of Terry Davis; your demand for a sequel made this happen. Thank you to the Chicagoland area for providing the perfect backdrop for this story. You will always be my home.

And to my Susie, I love you so much.

ABOUT THE AUTHOR

Clay Novak is a retired US Army officer and veteran of multiple tours in Iraq and Afghanistan. He is a graduate of the United States Army Ranger School, a master parachutist, and has been decorated numerous times during his twenty-five years of service, both in and out of combat.

Clay is a political analyst, a Hollywood military advisor, and donates time to support multiple veteran charity organizations. *Cross to Bear* is the sequel to his debut novel, *Keep Moving, Keep Shooting*, and Book Two in *The Terry Davis Series*.

AFTERWORD

Dear Readers,

Thank you for reading *Cross to Bear*. I hope you also read the first in The Terry Davis Series, *Keep Moving, Keep Shooting*.

You are the reason I wrote the first, as well as the second book, in the series. I continue to be inspired by your reviews, feedback, and messages.

I never realized how satisfying it would be to write about Terry Davis and have you respond so enthusiastically. You're my primary motivation in propelling me to keep writing and to release the next one.

As a thank you for your support, I have included a sneak preview of the upcoming third book in The Terry Davis Series, *Rebellis*.

If you enjoyed my books, please consider writing a short review and posting it on your favorite sites (Amazon, Goodreads, etc.).

Reviews are very helpful to other readers and are greatly appreciaed by authors, especially me. When you post a review, drop me an email and let me know. In turn, I'd be pleased to send a free chapter of the next book coming, *Rebellis*. I always read my emails and messages personally and am happy to hear from my readers.

Regards,
  Clay
  cnovakauthor@gmail.com
  ClayNovak.com

SNEAK PREVIEW OF BOOK THREE
REBELLIS

Sneak Preview of Book Three in The Terry Davis Series

———

Rebellis

"Take a look at that information," Vice President Andrew Miller said. He put a business card on the table. "There is a direct line to me on the back of that card. Use the phone inside the house; it's a secure line. Let me know if anything jumps out at you."

The trio walked through the front door and onto the porch. Terry could see the Polaris roaring up the drive. He offered the Vice President his hand. The younger man shook it and then smiled at Dana. When he reached the bottom of the stairs, Vice President Andrew Miller turned and looked at the two of them.

"One question," Terry said as the Polaris was pulling up. The Vice President nodded as if to say 'go ahead'. "This organization, Smith and Dawson, and the rest. You guys got a name for them?"

"It's in the book on the table," Miller said climbing into the Polaris with the young Army Captain behind the wheel. "I think you'll appreciate it. We didn't know what to call them, so the President came up with something." He waved at the two of them as the side-by-side turned around in front of the house. Terry could hear the rotors of the incoming Blackhawk as he followed Dana back into the house. They walked straight to Miller's folder on the table, Dana picked it up and unzipped the cover, and dropped it back on the table. Inside the black casing was a stack of manila folders, thick with documents and photos. The very top folder had bold, red letters written in marker.

ALSO BY CLAY E. NOVAK

The Terry Davis Series:

Keep Moving, Keep Shooting (2nd Edition)

Cross to Bear

Rebellis